ODYSSEY FROM ANTIETAM

ODYSSEY FROM ANTIETAM

A Medical Novel of the Civil War and Aftermath

Robert Hartley

While the major characters are fictional, some of the supporting ones are real indeed, and I have tried to portray them as realistically as possible. The depiction of events and battles are as accurate as I could make them, realizing that a novel of this type cannot be as detailed as a history. I have tried to be as accurate as possible in describing the medical practices and problems of the day.

This book was printed in the United States of America.

To order additional copies of this book, contact:
Xlibris Corporation
1-888-795-4274
www.Xlibris.com
Orders@Xlibris.com
30087

PROLOGUE

Summer, 2003

Betsy's mother passed away unexpectedly in April and left her a large stone house tucked in the shadow of the Blue Ridge Mountains of North Carolina. Her great great grandmother, Sarah, built it in the 1890s and named it Sanctuary. There Betsy spent her youth until she left for college and a career in public health in Washington D. C.

Legend had it that Sarah was a heroine of significant proportions, something to do with the Civil War, although Betsy didn't know many details. I told her in jest, "I certainly have no such distinguished ancestors. Only humble artisans. Maybe a horse thief or two."

She smiled, and then shook her head. "For a long time I was awed, and maybe a little scared of trying to live up to such a legend. Then when I got in my teens, I became skeptical. After all, the tales I'd heard were hazy—a nurse wandering Civil War battlefields saving lives right and left. I figured everything was wildly exaggerated."

"It would be interesting to research her life," I suggested.

"I've thought of that. Maybe some day . . ."

We stayed at Sanctuary for the funeral, but then had to return to Washington immediately to my job as a business professor at George Washington University. It was early July before we could come back down and look more closely at Betsy's inheritance.

She wanted to sell Sanctuary but first we needed to clean it up and sort through generations of accumulations crowding the attic. I had asked Betsy before, "Are you sure you want to sell this ancestral home?"

"Ken, I was lonely growing up in this big house with no close neighbors, and eager to escape. What could we possibly do with this place? We'll never live here."

I nodded. Reason was on her side. Still, for myself, heritage was something not to be treated lightly. Even the name of the estate, Sanctuary, had a mystical appeal. As rejection slips piled up for my manuscripts, I sometimes longed for a place to lick my wounds; to perhaps find fresh inspiration and be a sanctuary of sort. Besides, the Civil War intrigued me, growing up as I had on the prairies of the Midwest, with only a boy's dreams of the bloody yet heroic struggles far to the East.

The day threatened rain as we rummaged through the attic facing decisions of what to save and what to throw away. Late in the afternoon, Betsy called from a far corner with excitement in her voice: "Ken, you should see this!" I was glad to take a break, and moved to where she was staring at some papers she'd taken from a box.

She handed me a heavy stack of yellowed pages that smelled of dust and tickled my nose. It was a manuscript of some sort, written in rather neat script with most words surprisingly still legible. "I bet this goes back to my great-great-grandparents. See the date, 1879." I gingerly took some of the pages, and she touched my arm and her fingers dug into it. "Look at the title. What a great title —Odyssey from Antietam! Now I remember my grandmother telling me they met at Antietam." Her eyes were shining. "Ken, look how this starts: 'Antietam was the bloodiest day of the Civil War. Two lives cross there, then move on to difficult odysseys of hope and striving.'" She looked at me, trying to assess my reaction.

I tried to tease her and feign only lukewarm interest when in truth I was intrigued. I read the first five or six pages, and then skipped further into the manuscript. I was becoming excited too. "Your great-great-grandfather must have written this. About how they met and how the War affected them."

"I also found some old letters that seem to relate to that time," she said. "I wonder if there are more around."

I nodded. "We better be careful in our sorting. Even if it takes longer than we planned."

We took the material downstairs, quickly fixed something to eat, barely able to wait to start reading the manuscript. It would take another day to finish, but we were quickly hooked. "I don't think he was ever able to get this published," I told Betsy. "Else there would have been books around, and you probably would have read it as a girl. Don't you think you'd have found this story interesting then?"

"I would have devoured it, all the more so since it was written by an ancestor." She wrinkled her nose. "He must have been just like you."

I nodded. "An unpublished author. Yes, I already feel we're kindred spirits."

"Do you think it might be publishable today, maybe with your working on it?"

"I would like to think so. It looks like a dynamite plot. Now if we can only weave the words to do justice to it."

"It's based on facts, I'm sure," she said.

"Yes, it must be. But it reads like fiction."

So we spent the next six weeks at Sanctuary, rewriting an ancient novel to put it in the format of present-day publishing. Sometimes as I wrote or contemplated a better word or phrase, I thought I could feel the spirits of two intrepid souls resting on my shoulders, guiding my fingers in pursuit of a romance and odyssey that yearned to be told.

We had to get back to Washington by the end of August. There we finished the manuscript, and sent it on to a literary agent recommended by the English faculty.

CHAPTER 1

September, 1862

The land lay empty before her.

Sarah Lindsey realized she'd seen nary a soul, not even livestock, or chickens or dogs. The farm buildings seemed abandoned.

She'd ridden down Pleasant Valley from the north this morning, on a foolish impulse Pa would say. At first she'd been merely curious whether she'd see anything out of the ordinary. Well, now she had: this land should have been teeming with animals and people; instead, it was as if a giant hand had swept the land clean. Despite the warmth of the day, she shivered.

Adding to the apprehension, she could hear an increasing rumble, like distant thunder may sound on a summer evening as it brings menace to heat lightning. But this early afternoon sky was cloudless.

The threat of the unknown suddenly brought her to caution. As a solitary woman on horseback on this road in a lonesome land, she felt conspicuous, in danger maybe from marauders or scouts of either side. If she wanted to continue further on this adventure, she better leave these fertile fields and find a trail to higher ground rimming the valley.

A half mile farther on, she saw a trail and urged her horse onto it. It looked familiar to what she had explored of this country when she was a girl. She thought this old trail would eventually lead to a view of the valley to the south. It soon rose through trees and underbrush as it snaked ahead. This eased her concerns and now she felt concealed. She would continue to the lookout and then take a ridge trail back north and home.

She had left home this morning without telling anyone of her intentions. She'd not been sure herself, this morning, but thoughts of Solomon urged her on. It was September 1862 and word had come only a few months before of her dear husband's death in April at the terrible battle of Shiloh in the West. Now the rebels were invading Maryland, had occupied Frederick barely twenty miles to the east, and she was riding toward them.

She had come maybe a half mile into the trees when she heard something rustling up ahead. It sounded like animals. Could it be a cavalry patrol? The thought was frightening: If they were Rebs, they might be lying in wait and could capture her as a spy!

She eased the horse to a stop, trying to keep him calm. Still, he seemed agitated and she feared he would neigh and alert the ambushers. She struggled without success to convince herself that what she'd heard was deer.

Could she go back without being detected? She dismounted, and began to lead the horse down the slope. It occurred to her to examine the soft dirt of the trail for any prints that might indicate what was up ahead. The only prints seemed to be those of her horse. She looked more closely and now sensed that other tracks had been carefully smoothed over. This was a new worry. If Rebs were up ahead, wouldn't they have tried to hide their tracks, just like this?

She retreated a quarter mile and then tied the horse to a tree just off the trail. She spent a few minutes stroking and talking softly to him. Maybe the prudent thing would be to turn back for home, but she decided to investigate a bit more first, and carefully moved through the underbrush toward the ambushers, or hopefully the deer. She had nearly reached the spot where she first heard the animals when she heard a mooing sound. She almost collapsed with relief: these were cows, not cavalry horses!

Now she could see dozens of cows wandering the underbrush. Of course! The good people of Pleasant Valley had moved their cattle up the trail and into the trees to hide them from foraging rebels. Then they smoothed the tracks to hide the whereabouts.

Emboldened, she retrieved her horse and moved ahead. The trail became steep and rocky, and the horse dislodged stones as it clambered ahead. She turned in the saddle to see them showering downward.

As she climbed higher she could hear an increasing rumble—the sound of a great battle it surely must be—though the shoulder of the ridge still muted it. The trail leveled off short of the top, and to get a better view she dismounted, again tied her horse to a sturdy tree, and moved on foot through pines and scraggly bushes to the lookout.

She covered about fifty feet when it seemed as though a door to bedlam had crashed open, and she cringed as from a blow. She parted bushes and peered out. As far as she could see through dust and haze, masses of blue flowed across the valley toward the passes of South Mountain—thank the Lord they must have pushed the rebels out of Frederick. Smoke drifted from the heights like creeping fingers of doom, but it could not hide the flashes of guns and shells. She leaned against a tree, her pulse racing as she contemplated the battle, a battle such as Sol surely must have known. She could well imagine men charging and fighting hand-to-hand in a bloody struggle. Now she could faintly hear wild shouts carried on the breeze, and she wondered if these were the Rebel yells she'd heard Sol and Pa discussing before he left. They were supposed to strike terror as they charged against green troops. A little later the breeze brought the sound of distant cheering, and she wondered about that.

She thought of riding closer, but then decided not to. The sun moving behind South Mountain would soon cast its eastern slopes in shadow. From the hundreds of wagons moving toward the mountain passes the main battle must still be a day or two away. She was three hours from home and reluctantly turned back.

#

Now thoughts of Sol overwhelmed her, thoughts of their wonderful days together, only they were so few. She tried to shut out the bitter days, but they kept creeping into her mind like wolves on the prowl.

He was a young lawyer from Hagerstown, a much larger community twenty miles north of Pikeston, and had come down in early March last year to confer with Pa on some legal matters. Pa had been quite taken with him, and brought him home for dinner after they finished their business for the day. Solomon Lindsey was tall and straight, with blonde hair and mustache. As Pa introduced them, she was struck by his gentle manner and his courtesy. He smiled and kissed her hand, and seemed reluctant to release it. She stared up at his blue eyes. "I'm so glad to meet you," he said.

"Thank you," she murmured. She was aware of Pa watching intently.

"Your father tells me you're a school teacher, guiding young minds."

"More like struggling to get them to learn anything, I would say." He had laughed at her weak attempt at humor.

At the table and afterwards the men conversed, mostly about the war that seemed so imminent. Solomon tried to include her in the conversation as much as possible, despite Pa's reluctance to consider her ideas as worth anything. Several times she reddened at Pa's treating her like a weak-minded female. Once, Sol winked at her as Pa pooh-poohed her comments.

Over the next few weeks she saw a lot of Sol. It seemed his business with Pa was dragging on longer than expected. She sometimes wondered why this was so, but didn't want to flatter herself that she might be part of the reason. One warm and sunny day in early April, he came to the schoolhouse around noon and asked if she would like to take a ride with him and show him some of the beautiful countryside. "Shouldn't you be working?" she asked.

"I'll work late tonight. I didn't want to waste a nice afternoon when I could be with you." With no hesitancy she dismissed class, giving her students a reading assignment instead.

Later, they stopped at a meadow beside a gently flowing stream, and he took her in his arms for the first time, while the scent of apple blossoms filled the air. His mustache tickled as he kissed her, but she soon forgot about the mustache. His warm breath fanned her cheek and she could feel her heart pounding, and she craved the touch of his hands.

She still wondered what Sol had seen in her—so skinny she was, face too bony, hair straight and not curly. She had gone out with men only a few times before, and these were all clumsy country boys. Pa was even telling her that she couldn't be too choosy, that she might wind up an old maid.

Somehow, Sol thought otherwise. "You're so beautiful," he told her. "I can't believe some other man hasn't already claimed your hand." She murmured some denial of her attractiveness, something she was prone to do to a fault, but he persisted with his gentle flattery. "I love to hold your hands. And to have them touch me. Your fingers are so long and slender, so beautiful, so gentle, they mesmerize me," he would say. Well, her hands were her best feature, but that hardly made up for her deficiencies. Now the only man who ever called her beautiful was gone.

A few days later word had come of the bombardment and capture of Fort Sumter in the harbor of Charleston, South Carolina, and of Lincoln's call for volunteers. The sweeping tides of war hastened their wedding plans.

Solomon had just been given a commission, and appeared at the ceremony in his captain's uniform. She was so proud of him, and so much in love. In those early days, they neither understood nor anticipated the full consequences of the War that was to destroy one of them and forever brand the other.

The War took him from her, so soon after they were married. Barely two weeks later he had to leave and join his regiment. It was posted to the western frontier, and at first this was a relief since most of the early fighting was taking place between Washington and Richmond.

"Don't you think the War ought to be over in a few more months?" she had asked Pa last winter.

He rubbed his temple. "I once thought that, but not anymore. I think we have a long desperate struggle ahead. The rebels, the slaveholders, are not going to give up easily, despite their damned cause." He looked at her sympathetically. "I'm sorry, dear, but I think this will be hardest on you women—mothers and wives. We may wish you had never married Solomon."

"Pa," she shook her head furiously. "Don't say that. Not now, please. I live only in the hope that Solomon will come back. He just has to."

"I know, darlin'."

When word came of Sol's death, she'd thought her world had ended. Still, she doggedly went through the motions of teaching, and tried to keep from crying except in the privacy of her bed when the demons would attack and she would crush her face to the pillow. She'd not been able to bear his child in the short time they had together, and she regretted that so much. A child would surely have eased the torment.

The three-hour ride home had passed quickly, lost as she was in reverie. As she entered Pikeston, the thought came that was to change her life forever.

#

She was too late for supper. Sweaty and grimy, she found leftovers in the kitchen and sat down to eat alone. Pa soon found her.

"Where you been, Sarah? I've been worried about you."

"I rode toward the sound of the guns."

"Did you now?" He frowned. "Do you think that was wise?"

She fiddled with her spoon. "I want to go back tomorrow. Only this time closer to where the fighting is."

He stared at her. "What are you saying? I'm not hearing this."

"I want to try to help, however I can. Even if it's only to give a wounded soldier a drink. But maybe I can do more than that."

"A killing field's no place for a woman! It'll be a bloody mess, far worse than anything you've seen in your life."

"I know it will be. But I won't be fighting, only helping the wounded. Maybe I can make the dying easier for some poor soul, as I wish someone could have made Sol's easier."

"Yes, Sol." Her father sighed, then his voice hardened. "He wouldn't want his wife exposed to the horrors of war, any more than I do. To be killed or maimed. No, I'll not have that on my conscience!" His voice was rising now, and he pounded his fist on the table. More quietly he said, "Your mother would never forgive me, either, were she still alive, if I let you go back." He got up heavily from the table and walked to the window to look out at the night sky and the scattered lights of the peaceful village. He leaned his head against the window.

"I'm going, Pa. I'm not a child, and I feel I owe it to Solomon. You can't stop me."

He turned around, the veins in his neck distended. "I'll stop you, if I have to lock you in your room! I'll not sacrifice my youngest daughter to this unholy war!"

"Then I'll go out the window. This is something I have to do."

He glared at her, breathing heavily. She momentarily feared he would have a stroke, or a heart attack. Then he grabbed a glass from the table and she cringed, thinking he was going to hurl it at her. Instead, in his anger he crushed it in his grip.

In an instant, blood poured from his hand. He groaned and sat down.

"Pa, what have you done?" She rushed to him, panic-stricken. This was all her fault!

From somewhere a resolute strength took over. "Just sit there and let me take care of it," she told him. He stared at his hand as it dripped blood.

She grabbed a pan, filled it with water, ransacked the cupboards for clean cloths, and sat beside him at the table. "First we've got to get the bleeding stopped, then I'll pick the glass out and bandage it," she said gently. "I'm sorry, Pa, I made you so angry."

He didn't answer as she placed the back of his hand on the table and put a cloth over his bleeding palm and fingers. She didn't dare press on the wounds because of the glass still imbedded. In seconds, blood had seeped through and his blood was on her hands. His face was gray and perspiration beaded his forehead and rolled down his cheeks.

Again she felt herself panicking. She had to slow the bleeding! She fought off the panic. She must think clearly. There was no one else to help. But first she had him lean back and close his eyes, before he passed out.

"It's all right, Pa. We'll soon have it stopped." She had to reassure him, and herself. Quickly she rolled up a cloth and placed it around his arm just above the elbow and tied it tight. She managed to get the handle of a spoon through the knot so she could twist the cloth tighter. Then she groped around his wrist for a pressure point and pressed as hard as she could with her thumb.

She maintained the pressure for many minutes until her fingers were cramping. Dear God, let the blood be slowing, she silently prayed. Don't let me fail Pa. She eased the tourniquet and let up on the pressure point and gingerly removed the bloody cloth from his hand, fearful of what she would see. The bleeding had slowed to a trickle. Thank you dear Lord, she murmured, as she placed a clean cloth over the wounds, again afraid to press down.

He opened his eyes and looked at her, then at his hand and the bloody cloths, and his breathing was ragged. She knew he must be near shock. She dipped a cloth in cold water. "I'm going to put this on your forehead before I work on your hand. Just lean back again and close your eyes. Everything'll be all right."

A few more minutes and the bleeding had almost stopped. She held her breath as she loosened the makeshift tourniquet all the way, fearful that it would start up again. But it only oozed a little.

She blotted at the blood and could see the glass fragments imbedded in his palm and at the base of several fingers. With her thumb and forefinger she removed the larger shards, then peered closer to get at the tiny slivers. It seemed like it took forever to get all of the glass, and her fingers were bloody from the sharp edges she couldn't avoid. His palm began bleeding again, but the worst seemed to be over. She bandaged his hand and would bandage it again before they went to bed.

"I think I got all the glass, but you should let Doc look at it tomorrow. He may want to stitch some of the cuts."

"Thank you, Sarah," he murmured, and closed his eyes as he again leaned back in the chair.

She began cleaning up, the bloody rags, the mess on the floor and on the table, and the glass particles she had collected. Her hands were covered with blood, Pa's and her own, and blood had even gotten on their clothes. Afterwards she brought him a glass of water. "Drink this, Pa. You need some liquids."

He roused a bit. "A shot of bourbon would do me better," he tried to joke.

"That would make you sick right now," she frowned as she scolded him. Then she helped him to his easy chair in the living room.

She sat on another chair. "I still want to go tomorrow. I feel I must."

He took a deep breath, maybe of capitulation. "I hear Preacher Williams is after volunteers. To help with supplies and nursing . . . if there's a big battle. Can't you wait a few days?"

"If I know Preacher Williams, he'll spend so much time planning everything before doing anything that it'll be too late."

He sighed, and rubbed his eyes with his good hand. "How hard this is," he said at last. "Still, I suppose I know how you feel. Especially after Solomon . . . I just don't know if I could take it, to lose my youngest."

"I'll be careful."

"Jeremy should ride with you tomorrow, but I wish he wasn't so old."

"You think I need protection?"

"You may wind up near the fighting. You never can tell just how a battle will move. I'm not sure how much you can help. Even though you fixed me up fine." He was silent, marshalling his thoughts, and maybe his strength. "I've heard the docs have been badly short of supplies in other battles. They probably need more than just another pair of hands."

"I still have to go."

"Well, then, we better do some planning." His voice strengthened. "I imagine it'd be best if you have Jeremy load the carriage full of supplies as you can. It's too bad we don't have a wagon like the Preacher. Still, you can travel a lot faster."

She nodded, and he went on. "In the morning we'll look 'round to see what you can take. I suppose they'll need blankets, cloth for bandages. And water. That may be the most needed. Only you can't take much water because of the weight, but Jeremy should be able to load a couple barrels. We'll have to plan carefully . . . pick only those things most essential." He sagged in the chair, exhausted.

"Thank you, Papa." She examined the bandage. Some blood had soaked through. She had him close his eyes while she rebandaged. "Does it hurt much?"

"Not as much as you leaving."

"Please don't start that again."

"No, I won't." He got up slowly. "Sarah, I'm terribly tired. I'm going to bed now. Goodnight, dear."

She went over and kissed him. He put an arm around her and they embraced, then he slowly climbed the stairs to his bedroom. He hadn't noticed that she had cut her fingers in pulling out the glass, and she was thankful for that. It would only complicate things if he had noticed, and besides, they were just a few minor cuts.

#

It was late morning before the carriage was ready. At her impatience he told her, "Remember, girl, your work doesn't begin till after the battle. Promise me you'll be careful."

"I promise. Now see Doc about that hand." She kissed him. "Love you, Pa."

"All right," he said stolidly, then watched her climb onto the carriage seat and their groom Jeremy urged the two horses forward. She wished now she had assured Pa that old Jeremy would see that she came to no harm. He was a small man, now stooped with age and with a weathered face, but he had come to her aid several times in her childhood misadventures with horses and wanderings into unfamiliar territory.

She looked back as the road began to curve out of sight. Pa was still standing in the driveway, hitting his thigh with the fist of his uninjured hand.

The carriage moved down the road through Pleasant Valley, the same route she had partially traversed yesterday. Then the country had been empty of people and livestock, with the livestock hidden in the hills and foliage rimming the valley. Now the land was not so empty, and she could see farmers and animals, not in great numbers yet, but growing. She pointed that out to Jeremy.

"We got the Rebs on the run now, Miss Sarah, 'less they lick us agin the other side o' South Mountain. These farmers, they mus' think the danger's over."

"Maybe so."

"Still, dem devils, the Rebs, are hard fighters. If I was farmin' I'd still want my critters up the hills."

As the carriage moved toward the main road over the pass, Sarah stared ahead pondering what was to come. The episode with her father had drained her, and she'd slept poorly. When sleep finally came she'd dreamed of monstrous battlefield injuries, and woke sweating. Self doubt overwhelmed her—it would hardly be the last time for self doubt. Despite fixing up Pa's hand, what did she really know about medicine? She was just a simple teacher of children, and the only medicine she knew was bandaging cuts and scrapes. And here she was, determined in some way to help and comfort men with grievous wounds.

Was she making a terrible mistake? Did Pa's injury foretell God's frowning on what she was so impulsively undertaking?

Then another thought came to her, and comforted her. Had she not handled her father's unexpected injury as well as anyone could? She'd not panicked, though admittedly was close to it twice, but was able to steel herself to be calm and resolute. And the blood, it had not sickened her or made her faint.

They reached the National Road from Frederick by mid-afternoon, and eased into a massive wagon train following the Union Army as the road rose toward Turner's Gap at South Mountain. Progress was unbearably slow, and the dust from the wagons was a torment. Sarah in her restlessness got down and walked alongside the carriage.

As they inched toward the Gap, evidence of the battle the previous day was all around, while a fitful wind blew litter across the open spaces. Through shattered trees, horses and equipment were scattered about like the aftermath of the tornado that had passed near their house when she was a little girl.

Just ahead alongside the road a dead horse was lying on its side bloated with gasses and the legs were thrust out in rigor mortis. The body had been smashed by a cannon ball and scavengers were tearing on intestines and other innards. A putrid smell rose from the carcass and as she passed it suddenly was more than she could bear. She retched helplessly alongside the carriage.

Now Jeremy was beside her, supporting her. "Let me help you back up, Miss Sarah. These not be sights and smells for the likes of us. An' it's goin' t'get worse, it is."

Sarah sat ashamed, hardly able to talk, as her thoughts churned. Pa was right. This was no place for a woman. How could she help men when a dead horse was more than she could bear? She wanted Jeremy to turn back, but there was no way they could on this narrow mountain road. Even a huge herd of cattle was catching up with them.

As they crawled upward they saw more remains of the battle. Even bodies of soldiers.

The bodies were being collected from the woods and rocks and brought alongside the road. In a now-stormy sky dozens of carrion birds circled. Just ahead, wagons were being loaded, and Sarah stared in sick fascination as soldiers lifted bodies and tossed them like firewood into the wagons. Somehow, the sight of the bodies strengthened her resolve to continue with this.

They neared the top of the pass. The road would soon be turning downward and maybe things would speed up a bit. Not all the wounded had yet been picked up by ambulance wagons, and she had Jeremy stop on the side of the road hoping to help and atone for her weakness.

She got down to comfort a soldier, offering him a drink from her canteen. "Don't they know you're here?"

"The ambulances have been takin' only the bad wounded first," he said wearily. "They didn't think I was bad 'nuff, so I have to wait, but they didn't have no water left."

"You can keep the canteen," she told him, then realized the air was chilling in the dying sun. She fumbled with the supplies and came back with a blanket. "Let me tuck this round you. And I pray the rain will hold off."

"Bless you, ma'am," he murmured. "There's another angel like you jus' up ahead, and oh how we need such angels."

Sarah, in wonderment, questioned the young man and learned a woman with a wagonload of medical supplies had passed not long before. She felt strengthened to think she was not the only woman in this hell, and hankered to join up with her. But the road ahead remained clogged and cattle began catching up with them again.

They made camp that Monday night on the western flank of South Mountain. The land had begun to level out as it fell away from the pass, and they found an empty space among the horde of wagons that were congregating. It was rocky and slanted, and the carriage listed more than she was comfortable with. She thought it would be better to be farther ahead and not trapped by these ponderous wagons and the oxen and horses.

"Miss Sarah, we don' know der's anything better up ahead, or even any space a'tall for us. We better stay here, 'n be glad to have it."

"You're probably right, Jeremy." But she was still chafed at their inability to catch up with that woman up ahead.

Now the campfires of the massive army spread before them. She helped Jeremy in taking care of the horses, then he started a fire for coffee while she put together two tins of cold ham and biscuits. Afterwards she asked, "Would you go with me to visit some of the troops, Jeremy? I'd like to see if I could find who that other woman is, and where she might be. Maybe we can join her."

"I sure can't let you wander 'round by yourself, Miss Sarah."

So they moved from campfire to campfire, inquiring. Most men knew nothing about such a woman, but then a sandy-haired captain came out of a larger tent and approached her. "Miss, I'm Captain Reddig, aide to Colonel Kimball. We've heard you're inquiring about the woman ahead. She's Clara Barton."

"My groom and I would like to join her if we could only find her."

An older man came to the tent's entrance. "Miss, a battlefield's no place for a woman."

"This is Colonel Kimball," the captain said. "We're the 7th Ohio."

"I'm Sarah Lindsey. My husband was killed at Shiloh. I live near here and brought some supplies." She took a deep breath as they stared at her. "I just want to help, however I can," she said softly.

The captain touched his cap in a salute. "I'm sorry ma'am. So many widows . . ." His face looked stricken as he tried to gather himself. Then he said, "The woman you're looking for is no stranger to battlefields. She's been at Culpepper, Bull Run, now she's here. I wish we had a hundred like her."

"Then we'd have women casualties to worry about as well as men," the colonel said, his voice bitter. "All right, Mrs. Lindsey, you can camp with us tonight. You'll be safe here. At first light, we'll try to find out where Clara Barton is." He started back into the tent, then turned around. "Captain Reddig will see to your comfort. And please accept our regrets at your loss."

The captain ordered their carriage moved close to the command tent where there were sentries. He touched his hand to his cap again, and started to bid her goodnight.

"Please, Captain Reddig, could you tell me where the wounded will be taken, where I might be most useful?"

He started at the question, and she could see his hand trembling. "They'll be taken to every shelter, barn, farmhouse, shed, under trees, every place that can offer any kind of shelter. If the battle is huge, as this promises to be, there won't be enough shelter within twenty miles for all the wounded. Many will have to lie out in the open, without shelter."

"What if it rains, or storms?"

Captain Reddig thought about that. "It will help some of us die quicker, and maybe that would be a blessing." He was staring at her in the flickering light of the campfire.

Then he shook himself briefly away from his morousness, as Sarah looked at him horrified, yet fascinated. "Mrs. Lindsey, on the battle day, whether it's tomorrow or the day after, you should look for any farm buildings. That's where the surgeons should be busy cutting off our limbs."

#

Though her eyes felt gritty and her body weary, Sarah couldn't sleep. Anxiety knotted her stomach and kept her mind full. Wrapping a blanket around herself, she rested her back against a wagon wheel, trying to ignore the thunder sounding in the distance. She wondered again what had ever possessed her to undertake this. It wasn't just because she was a recent widow. There were hundreds, nay thousands, of such widows in the War so far. She realized that in all this vast encampment of men, there were probably only two women, Clara Barton up ahead somewhere, and herself. She wondered whether she had the strength to go through with this. She prayed that she did.

The faraway lonesome sound of a harmonica wafted through the air. It was somehow both comforting and chilling, and she held her breath as thunder tried to blot out the sounds of the harmonica. But the harmonica prevailed this night. Now she marveled at how quiet these thousands of men were, probably thinking of the battle tomorrow and of what might happen to them. She wondered how many were praying. Surely most were.

Could Sol be nearby in spirit? Somehow, she thought he might be. If so, she prayed she would not disappoint him on the morrow. She still felt ashamed at having gotten sick just passing a dead horse.

CHAPTER 2

Frederick, Maryland loomed just ahead on this invasion of the North. Word passing down the line was good: the people of Frederick were welcoming Lee and the Army of Northern Virginia with open arms, with flags, flowers, kisses from pretty girls. And food, wonderful food. How good it would be to taste home cooking again after the drab field rations and occasional scrawny chicken gained from foraging. He'd believe it when he saw it. The good people of Frederick could hardly give out home cooking to all the men of the Army of Northern Virginia.

Major Thaddeus Barrett looked back at his steadily plodding regiment. Coated in the dust raised by thousands of feet, the men of the 20th North Carolina did not look like victors, destroyers of the Union Army barely ten days before at Second Manassas. No, they were gaunt, ragged, dirty. Many were shoeless. These rocky roads of Maryland were particularly hard on bare feet accustomed to the soft dirt roads of Virginia. He hoped, more than food, the people of Frederick might let loose of some shoes.

He could hear cheers now, ahead. Captain Tom Ross galloped up beside him. "Thad, the men want to know if we'll be stayin' here for a few days. Some of their feet are bad."

"I don't know, Tom. The generals don't confide in me, you know."

"Shucks, Thad, the word is they'll be makin' you a colonel, any day now. An' colonels get confided in, don't they?"

Barrett laughed. "Probably only by other colonels, not by generals." He turned serious. "Pass the word again to your men. General Lee wants us to be on our best behavior. That means no looting, nor foraging . . ."

"An' no raping?" Ross interrupted, with a twinkle in his eye.

"No!" He was horrified at this idea, even though given in jest. "We're supposed to be liberators, not conquerors." His face was stern. "Be sure your men understand this, Tom! Don't even let them joke about it! Understood?"

Ross saluted, "Right, Major, suh." Thad watched as Tom Ross spurred his horse back to his company. Of the officers under his command, Tom was his favorite. He envied the younger man's youthful exuberance. In contrast, though only a few years older, Thad felt like an oldster, seasoned to the point of tiredness and skepticism. Despite their victory ten days ago, he had forebodings.

He tried to hide such pessimism from his troops. He mustn't erode their confidence. That was probably the greatest strength of the Army of Northern Virginia: confidence in itself and its leaders. But Thad wondered how long such confidence would last in the days to come. Nagging thoughts pursued him lately, interrupted his sleep: The great generals of the Confederacy, Lee and Jackson, were they so great really, or simply finding pleasure in bloodletting, in the power over men's lives?

As his men came into Frederick, provost marshals directed them through the downtown toward a bivouac northwest of the town. People lining the route were offering cakes, pies, bread and other treats. However, supplies were becoming depleted and regiments farther back would find precious little left.

A loud-voiced civilian yelled at him, "Hey soldier, is Stonewall Jackson still behind you?"

Thad shook his head. The man yelled again, "You're not Stuart, are you?"

He shook his head again and shrugged his shoulders. He realized now that the crowds had come to see the famous heroes of the Confederacy: Lee, Longstreet, Jackson, Stuart. He tried to banish his heretical thoughts of their passion for blood, these famous heroes.

All the flowers and festooning and people waving and cheering meant little. What his men needed was shoes, and nowhere could he see any of these being handed out.

As they reached their campsite in the midst of thousands of other men already bivouacked, a provost marshal approached him and saluted. "Major, I'm to tell you the General has put the town off limits for all troops, 'less they have a pass. We'll be patrollin' the streets to stop trouble. Also, anything needed must be paid for with our script. You'll notify your men, suh?"

"Certainly. Tell me, do you know if the Army has been able to buy any shoes? Some of my men are in bad shape."

"I don' know, Major. But suspect not. The stores wouldn't 'ave enough for more'n a few dozen, anyways."

He grimaced, sympathetically. "We're not even gettin' much food, 'cept some sweets." He paused, seemingly reluctant to leave. "An' what's more, Major, I hear we're gettin' scarce any recruits. The General thought thousands might want to join our cause."

"Maybe we look too much like pirates, dirty and foul mouthed."

The man looked surprised. "I hadn't thought 'bout that, Major." He laughed sheepishly. "I guess we've all grown used t' each other." He looked around. "Maybe we'd scare ordnary folks."

"Well, there's nothing the Army can do about it now, soldier."

That evening, Thad and his company commanders and officers of nearby regiments conversed around a campfire. This early September night was balmy, the breeze was gentle, night birds sang in the darkness beyond the camp, and the sky was a feast of stars. Thad's mind drifted to the peacefulness of this night, and how he would have liked to leave this campfire and find some stretch of ground where he could lie down and gaze at the heavens, and forget this damned war. But, of course, as commander of a regiment, he could not indulge his fancies. He looked around. Nobody here saw this brief respite as a chance for appreciation of life and contemplation.

Several of his fellow officers now were producing flasks of whiskey that were generously passed around.

"This Maryland invasion should bring the North to its knees," Colonel Randall in command of the 29th Georgia pontificated. "Now we can give 'em a taste of what it's like."

Maynard Lassiter, commanding one of Barrett's companies, agreed. "I've heard people in Washington City are callin' for Lincoln's impeachment. One more decisive victory should win the War for us."

Thad observed with interest Tom Ross's disagreement.

"The Yanks are tough. They're no pushovers. Maybe we were lucky to beat 'em at Manassas." He saw Tom Ross looking in his direction, perhaps to gauge his approval of such views. Had his pessimism been all that transparent? He shuddered to think that.

"Young man, don't be a defeatist. There's no room in this army for such," the Colonel admonished sternly. "We've got the best fightin' men and generals in the world."

Thad listened to the conversation as the flickering flames cast distorting shadows. The unaccustomed whiskey gave him a temporary euphoria. A whiskey euphoria, he recognized. Perhaps this was affecting the other people here, too. Giving false optimism. How could this situation really be all that promising? He was suddenly aware of Colonel Randall addressing him.

"Major Barrett, have you nothin' to say about the great fightin' abilities of the Confederate soldier?"

Thad pondered this, reluctant to be negative in this circle of whiskey optimists. "I certainly can't fault our soldiers. They've performed beyond all expectations." He paused. "What bothers me is that the soldiers of the North, many of them, are like us. They have the same bloodlines, even brother fighting brother." He looked around the fire. "How can we possibly think that we're the epitome of bravery, and they're hopeless incompetents?"

This statement aroused a flurry of denials and wild discussion. He leaned back wearily. He wished he could share in the confidence and optimism of most of these fanatics. In truth, he sensed that the Confederacy was overmatched. He briefly wondered if any generals entertained such thoughts on occasion. Even Lee, did he ever think they were overmatched? In the darkness of the night, maybe?

#

The stay around Frederick was brief. Next morning they received orders to move out, to move west, to cross the mountains looming blue on the horizon. No one was sure what this meant. Some thought it a feint to disguise a power thrust into Pennsylvania; a few suggested it was a strategic withdrawal back across the Potomac, although these sentiments were condemned by most as being too negative; the majority predicted it was a flanking movement aimed at Washington City itself.

The encampment slowly roused and prepared to move on. A courier from Thad's commanding general, Daniel Hill, directed the regiment to assume the rear guard position, to be the last in line as the columns turned toward the mountains. The dispatch concluded, "Union forces may be moving on Frederick. You must delay them if they turn west before we have crossed South Mountain."

He asked the courier, "Does General Hill really think the Yanks can move that fast?"

"Sir," the courier said, "We hear they've changed generals. McClellan, again. Stuart's cavalry reports uncommon movement toward us." He saluted and rode off.

Thad summoned his company commanders and read the dispatch. "While I don't think McClellan can move fast enough to catch us before the mountains, we have to be alert to cavalry probes. Instruct the men."

"Does this mean we're the sacrificial lambs?" Lassiter wanted to know.

"I hope not. But if necessary, yes."

Ross piped up, "This is the honor spot, isn't it?"

"Maybe so," Thad encouraged him.

"Not at all," Lassiter disagreed. "It merely means we're the expendables, those least valuable."

He and Ross began arguing, and Thad had to intervene.

"Save your energies, men. If the rest of the Army moves at its usual speed, we'll probably have little action. But let's take it as it comes."

He had to admit, though, as the afternoon progressed, that the main body of the Army was unduly slow. Perhaps the passes at Catoctin and South Mountain were slowing things down. But he fretted. Several times he could see through his glasses blue horsemen only a few miles away. And still the Army ponderously stretched toward the mountains.

By evening they had moved a few miles west. Still too close to Frederick, if indeed the Union Army was on their tails. He ordered pickets placed, while he wondered about Stuart and his cavalry. They should be out there, somewhere, keeping tabs on the enemy.

He had trouble sleeping that night. He felt the weight of command with his responsibility for the whole regiment, decimated though it might be. These North Carolina boys had come through the major battle at Manassas a few weeks ago, only to lose their colonel at a skirmish near Chantilly several days later. As the senior officer remaining he had been given command of the undermanned regiment. But weren't they all undermanned, after these weeks of fighting?

He sometimes wondered what he, a college professor, was doing in such a command. Yet, Thomas (Stonewall) Jackson had been a professor. And rumor had it that Daniel Hill, the divisional commander, had also been a teacher as well as being brother-in-law to Jackson.

No incidents occurred during the night. For the next several days they moved up over Catoctin ridge and down into the green valley they learned was called Pleasant Valley. Beyond was the high outline of the long ridge of South Mountain and its several passes that would lead them to the main body of the Army of Northern Virginia.

They found no welcome in this country. Villages they passed through were shuttered, without even dogs to welcome them. Attempts at foraging were not successful. Livestock had been driven off and hidden. Barns were empty with the grain not yet harvested. Not even stray chickens could be found. Perhaps they had already been confiscated by the troops ahead. The men of the 20th North Carolina plodded stolidly ahead in the heat and dust, on their bloody feet.

The voices of cannons lent some urgency to their march, although no shells had yet fallen nearby. Now Stuart's horsemen were ranging behind them, between them and the enemy.

A contingent of his troopers stopped. "Are you the commanding officer?" the captain asked.

Barrett nodded.

"The enemy is pressing us. They have superior numbers. I'm not sure we can hold 'em off till you reach the gap."

"How much farther do we have to go?"

"You'll be starting to climb in a mile or so. Then it's about two steep miles to the top. Once you're in among the trees you'll be safer. But they're unlimbering their cannon behind. So you may want to spread out more."

"Thanks, Captain."

"We'll do our best to keep 'em off your heels till you get to the trees." With that he saluted and dashed off with his troop.

"Major, could'ya transfer me to the hosses?" a grizzled veteran, Jed Johnson, asked, tongue in cheek.

"Can you ride?" Thad asked.

"Oh, suh, ah could learn real fast."

He laughed. "Then we'll have to see about getting you transferred, won't we?"

#

Their mettle was tested before they could reach the trees. "Major!" came an urgent cry. Blue-clad horsemen were thundering down on them from a knoll a quarter mile to their north.

Thad spurred among his foot soldiers. "Off the road, men! Quickly! Scatter! Find shelter!"

Spying Ross, he shouted, "Tom, have some of your men watch the other side! They may be trying to pincher us!"

Rifle fire was steady now. He was pleased at how quickly his men reacted to the surprise attack. But the blue horsemen were almost on them.

Corporal Davey grabbed his horse. "Major, suh, take shelter yr'self! I've got the horse."

"Hold steady, men," he yelled. "Let them come through us."

The wild-eyed horses and their yelling men with flashing sabers quickly poured over them. A number of horses were down, but he could see casualties from the trampling horses. One of his men had his head neatly severed by a saber. He could see it rolling in the dust of the ditch.

Now a bearded horseman bore down on him with saber raised, screaming something. Thad raised his pistol, vaguely aware that he was too slow.

A rifle sounded in his ear.

The horseman toppled, the saber falling almost at his feet. The trooper's foot was caught in the stirrup and the frantic horse rapidly dragged the corpse or still living man off.

As suddenly as they had come, the attackers were gone.

Thad turned around. "Johnson, was that you that saved my life?"

"Wal, Major, ah just reckoned to keep ya alive so's to transfer me to dem hosses."

He put his hand on the man's shoulder. "Thanks, Jed."

The respite was short-lived. Another batch of cavalry approached from the other side, and began dueling at long range, occasionally feinting as though to charge, and then backing off. Then they were gone.

His officers approached to report on casualties of the skirmish. "We bloodied them pretty good, Major. There must be twenty, thirty horses down out there."

"Your casualties, Tom?"

"I've got three dead and six wounded, two seriously."

He added, "I'm proud of the men, suh. They stood firm, didn't panic."

The other companies reported similar statistics. "Dammit, we've lost almost ten percent in this skirmish," Thad muttered.

"But some of the wounded can still fight," Ross pointed out.

"Make arrangements to bring the dead and wounded with us," he instructed his officers. "We're going to high tail it up the mountain, before we're attacked again."

As if to emphasize his concern, the regiment was coming under ranging cannon fire. Thad scribbled a note to General Hill, telling him that the Feds were pressing hard on their heels with cavalry and cannon, and gave it to an eager lieutenant.

This Old National Road zigzagged up to the pass, Turner's Gap. After marching all day, and with the letdown from the excitement of fighting off the attacks, the long climb severely taxed the men. Thad got off his horse several times to tramp with them, but his men prevailed on him to save his strength and mount up again.

They approached the final incline leading to the highest point of the pass. Feverish preparations were being made to build some sort of barricades. He could see two cannon being positioned on higher ground that could sweep the roadway. Unless the Feds got their own guns in position to destroy these batteries, they would have to content themselves with attacking through the wooded terrain on either side of the road.

A staff officer rushed up. "Major Barrett, Colonel Colquitt wants to see you. I'm to take you to him."

He had met Colquitt at Chantilly shortly after taking command of the regiment. The Colonel was a big man with a florid face, seemingly a commanding presence, but appeared prone to becoming rattled and impulsive under stressful conditions.

Colquitt was indeed highly agitated when he saw Thad. "We need your men to reinforce our troops defending the pass. We're making a line a half mile short of the pass. General Lee believes it's urgent we hold this pass as long as possible. Our Army needs time to come together on the other side of South Mountain 'fore the Union attacks. The generals expect they'll try to break through tomorrow. Ours may be a suicide mission." The Colonel strode back and forth, clasping and unclasping his hands.

"How can we help?"

"I want you to take responsibility for the far left of our line. You will be our ultimate outpost. If they overrun your troops, our whole position will have to cave in."

"I see."

"General Hill is taking personal command, and bringing up reinforcements and some cannon, sometime tomorrow. But from those lights down below, looks like the whole damn Union Army is waiting to come up."

"I didn't think McClellan could move this fast," Thad commented.

"Wal, he seems to have a burr in his saddle this time."

#

The 20th North Carolina moved to the far left position on wooded heights above the pass. Although night was upon them, Thad summoned his company commanders for a strategy assessment. Their front was heavily wooded with scattered boulders.

"Good cover for us," Tom Ross observed.

"And for them, too," Thad soberly noted. In truth, the terrain scared him. It seemed indefensible against superior numbers who could creep up, and then overwhelm them with brief charges.

"There's an old stone fence down there 'bout fifty yards," somebody said.

They went down to examine it. It ran parallel with the valley, the direction from which the attack was bound to come, for some distance. But just beyond the fence was heavy underbrush. "We have to clear that underbrush, as much as possible," he told his company officers. "We can't give the Yankees so much cover."

Several winced, and Lassiter reminded him how much the men had been through this day.

"I know the men are beat, but this has to be done tonight. Otherwise, our position is doomed with the first Union charge." They nodded tiredly. "Now let's look at the situation on our north flank."

The situation there was worse. A higher knob loomed a quarter mile away. "If they can get one or two cannon up there, they'll roll up our entire line," he mused. "But even without that, we're vulnerable to any flank attack." He turned to Sam Evans, commander of his third company, a quiet but competent man. "Sam, at first light, deploy your men into those trees on our flank. Not too far out, so we can retrieve you if need be." Thad clenched his fist for emphasis. "You'll be our strategic reserve, unless they come your way. And Tom and Maynard, you'll want to place your men at the fence. But not all. Keep some behind to try to contain any penetration."

"How about pickets, sir?" Tom Ross asked.

"I don't think they'll try to come up the mountain at night, so a few pickets should be enough. But at first light, I'd like each of you to send out about a dozen skirmishers." He looked at them grimly. "Anything else, at this time?"

They had nothing else. "Then get your men clearing that underbrush. You better fix up some lanterns, and you may want to spell the men. We don't want anyone too exhausted to fight tomorrow."

"You think it'll be tomorrow, then?" Ross asked.

"From the looks of those fires below, I think so. Maybe not at first light. But we need to be ready in case."

Near midnight, the regiment sprawled in a clearing surrounded by boulders and trees. They had done all they could to remove underbrush, and at one end of the clearing had piled the brush and small trees they had gathered from below. Some rocks had also been added to the stone fence. Now, small fires cast shadows like a macabre dance of phantoms. Thad wandered among the men, listening, but saying little. They were in reasonably good spirits, despite their losses in the valley and the fatigue of the march and from these defensive preparations. Probably they felt they had given better than they got in the skirmish with the Union cavalry.

Thad had always been a quiet man, not very sociable. Some would call him moody, he knew. But it was not that. He just didn't always enjoy company, and never partying. Sometimes he preferred to be alone with his thoughts. He smiled ruefully. Maybe that was why he'd never married. He wasn't jolly enough. He wondered if that came from growing up in western Carolina, among those hills that could make a man silent among God's majesty. And now he was a commander of men, he, a humble professor.

Early the next morning, General Daniel Hill with several aides galloped up. The general seemed agitated, just like Colquitt. "The Yankees are coming up the hill, Major. We're badly undermanned, for the time being. I've reinforcements coming up from Boonesboro, but they probably won't get here before noon. Your regiment is holding the far end of our left flank. I'm depending on you."

He started to ride off, then turned, "I hear, Major, that your Carolinians bloodied the bluebellies yesterday." Before Thad could respond, he said, "Well done!" and galloped away.

Now they could hear shouts of attackers climbing toward them. The sharp crack of skirmishers' rifles began intensifying. Cannon shells shredded trees and plowed into the ground or screamed over their heads. Thad saw his men piling more rocks. This would be a good place to defend if only they had a decent field of fire with open space in front of them. Despite the clearing efforts last night by exhausted men, the field of fire was barely acceptable, and he didn't see how this small undermanned regiment could hold its position against superior numbers in a relentless attack.

Thad sighed. Well, they would have to do their best. And probably die trying. He wondered what it would be like, the dying that is.

Jed Johnson seemed to have taken responsibility for his protection, he observed as he moved along the line to check on his men. Well, Jed had saved his life down below. Maybe that made for a special relationship.

A young man, almost a boy, asked plaintively, "I've never faced bayonets, Major. I'm not sure I can, suh."

Thad reminded him, "They're not nearly as bad as horses and sabers, son. And you did well against them."

He went along the line, instructing his men to aim lower than usual since the tendency is to overshoot when firing from a higher elevation. He wanted to reassure his men, bolster their confidence. But they were the victors at Manassas. Did they need reassurance? But such a thin line, such a damn thin line to hold. He wondered about Evans' company out there in the woods on their north flank.

Now he told his troops to fire at will. Volleys would be useless in such terrain.

They were coming under heavy fire from the trees below. A man pitched backward near him. Another clutched at his throat, trying to stem the blood. But their fire was telling, as bodies were piling up down the slope near the woods.

The blue tide emerged from the woods, the dreaded bayonets flashing. He groaned as he realized from the battle flags that several regiments must be massed down there. Against his pitiful one.

Smoke drifted over him, obscuring the scene, making it dreamlike. But bullets thudding all around brought reality. Despite their losses, the enemy kept coming. Both sides were screaming now, elemental animal sounds. God, where was the glory in this?

At last the Union charge faltered. A few reached the stone barrier and fought with his men hand-to-hand. But they did not break through, this time.

The survivors flowed back down to the safety of the trees, the ground covered with their dead and wounded. But his men had suffered badly, too.

Lassiter was mortally wounded. A Lieutenant Moore had taken over what remained of his company. Tom Ross was all right, but one-third of his company was down.

Thad realized they could never hold off another full-scale attack without more men. He had to bring in Evans and his company guarding their flank. There was a risk in doing so, but their greatest danger was in front. If he guessed wrong, they were doomed. But they were doomed if he didn't use these reserves. Maybe they were doomed anyway. The thought crossed his mind that he who so loved the mountains should find it fitting to die on a mountain.

He placed the fresh reserves of Sam Evans up in the trees, back from the stone barrier. "I'm sure you'll be needed the next charge. We can't hold them at the fence. If they attack in any numbers they'll break through, and you and your men will be our only hope. You'll sure to be outnumbered, Sam," he told him. "But instruct your men to yell like the very devil himself as they charge pell-mell out of the trees. Maybe you can scare the bluecoats, make them think you're a bigger force."

Evans nodded, then asked, "How will I know when to sound the charge?"

"I'll leave it to you. You'll have to decide when they have broken through our defenses in sufficient numbers, and have us about beat. Again, remember those rebel yells!"

As the smoke dissipated, he could see more blue uniforms massing below. They were not giving his men much breathing room. Bullets whined, whispers of death.

Thad again went down the line behind the fence, stepping over bodies, trying to bolster his men. Jed Johnson stuck with him, like a leech. Once he turned to him, "Jed, I'm not a maiden to be protected."

"Major, suh, you're all we got. To bring us through this. We gotta protect you."

There was no reasoning with the man, he realized. And maybe he needed protection. But what could possibly protect a man from cannon debris or a minie ball?

This time the Feds charged en masse up the hill, even disregarding the shelter of trees and boulders in a massive frontal attack.

His men fired steadily, but they were too few to blunt the attack. From the battle flags dimly seen through the smoke, Thad raised his estimate from several to at least three and maybe four regiments facing his lone regiment. Thank God he had brought in Evans.

The bluebellies poured over the center of the stone fence. Hand-to-hand fighting ranged up and down the barrier, and his men were forced back, many of them falling under the blue uniforms.

Jed pulled him away from the fence. "Suh, don't sacrifice yr'self. You can't handle bayonets with a pistol."

Suddenly he heard wild yells behind them. Evans' men were bounding down the hill, screaming like they were several regiments, instead of one depleted company. They threw themselves on the enemy thrusting their bayonets and wielding their rifles as clubs. He saw with wonder the enemy falling back, retreating down the hill.

He momentarily slumped to the ground, exhausted. "Are you all right, suh?" Jed asked anxiously.

Thad roused himself. He mustn't show weakness before his men. He touched Jed on the shoulder, "I'm fine, Jed. Your help is appreciated."

He congratulated Evans and his men. "You saved the day, Sam. The way you yelled I bet those Yanks thought you were a thousand men."

He surveyed what remained of his regiment, and it was sobering. They had lost more than half. All the reserves had been committed. They could not survive another attack.

Ross approached him, his face blackened and blood showing on his sleeve. "Tom, are you wounded?"

"Just a scratch. I'm okay. But we're in a bad way." He paused, looking at the bodies along the fence. "Should we withdraw, suh?"

Thad took a deep breath. "Tell your men to hold their positions." Tom started to protest, but he motioned him to listen. "Maybe reinforcements will get to us before another attack. And maybe the Yanks will want to think awhile before they try again. We mustn't abandon this position, and simply hand it to them. After all the men who fell protecting it."

Tom Ross collapsed on the ground. "The men are almost out of ammo, and water. I don' think they can do this agin."

"I hope they won't have to. But tell them to search the bodies for more ammo and water." He peered at the younger man. "Tom, we must stay here until relieved. Tell the men that. May Heaven help us."

Thad looked at his watch. It was only 10:00. What was it General Hill had said about reinforcements? That they wouldn't be here till noon? He decided not to tell anyone that relief was at least two hours off.

#

Somehow, the Union forces did not attack again that morning. By early afternoon fresh troops began arriving. Colquitt instructed Thad to vacate his position, but hold what men he had left as reserves.

"Our flank is very vulnerable, Colonel," Thad reminded him.

"I see it is. But I'm not sure we're getting enough men to extend it very far. We'd be spread too thin, if we try to."

"That high spot over there looks down on our entire line."

"I know, I know, Major. But it can't be helped."

The Union did not attack again until late afternoon. But then they mounted a furious assault, driving to within a stone's throw of Turner's Gap itself, and bringing the flanks under heavy pressure. As daylight waned, the Confederates were forced back from most of their positions. The fighting sporadically continued into the night with men firing at gun flashes. Thad's decimated regiment was moved into battle positions several times during the evening, but no longer had major responsibility for holding the line.

In the night, a courier brought a message ordering the 20th North Carolina to join the main body of Hill's forces down the hill toward Sharpsburg, a small town six miles away, close to the Potomac. Thad reflected, though he dared not tell his officers of his concerns, that this battle placement—with their backs to the Potomac—meant that defeat would mean the destruction of the Army. He wondered whether Lee had thought about this. Probably so, but the man had such confidence in the fighting ability of the Confederate soldier, even against overwhelming odds. Thad hoped Lee's wasn't misplaced confidence.

#

Tuesday night, with thousands of men around, contrasted sharply from the situation on South Mountain. Thad found little comfort in this. The forces arrayed on both sides were massive indeed. This was setting up as the heroic struggle of the War. He feared, not so much of dying but of not doing what was expected. In the drizzle and cold rain of that night, he went among his men trying to embolden them. They were no longer alone but part of Stonewall Jackson's overall command, Stonewall, the legendary hero of second Manassas. He was amazed how high their spirits were. Was he badly misjudging the steadfastness and heroic ability of these outnumbered men with their bloody feet, and with a professor as their leader?

The battle day, Thad and his men occupied the center of the Confederate line. They found protection in a road eroded by the elements and by heavy use, a road to be forever known as the Sunken Road. It provided shelter of sorts for defending against the attacking Yankees. General Lee, himself, rode up to tell them to hold at all costs. How many times had they heard similar exhortations?

#

The bloodletting turned out to be worse than Thad could ever have imagined. His mind was numbed by the number of Yankee charges, by the red hot barrels of his men's rifles, by the pile-up of Confederate bodies in this sunken road, and, of course, the blue corpses beyond. Eventually the bodies became so numerous that the sunken road no longer offered sufficient protection. His men had to crouch and prostrate themselves on bloody bodies, and even then were not adequately shielded.

Time after time they beat back federal charges, slipping and sliding on bodies as they fought hand-to-hand.

His regiment was practically gone. He had lost his favorite, Tom Ross, earlier in the morning. Sam Evans who had saved them on South Mountain was gone.

He knew he was on borrowed time. The odds of escaping the final blow were not infinite. He was overdue.

Still, the men remaining in the Sunken Road rose to repulse the enemy. Ragtails of many companies and regiments, fighting to preserve . . . what? Their pride, their manhood . . . what? Thad found himself in command of the keypoint in the center of Lee's line. He knew few of these men, now. But Jed Johnson was still with him.

"We're almost out of ammo, Major," they urgently complained.

"Take it from the wounded, and the dead," he told them time after time. Such a pileup of bodies, once living, caring humans. How much more could men stand of such bloodletting? Before becoming animals without consciences? Merciful Lord, where are you?

A final desperate Union charge carried the Road. Thad saw his men fighting to the end, not surrendering.

He was not to know that the Union advantage would be short-lived. Confederate counterattacks would soon nullify the advantage gained at the cost of thousands.

A crushing weight on his leg and chest gave him merciful oblivion. His guardian, Jed Johnson, died in the same volley. He lay on top of Barrett, protecting. But it was, of course, too late.

CHAPTER 3

The battle did not materialize the next day, Tuesday. The huge army was still gathering itself.

In the morning, Captain Reddig came to the campsite as they were finishing coffee. "Mrs. Lindsey, the Colonel wants me to tell you that as best we can determine the other woman, Clara Barton, is several miles ahead. It seems she moved her wagon during the night, and wound up just behind the front lines. We don't think you can reach her before the fighting starts, so maybe you'd best stay with us as we move up." He took a deep breath. "Mrs. Lindsey, all indications are the full battle will begin tomorrow." He hesitated, and Sarah could see his hand trembling. "Ah, the Colonel wanted me to tell you, no, to ask you . . . would you consider, being our nurse?"

Sarah's eyes teared. This was beyond anything she could ever have hoped for, to feel so needed.

"I'd be honored to," she softly said, trying not to break down.

"I'll tell the Colonel, then. Thank you." The captain touched his cap and moved away.

All that day the army edged southward. Now cannon could be heard.

"Miss Sarah, we're gettin' awful close to dem rebs," Jeremy said that night as the 7th Ohio settled in.

"Are you afraid, Jeremy?"

"I guess so," he admitted. "Not s'much for myself, but for you." With the toe of his boot he traced in the dust. "Your father, you know, trusted your safety t' me." He shook his head. "He tol' me not t' come back if anything happens to you."

"He did? Oh Jeremy, poor Jeremy," she murmured. She touched his bony shoulder. He had been with them as long as she could remember and had put her on her first horse when she was a little girl. "Such a burden I am. I didn't want this."

"It's all right, Miss Sarah. If anythin' should happen t' you, under my care, I wouldn't want t'go back. It'd never be the same."

How unfair this was, this decree of her father. Now he had placed on her the responsibility for Jeremy, so that she not expose herself to any danger. How clever of him. If she let anything happen to herself the innocent Jeremy would be blamed. She could understand her father's concern and his distorted way of protecting her, but she must be steadfast.

That night, anticipation of the coming battle seemed almost palpable. Cannon could not keep quiet, even during the middle of the night. To add further misery, a cold rain began falling before dawn. The carriage provided some shelter, but the rain found them anyway and there was no escape. In her wretchedness, she pictured the thousands of men who were trying to rest. For many it would be the last night of their lives. The marvel of it all kept rattling in her mind: how she had managed this, to be among them this night. She hoped Sol approved, but was not sure. He might feel as Pa did.

With the wonderment came a surge of fear that left her trembling, and she thought of God. She had seldom thought of Him in her comfortable life as the daughter of a small town lawyer. Even Sol's death had left her not close to God, but only resentful. Of course, she'd faithfully gone to Sunday services with her family as long as she could remember. But, somehow God seemed remote, a fiction. Suddenly she realized He was becoming very real. It started when she had desperately prayed during Pa's accident with the glass, and continued on the road over South Mountain to here. She felt His presence, like an Almighty Father observing his wilful and unruly children. She fell to her knees, praying. "Dear Lord, please give me strength for the ordeal ahead. Let me help, somehow. Let me not fail these brave men."

#

The morning started foggy. Morn of a great battle, and visibility only a hundred yards. If it would only last, maybe the full measure of bloodshed could be thwarted. In the half light, the huge camp was stirring, although the fog muted the sounds.

As Sarah and Jeremy loaded their carriage and began hitching the horses, Captain Reddig approached her. He touched his hand to his cap. "Mrs. Lindsey, you must go no farther. We probably have already brought you too close. Colonel Kimball is worried about that. We think you should look for shelters nearby. Someplace where the casualties can be brought, such as farmsteads."

As he turned to go she said, "Captain, I pray you and Colonel Kimball will be safe in the hours ahead."

He hesitated and turned back. His hand was shaking again. "And we, you," he said. "May God help us all."

Soldiers of the 7th Ohio, and others, filed past them toward the insistent cannon. During a break in the mass of troops moving past, Jeremy pointed out some farm buildings a quarter mile away.

"Maybe we should head over thar, Miss Sarah. It sure looks like a place fur a 'ospital."

Sarah agreed. But then they were again stymied by the traffic surging past. All the while guns behind and ahead blasted away. A few rebel shells tore into horses and wagons on the roadway in front of them, and she flinched.

Jeremy became agitated. "Miss Sarah, we're too close. We need t' move back!"

Sarah tried to calm him. "If our troops move on the rebs and drive them back . . . then we're in the best place to take care of casualties."

"What if the rebs ain't driven back? What if they attack?"

"God help us then."

"But you won't move back?"

"Not yet. Maybe we'll have to later."

Jeremy moved away, muttering to himself.

The fog began lifting, but the smoke of battle replaced it. Occasionally through the haze Sarah could see a distant white church building around which flags were moving back and forth.

Now the noise of cannons was almost blotted out by the hammering of small arms fire and men yelling and screaming. The troops pouring past were more driven.

It seemed hours before they could move their carriage across the road toward the farm buildings. Now they could see the gathering of wounded. Stretchers littered the grounds, with more coming by the minute, while cries and moans like a macabre chorus filled the air with every lull in the shelling.

They parked the carriage on the edge of this great gathering of wounded, and Jeremy unhitched the horses and tied them to a wheel. Sarah wandered among the wounded, moistening lips with water from her canteens, which Jeremy had to refill constantly from the barrels in the wagon. So many had wounds bloody and untreated that she soon turned to bandaging and trying to help those more profusely bleeding. She witnessed death at first hand, as some succumbed to their wounds while she knelt nearby. She realized that weak though she might have been with the dead horse, she was not weak and faint now.

She questioned those able to talk. "Are you from the 7th Ohio?"

Many turned out to be. "The Rebs were waitin' for us. They wouldn't fall back," they told her.

"Were Captain Reddig and Colonel Kimball all right?" she asked.

Most did not know. But then one, a sergeant murmured, "I saw the Colonel . . . fatally struck down. Captain Reddig . . . he's wounded. Maybe he's here, somewhere." Suddenly a spasm of pain from an abdominal wound made him cry out. His eyes were glazing over. But he moaned, "Miss . . . thank you . . . for being our nurse."

She moistened his forehead with a wet cloth. He sobbed now, "Would you hold me . . . please?"

As she held the young man in her arms, his blood seeping through to her dress, she felt strangely fulfilled: she had eased a brave man's final minutes. His breathing stopped and she laid him on the ground and closed his eyes and covered his handsome young face with his tunic. She wondered about those who would mourn him. But she well knew the mourning. She felt close to Sol, and hoped he approved.

Rising, she looked around for whatever formal medical help there might be, but saw only a few male attendants bent on moving stretchers. She instructed Jeremy on distributing their remaining supplies and asked him to look for Captain Reddig among the hundreds awaiting treatment.

The barn seemed the center of activity, and she went inside. It was one big room with stalls ripped out to give more space, and stretchers lined the perimeter, while in the middle . . .

A single surgeon with a male nurse was so engrossed in his sawing that he didn't notice her at first. Like a creature from Dante's hell, his clothes and arms were covered with blood. Even his face was a macabre blood-smeared mask. Contorted arms and legs were piled alongside the butcher table and the floor was slippery with blood. As she watched, the attendant began tossing these bloody limbs out the open back door, like junk to be discarded.

She felt faint and nauseous and wanted to flee this terrible scene. She leaned against a wall to gather the strength to do so.

Before she could get her body to move, the surgeon looked up. He started, then thundered at her, "Woman, what are you doing here? This is no place for a woman! Get the hell out of here!"

She cringed, but from somewhere calmness came over her, and her light headedness disappeared. She was aware of moving farther into the room, toward that awful table and the monster who glared at her. "I want to help." She tried to keep her voice steady, to still the tremor barely beneath the surface.

The attendant had turned his attention to the body being operated on. Before the doctor could further berate her, the man said, "He's dead, Doctor."

The surgeon took a deep breath, wiped his bloody hand across his forehead, and leaned against the table. He peered long at her, weariness evident in every line of his face. Then more softly he said, "We could use help if you're strong enough to handle this."

"I think I am, Doctor. Please let me try."

"So many, so many . . ." he muttered. He roused himself. "Well, we can see, if you're really up to it. All these shattered arms and legs, they have to be cut off. You could help with the tourniquet and giving chloroform."

He showed her how to fix the tourniquet and administer chloroform, and she watched as he amputated. Tying off the arteries seemed to be the major bottleneck. She leaned over him as he was bent down trying to clamp a particularly difficult flow of blood. He stopped, straightened up, and looked at her. She braced herself for a harsh reprimand.

Instead, he said, "I wonder, young lady, could you help me clamp and tie off the arteries after I've amputated? Are you up to this?"

"I think so, Doctor. I've been watching you do it."

He looked at her rather wild eyed, she thought. He muttered something. She could barely hear it, but thought it was, "Has the Lord brought you to me?" And a chill went through her.

He showed her what to do, and they worked side by side. She was surprised how quickly she adjusted to the primitive medical conditions, and how quickly she became inured to the blood and pain.

A door laid upon four barrels served as the operating table. Several tubs were alongside to catch the blood. Nearby also were pails of water, rags, and sponges to be used to swish away the bloody slime after each operation. The surgeon dipped the smeared instruments in these pails, then wiped them with his hand. And Pa was right, she quickly realized. Fresh water either for drinking or for medical purposes was terribly scarce, adding to the misery and the fatalities.

At first she shuddered at the callousness of the procedure, but the doctor quickly changed her mind. "We don't have time to be respectful or compassionate. Our goal is to save as many lives as possible."

His amputation procedure, which she later learned was standard practice, was to use a large knife to slice the soft tissue to the bone just above the damaged area and below the tourniquet, then finish the job with a hacksaw. In the process, the blood vessels needed to be clamped and tied off with oiled silk. Sarah's nimble fingers soon proved adept at this in the slippery mess of blood.

After a while she became aware that the sounds of battle were intensifying. Union guns seemed to have moved closer, and their thundering shook the operating table. With increasing frequency, retaliatory Confederate shells landed nearby. From the screams outside, she knew some must have fallen among the wounded waiting their turn at the table. Several times they winced as a shell barely missed the barn.

The noise reached a crescendo. The surgeon gritted his teeth, "If the shells don't get us, we'll be lucky not to be captured by the Rebs. You've done far beyond . . . Please leave now. While you can."

She looked at this bloody man. She asked, "Are you staying, Doctor?"

"Yes. But I have an obligation to these men. It's my job."

She gritted her teeth, and wiped her forehead with her own bloody hands. This was far worse than she'd ever imagined, yet she was so needed. Was she strong enough for all this? Somehow she felt she just might be. "I feel driven to help, too," she heard herself saying.

"Holy Lord, what are we coming to," he muttered.

#

Sounds of battle lessened by late afternoon as fighting shifted to the far left of the Union front. Sarah went to the door in a brief respite between amputations. She looked down at herself. She was as bloody as the surgeon. She knew she should be exhausted, but somehow had found reserves of strength she'd never known. Then she looked out. The wounded stretched almost forever, it seemed, around the farmstead.

The doctor came up behind her. "You performed real good. And I don't even know your name. I'm John Rizzo."

"Sarah Lindsey, Doctor."

"What could have brought you to this hell on earth?"

"I wanted to help. My husband, well, he was killed at Shiloh. If I were a man, I would have fought."

"You've done far more good as a physician's helper."

She looked at him. "Do you really mean it?"

"Yes, I do." He put his hand on her shoulder. "C'mon, Sarah, let's go back to the butcher shop."

She lost track of time during that longest day. Sometime toward evening they ran out of chloroform. He instructed her, "Place this leather strap in their mouths, so they can bite down on it in their agony."

As she looked at him in dismay, he continued, "We can't stop. These shattered limbs have to come off, regardless of the pain."

At least the leather gag muffled their screams. Several men had now been recruited to help hold down the patients before they lapsed into unconsciousness. She wondered whether Sol had been exposed to such a demoniac finish to his life, or whether he had died outright, with no pain or suffering. She was never told.

Sounds of battle faded with the night. But in the darkness, they had to stop. The few lanterns didn't provide enough light to operate.

"We would try it under the moonlight," John Rizzo told her. "But there's no moonlight. I've sent men out to get more lanterns, but they haven't found any."

"I should have brought candles," she told him. "My father and I wondered what supplies to bring. We didn't think of candles, or lanterns."

"Nor did the U. S. Army," he said.

#

Dr. Rizzo insisted she get some sleep. "There'll still be plenty to do tomorrow, and things will go better if you're not too exhausted."

Sarah found her way back to the carriage and Jeremy. He roused briefly. "I gave out all dem supplies. We coulda' used ten wagons of 'em. Are we goin' back tomorrow?" he asked sleepily.

"I don't think tomorrow. Maybe the next day. Did you ever find Captain Reddig?"

"I couldn't find 'im. Maybe he was taken somewheres else."

"Or maybe he's still out on the field," she said. "Go back to sleep, Jeremy. Tomorrow's another long day."

She was bone tired, but couldn't sleep. Finally she got up and wandered over toward the edge of the battlefield. In the blackness, the field was lit by torches held by small groups searching for more wounded among the piles of dead. She wondered whether Captain Reddig could still be lying out there somewhere.

Reluctantly she turned back toward her shelter, trying not to step on bodies, and fell exhausted alongside the carriage. But she still couldn't go right to sleep. Her last thought was of the marvel of Pa's bloody hand toughening her for what she had just been through.

#

Dawn, and the din of the great mass of men stirring awakened her. Jeremy was still sleeping, and she didn't want to take time to make coffee. She felt guilty at sleeping so long as she made her way back to the barn where Dr. Rizzo was already operating.

"I'm sorry," she told him. "I overslept, and there's so much still to do."

He looked up and smiled at her. "I was afraid you'd had enough and fled during the night, and I wouldn't have blamed you. But I'd have truly missed my number one assistant surgeon."

She was touched by his praise. Now he looked closely at her. "Your dress is ruined. Do you have a clean one for when you're through here?"

She looked down at herself, shocked at what she saw. She'd not realized how bad it was. Stains and dirt had made its original color and fabric unrecognizable, and the day had barely begun.

He asked again, "Do you have a clean dress?"

"No. I didn't think about clothes when I decided to come." She could feel her face coloring.

"I see," he said. Soon the question was forgotten as they became absorbed in the surgery.

#

This day went better than the previous one. A truce seemed to have been declared. Firing had stopped, and both sides were gathering their wounded and identifying the dead. Several surgeons and nurses arrived early afternoon.

An older woman told Sarah that Preacher Williams had brought three wagonloads of supplies and twenty people to the eastern end of the line. The woman added, "They said you had come on ahead. They wanted me to watch out for you. They're praying you're all right." The woman looked at her strangely. "From what I've heard from the doctor, you've helped, so very much." She was still watching her intently.

Sarah felt embarrassed again. Her dress was completely covered with blood, her hands were bloody. and she reckoned her face most likely was bloody, too. And her hair.

The woman continued. "Dr. Rizzo was concerned you didn't have a clean dress to put on after this is all over and he asked if I could find one for you." She smiled.

"I think I have one that should fit you just fine."

Now, with wonderment, Sarah realized the woman was viewing her with genuine admiration and respect.

#

Later that afternoon, Sarah bade farewell to Dr. Rizzo. Her services were no longer needed with all the replacements that had arrived, and she'd changed to the clean dress. "I think I'll always remember this, working with you and all these poor soldiers," she said. She realized she had never really seen his face without it being smeared with blood. Now he had made a reasonable effort to clean up, and was darkly handsome. She noticed that he had not gotten all the blood out of his beard, though. Well, she probably still had blood in her hair, too. She felt close to him in spirit, somehow closer even than with Sol. They had shared so much.

He was staring at her. "I'm being transfered to the base hospital in Baltimore in a few days. This place should be closed by then and the men who are still alive shipped to permanent hospitals." He continued to study her. She looked down at her dress wondering if she'd gotten it dirty already. "Sarah, I'll always remember you," he said. "Your grit. Your remarkable dedication. And, yes, your nimble fingers."

She thanked him, and turned to go.

"Sarah, let me give you a thought."

She turned back. Suddenly a premonition struck her that something momentous was about to happen. Her eyes were large as she managed the words, "A thought?"

He nodded, very serious. "I know it's unheard of for a woman to think of medical school. Of becoming a doctor. Much less a surgeon. But I understand a few woman are becoming trailblazers."

A thrill went through her.

He continued. "I would be very happy to give you a recommendation. Think about this, long and hard."

She struggled not to break down. Physically she was so beat. And now this . . . this wonderful idea. Such an all-consuming quest this could be. "Thank you, Dr. Rizzo," she murmured. "I hadn't dreamed . . ."

He squeezed her arm. "Please call me John. If you should get to Baltimore, look me up there. We could talk more about medical school then. And you might want to try nursing for a while in one of the big base hospitals." He smiled, "Of course, it'd be a lot tamer than a field hospital just behind the front lines."

Dazed, she left to find her way back to Jeremy and the carriage.

CHAPTER 4

After the euphoria of her last conversation with Dr. Rizzo, Sarah found it difficult to tear herself away from the most momentous experience of her life. She and Jeremy should go home, to Pa, to relieve his concerns and to the comfort of normal routine. But was she ready for that? Two days had changed her life.

She went back that early evening to the wagon and Jeremy. "Are we goin' back now?" he asked.

"Maybe in the morning. I want to wander the battlefield one more time."

"What can you 'spect to find there? Only dead men, for sure," he said, sounding concerned.

"I don't know, Jeremy. Please bear with me. This is a new experience . . . for both of us."

He didn't approve, she could see that. But who would approve what she was doing? Not her father, certainly. Not Preacher Williams. Anybody? She made an effort to mollify Jeremy. "We'll head back tomorrow morning."

Near the end of this day after, the guns still remained silent. In a kind of tacit truce, throughout the day both blue and gray scoured the fields looking for survivors and burying the dead in shallow graves. But the task was overwhelming. Many dead were still on the field. Could there be any living men out there, among these bodies?

Earlier in the day she had thought as many gray as blue were searching the fields for their fallen. Now the Confederates seemed to have abandoned the grounds. She wondered about this. Did it mean they had already recovered all their casualties? Somehow she doubted that.

She went out into the fields again as the sun moved closer to the horizon. Of a sudden, she realized her hatred of the Rebels had diminished, even vanished. They had surely suffered as badly as the men in blue. In the operating room, she had not even been aware of the color of a man's uniform.

She decided to make one last effort to locate Captain Reddig, just in case he might still be on the field unattended. She knew the 7th Ohio had fought mainly on this end of the line, toward the white Church in the distance, that she now knew was called the Dunker Church, and on the sunken road lying before her. As she picked her way among the bodies she wished she had started earlier, while there was good light.

Many of the bodies were stiffening and the smell of death was pervasive. She tied a kerchief over her nose and mouth to keep out the sickening odors. Around her the wounded seemed to have all been removed. But in the sunken road, the bodies still lay two and three deep. There could be wounded under the dead.

She gingerly made her way along the road. Impossible not to step on bodies. If someone were unconscious underneath, she wouldn't know. But if there was even a slight noise or moan . . .

The battlefield was quiet tonight, except for crows in the distance giving their final cries before the dark.

She bent down often to listen for any faint sounds, but could hear nothing. Night was almost on the field but a half moon gave an eerie light over this ghostly landscape. In a few more minutes she would have to give up and go back to the wagon and Jeremy. She hoped Captain Reddig had been found.

Then she thought she heard a faint moan. She wasn't sure. "Please," she cried out, "Is anyone there? Please make a noise. So I can help you."

She heard it again, underneath the bodies, somewhere to her right.

Frantically she tugged at the stiffened corpses, trying to pull them off the survivor.

Now, in the dim light she could see he was a Confederate officer. Badly wounded. Her trained eye took in what must be a chest wound and another shattered leg waiting for amputation.

"Water," he whispered.

She had brought several canteens, just in case. She moistened his lips, then tore off part of her skirt and wet it and wiped his face, shuddering at the heat of his fever.

He was trying to say something. She bent down. "Am I in heaven?" she thought he murmured. She had heard that question before, and a thrill went through her: these men thought she was an angel, and not just a homely country girl.

"No, you're not," she managed to say. "Now I'm going to try to get some help."

Small groups still roamed the fields with torches. None were close, but she had to attract attention, for the hospital was too far away. This man might well be dead before she could make it back to get help.

She stood and shouted, "Help! Help! Over here! We need help!"

Now several torches moved in her direction. She heard a man yelling, "Where are you? Keep shouting!"

"Over here! Here!" She was almost crying as the torches came nearer. "We have a wounded man here."

"Miss, what're you doing out heah alone, on this death field? An' no light with you?"

"When I started it was still light. I'm from the hospital, looking for anyone still alive. And here's a badly wounded Rebel officer. Do you have a stretcher?"

"We have one comin'. Over here, Lucas!" the man shouted. He directed the torch down. "Looks like a Reb major. Pretty high ranking to be still on the field."

"He was under some of these bodies. I heard him moan."

"An' you pulled the bodies off, by yourself?"

She nodded in the flickering light. The man was appraising her now. She could see she'd gotten her clean dress all bloody again. The Rebel moaned. She bent down and gave him more water. "We're going to get you to the hospital real soon."

Other torchbearers approached with a stretcher. "We've a Reb major here, boys. Looks bad hurt, but still alive," the first man said. They eased him on the stretcher. "Why don't you lead the way, ma'am, to that hospital. Here, you take this torch."

#

Dr. Rizzo was still working, as were several other surgeons. "We have a badly wounded Confed major, Doctor . . . John. I don't think he can last without immediate attention. And he's burning up with fever."

"Holy . . . !" He stared at her incredulously. "Were you out on the field tonight?"

"I thought there might be some wounded still there."

"And where was this man?" he asked as he made preparations for the examination. "How come nobody found him?"

"In the sunken road, under bodies."

Rizzo took a deep breath. "I'll be damned," he muttered. "Well, if we save him he's got you to thank for his life."

But after looking him over, Rizzo shook his head. "I don't know that we can save him." He studied her. "I see your dress is bloody again. Do you want to assist me with this man?"

"Yes."

"This will be more than a simple amputation."

"I'll help however I can."

They cut away his uniform, and bared the ugly chest wound. "Sarah, give him the chloroform now. And move that lantern closer so we can see better."

She was fascinated as Dr. Rizzo probed the chest wound for fragments of cloth and bone. The bullet had not exited, so he had to find it and remove the distorted metal. Sarah worked at his side, sponging up the blood and giving him the instruments he demanded as quickly as she could.

"I think we've gotten all the foreign substances," he muttered finally. "All we can do is close him up and hope for the best. Here Sarah, your nimble fingers can do this. Thusly."

Her hands were remarkably steady as she followed his directions. "Now Sarah, we have to remove his leg." He looked at her reflectively. "Would you like to do it?"

She stared at him. Dear Lord, she couldn't believe what she'd heard. "Yes," she said firmly.

"Then I'll assist," he said.

She placed the tourniquet, and took a deep breath before making the incision, willing her hands to be steady for this cut to the bone, above the grievous wound on the thigh, as she'd seen him do so many times. They tied the arteries, working together. Then he handed her the saw. She grasped it, but shivered at the feel of sawing human bone. Still, the saw's violation was easier than she'd expected. This did not require great strength, only a good saw. The shattered leg was quickly severed. And they turned their attention to the stump.

"Well done, Sarah," he said at last. "I knew you could do it. I couldn't have done it better myself."

She felt exhausted. On the verge of fainting. "Sit down, Sarah. Lower your head to your knees, for a few minutes. You'll be fine." He instructed the male attendants to prepare a lean-to outside near the building for this special patient.

"Will he live, Doctor?"

"It's in God's hands."

"What will happen now, to him, if he lives?"

"We certainly can't move him, for at least a few days and maybe longer. If the fever breaks and he survives the next forty-eight hours we'll see about getting him to Frederick, and eventually to Baltimore. If he gets better he can probably be paroled and sent home. Of course, he'll never fight again."

"Would it be all right if I stayed a few days more to try to help him?"

"Dear Sarah. You saved his life. I'm not surprised you feel an attachment for him. But he's likely to die. Do you really want to be around for that?"

"I . . . I think I do. Do you think, John, I could make a difference?"

He looked at her and started to shake his head. Then he hesitated. "I don't know," he finally said.

#

She broke the news to Jeremy late that night. "I found a badly wounded rebel officer on the field, and I want to stay another day or so, to see if he makes it. But I think you should go back. Father will be frantic with worry."

"He won't like this, your stayin', you know."

"I know," she said, realizing the depths of her exhaustion.

"How you gonna get back, Miss Sarah? If'n I leave?"

"Maybe you can leave me one of the horses. With the carriage empty, you won't need both horses."

"But dere's no saddle."

"I'll ride bareback."

He shook his head. "Twenty miles, bareback? Golly, Miss Sarah." He scratched his head. "Maybe I can come back wit' a ridin' horse for you."

"That would be nice." She couldn't keep her eyes open. "I've got to sleep now, before I fall down."

"Sure, Miss Sarah. Can I heat you some stew 'fore you lie down?"

She nodded, but was asleep before he could.

#

She woke early the next morning amid cries of crows and vultures. She moved quietly around Jeremy, trying to fix a bit to eat and the much-needed coffee. She gathered her few belongings, and prepared to depart, but he roused.

"Miss Sarah, where you gonna stay if'n I take the carriage?"

"I'll bed down at the hospital. Now don't fret about me. Tell Pa I'm fine. The battle's over. There's no danger anymore. But I have something I have to see through. Tell him that, Jeremy."

"He'll be mad that I left you."

"Tell him I insisted. Tell him I've found great comfort in what I've been doing these past few days. Tell him that I have some ideas I'd like to discuss with him when I get home."

#

She made her way to the hospital and to the tent they erected for the Reb major alongside it. She feared he'd died during the night. If he had, probably no one had noticed. She would be the one to make the discovery, and she would be devastated.

Somehow she felt a powerful interest in this man whose life she'd saved, if even for just a few hours. She steeled herself before moving into the flimsy shelter and was almost afraid to look at him. She heaved a sigh when she saw he was still alive, though unconscious. His fever had not broken. His cheeks were slightly flushed and his breathing was labored.

She made her way to the barn and Dr. Rizzo, and told him the situation. "I won't be here much longer," Dr. Rizzo said. "But your Confederate major should either be dead or a survivor by then."

"John, what if it storms on these poor wounded men tonight or the next few days?"

"You know shelter's terribly scarce. Your major, well, we should be able to bring him inside, if that happens. If he's still alive." He sighed. "If he were a private, Reb or Union, God help him, he'd have to take his chances out in the elements."

"You're going to Baltimore, then?"

"Yes, I'm to report Monday. We have enough medical help now, and this place will soon be shutting down." He looked at her. "Sarah, remember what I told you."

"I remember. I can't get it out of my mind. It's almost like you've branded me. With an idea. And letting me operate last night . . ."

"You're a natural." He paused, considering this. "Maybe you're one of the chosen." The pulse pounded in her ear at this idea. "Please, come to Baltimore when you can."

"I will, Doctor . . . John. I surely must."

#

Now she devoted most of her time to the major, dressing his oozing wounds, the terribly defiled stump, placing cold cloths on his hot forehead, forcing sips of water into his mouth. There seemed little improvement and he had not regained consciousness.

"He's still alive," John Rizzo observed several times during the day. "That's encouraging. Now if that fever would only break."

Toward evening, the major began shivering violently. Sarah scronged around for anything to cover him. Rizzo joined her. "I think, Sarah, this may be the breakup of the fever."

"Do you think so? I was afraid this might mean the end."

"We must let him sweat, so keep him well covered. Don't let him get chilled."

As darkness approached, he became drenched in sweat and extremely agitated. She toweled him off and his body seemed cooler, although the shivering would not stop. Dr. Rizzo instructed an orderly to bring fresh bedclothes. "I think if we're careful and don't let him get too chilled, he may make it. Next, we'll need to get some food in him."

She sat through that night, toweling off the sweat, moistening his lips, trying to force water. In the flickering light of the lantern she studied his face. It was a nice face, good bones, dark hair shielding a high forehead. He had been clean shaven, but now his face was stubbled. He appeared younger than she'd thought, probably only a few years older than herself. She picked up a hand and was impressed with the long slender fingers. She absently stroked it.

"Hi," he whispered. She started. He was conscious and coherent. She dropped his hand embarrassed. "Is this a dream? Are you real?"

She smiled. "I'm real."

His eyelids closed. "I'm glad." He sunk back into sleep. But the coma was broken, as was the fever. In the morning he roused again. She was able to get some hot soup into him.

"You need food if you're to get back your strength."

His eyes followed her. "Are you . . . the one . . . who found me?"

"Yes." She hesitated, wondering how much to tell him. "I found you on that bloody lane, under dead bodies."

"I didn't . . . think . . . I'd ever . . . be found. Then everything . . . went black." He took a ragged breath, and struggled to say more.

"Don't talk for now," she cautioned.

"I remember an . . . angel," he murmured. "Was that . . . a dream? Or you?"

"I guess it was me. You were barely conscious when I found you. But then you lapsed into a coma." She stroked his cheek. "Now be quiet, and rest."

"Did they take . . . my leg?"

"Yes."

He groaned, and closed his eyes. His hand gripped the blanket. Then he opened his eyes. "What is . . . your name?"

"Sarah. Sarah Lindsey."

"Thad Barrett." Now he seemed exhausted, and soon lapsed into sleep.

With his improvement, she realized how tired she was. She'd slept little in twenty-four hours. She wrapped herself in a blanket, and lay down besides him. A thunder clap woke her toward noon. Dark clouds were rolling across the western sky with their premonitory rain drops.

She hurried inside the barn to get help. The flimsy lean-to over Thad Barrett would hardly be adequate protection in a storm. She looked around but didn't see Dr. Rizzo. She hoped he hadn't left yet. Two male nurse attendants were standing around talking.

"Can you help me bring the Confederate officer inside?" she asked urgently. "Dr. Rizzo said there was space in here in case of a storm."

"We have no space here for a Reb," one said curtly. "Let the bastard get rained on."

"Please," she pleaded. "He's seriously wounded, has almost died."

"Good riddance." The man turned away.

"Jake, loosen up," the other man spoke up. "This woman worked with the Doc. During the battle. All the next day, too. She's the one that found the Reb. Under a pile of bodies."

"So what," the other man retorted. But he had turned back and was staring at her.

"Jake, we owe her something. She didn't have to do this. She saved lives, man."

Jake thought about this, and shrugged. "Only for you, miss," he told her. "I still don' cotton to saving any Rebs, though."

So they carried Thad inside, just as the storm broke. Wind and rain pelted the windows and the sides of the building. But he was safe from the elements, if not from his festering wounds.

#

That evening Dr. Rizzo bade her a last goodbye. "I'm on my way to catch the train at Hagerstown. I think the Reb is going to make it, thanks to you. He's scheduled to be sent to Baltimore in a few more days. Unless he takes a turn for the worst." He paused. "When are you going back home?"

"Probably tomorrow morning. I'm expecting our groom to bring a riding horse, then."

"How long a ride?"

"About twenty miles. But it's on the other side of South Mountain. In Pleasant Valley."

"Pleasant Valley? It sounds like a refuge." He swept his hand around. "From all this."

They stood silent, assessing each other. Then she softly asked, "Would you hold me, for a moment, Dr. John?" He moved to her and stroked her hair as her chin rested against his shoulder. He kissed her cheek, and she fought to keep from breaking down and crying. But she wouldn't let herself. "I'll always remember these few days, John. To feel so needed, so useful, terrible though it was." She moved away a bit. "Thank you."

He sighed audibly. Then he grinned. "All this hasn't been good for your dresses. We can't keep you in an unbloody one, can we?"

She returned his smile. "It seems not." She heard someone calling for the doctor, from the doorway.

"It's my driver," he told her. "I have to go." He took both her hands and drew her to him again, and kissed her strongly on the lips. She tried to pull away, but then pressed against him and felt her heart racing. The moment passed, and they drew apart. He gathered his valise and followed the driver to the carriage. There he turned and mouthed a single word as she stood in the doorway: "Baltimore."

As the carriage moved away, taking John to a distant city, she realized she didn't know whether he was married or single. She'd never asked, and he'd never said. But why should it matter?

Incredibly, under the demands of the last few days thoughts of Sol had faded, the pain of his loss seemed to have crusted over, at least temporarily. Was her love so shallow? Her conscience bothered her that she felt some attraction for John. Surely this must be the result of their working side by side during these terrible days. Wasn't it? Could it also be due to the dream he had proferred her? She tried to regain her closeness to Sol.

She turned back inside. It was time to see how the Reb major, Thad, was getting along. Maybe he'd be able to take some solid food now.

He was awake. "I was afraid you'd . . . gone."

She smiled down at him. "I'll probably be leaving tomorrow morning. I understand you're likely to be moved to Baltimore in a day or two. To a regular hospital."

"Might you be there?"

She started, thoughts jumbled. This was the second man in this short space of time who wanted her in Baltimore. "I don't know," she whispered, as she dipped a piece of bread in the broth and carefully placed it in his mouth. "Maybe."

He seemed so vulnerable, so boyish. She realized now his resemblance to Sol. Except Sol had been blonde, and this man was dark. The thought of Sol reminded her how she had judged these Confederates as inhuman monsters who had killed her husband. And she had so hated them.

He was saying, "Did you . . . get them to bring me in . . . before the storm?"

"I thought your life was in danger."

"Did I dream that . . . you were lying beside me . . . when the thunder crashed?"

Her face reddened. "I was exhausted. I'd been up all night."

"Taking care of me?"

"We thought you might die."

He studied her face. "Sarah, I am so much . . . in your debt . . . how can I repay? . . ." his voice faded.

"Shush," she said, stroking his forehead. "Don't wear yourself out talking. You're not a well man, yet."

"Please tell me . . . about yourself."

So as the daylight faded, and lanterns were lit in the cramped interior of a barn turned field hospital, she told about herself. About growing up in Pleasant Valley, daughter of a lawyer. About being a school teacher, and then meeting and somehow marrying Solomon, a dashing Union captain, who was killed last spring at Shiloh. When she told him about Sol being killed, he groaned.

"I'm so sorry . . . this bloody war," he said.

She told him of her dream, maybe an impossible dream, of becoming a doctor.

"Don't ever believe it's . . . impossible," he murmured. "I have a dream . . . too. To become . . . a great writer."

"Ah," she said, impressed. "What were you, before all this?"

"A professor . . . of rhetoric. At a small college, in North Carolina, in the mountains." For a moment his face became wistful and his eyes faraway. "I didn't think . . . I'd ever see those green and purple mountains again." He shook his head. "You know, Sarah, I thought I'd be killed . . . in your Maryland mountains, at South Mountain. We were outnumbered three to one, defending the pass . . . I thought how fitting it would be . . . to die on a mountain."

Now he sighed, for the moment worn out from talking. Sarah stared at him, profoundly moved by this man. She asked gently, "You must have someone waiting anxiously for you, back in Carolina?"

"Only an old aunt, Aunt Abigail. She's a real character . . . likes to chew tobacco and spit it at beetles and other critters. Occasionally she hits one." He smiled at the recollection, but then a sharp jab of pain contorted his face.

Concerned, she reprimanded herself. "Enough of this. I've been wearing you out, with all this talking. Try to sleep."

"Would you . . . hold my hand? For a little while?"

He soon fell into an exhausted sleep.

God help her. She was becoming too attached to this patient. This crippled but heroic man, who might yet die of his wounds, and who reminded her of Sol. He evidently had not been married, or at least was not now. She wondered about that, then scolded herself for such thoughts. Like a school girl she had suddenly become.

She had read some place, or maybe Dr. Rizzo had told her, that doctors and nurses shouldn't let themselves become too emotionally attached to a patient. If they do, they lose objectivity. Well, she was not a doctor yet. Just a naive small town girl, awestruck by the violence and vast canvas of war.

#

Her father arrived with Jeremy the next morning. She was glad she'd washed out the worst of the blood from her dress, but stains remained.

"Papa, I didn't expect you to come."

"It 'pears I should have come sooner. Jeremy tells me you were practically on the front line."

"But only for one day. I was so needed."

"I also heard from some of Preacher Williams' folks that you were covered with blood from head to foot. At first, I was afraid some of it was yours. But they assured me it was not. That you were assisting a doctor with amputations." He looked more closely at her. "From the condition of your dress these wild tales must be true. Were you?"

"Were I what?"

"Doing surgeon's work, my impulsive and reckless daughter." But he said this gently, she thought.

"I've found a purpose for my life, Pa. To help the sick and injured."

"You want to be a nurse, then? They're not held in very high regard. Isn't teaching school good enough for you?"

"The war is changing the image of nursing. Florence Nightingale started it a decade ago. But I want to do more."

"More?"

"I want to become a doctor. Go to medical school."

He stared at her, unbelieving. "What are you saying, girl? You know that all doctors are men. That medical schools only accept men. It's too hard for a woman."

"That's changing, too. It won't be easy, but a few schools will now accept women." She could hear her voice rising. Calm down, she told herself. Men are so eager to label women as emotional, every chance they can get. And they equated being emotional with unfitness for many things. More quietly, she said, "The doctor I worked with during the battle days suggested I consider becoming a doctor, even a surgeon. He said he'd write a recommendation to help me get into medical school."

"Really?"

"Yes, truly so."

He grunted, "What a wild spirit." Then he turned ominous. "Jeremy also tells me you found a Rebel officer, probably saved his life. One of those who killed Sol. Have you forgotten whose side you're on?" He was slapping a fist against his leg.

She struggled to find the right words. Blast Jeremy. Why couldn't he keep his mouth shut? He knew how Father felt about Rebs. Why was he so quick to tattle? "I found him on the battlefield that night, under a pile of bodies, at the bloodiest part of the whole fight, where more men died than any other place. He'd been there for more than 24 hours, near death." She paused. She could see no compassion in her father's face, only anger and cold incomprehension.

"He was burning up with fever, had a terrible chest wound, and a shattered leg. Doctor Rizzo and I operated on his wounds. Afterwards, I sat with him trying to ease his raging fever."

"He lived, I gather," her father said sarcastically.

"Yes, he's still alive. They expect to ship him to a base hospital in a few days."

"Well, let's forget about this, and go home, Daughter."

"Only for a few days, Pa. I want to go to Baltimore, where Dr. Rizzo will be. I may work there a while as a nurse. Then, we'll see."

"Is that where that Reb is getting sent to?"

How perceptive her father was. She wished he were more flexible in his attitudes. Once he formed one, he was like a bulldog, unwilling to bend or compromise. "I don't know. Possibly, although it could be Frederick, or Washington City. Eventually, if he lives, he'll probably be paroled back to North Carolina. To start life over, as a professor."

"You know a lot about this Reb. I suppose you even know whether he's married or not."

Sarah didn't want to answer that, didn't want to fan the fire.

"Well, is he married?" Pa demanded, his voice rising.

"No," she said in a little voice.

"Ha, I thought as much."

"I need to tell him goodbye. Please, Pa, will you come with me to meet him? Thad's a nice man."

"So, you're on a first name basis with him. Gawd help us!" He was icy still, a vein in his forehead standing out.

"Pa, please bend a little. In this terrible war brothers are fighting brothers. Both sides are sorely afflicted. Thad didn't kill Sol. Their cause did. It's killing them as much as us." She touched his arm, but he shrugged it off. "Please, Pa, come and meet him."

"Never, Sarah! I can't accept this. You should've left him under those bodies. You're betraying your own husband. He was a martyr for your country, and you're betraying him," he said bitterly.

Sarah shivered at this savage portrayal of her actions. "Good God, I'm not betraying Sol. Pa, your prejudices make you seem inhuman. Things are not black and white." She was tearing. She couldn't help it.

His face remained grim. "Say goodbye to this Reb . . . this enemy, if you must!" He spat out the words. "But make it fast! We leave in fifteen minutes."

She left before he could change his mind. He was so quick to anger. She had hoped his crushing the glass in his hand would have toned down his uncontrollable anger. But it hadn't. She could imagine him dragging her bodily away from this place.

She hurried into the building and threaded her way between the wounded to Thad in a quiet corner. She was afraid he'd be sleeping, but he was awake, watching for her.

"I hoped you'd stop by . . . before you left," he said.

"I thought you might be asleep. I wouldn't have wanted to wake you."

"I was afraid you'd feel that way."

"So you wouldn't let yourself sleep."

"No." He smiled weakly. "I can sleep when you're not here."

She held his hand, and laid her other hand on his cheek.

He sighed. "I think I'm falling in love."

"Don't."

"Yes, I know I shouldn't."

"Thad, I have to go." He nodded but didn't release her hand. "My father is here. He hates the Confederacy."

He squeezed her hand gently before releasing it. "I understand. Thank you, dear Sarah."

She bent down and kissed him on the lips. He took a ragged breath. "Goodbye Thad. I hope you'll become a famous writer."

"And you a wonderful doctor."

She fled the building, emotions threatening to get the best of her. She must fight this off, not let Pa and Jeremy see her weep after leaving the enemy. That would be the final straw in Pa's all-consuming hatred.

CHAPTER 5

Thad Barrett felt Sarah's departure keenly. He realized his dependence on her. Or was it a lot more? He could not expect her or anyone to personally nurse him in these days of thousands needing care, and he a Confederate in Union hands. Her soft and gentle touch, her quiet voice, her lovely face—how could he forget these? And the tender kiss she had given him before she left that morning?

As he lay in the crowded shelter that served as a field hospital, he tried to analyze his feelings. Maybe there was something to be learned from all this, something profound. But he couldn't grasp it. We are all pawns, he decided, to be manipulated by those enamored with their authority—while a merciless God looks down, seemingly unconcerned. Still, his thoughts kept coming back to the one shining interlude in all this horrible war, and he tried to imagine again the feel of her lovely presence. He had told her he was falling in love. He remembered her staring at him at that announcement. Now in the harsh light of reality he knew the futility of his love, he not only an enemy but a legless man with the further infirmity of a bad chest wound and an uncertain prognosis.

The next day a doctor examined him. "Major," he was told, "You're doing reasonably well if you don't get an acute infection. We'll be sending you on to Baltimore shortly."

"I appreciate . . . your care . . . for me an enemy . . . I'm deeply in your debt . . . sir," he whispered.

The doctor said, "We are all brothers in the aftermath of battle." He hazarded, "I'm sure your medical people are treating our wounded with the same care."

After the doctor left, Thad wondered whether any cause was worth all this pain and death. The thought again flickered across his mind: Did Robert Lee ever wonder whether all the killing was worth it, whatever the cause?

They moved him the next day. Now began the agony of the ambulance to the closest rail site at Hagerstown. On the jolting journey, he let himself sink into a red haze of pain, comforting himself that he was one of many. At least the pain meant that he was still among the living. At times he doubted the desirability of that.

He thought things would be better once they reached the train. But the jerking and swaying was little improvement. He floated in and out of consciousness. Sometimes his dreams were wild: such as those of the angel, Sarah. Once he was amazed. He felt himself aroused by his thoughts of her. Yet, he was barely beyond death's door. What a marvel!

Eventually the train reached Baltimore and the ambulances waiting to transport them to hospitals. In his stupor he was barely aware of the logistics. He was only a hunk of beef to be manhandled in whatever manner suited those in authority. Was there really any system in all this chaos? Whether as efficient as possible under the circumstances or the utmost of neglect and disorganization, he couldn't rightly tell. It would make no difference, that was for sure.

#

The hospital was a sprawling place, an impersonal waystation between life and death. While inside protected from rain and storms, the smells were the vapors of hell. There were not enough nurses and attendants to care for all these grievously wounded men, even for their simple body needs. He even missed the more primitive conditions at the field hospital. He sank into a deep and troubled sleep.

Some days later he was roused by a Federal officer, also a major as it turned out. The man seemed somehow familiar. Maybe from the field hospital?

"Major Barrett, I'm Major Rizzo, Dr. Rizzo. I took care of you, with Sarah, at Antietam. I wanted to stop and see how you're doing. From your chart it looks like you're getting along quite well. If we can keep your stump draining and any fevers away."

"Were you the one . . . who operated on me?"

Rizzo looked at him, without saying anything.

"Were you?"

"I took care of your chest. Sarah took care of your leg."

"She did?" Thad was incredulous.

"Yes."

"And she found me on the battlefield."

"You owe her your life."

"I thought as much."

"I needed to see how fares the man she saved."

"I imagined an angel. And I think I fell . . . in love with that angel."

Now it was Rizzo's turn to sigh. "I feared that, if you lived. Major Barrett, I think we're both in love with the same woman." He hesitated a moment. "Did you know she's a recent widow, that her husband was killed at Shiloh?"

"Yes, she told me," Thad whispered. He groaned, then roused. "And she still saved me, an enemy. What a marvel."

"Yes, a marvel." Rizzo sighed. "I don't know how this will work out. Whether she could be interested in either one of us."

"How could she be interested in a . . . Reb?"

"Saving your life, nursing you, that's a powerful attraction." Thad's heart leaped at these words. Could it be? Rizzo went on. "I thought you'd die. Didn't think you had a chance."

"But you didn't give up taking care of me."

"No, I couldn't do that and be able to live with myself. Major Barrett, you received the best care Civil War medicine could provide. And you'll continue to."

"I'm truly grateful, to you, and Sarah."

"Yes, well . . ." the surgeon turned away.

"Tell me, Doctor, do you think we'll see Sarah again. Is she likely to come here?"

Rizzo turned back to him. "I thought she might. I'd hoped she would. Now I'm not so sure." He hesitated. "I told her she ought to consider medical school and train to be a doctor. I would try to help her get accepted."

Thad remembered her telling him this dream. But didn't it shatter any hopes he might have? He managed to say, "A wonderful thing, that. She would be forever indebted to you, I'm sure."

Rizzo stared at him, eyes narrowed.

Thad tried not to let his dejection show. He murmured, "I wish her only the best. She truly deserves it. And I fear the best for her does not rest with being with me. In these times."

"Women are seldom rational." Then Rizzo smiled cynically. "Major Barrett, perhaps we are kindred spirits."

#

As the weeks of convalescence flowed by, Thad had little to do but contemplate his bleak future. A hopeless cripple, the leavings of a lost cause. John Rizzo came to see him a few times although the momentary closeness of the first meeting was never regained. The doctor had met his suspected rival and had no reason to further the relationship.

As Thad's medical condition improved they fitted his stump with a pegleg. How great this was. Now he could learn to clump around, and try to cope with the humiliating falls that plagued many of the men here, the ones who lived that is.

The time came when they told him he was soon to be paroled and transported with the cooperation of the Confederacy back to his home. His memories of Sarah were not fading, though he was reconciled to never seeing her again. He was sure his departure from this hospital would guarantee that.

#

A day before he was due to leave, he sat in a wheelchair looking out at the gray winter landscape with its detritus of dirty snow. The view outside was almost as depressing as inside. Now he became aware of a stirring in the ward. Maybe a collective intake of breaths. He looked up curiously, and idly noticed that a woman had come into the room from a far door. She was not a nurse for she did not have a uniform on, and she was evidently looking for someone. Several men pointed in his direction. As the woman turned, he looked more closely. Suddenly his pulse quickened. It was Sarah! He hadn't recognized her in good clothing but, dear Lord, she was looking for him!

She was more beautiful than he had imagined. But, of course, she was covered with blood and near exhaustion when he had seen her before. And he was at best only dimly conscious.

With a soft rustling of her green dress she rather hesitantly approached him. A faint fragrance of perfume surrounded her, a wondering relief from the smells of this place. He sensed this huge room had become silent, waiting. She smiled down at him and offered her hand. He took it in both of his. So slender and soft it was, but cold and trembling as he gently squeezed. "Sarah, you came," he managed to say. Someone brought a chair for her. She turned and murmured a thank you. Then she turned back to him. He was still holding her hand and, embarrassed, he released it as she sat down.

She looked at him, now soberly. "I wanted to see you, Thaddeus, before I left. I'm so happy you survived. I wasn't sure . . ."

"I'd hoped you'd come. But then despaired of seeing you again."

She was still staring at him, her lips slightly parted. He wanted to reach over and kiss them. "Are you going to be working here?" he asked instead.

She grimaced. "It doesn't look like it. I can't seem to meet the standards for nurses."

He was shocked. "How can that be? You were a nurse practically on the battlefield. No other women were that I know of. Dr. Rizzo even told me you helped him with my wounds . . . even operated on my shattered leg. All this, after you found and saved me on the battlefield."

"He told you that?"

"Yes."

She sighed. "I felt so vital and needed, then. But now . . ."

"Can't Dr. Rizzo help?"

"It seems not. The Superintendent of Nursing, Dorothea Dix, holds a commission from the Surgeon General and can dictate who's to serve in military hospitals. And I," she said bitterly, "do not apparently meet her standards."

"Dr. Rizzo is really on your side, you know."

"I'm glad you met him."

"He told me about your husband. But then you had already told me."

She was surprised. "How did he know? I don't think I ever told him." She crinkled her brow. "Maybe I did, in that terrible battle day. I don't remember. Or he may have heard that from one of the women who came with Preacher Williams the day after the battle."

He reached for her hand. "Did I tell you how very sorry I am."

She squeezed his hand. "That was what brought me to the battlefield. To try to help in some small way," she said softly, her eyes tearing.

"And you saved my life." She sighed and at last removed her hand.

"Dr. Rizzo said he was in love with you."

"Did he now?"

"I said I was, too. As I told you before."

She put her hands over her eyes. "I'm overwhelmed," she murmured. "I didn't want this."

As she seemed unable to understand how two men could have fallen in love with her, he changed the subject. "Dr. Rizzo told me he was going to help you get into medical school. He thinks your destiny is to be a doctor."

She looked up at him, her eyes luminous. "I'm so beholden with that idea. Yet, it may be an impossible dream."

Thad felt compelled to encourage her dream, such a wonderful quest, even though it probably insured his losing her. Still, this lovely person deserved to have her dream nurtured. "Dreams have enabled us to rise above the muck of animal existence," he said.

He wryly realized that his professorial manner was emerging. "They've brought us ideas . . . and ideals . . . and striving for the best we can be."

"Oh Thad, I'm so glad you survived."

He took her hand again and raised it to his lips. "I'll be leaving tomorrow, shipped back to Carolina. As a sorry cripple, unable to bear arms ever again."

She looked at him and shook her head. "Not a sorry cripple, Thad. A hero bearing the marks of battle with honor. Don't you see?"

"Dear Sarah. If only our paths could cross again."

Her eyes were tearing. He reached for her face and gently wiped a tear away. "God only knows, Thad," she whispered, "and He determines whether our paths will cross again."

She left then, threading her way through the ward as the men stared up and after her and inhaled her gentle fragrance and then looked over at him, their faces wistful. The next day he began the long exhausting journey back to Carolina.

#

The visit to Baltimore was an acute disappointment to Sarah. She had expected an eager demand for her services, especially since Dr. Rizzo was there. But the bureaucracy was stifling, as stifling as the air inside the mammoth hospital.

It had taken her weeks to get her father's permission to make this pilgrimage to Baltimore. Of course, she could have gone without his approval, but as a dutiful daughter she was reluctant to do that, especially since she was sure his permission would eventually be forthcoming. The lurid tales Jeremy had told Pa about conditions at Antietam had not helped the situation. She was still mighty put out at Jeremy.

The hospital at first awed her, and then disgusted her. By now winter was in its fullness and the building was cold, damp, and dirty. And full of the vilest odors imaginable. It smelled like a gigantic cesspool. And she could see why. Buckets of waste lined the walls, waiting to be collected, and some had spilled on the floors to add their mess to that yet to be mopped up. She could well imagine the weaker men lying in their own filth. If this were summer, this place would be infested with flies. Where were all the nurses and attendants?

More disappointing, however, was the lack of welcome. "Miss, you will have to get the authorization of Superintendent Dorothea Dix in Washington before we could use you as a nurse." She had sought out the nursing supervisor, an older woman who seemed impatient to get rid of her.

"Dr. Rizzo will vouch for me, will give me a recommendation. I helped him near the front lines at Antietam."

The woman stared at her, but shook her head. "The Superintendent still has to approve," she said doggedly. Sarah shrugged her shoulders in frustration. "Very well, I'll go down to Washington to see her."

"I don't think it will do any good. Superintendent Dix's policy is that all applicants must be over thirty, plain looking, and modestly dressed in brown or black, with no bows, no curls, no jewelry. I don't think you'll meet her requirements, Miss."

"It looks to me like you badly need more nursing help," Sarah couldn't resist saying. "I've never seen a more filthy place."

The woman's face hardened. "Superintendent Dix is busy screening for more nurses."

"But you don't think she'll accept me."

"No, she's very selective. We want only the fittest for our men."

"And I'm not the fittest? Despite nursing almost on the front lines?"

"Good day, Miss." The supervisor abruptly walked away.

#

"This isn't going to work out," she later told John Rizzo. "They don't want me."

"I'm so sorry, Sarah, but I'm powerless. I truly wish I could help."

"Do you think it might be different at other hospitals?"

"I doubt it. Dix has complete authority to recruit female nurses for all general or permanent hospitals." He grimaced. "We doctors have no say regarding nurses."

"Will it be the same thing when I try to get into medical school? An impossible bureaucracy?"

He tried to reassure her. But she now was becoming skeptical about the realization of this dream; was it just a forlorn hope? "Please don't give up hope about this," he pleaded.

"I'll believe it when I see it," she said tight-lipped.

He sighed. "What are you going to do now?"

"I'm going to make one last effort to get in the Army nursing corps. I'll go down to Washington and try to see Miss Dix, and hope to somehow persuade her."

"If you can't?"

"Then I'll try to find Clara Barton and see if she'll take me on as a helper. As long as this frightful War lasts. After that . . . well, maybe I'll seek you out about medical school."

"Sarah, please stop back here after you've been to Washington? To let me know how things went." As she hesitated, he said, "Look, Sarah, I'd like us to get to know each other better. After all, we've hardly seen each other without both of us being covered with blood." He laughed without mirth. "Why don't you let me take you out to dinner tonight? Also when you get back from Washington?"

A day or so ago she would have been pleased with such an invitation. Now with the disappointment here in Baltimore and the probable further disappointment waiting in Washington her ardor had cooled. At least temporarily. "John, I'd love to. But let's wait till I get back from seeing Miss Dix. I plan to leave early in the morning, and stay until she'll talk with me. I'll probably need some comforting and advice when I get back."

"It's a deal. And why don't you stay a few days then. I suspect we'll have a lot to talk about." He looked at her pensively. "I'll inquire around, Sarah, and see if any of my colleagues have ideas for bypassing Superintendent Dix. I'll also try to get some material on medical schools, though this may take longer than a few days."

On impulse she kissed him on the cheek. "Thanks, John, for being so supportive. You're a very dear friend."

He took both her hands and gently squeezed them. "Dear Sarah, I wish you the best down in Washington. When you get back, we'll forget the War for an evening or two."

She didn't ask John about Thaddeus Barrett. But she found out at the registration desk that he was indeed at this hospital. She was so thankful that he was still alive and had not succumbed to infection or other deadly consequences of injuries and contamination. This deep feeling of relief surprised her more than she thought it should.

When she saw him just before she left she was encouraged by his physical appearance, but his mental state was poor. And why shouldn't it be? Sitting in a wheelchair with a stump and a peg. But what had he told her? That Dr. Rizzo was in love with her. Then he reaffirmed his own murmurings of love that she'd thought were only his delirium back at Antietam. Her heart quickened at these revelations.

But she still couldn't understand how these men apparently found her attractive. They must still be fixated by the blood masking her plain features. She realized now, with some surprise, that her memories of Sol and her almost unbearable grief before Antietam were fading, and she felt a sense of guilt about that. She wondered if she indeed was capable of finding love again?

How could she forget Thad's gentle encouragement of her dream to become a doctor and how he had tried to hide his disappointment that this probably meant they would never see each other again? Please God, must I choose between a wonderful career or love, only one and not the other? Or maybe neither?

#

In Washington City she dressed conservatively for the hoped-for meeting with Dorothea Dix. But her youth could hardly be disguised. From what she'd heard, this was the death knell for getting into Army nursing. She now worried that Miss Dix would not be in Washington, that she might be visiting distant hospitals and not be back for weeks. With a faint relief she learned that the woman apparently was in.

The receptionist took her name and a few vital statistics, including her age. Sarah momentarily thought of lying about her age, but then realized the futility of this. She would be caught up in a lie and any faint hope would be dashed. "I'm not sure Superintendent Dix will be able to see you today," the receptionist told her. "Many other women are waiting."

She was directed to the waiting room and it was indeed full of eager candidates. She was at first surprised but then realized that many women would want to contribute to the war effort to augment the efforts of their men.

Most of these women were older and unattractive. Evidently the policies of Dix were well publicized: young, even modestly attractive women need not apply. She felt she knew the verdict without even going through the motions, and wondered what she was doing here.

Her turn came early afternoon the next day. Full of trepidation she entered the spartan office. The room matched Dix's appearance. She was older than Sarah had expected. Probably in her sixties, she was tall and thin, ramrod straight, and her face was stern, austere, forbidding. Her voice was sharp and incisive. Sarah could well imagine how this woman had intimidated the Army brass to her cause. But it was a noble cause: to bring women into nursing, a field that in this country had always been dominated by men. Often not very good men at that.

After a brief introduction Dix peered unsmilingly at Sarah. "I see on your application you report that you assisted at Antietam in a field hospital."

"I did, yes."

"What were your qualifications for such a battlefield assignment? Did you have permission from the Army, from the Sanitation Commission, from the Surgeon General?"

"No. I only wanted to help the poor wounded in that terrible battle near my home."

"I understand you even assisted in amputations." The stern visaged Superintendent stared at her.

Now Sarah stared, surprised. "How . . . ?"

"Well, did you or didn't you, Lindsey?" Her voice was like a glacier.

"Yes," Sarah whispered. As Dix continued to stare at her, she said more firmly, "Yes, I did. But I don't know how you knew about this."

"Young woman, you overstepped the bounds of acceptable nursing behavior. If indeed you really did what you claim."

"I only did what needed to be done, under terrible battle conditions, when men were dying without adequate medical attention. Dr. Rizzo was the only surgeon at the field hospital, among hundreds and hundreds of injured. He asked me to assist him."

She frowned. "I bet he did."

"He's at the base hospital in Baltimore. He would certainly confirm this."

The older woman continued to stare at her. "You made the papers, Lindsey. Did you know that?"

Sarah was shocked. "Made the papers? Me?"

"The Washington Post. The Baltimore Sun. Others, I'm sure. Young woman, you disgrace what you say you want to be," she spat out the words. "We have no room for publicity seekers and opportunists. I'll not have any such!"

"Please, I know nothing of any newspaper articles. What on earth were they about? How did they get my name?"

"You must have shrewdly planted the information, probably exaggerated your role. And any story about a young woman on a battlefield was bound to make the papers. All you had to do was write the editor."

"I did no such thing! I know nothing about this. Why don't you believe me?"

"To make things worse, the articles claim you rescued a wounded Rebel officer from under dead bodies."

"I did that," she murmured. "But certainly not to seek publicity."

"You know, there's a lot of hatred for these Rebs up here. Too many families have lost loved ones, and your alleged actions have made you hated."

"There's no hatred on the battlefield, after a battle," Sarah said. "In the field hospital we worked on the wounded of both sides."

The woman continued to peer solemnly at her. Sarah tried to meet her eyes, but had to drop her's. "Lindsey, you state that you would now like to be a nurse at one of our base hospitals. Is that right?"

"Yes. I want to help the wounded."

Dix shrugged. "Humph. I hear the same thing from all these women out in the waiting room. You're no different. Only younger, pretty, a temptress to bring false expectations to these men." She paused, and tapped a pencil. "Lindsey, there's no place for you, or your kind, in the Army nursing corps."

Sarah could feel her anger rising, but it would do no good. She took a deep breath. "Please, ma'am, I want to help, so much."

The Superintendent gave a small bitter chuckle. "Then, Lindsey, if you truly want to help so much, I suggest that you offer your services at any one of our fine institutions, as a cleaning woman, to mop and sterilize the rooms, hallways, and kitchens. There's a real need there." She smiled sardonically. "Lindsey, if enough of you women had a dedication to cleanliness and hygiene, this could well make a bigger contribution in saving the lives of our men than any amount of nursing expertise."

She looked steadily at Sarah. "So, I give you this challenge. Humble yourself. Dedicate yourself to clean wardrooms and hallways. And you don't need my approval for that. Good day, Lindsey."

Dazed, Sarah left the office. As she'd feared, the effort accomplished nothing. Except to humiliate her. But, of course, Dix was right. There was a tremendous need for greater cleanliness and sanitation in the hospitals. But weren't her talents beyond such mindless tasks?

She went to her room that night utterly confused and disoriented. She wanted to help. But weren't there better things for her to do? Dr. Rizzo surely thought so. In the dark hours before dawn she knew that her future did not lie with the Army nursing corps under Dorothea Dix. But where did it lie?

Now she was intrigued with Clara Barton. Could she join up with her? But she had not been able to catch up with Clara at Antietam. Would she be more successful now?

The next morning Sarah tried to find out Clara Barton's whereabouts. The Patent Office seemed the best source for information since Clara had worked there and had strong ties. However, the only information they could provide was that she was believed to have sailed south toward the Carolina coast. Clara had been involved in a fearsome bloodletting at Fredericksburg the previous December, but the consequences of that battle were resolved by early 1863, and she had moved to other areas of need. Still, as far as Sarah was concerned, Clara Barton was as inaccessible as she had been at Antietam.

CHAPTER 6

Sarah returned to Baltimore dejected. Not only were her efforts with Dix unsuccessful, but even Clara Barton seemed a lost cause.

"John, I'm so depressed," she told him that night over dinner at an elegant restaurant. "Every way I turn to try to be useful and make a contribution seems blocked. Unless I want to mop floors and wash dishes. On top of this, Dix claims I've become notorious in the public press."

"You did receive some newspaper coverage," Rizzo admitted.

"How did they find out about me?"

"Reporters were ranging about in the days after Antietam. I told them about a remarkable young woman. I certainly didn't intend anything but the best for you. You deserved such publicity. It did hit the national press."

"Superintendent Dix didn't see it that way. She thought I'd set everything up for my own personal gain."

"Well, curses on that woman, then."

"She suggested that some people hate me for saving the Rebel officer."

Rizzo shook his head. "I'm sorry to think there's such hatred. One would think all this bloodshed would have cleansed it." He rubbed his eyes. "But it's even made it worse, it seems. Still, we know it wasn't there on the aftermath of a battle."

"That's what I told Superintendent Dix."

He steepled his hands. "How difficult we mortals can make of things, can make of best intentions." He looked up. "Would it have made any difference, if there'd been no publicity?"

"I don't think so. Her mind was made up as soon as she saw me."

"Well, that makes me feel better. I still think you deserved the publicity."

"I didn't do it for that."

"I know." Then he took her hand, and squeezed it. "I've been inquiring since you've been away. Several possibilities seem far better than mopping floors. I heard of a wonderful woman, Mary Ann Bickerdyke, working in the West. A strong woman, she, who's making a big difference. You may want to consider going to her. Though, God knows, I would sorely miss you. I'd rather have you in central Maryland than out in western Tennessee.

"Another possibility is medical school now, rather than after the War. There's a Doctor Elizabeth Blackwell, the first woman to earn a medical degree in America and the founder and head of New York's Infirmary for Women and Children. You should talk to her. She might not only help you get into medical school but even persuade Dix to use your services. I understand they've been in contact during this whole effort to bring women into nursing."

Sarah listened to these suggestions, her food forgotten. She took a deep breath to calm her racing pulse. "You give me hope, John . . . when all I had was despair." She smiled tremulously. "You've been so good to me. You've inspired me to be more than I ever thought possible. How can I ever thank you?"

"Don't you know why I'm doing this?" he asked quietly.

She contemplated this. Now a streak of humor tempted her: "Because you're a good Samaritan?"

"Don't you know? . . . That's not it."

"Know what?" She breathed the words, a thrill, and a chill, going through her.

He sighed. "Don't you know, haven't you suspected, that my interest in you, in your dreams, is more than merely platonic?"

She slowly nodded. At that moment the attendant came to clear the dishes and offer them dessert and coffee. She was glad for the interruption. She declined the dessert, but asked for coffee, black, to try to clear her head from the bottle of wine they had shared on this night when she was so depressed. She should have known and been prepared for this declaration by John.

"I suspected, and felt wonderfully honored. But I wasn't sure if I was seeing things right." She looked away. "You see, I'm not very experienced in these things."

"That's what makes you so extraordinary, you know. The wonderful blend of naivete, with all your remarkable strength and dedication." He smiled and took her hand again. "Sarah, you're something special. I've fallen in love with you."

This should have been no surprise. After all, Thad had told her—warned her—that they both were in love with her. Yet, somehow, it still was a surprise. She had not anticipated her attractiveness to men and certainly had not sought it. She was deeply moved. John was such a splendid man . . . to want her. Yet, an even stronger longing than love seemed to control her. She wondered how best to answer him.

"John, I'm so truly grateful. Such a wonderful friend, and mentor." She knew the words were too trite.

He frowned slightly. "Sarah, some things are foreordained. Perhaps this is."

"Our paths do seem to be solidly linked." She smiled now, thinking back. "I would never, in my fondest dreams, have expected such to happen. A simple naive small-town girl, one barely married before her husband was killed. You a successful surgeon. How could this have happened?"

"You're no simple naive small-town girl, you know. You deserve to be loved." He sighed. "Maybe we both . . . deserve to be loved."

She was silent, too long, she suspected. Why this hesitation? "Thank you, dear John," she murmured. She knew this was not quite what he wanted to hear.

She stared down at the tablecloth and her half-emptied coffee cup. Then she realized something: He had expressed his love, but he had not asked her to marry him. She vaguely wondered about that. But there was more to her hesitancy.

Perhaps it was because the battlefield still beckoned. Had she fulfilled her destiny as a battlefield nurse with this one battle at Antietam? She didn't think so and suddenly doubted that she could be content to abandon it. At least not yet, not while this War was still on.

"Let's dance, Sarah. I need to hold you, to feel you, the woman I love who is so gentle yet tough."

A three-man ensemble was playing soft music. He led her to the small dance floor and they joined two other couples. She rested her head against his cheek and could feel the lean strength of his body. In the embrace of his arms she had a sense of comfort and security, She knew the temptation to submerge herself to his personality and gentle authority.

Later back at their table, the thought burst forth. Of a sudden she said, "John, I've never asked you. Are you married?"

He was silent so long she wasn't sure if he'd heard her. She was about to repeat the question, when he muttered, "If you can call it a marriage."

"Tell me about it, John," she urged. "I need to know."

"Yes, I guess you deserve to know."

"Go on," she encouraged.

"She was having problems . . . great periods of depression, before. Then we lost our only son, at Fort Sumter, at the beginning of the War. She became suicidal and I had to put her in an institution."

"How awful."

"I try to see her every few weeks. Most of the time she doesn't even recognize me. She's living somewhere else, maybe in a happier time. She sometimes thinks I'm our lost son, Jacob.

"Maybe this is why I've dedicated myself to medicine, to trying to lose myself in human need." He gripped the edge of the table, and she could see his white knuckles. "Sometimes I was almost glad the War continued, to forget my personal troubles." Now he paused, and tenderly touched her face. "Until you came into my life."

"You haven't divorced her?"

"No. Even though much of the time she's barely lucid, I thought this might be too hard on her. And I've had no reason to until now."

They danced some more in this quiet elegant room. He held her close, almost suffocatingly so, she thought. With the disclosure of a wife, her mind had distanced itself from him, even while her body was pressed against his. "It's late, John," she finally murmured. "Would you take me back to my hotel?" He looked at her strangely, but nodded.

In the hallway at her door he took her in his arms again and kissed her strongly. She felt herself responding, but she pushed away. "I must go in now, John." She brushed her lips across his cheek.

"Sarah, can we meet for breakfast before I go to the hospital? I may have some other thoughts for you."

"Of course. I'd like that. Thank you for a lovely evening."

He stared at her as she began to go in. As she looked back, she thought he looked so sad. As though he knew this was not meant to be.

The next morning over breakfast, he suggested, "Won't you consider staying with me here in Baltimore? It would give you a chance to take a breather. You could investigate other possibilities at more leisure."

"I don't know."

"We could, you and me, take a trip up to New York and talk personally with Dr. Blackwell about getting you started in medical school."

"This is too sudden. Let me think about it for a day or so."

He looked at her, unsmiling. "All right. I have to go to work shortly. We can discuss it further tonight."

She placed her hand on his arm. "No, John, I need to think about this away from emotional involvement. I think I should stay in tonight. Do you mind?"

He muttered, "Don't punish us this way, Sarah. We've just really found each other. Now you want to separate us."

"I'm not sure that I'm ready for a relationship. I have to think about this and the other parts of my life. Bear with me, please."

He rather grudgingly prepared to go to the hospital. She promised she would meet him for dinner the following day. "Beyond that I don't want to make any promises. You see, I haven't ruled out trying to meet up with Mary Ann Bickerdyke out West."

At his protests, she gently chided, "Maybe it's all your fault, John. You introduced me to battlefield medicine. After that everything else pales in comparison. Maybe a battlefield nurse is what my real calling is."

"I thought you were interested in medical school."

"Oh, I am. Truly. But I think I'll be more ready, maybe more deserving, after this conflict is over."

They left the issue at that. After he had gone to the hospital, she wandered around the city trying to sort out her thoughts from her emotions. She had a major decision to make as to what direction her life should take at this point. Despite the physical attraction to John, she knew living with him was out of the question. Not yet, not unless she was his wife. Now she wondered whether John had fully adjusted to his wife's illness.

The idea of medical school was so intriguing. Whether realistic was another matter. At this point in her life she realized it was best kept as an ultimate dream. Not to give it up, but something to work toward when she was more worthy. By the time she was ready to go down to eat that evening her mind was made up. She must somehow find a way around the formidable obstacle of Dorothea Dix.

She spent a quiet evening in her room reading the Baltimore newspaper. It devoted a full page to describing the activities on the Western sector. General Grant was moving in on the Confederate bastion of Vicksburg that commanded the Mississippi. But achieving this military objective was months away and it was far from certain this fortress could be captured. Grant was working his way across southern Tennessee and Mississippi, sparring with enemy troops trying to stymie his approach to Vicksburg. The army was living on salt beef and hardtack as supplies failed to keep up with the advance. While no major battles were yet taking place, still a stream of wounded and sick were flowing back to Memphis. On top of this an outbreak of scurvy had filled the 11,000 beds at Memphis.

A brief paragraph in the article mentioned "Mother" Bickerdyke. She operated under the auspices of the Sanitary Commission. The article mentioned that at one terrible battle, she, in the blackness of the night, moved up and down among the dead to make sure no living man should be left alone "amid such surroundings."

A thrill went through Sarah. Hadn't she done the same . . . when she found Thad? She reread the article. Apparently Mother Bickerdyke was highly thought of by such important generals as Grant and Sherman. The article even intimated that President Lincoln was a strong supporter.

Sarah now felt that this was where her immediate destiny should be: on the Western sector. If Mother Bickerdyke would have her. Somehow, she thought she would, that they were kindred spirits.

A soft flutter of a thought of Thad Barrett came to her that night. She wondered how he was faring. Had he reached his home in North Carolina? How was he adjusting to his infirmities? Out of nowhere the question came to her: Did he ever think of her? But he had told her that he was in love with her, as had John. He must still be thinking of her. She remembered him telling her that only Aunt . . . Aunt Abigail would be waiting for him back in Carolina, in those mountains that he loved, so he must not be married or even close to it. She was so confused with these men who professed to love her, and of her feelings toward them. How complicated life could be!

The next morning she inquired about Bickerdyke in a Sanitary Commission office in Baltimore. This was a small office, and they could give no help in locating Mother Bickerdyke. They directed her to the Washington headquarters. "They should know her whereabouts, Miss," they told her in Baltimore.

It was too late to go down to Washington City, and still meet John that night as she had promised. Well, she could do this after she saw him. Or simply go to Memphis, where Bickerdyke most likely was. But not for sure. Furthermore, she needed to stop home, and apprise Pa of her goings-on.

#

"You don't have to tell me," John Rizzo said that afternoon, as she met him at the hospital. "I know what your decision is."

"How could you know that, John? I barely know it myself."

"You want to go West, don't you?"

"Yes," she said slowly.

"I knew it."

"How . . . could you?"

"I know you . . . maybe better than you know yourself. I was sure you'd want to go West. Where the action seems to be."

She massaged her temples. "Am I so transparent? So easily predictable?"

"Only to someone who loves you," he said seriously.

"Ah."

"I have some information. Where you might find her."

"John?"

"Yes. Grant himself has ordered her to take a two-week rest. She should be in Chicago or at her home in Galesburg, Illinois. The Sanitary Commission people in Chicago will know."

"I'm so grateful."

"There's more. I've written a letter to introduce you to her. I wrote it last night when I was lonely thinking about you. I told her about your battlefield experience, your dedication, and your great promise. I hope it will make things easier."

"How can I ever thank you for all this?"

"You can thank me by coming back to me when this is all over, my dear Sarah."

She stumbled with her words. "Your unselfishness in helping me . . . such a great gesture of your love. What more can I say, John? I'm so beholden to you."

"Just remember, I want our futures to be together. You and me. All right?"

"I'll cherish that thought."

#

Sarah stopped to see her father before journeying west to find Mary Ann Bickerdyke. The experience was far from pleasant.

She had hardly arrived home when he confronted her, "Daughter, how could you disgrace our family this way?"

"What do you mean?" Her heart sank as she guessed what was to come.

"What you did for that Reb, saving his life, befriending him—this made the papers. All the people here were shocked to hear about it." He looked at her sternly. "Damn it, Sarah, how could you do this for one of those who killed your husband?"

"Pa, as I told you before, he was badly wounded and would have died. I only helped another human being." She shook her head. "Some reporter got word of this and played it up. More than it should have been. To sell papers."

"It sounds to me like you're proud of it."

"I didn't go out on the field to save Rebels. I was looking for any of our own wounded who might have been overlooked. Why is so much being made of this?"

"Daughter, you if anyone should know! Our boys, and your Sol, undertook this struggle to preserve our way of life. To protect their sisters, wives, and mothers. The enemy, well they're trying to preserve that abomination before God of slavery. They're not like our boys. They're butchers, the agents of the devil!"

"And you aided their cause. Shame on you, daughter! I shouldn't have let you go to that field of battle, even though my hand was bleeding like hell." He beat his breast. "You caught me at a weak moment, and may God forgive me, I gave in to your unholy ideas."

"They were not unholy, Pa! Maybe I've never done anything in my life so holy, that God would so approve."

"Don't blaspheme before God. This is Satan talking, not my daughter."

She stared at him, incredulously. "You accuse me of being in league with Satan? You're the one, your hatred is not God's work, but the devil's."

"Damn it, Sarah, don't lecture me about right and wrong. You sound like you've been converted to the slaveholder cause."

"Of course not! I simply see these men, blue and gray, as innocent victims of a cause greater than they are. And, incidentally, most of the Rebs are not slaveowners. The major isn't—he's a simple professor in a small college in Carolina. So how can you accuse them of being in league with the devil?"

But there was no dissuading her father of his hatred of the enemy, of her sins, and of his guilt in letting her go to the battlefield in the first place. She wondered how widespread such attitudes were. Now she remembered Superintendent Dix's comments about hatred sweeping the country.

"Aren't you going to let me go to church with you?" she asked him Sunday morning, as he prepared to leave without her.

"I don't think you'll find yourself welcome at our church, daughter."

She stared at him, aghast.

"No, not welcome. Preacher Williams has singled you out for giving comfort to the enemy. Most of the congregation agrees with him."

"Didn't you stand up for your own daughter?" she asked, stricken.

"I couldn't condone what you did."

"Pa, I did nothing wrong! How many times do I have to tell you? I only saved a poor soldier who would have died otherwise!"

"But he was the enemy, the devil's spawn," he insisted.

She shook her head at this unreasonable hatred, and felt like weeping at the injustice of it all.

Against his advice she went to church with him that Sunday, and the full realization of the hatred engulfed her. Preacher Williams had somehow gotten word of her presence in the congregation and directed his sermon at her.

"There is one among us today," he thundered, "who has lost her soul by giving comfort and solace to the enemy, the agents of the devil on this earth. If it were not for the presence of her father, a good and honorable man, I would urge you to drive this witch from our house of worship. As it is, I ask Sarah Lindsey to remove her sinful presence. Before her presence blasphemes the Lord."

"Sarah, you'd better leave now," her father whispered.

Suddenly, her anger ignited at this narrow-minded hatred. She stood up, her eyes blazing. "Preacher Williams, let God above be the judge of what I have done. Not you, sir!"

The Preacher recoiled from her outburst. "He has spoken to me," he said more quietly.

"Ha. Prove it! He has spoken to me, you know, to help the wounded and dying, of whatever cloth."

The congregation were on their feet with this exchange. Most supported the Preacher, screaming, "Remove the witch!" and "Banish the Rebel lover!" But Sarah saw a few people restraining themselves, not going along with the mob psychology of the moment.

The Preacher, somewhat shaken by the violence of the confrontation and the ensuing outburst, raised his hands to bring some order to the situation. Finally, when he could be heard he said, "Let her stay if she wants to. We'll leave her judgment to the Lord above. May God have mercy on her soul."

So Sarah stayed through the service, staring tight-lipped ahead, while the busybodies whispered around her. If they could have painted a scarlet letter on her, they would have, she knew. There was no tolerance here, only hatred and unbending smugness.

As she and her father left the church it was as though she were an invisible person, a pariah. No one looked at her or spoke to her. Except for Julia, her best friend from high school.

She had always thought of Julia as a soft and gentle lap dog, deserving of sheltering and pampering, but a dear contrast to her own more adventurous personality. Never one to make waves, Julia sought her out after the service as Sarah and her father moved through the silent and frowning congregation to their carriage. "Sarah, please wait a minute," Julia called out.

Sarah turned around, and she and Julia embraced. "Aren't you afraid of being seen befriending me?" she asked.

"Oh, Sarah, these people are so wrong. I know you're right." She was breathless. "But I never could have stood up to Preacher Williams like you did."

Sarah laughed sheepishly. "I didn't think I could either. But I got so angry at his prejudice and his pompousness. He knows more about God's views than God Himself knows." Now she sighed. "But I'm afraid he's swayed virtually the whole town. Except you, dear Julia."

"Hurry up, Sarah, we must get home," Father urged.

"Go ahead, Pa, I'll walk home. Julia and I have some catching up to do."

He didn't say anything further, but whipped the horse and galloped away.

"Sarah, come home with me. We can have some tea and talk."

"Are you sure, Julia, you want to get involved with me? What will your folks say about inviting me into your home?"

"Sarah, we've been friends since childhood. That can't be destroyed just because of a few embittered neighbors."

"Julia, didn't I hear that your Ben was killed at Fredericksburg?"

Her friend had tears in her eyes now. "I can't blame you for that, Sarah. Nor the Reb major you saved."

They hugged again. "This terrible War. When will it ever end? Can things ever be the same again?"

Over tea, Sarah told Julia about her frustrations in getting into nursing, of her dream of becoming a physician, impossible though this might be.

Julia wanted to know about the Rebel major. "Did you really pull him from under dead bodies, in the dark of night, on a haunted battleground?"

"Haunted?"

"Well, you know, with death all around. That's how the newspaper described it."

"I didn't think about it being haunted. I just wanted to save anybody still alive that night. And yes, I pulled him out from under dead bodies. Then some men came to help me."

"Was he handsome?"

"He certainly wasn't then. At least I didn't have time to examine his bloodstained begrimed face. His wounds were bad. He was near death. We thought he would die."

Julia was looking at her wide-eyed. "The paper said you operated on him, saved his life."

"The surgeon and I saved him that night. Afterwards, we thought we'd lose him to infections."

"My, Sarah, what an adventure." She looked at her fondly. "Do you love him?"

Sarah started to say, "Of course not." But the words stuck in her throat as Julia stared intently at her. She put her hand on her friend's arm. "God help me. I don't know. I had thought Sol would be the only man in my life." She gave a soft laugh. "He told me he loved me. I thought he was delirious." She sighed. "But he told me again, in Baltimore."

"What a magnificent love," Julia breathed.

Sarah snorted. "Our paths will probably never cross again. He was just recovering when he thought he was in love with me, and any woman probably looked good."

"This is the stuff of legends," she gushed.

"Nonsense," Sarah said. "Just an impossible affair, one of tens of thousands coming out of this War."

"Does your father suspect?"

"I don't know."

"I bet he does. Or at least he fears it."

Sarah started to protest. But then she paused. This could be why he was so violently upset by her deeds at Antietam. He was afraid she was in love with a Confederate. "You may be right," she admitted.

"What a wonderful romance!"

"Stop it, Julia. Please don't let on to anybody that I even had faint thoughts about love. Tell them he's homely, has a wife and ten kids in Carolina. And you know he's lost a leg." She searched her friend's face. "Please, Julia, let's just keep this as our little secret."

"I won't say anything to anybody. On one condition."

"Yes?"

"That you have me as your bridesmaid, when the time comes."

Sarah laughed. "I always knew you were a romantic of the worse kind. But it's a deal. Don't count on anything materializing, however."

CHAPTER 7

"Miss Lindsey, Sarah, this is sure a remarkable letter that Dr. Rizzo wrote." Mother Bickerdyke looked at Sarah intently. They were in her small apartment, plainly furnished, in Chicago. There was a desk in one corner, and a bed in the other, and one comfortable chair. Evidently she was not used to having company, for they were sitting on straight back chairs at a small square table. Dr. Rizzo's letter was on the table, and Mother Bickerdyke had read it, then looked at her, then reread it, then got up and read it again, and had just now sat back down. She seemed very kind, but rather strange, as though, could it be, that she was deeply moved? By Dr. Rizzo's letter? The woman unobtrusively rubbed her eyes.

Mother Bickerdyke was just about as Sarah had imagined her to be. She was dressed in a shabby calico dress. Her face was plain, and her graying hair was tied in a tight bun, but still some strands had worked loose. Her hands were big and work-reddened. She was blunt, almost crude, but somehow conveyed an image of selfless confidence. A person not concerned with making an impression or with ambition. Or with prejudices. So wonderfully different from Dorothea Dix.

Sarah said softly, "I want to serve, as best I can." She sighed. "Superintendent Dix thought I was only qualified to be a scullery helper, and mop floors."

"You certainly can do much more than that," the woman said, almost harshly. "Much more than that." She was quiet for a few moments. Sarah held her breath. Then she asked, "Dr. Rizzo says you should eventually go to medical school. Why not now?"

Sarah tried to find the words, to marshall her thoughts in some coherent fashion. "I feel . . . I'm not ready for that, yet. Not with this War on. I feel I can do more good as a battlefield nurse, now, than studying anatomy textbooks."

"Dr. Rizzo says you lost your husband at Shiloh. Is that your great motivation for this?"

"It was at first. At Antietam. Not anymore." Again she tried to find the words to express her deep feelings.

"At Antietam I learned the full extent of our men's sufferings. Also, how much better they could be served by the medical profession. How ill-used they frequently were. And I learned I could make a difference. Even if only for a few soldiers. To ease their pain, maybe even to save a life." She was breathing heavily and massaged her forehead, trying to subdue the raging emotions these thoughts brought. She hoped Mother Bickerdyke hadn't noticed her momentary loss of control, and didn't think she was a weak female, not suited to battlefield nursing.

But if Bickerdyke had noticed her lapse, she didn't let on. She also took a deep breath and looked down at the letter in her hand. "Dr. Rizzo also writes that you went out on the battlefield. That you found a Reb officer. Saved his life, he says. Did you really do that?"

Sarah nodded soberly.

"He says you even amputated his leg, with the Doctor assisting. As you had assisted him with hundreds of poor men."

Sarah was overwhelmed. Despite herself, tears came into her eyes. She took a deep breath. "He wrote all that?"

Bickerdyke moved closer to Sarah, and took her hand. "Yes, Sarah, he did. I can't think he'd lie about that."

"I couldn't be a scullery maid, after all that," she whispered.

"Of course you couldn't, my dear. Your talents, well, they sure would of been wasted, if you had." She smiled now, and squeezed her hand. "My dear, I think we should get you appointed by the Commission as my assistant. Would that be all right with you?"

Sarah couldn't restrain the tears. This was more than she could have hoped for. What a powerful letter John must have written in her behalf. "Please excuse me, Mother Bickerdyke. I'm not usually this . . . emotional. Certainly not when it matters on the battlefield."

"I understand, my dear, and please call me Mary Ann." But then she frowned. "Sarah, you have to realize. Not all our jobs are to nurse men. We have to be sure the facilities are clean. That adequate food is served. Sometimes the docs are not too cooperative. Though that's changing now. Since we've got the support of the top generals. Do you understand, dear?"

"I understand. After seeing the conditions at Antietam, and even at the base hospital at Baltimore, well, I know how important good sanitation and food and ventilation are." She nodded her head. "I certainly wouldn't object to taking a mop in hand, or doing kitchen duties."

Mother Bickerdyke smiled broadly. "I don't think that'll be necessary, my dear. But let's see about getting you officially on the roster. We'll leave in a few days for Memphis, and who knows after that. The Army of the West is moving on Vicksburg. Then, it'll probably turn east. And I sure can use an assistant like you."

#

They did not stay long at Memphis, that spring of 1863. Field hospitals were being set up as the fighting moved closer to Vicksburg. By May, Grant was able to launch two direct assaults on the city. Both failed in heavy fighting. Then he resorted to a siege of starvation. Union gunboats now controlled the river, and on the land side his forces maintained a tight ring around Vicksburg, closing all access to the outside world. The people there were forced to eat their horses and mules, even dogs and cats. On July 4, the starving city fell.

From Vicksburg on, Mrs. Bickerdyke became closely associated with General Sherman. He was a fellow Ohioan; actually they came from adjoining counties and were nearly the same age. They were both energetic and practical people, both concerned with the welfare of the men. General Sherman trusted Mary Ann Bickerdyke as he trusted no other civilian. At Vicksburg he made a formal request to the Sanitation Commission asking to have her permanently assigned to his Fifteenth Corps.

So it was that when Sherman and his troops left their Vicksburg camp in late September, Mother Bickerdyke and Sarah went with them. Their destination was Alabama and they would ride the Memphis & Charleston railroad. Which seemed to the soldiers a vast improvement over the customary marching.

But the enemy had wrecked havoc on the tracks, and the troops had to rebuild these as the trains crawled along, sometimes making less than three miles a day. By early November, with the weather bitterly cold, Sherman received orders from Grant to abandon the railroad and march north to Chattanooga.

So the troops marched across northern Alabama and up into Tennessee. Sarah and Mother Bickerdyke either rode horses or used a hospital wagon, but it was soon apparent they would receive little rest once the march had stopped each day. The army boots were proving too flimsy for the rough trails. A steady flow of soldiers sought them out, plaintively pleading for help for their blisters and stone-bruised feet.

"Can't we do anything to get them decent footwear?" Sarah asked.

"I'll go talk to General Sherman," Bickerdyke said.

She came back crestfallen. "There're no replacement boots. Or much of anything else either. Our supplies have not caught up with us. Maybe won't." She shook her head. "The General says it may not be much better in Chattanooga. Our men have the town, but the Rebs got all the heights. One in particular, Lookout Mountain, has artillery commanding the town. So supplies are tough to get in."

"Maybe we can improvise," Sarah said. "I've been thinking of what we might use to help these men's feet. What would you think if we showed them how to make moccasins. Cutting up some of their blankets."

"Moccasins are a good idea, Sarah. Except . . ."

"I know, Mary Ann. How can they keep their soles from wearing out, inside a quarter mile? I'd thought of wood, for soles. But it's too stiff."

Mother Bickerdyke pondered this. "Wood might work. If we can get the right kind. We've certainly got plenty of trees around here." She paused and looked searchingly at Sarah. Then they both smiled. "Sarah, are you thinking what I'm thinking?"

"Tree bark. That should be flexible and reasonably durable." Bickerdyke nodded. "Do you think the bark can be peeled without too much trouble?"

"Let's ask the men."

The moccasins soled with tree bark proved a real blessing for marching. The only trouble was that sleeping became less so as the men's cover for cold nights had been put to another use.

The weather was cold. Most men had only summer clothing. The belief among Northerners was widespread that the South had a warm winter climate. It was true that there was little snow, but bitterly cold winds and pellets of sleet brought misery. The country was poor, ravaged by war, deserted.

Sherman's troops dragged into Chattanooga shortly after the middle of November to join up with Grant. They had hoped to find roofs to shelter them, but had to pitch tents outside of town, behind log and earthen breastworks, and tried to keep warm with campfires.

The wait was not long. Four days after their arrival, Grant ordered the assault of Lookout Mountain. Sarah and Mary Ann supervised the preparation of tents for a field hospital. But medical supplies, and even food, were very short.

Sarah could see nothing of the battle that day. Thick mists obscured the mountain. But by early afternoon stretcher bearers began bringing in the first casualties. By late afternoon the tents were half full. Then as the fighting eased off with darkness, casualties began flooding in, filling the tents, then being laid on the frozen ground, propped up against trees, even dropped on the path where exhausted bearers could go no further.

Outside the operating tent, the usual pile of amputated limbs began growing. As Sarah was helping one of the patients after his amputation, he pleaded with her, "Can't my leg be buried like a Christian?" She suddenly realized that she had never really thought about what happened to these shattered limbs. She knew that bodies, even those of the Rebels, were given a Christian burial, with prayers and a psalm. But what about the severed limbs?

She asked Mother Bickerdyke about this.

"Didn't you know, Sarah? After being on the battlefield at Antietam?"

"I guess I was so busy in the operating barn I never noticed. I know the limbs were tossed outside, but what happened then? I gather they were not buried."

Bickerdyke patiently explained, "Arms and legs, as well as horses, are piled up, doused with kerosene, and burned. No prayers are said over them. Most of these men know that. Some must have even participated."

Sarah sighed. "Maybe I can fib, just a little, and tell them that someone will say a prayer before they are burned."

Mother Bickerdyke put her hand on Sarah's arm, and smiled at her. "If it would comfort some poor devil, I don't think God would mind a little fib." Then she said, "I told the head Surgeon about what you did at Antietam. He might want your assistance tomorrow. The heaviest fighting should be then, They'll probably be a deluge of casualties. Are you up to doing this?"

"Mary Ann, I'm grateful to help. Thank you."

"He wants to meet you."

"All right. When?"

"How about now?"

"Sure."

Bickerdyke led her into the surgery tent. A gray haired bearded man was working on an amputation, assisted by a male nurse. They waited while he finished. Then he looked up. "Ah, Mother Bickerdyke. Is this your young surgical nurse?" He looked severely at Sarah.

She met his gaze steadily.

"Yes. Dr. Randall, this is Sarah Lindsey."

He wiped a bloody hand on his apron, and extended it to her. She took it firmly without flinching.

"Ah," he said, "Hand strength is good. Now if you have the nimble fingers to go with it."

"I guess you'll have to judge that," she said, smiling slightly.

"Mother tells me you worked with Dr. Rizzo at Antietam."

"Yes. For two days."

"You assisted him?"

"I did the tourniquets, administered chloroform, and tied off the arteries during amputations."

"She tells me you even did an amp, with Dr. Rizzo assisting."

"Yes. He invited me to."

"Of the Confederate officer you saved?"

"Yes."

The surgeon gave her a strange look. Sarah shivered. Had she done the unthinkable? Then he gently said, "I know Dr. Rizzo. A fine man. If you impressed him so mightily, you must truly be a special young woman."

She said nothing, only lowered her head slightly. Mother Bickerdyke touched her shoulder.

She heard his words then. "Sarah Lindsey, would you be prepared to assist me at eight o'clock tomorrow morning? I think we'll have an abundance of subjects."

"I'd be most honored, Doctor," she said humbly.

Afterwards, she could hardly express her feelings to Mother Bickerdyke. They hugged. "I'm so grateful to you, Mary Ann."

"It'll be hard work." She smiled. "Harder than mopping floors."

"Much more satisfying," Sarah murmured. But she wondered. "Tell me, Mary Ann, why did you go to such lengths in promoting me?"

The older woman studied her before replying. "We need to raise the stature of womankind, to show the world our strengths. I did this for you. But also for all women." She paused. "This War, terrible as it is, gives us a great chance to show our worth. Beyond cleaning house and raising kids." She sighed, and wiped a surprising tear from her cheek. "My dear, I can see the time, somewhere in the future, where more than half the docs will be women. We have the compassion, the intelligence, and the dexterity to be good. Even damn good. All we lack is acceptance . . . by a male-dominated world."

Sarah felt a chill going through her, as she was mesmerized by this vision.

"So, my dear, you can be one of the trailblazers. You've impressed Dr. Rizzo. Now impress Dr. Randall tomorrow." The two women again hugged each other.

#

Sarah arrived promptly at the surgical tent. The weather had worsened, if that were possible. A fierce gale with driving sleet was building up. The wind threatened the tent, and men were hurriedly tying it down with additional stakes.

Dr. Randall greeted her. "Well, Miss Lindsey, you're on time. The major flood of casualties is not here yet. So let's go over procedures."

He showed her, but it was little different than that of John Rizzo at Antietam. "You do have superb finger dexterity, Sarah. I can see now why Dr. Rizzo wanted you to assist him. I think he trained you well." He stroked his white beard. "And I have to believe that you're inured to blood and suffering."

"Not inured, Doctor, but I can handle it." She smiled whimsically, "I'm not going to faint, if that's what you're afraid of."

"Well said, Sarah. I think I'm going to enjoy working with you, more so than with these clumsy-fingered male assistants." He paused. "That is, if you have the stamina."

"My stamina should be as good as yours, Doctor."

"Yes. Well, we'll see. But I'm still glad to have you."

The casualties soon began arriving. Then later in the afternoon they became overwhelming. There was little time for Sarah and Dr. Randall to talk. They worked as speedily as they could, amputating the shattered limbs. Most chest and head wounds were deemed too serious to take up precious surgery time, and were left to die or to somehow survive until later treatment might be forthcoming.

They worked through the night with little letup. The welcome word had come down that the conquest of the mountain was completed. By morning the mists had cleared and Dr. Randall and Sarah took a brief respite as the sun was rising to see the Union flag flying from the summit. Sarah was exhausted but no way was she going to admit it. Not as long as Doctor Randall was still functioning.

"Aren't you tired?" he asked her once.

"No more so than you," she said.

The human need was so great, it seemed a sin to let their fatigue interfere with the saving of lives. She worked on in a fog of weariness. Her fingers were becoming more clumsy in tying off the arteries. But she could see Dr. Randall was even more tired. Once his saw slipped, and she helped him get it reset. They both were drenched in blood and they had to watch their footing on the slippery floor.

At last he said, "Sarah, we have to take a break. Can you get a bite to eat and a little rest, and come back in three hours?"

"I'll be here, Doctor."

She could hardly manage it back to their tent, she was so tired. Her legs felt they were no longer hers. Her clothes were covered with blood, but there were no cleaning facilities. And she needed some nourishment. But she must not be late in getting back. Dr. Randall had said three hours. She wound up collapsing on a cot without eating or changing her clothes. She roused when Mother Bickerdyke came into the tent.

"When does he want you back?"

"In another hour."

"Let me help you, then, change your clothes and get a little soup in you. That's probably more important than an extra hour of sleep."

With Mother Bickerdyke's help she made it back before Dr. Randall showed up. He was surprised, then embarrassed.

He sternly said, "Young lady, are you trying to show me up?"

She wasn't sure if he was serious. "Mother Bickerdyke helped me get ready. If you'd had her to help you . . ."

He laughed. "Right. You had an unfair advantage."

They worked throughout the day. Now the inflow of casualties requiring their surgical attention was finally dwindling. At last they could take a rest and rely on the nursing staff to handle the wounded.

It came time to dismiss her. He clasped both her hands in his large ones, and smiled tiredly at her. "Young woman, you have exceeded my expectations. Greatly. I discharge you from this assignment with profound thanks. You made a significant contribution, and I will write this up."

"Thank you, Doctor."

She started to leave, the weariness suddenly overwhelming her. "Sarah," he called.

She turned back. "Mother tells me you're thinking of medical school, after the War. This is practically unheard of for a woman. It will be tough. But I believe you can do it. And will be a credit to the profession."

In her exhaustion her eyes filled with tears. "Thank you, Doctor. I deeply appreciate that."

"I'll be delighted to give you a strong recommendation."

She nodded gratefully, and groped her way to her quarters. The perverse thought crossed her mind: I hope nothing happens to these two willing references, John and Dr. Randall, before I try to apply to medical school. Please God, don't let a cannon ball get 'em.

#

They spent Christmas of 1863 in Chattanooga. Not a single Christmas box from home got through to the men eagerly awaiting them. These were piled high at the railroad yards in Nashville. But only a single track ran into Chattanooga, and military equipment had priority as Sherman prepared for a spring offensive that would split the Confederacy and capture Atlanta and then Savannah on the coast. Sarah and Mrs. Bickerdyke did their best to provide the men with baking and with molasses taffy. But the weather was unbearably cold, with high winds and no way to heat the hospital tents except to leave the flaps open for such heat as could be gained by the central campfire. On New Year's Day, the thermometer touched zero, and the supply of logs gave out.

"Our men are in danger of freezing," Bickerdyke told Sarah. "I'm going to have them tear down that line of breastworks over there so we can use the dry timbers to keep our patients warm."

"Mary Ann, destroying military fortifications without orders could get you court-martialed."

"These wounded heroes have to come first. Besides, the fighting has moved far away from Chattanooga."

Sarah watched in awe as Mother Bickerdyke moved to acquire the needed wood for fires "for her boys." She confronted a captain with her demands. "Captain Thomas, in this cold, our patients must have more heat. In their weakened condition, their very lives are at stake. I need those barricades taken down, and the wood used to keep our brave men warm."

The captain was flustered. "Mother Bickerdyke, our orders are to preserve the barricades, case of enemy attack."

Mary Ann snorted. "The enemy is a hundred miles away, fleeing fast as they can. They pose no danger anymore."

"I . . . still can't permit this. I'd be subject to court-martial. And you might, too, you know."

"Our brave men's needs got t' come first to old out-of-date orders. If you can't do this, I'll see Colonel Dixon, or even General Sherman hisself."

The captain after consulting with the colonel bowed to Mary Ann's demands. Later, there was an official inquiry about destroying Army installations. There, Mary Ann coolly admitted her guilt. "The urgent needs of our boys have to come first," she told the board. Any skepticism they might have had was quickly dispelled by a communication from General Sherman: "Mary Ann Bickerdyke has a better pulse on the needs of our men than any of us. If she thought the wood was badly needed, in a time of severe weather, she should not be criticized, but rather commended." The result was that the board warmly commended her.

Later, Sarah told Mary Ann, "I could never have stood up to the officers, and to that board like you did. Even though the need was so great. I would have been completely intimidated."

The woman smiled at her. "Well, an old crusty woman like me can get away with some things. But, dear, if you thought the need was great, I think you would have acted as I did. Although I'm not sure you would have pressured them as well as I did. But then I know the General pretty well."

Sarah still was sure she could never have the audacity, and courage, to defy authority, despite the rightness of the cause.

#

By spring, Grant had been promoted to commander-in-chief of all Union forces, and moved to Washington. Sherman took over as commander in the West. On May 6, he moved his 98,000 men into Georgia. The women followed the vast army in their ambulance wagon.

The greatly outnumbered Confederate troops now were little match for Sherman even though some sharp confrontations occurred en route to Atlanta. A bitter battle on the outskirts of Atlanta was fought on July 22. It led to the beginning of a siege that lasted until early September. All these contributed to wounded, but not to the extremes of the fighting around Vicksburg and Chattanooga, and weather was far better. The Confederacy was rapidly falling to its knees in this autumn of 1864.

A few weeks after the occupation of Atlanta, Mother Bickerdyke said, "Sarah, everything's under control. It looks like the General isn't going to move for a while. I've decided to go back to Illinois for a bit. See my family and all. Would you like to come with me?"

Sarah shook her head. "I'd like to get back to visit Pa in western Maryland. And also Dr. Rizzo in Baltimore. But I don't think it'd be easy to get there from here."

"I'm sure you'd have to go back to Nashville, and maybe even Memphis. Too many stray Confeds between here and north."

"So I think I'll stay here, until things get more settled."

Mother Bickerdyke nodded. "The War may be over by spring. Are you still thinking about medical school?"

"Yes." She sighed. "But most people I talk to say this is unthinkable, for a woman to try to go to medical school. All the doctors say that, except for Dr. Randall. And my friend, John Rizzo up in Baltimore. So, I don't know."

The older woman placed a hand on her arm. "It's high time more women broke the ice and became doctors. You and I both know they can do it, be good doctors. Even surgeons. Don't you dare give up, Sarah. If all else fails, let me know. I'm not sure how much influence I've got, but you never know till you try." She smiled. "So, dear, be of good heart."

Sarah smiled, too. "I will. Thanks to you."

"Meantime," Mother Bickerdyke chuckled, "I prescribe you do a little partying, while the army remains in Atlanta. Go out with a nice officer. There ought to be some balls and you deserve a little fun. You know, maybe I should find a nice officer for you."

"Wow," she said blushing. "You're acting like a dear aunt who's trying to marry me off. A widow woman."

Bickerdyke tried to look contrite. "You'll have to excuse an old woman. But I still think every good woman deserves a good man. Specially the pretty ones."

Now Sarah found herself saying things she'd not even revealed to herself. "When the War's over I'd like to try and locate a man. A Confederate officer. I believe he's from some town, a town with a small college, in the hill country of North Carolina."

"Mightn't that be that wounded officer you found at Antietam? Whose life you saved?"

"Yes."

"Do you think you have a romantic interest?"

"No . . . yes . . . I don't know." Sarah was confused. She had never succeeded in sorting out her thoughts about Thad Barrett. "I just wondered how he was doing. But I sometimes find myself thinking about him, maybe more than I should."

"You also have a close friend in that doctor up in Baltimore. Who wrote me the letter about you. Is there a romantic interest there?"

Sarah blushed again. She almost wished she'd never brought this up. But Mother Bickerdyke was someone she could confide in. Maybe she might help her sort out her feelings. "He told me he loved me and wanted me to stay with him up in Baltimore. But he's married and his wife's an invalid."

"Ha," Mrs. Bickerdyke snorted. "I wonder how many invalid wives husbands with roaming eyes have."

"Mary Ann!"

"Sorry. Maybe this is an honest fact. You certainly don't want to lose his friendship. He could be your ticket to getting into medical school." She looked at Sarah appraisingly. "I sense you have deeper feelings for that Reb."

Sarah felt confused. "I don't know . . . Maybe."

"Remember, dear, when this War's over, they'll be our brothers again."

The conversation with Mother Bickerdyke did help to clarify Sarah's feelings, she realized later. She now felt that her interest in Thad might indeed be deeper than she had admitted to herself before. She was sure that his feelings toward her were strong. At least they had been back in Baltimore. That didn't mean, of course, that they would be enduring. But she needed to see him again, she knew that now. But would he be that easy to find?

#

Mother Bickerdyke did not carry out her threat to find a young man to squire Sarah around Atlanta. At times over the next weeks Sarah rather regretted that she hadn't. Evidently her disclosure of her possible love interests dissuaded Mary Ann. Still, a young physician asked her for a date for some social event, the Harvest Ball or whatever. Without Mother Bickerdyke's help, Sarah reflected. She could do some things without the dominant personality of her mentor.

Her escort was a young captain who had recently joined the medical staff of Sherman's massive army. As one of the few young female nurses, she supposed she was fair game for such a young man on the prowl. But she said yes, most willingly, to the invitation. After all, he was an attractive young man, just out of medical school. And she hoped to tap into his experiences.

The feeling of being held closely by a young man was something she had not experienced for a long time. Obviously he had not experienced it with a woman for a considerable time, either. For he hungered with passion. She pushed him off, and tried to steer the conversation to more prosaic topics.

She told him she was thinking of applying to medical school after the War was over.

He was aghast at this idea. "You can't mean this, that you're thinking of applying to medical school? Good God! What are you females thinking? That you're men?"

Any brief ardor that she might have had quickly faded with that remark. She pushed him away. "I think we'd better sit down."

"What the hell, Sarah?"

As he reluctantly led her back to their table, she asked, "Is everybody at medical school as prejudiced as you against women?"

"Sarah, this isn't prejudice," he vehemently retorted, his voice rising. "It's a well known fact that females don't have the stamina and objectivity to perform well under the stress of medical emergency situations." He smiled smugly. "They're too emotional. But, of course, they're well suited for soothing and comforting after operations and medical emergencies."

"Is that what they teach you in medical school?"

"Everybody knows this."

"Did you know that I assisted a surgeon for 36 hours straight in major operations, both at Antietam and Chattanooga?"

He stared at her. "But . . ."

She asked again, intently and tight-lipped, "Is that what they teach you in medical school? That females cannot handle such stressful situations?"

"Well, they don't actually talk about females. But this is common knowledge."

"Among the professors, too?"

"Sure."

The promise of the evening was destroyed on this sour note. If such attitudes and prejudices existed with recent medical school graduates, what possible chance did she have? She was doomed before she even had a chance to prove her worth. Damn! Damn!

As soon as she could reasonably end the evening she did. "I have a bad headache. I think you should take me home."

"So soon," he said, irritably.

"Yes."

As he took her to her door, he said, "I guess this proves that you females and your headaches and female complaints are not able to cope with situations that require some degree of strength and endurance."

"If you say so, Todd." She felt like slugging him.

"Tell me, Todd, have you ever assisted at twenty amputations in an hour?"

"Good God, no!" He stared at her. "You're not telling me . . . ?"

"In the midst of major battles, yes, for many hours at a time. As I told you before, but you didn't believe me."

He looked at her. She could sense that his ardor had cooled completely at this disclosure. If he was indicative of men in general, she realized now that they did not want strong women. They only wanted the docile and fragile, those who needed protecting, who had no minds of their own. She was the anomaly in this society. For she was not like this, nor ever would be. But she could comfort herself that Mother Bickerdyke was not either, and she was sure that Clara Barton wasn't. There must be others like us, she thought. Though few in numbers we be.

#

Sherman's main army moved out of Atlanta in mid-November, far sooner than most expected. Mother Bickerdyke did not return in time, and would probably have to catch the army in Savannah. For that was where Sherman was heading.

On November 12 he broke his railroad and telegraph communications. Now he was out of touch with the Union. Three days later he burned Atlanta's war industries, just before departing for Savannah and the sea. On a bracing morning, 60,000 Federals headed south, prepared to live off the land.

The vast army spread out in four parallel columns, marching 10 to 15 miles a day, and picking clean an area up to 60 miles wide. They encountered little opposition and destroyed anything that might aid the Confederate's military efforts, wrecking bridges, factories, ripping up railroads, confiscating vast quantities of food and livestock.

Sarah shuddered at the destruction: a land picked clean, with no regard for the women and children, innocent victims. This was total war. So much food was obtained, more than needed, that a good portion was left to rot.

Sherman entered Savannah before Christmas, and telegraphed President Lincoln: "I beg to present you as a Christmas gift the city of Savannah."

Then he turned his attention and destructive path north, with the objective of joining up with Grant in front of Lee. About mid-January, the last major Confederate port, Wilmington, North Carolina, fell. The death knells of the Confederacy were near at hand.

But something occurred at Wilmington that profoundly affected Sarah. Mother Bickerdyke joined her there, coming in with a ship originally loaded with supplies for Sherman's troops at Savannah. But they never reached Savannah. She had found a better use for these supplies farther north at Wilmington: the released prisoners of Andersonville were pouring into Wilmington on their route to Annapolis and then to Washington.

These survivors of the worst prison camp in America had been turned over to Sherman in Georgia, then taken to Savannah and sent by steamer to Wilmington. As the survivors came ashore at Wilmington they were a shocking sight: walking skeletons, covered with the ugly running sores of "prison pox," and the stretcher cases with their more grievous afflictions. Many of the men were absolute mental wrecks, destined for the asylums of their home states.

With such need, the army authorities were making fairly good preparations for the released prisoners, utilizing churches, schools, and private homes for hospitals. Sarah and Mother Bickerdyke provided needed supplies and devoted themselves to bathing, bandaging, and feeding the survivors. They wrote letters to their families, ending their long suspense.

"This is not like amputations on the battlefield, Sarah," Bickerdyke said through tight lips.

"The need is just as great, Mary Ann." She wiped her eyes. "And I think the satisfaction of contributing is far greater for me. I never dreamed of such as this."

"Nor I, dear."

#

On April 9, Palm Sunday, Lee surrendered at Appomattox Court House. The War was essentially over. Sherman's army was ordered to concentrate itself near Washington City in preparation for a great victory celebration. Sarah wanted to detour to try and find Thad, someplace perhaps in western North Carolina.

"I don't think it's safe yet, Sarah," Mother Bickerdyke told her. "Not without a military escort. And I don't think they're be giving you one."

Sarah looked at her questioningly.

"Some of the officers tell me they suspect small bands of Rebs are still wandering around. Some may not have heard of Lee's surrender. Others, well they mightn't be ready to accept it yet."

"I see," she said disappointed.

"So, come with me, Sarah. To Washington. They want me to ride with Sherman in a grand parade."

"How wonderful. What great recognition!"

"Yes. Well, I could do without it. But they said it was an order." She smiled sheepishly. "They even want me to ride a fancy horse and be all dolled up."

During that first spring of peace, the Union troops poured into Washington. Miles deep outside the city their tents whitened the hills. The Capital was slowly getting over the death of Lincoln and the horrific casualties of the struggle, and was turning itself to exuberant celebration. The black bunting of mourning on building fronts and lamp posts was replaced with red, white, and blue. On May 23, the first day of the Grand Military Review, the marchers were the Army of the Potomac. Sherman and the westerners would take over on the second day.

Mary Ann's horse had been prettied up. Even his hoofs had been polished, and his tail was tied with ribbons. Despite the New York finery that had been prepared for her, she joined the parade in her everyday calico dress, with a sunbonnet dangling at her neck.

Sherman rode at the head of the procession. He and his staff rode past the reviewing stand, saluting the President. The horses were left at the White House grounds and he returned to stand behind the President, Grant, and members of the cabinet, as his troops marched past for hours. The Fifteenth, Sherman's old corps, came first, with its regimental band lustily playing, "Marching Through Georgia."

Just behind the band rode General Logan, with Mother Bickerdyke at his side.

Sarah watched with awe. No one she had ever known deserved the honor more than Mother Bickerdyke. She was proud to have been a part of this heroic effort and this stalwart woman's remarkable contribution. But she wondered what the future had in store for herself: acute letdown and disappointment, maybe?

CHAPTER 8

He came back to his home town, Chalfant, North Carolina, a little college town nestled deep in the foothills of North Carolina, broken in body and spirit. He had been exchanged at City Point, Virginia, early in 1863. Only later did he learn that such exchanges of Union and Confederate prisoners, man for man and officer for officer, had broken down after Lincoln's Emancipation Proclamation brought Negroes into the Union Army. The South refused to recognize colored soldiers as prisoners of war; instead, they were considered runaways. In the face of such an irreconcilable dispute, the U. S. Government suspended the agreement to exchange prisoners.

Whenever Thad felt particularly depressed, he had only to remember how lucky he was to have been exchanged before the suspension. Otherwise, he would be languishing in some wretched Union prison, or be dead.

Still, he was released from the hospital too soon. He was barely able to drag himself across a room with crutches and his stick of a leg, before he was thrust out in the world. If he had not been an officer, he knew he would never have made it. As it was, civilians and soldiers alike helped him. He often had to be carried. And food was scarce enough for the Southern combatants, much less for a man who could never fight again.

It took him three months to make it back home. There was no family waiting for him, no estate or farmstead. Only Aunt Abigail, and she must be in her 70s now. She was still spry when he left, but he wondered what three years of wartime and deprivations had done to her. He wondered whether she would or could take an invalid into her small house on the outskirts of town. But he had no place else to go.

The blacksmith offered to drive him out to her place. "It's the least I can do for a wounded hero," he said.

"Is she in good health?" Thad asked anxiously.

"As tough as a sackful of varmints."

"I wonder if she'll be able to put me up."

The blacksmith looked at him and chuckled. "Major, people'd be standin' in line to put you up. You're the town's hero, you know."

As they approached her little unpainted house in the woods, she came out on the porch, shading her eyes against the glare of the sun. She waved vigorously when she recognized him. She looked the same, a thin wisp of an old woman, with lively eyes and energy to burn.

"Abigail, can I stay with you?" Thad asked as she came over to the wagon.

"I'd be real put out if you went somewheres else, dear nephew."

She and the blacksmith helped him down. The blacksmith took his one small valise and carried it to the porch as Thad worked to get his crutches under control. "Thank you, Isaac," she said, "For bringin' my dear nephew home to me."

Isaac clasped Thad's hand. "Don't let Abigail be too bossy, Major. I 'spect she'd be bossin' Robert Lee, if she had the chance." His eyes crinkled. "If she gets too bad, you just let me know." With a final wave, he drove away.

"Thad, you look poorly," Abigail told him then.

Thad took a deep breath, trying to fight off waves of weariness, for just a few more minutes. "I was afraid you'd no longer be here," he said weakly.

"No longer be here? Where would I be?" She spit some tobacco, and looked fiercely at him. But then she winked. "Bet you thought I'd have dried up and blown away by now, didn't you?"

"The thought occurred to me."

"Wal, youngster, I'm a tough old biddy. A lot tougher than you, it 'pears. Here, let me help you up the steps."

They somehow made it. "I think we should get you to bed," she said quietly. He had no strength to object nor desire to. "An' you're so thin. We gotta get some food in you."

She helped him undress. "I bet you haven't been out of them clothes for weeks. Nor had a bath either. An' with that shaggy beard and long hair, I hardly knew you. Wasn't sure but that Isaac was bringin' me some wild creature." She peered at him. "You don't want to keep all that beard and hair, do you?"

He shook his head.

"Then I'll do some trimmin' after the bath. Shall I help you take off your leg?"

"Please. The stump's really sore."

He fell asleep before she could help him with a bath and spoon some nourishment into him.

The next three months were hazy. He had a recurrence of the fever. Without Aunt Abigail he would have died. She would not let him. "You have to fight this! Don' give up now that you've made it back home," she told him time and again. Sometimes he could barely nod at this exhortation.

At last the fever subsided, leaving him still weak and helpless.

"We need t' build up your strength, nephew Thad." As he weakly protested some of her offerings, she told him, "Don't fight me, Thad. Food, fresh air, sleep, that's what you need to put you right agin. Your old aunt knows, even if those docs swear the knife and strong medicine is all that's needed." She sniffed. "What do they know? Only to amputate and burn still twitchin' limbs. Our great medical professionals."

It was fall before Thad had gained back reasonable strength. With Abigail's constant prodding, he reached enough facility with his crutches that he and Abigail could make a few short trips into town. He was surprised that townspeople greeted him with respect, more respect than he deserved.

One day as he was sitting on the porch watching squirrels gathering acorns, Abigail sat down beside him. "You know, Thad," she said, "You'd be a lot better off with a wooden leg instead of that stick. There's a man hereabouts who makes wooden legs. His name's Rafe Kessler. I think we should see him."

"A wooden leg's expensive. I don't have any money. And I don't think you have either."

She sighed. "No, my only asset is this rundown shack."

But she brightened. "I bet the bank would give you the money. A fine, upstandin' officer like you."

"Right," he said sarcastically. "A fine, upstanding officer, with no resources, and no job. I'm sure bankers would be standing in line to give me money."

Aunt Abigail vigorously chewed her tobacco. She spit toward a fly, but missed. "Wal, I still think we should see Rafe. There's nothin' to lose. Are you up to takin' a little ride tomorrow?"

"I suppose," he said. In truth, he was more excited about seeing this man than he let on to Abigail. A wooden leg, instead of this peg. He might even be able to walk without crutches, after a while.

#

Rafe Kessler lived in a house that backed up against a raggedly forested hill, about two miles from town. He could have been 50 or he could have been 70. He was almost completely bald, but had a white luxuriant beard, badly stained with tobacco juice. Thad could see parts of artificial legs scattered seemingly in confusion in the one large room. Several young women were working on them in this barn that served as a factory.

"Rafe, look's like business is good," his aunt greeted him.

"Abigail, I could work twenty-four hours a day, 'n not keep up w' it." He looked keenly at Thad. "Are you bringin' me more business?"

"This is my nephew, Thaddeus, lately a major of the 20th North Carolina. They finished him at Antietam."

"Major." He touched his hand to his forehead. "Is it off at the thigh?"

"About eight inches above the knee."

"Wal, that's not too bad. You'll still have a decent stump. Course, you'll still need a good knee joint. An' that makes these things 'spensive. An' a long time to make."

"How much?" Abigail asked.

"Right aroun' two hundred U. S. dollars. Half down, and the rest when finished. But it'll take 'bout six months."

"I don't have that kind of money now. Will you accept an IOU?"

"I'm sorry, Major." Again he touched his forehead. "I've been burned too many times. Where men promise to pay, an' never do. I don' make any exceptions now. But I will try to do this faster for you, once you come up with the downpayment. An' my legs are good ones, Major. Most men are able to walk without crutches, after a while with 'em."

Thad could see that there was nothing to be gained by pleading, or coaxing. Certainly not by appealing to patriotism. This man had far more business than he could handle. Thad believed him when he said he'd been burned with people not paying. "Come on, Abigail, let's go, and let this good man get back to work."

#

A few weeks later, Aunt Abigail drove her buggy back from town and pulled up in a whirl of dust. Thad came around the corner of the house, curious at this unaccustomed urgency.

She jumped off the buggy and rushed over to him. "I ran into Dr. Turner today. He wants to see you, dear nephew." She whispered conspiratorially, "I think he wants to see you 'bout comin' back to the college."

Thad looked at her. "Are you sure he wants to see me about that?"

"You may have lost a leg, and had a few other injuries, nephew, but you still got your mind, and your voice, haven't you?"

"Yes, but . . ."

She sniffed. "I'm tired of you mopin' 'round here. It's high time you was up and doin'. Be damn thankful Dr. Turner is still interested."

Thad was thankful. Indeed he was. The life of an invalid had become unbearable. Especially since he wasn't a true invalid, now. He could get around some, was not completely dependent.

"He's comin' out here this afternoon," she said.

#

Dr. Sam Turner, president of Mountain View College for Men and Women, was a little more stooped, a little more white haired than Thad remembered. His beard now was all white. But his eyes were still warm and kind. As Thad was leaving for Virginia in the early days of the War, Sam had told him, "I'm afraid, Thad, this war will be worse than anybody thinks—long and bloody. But remember, you'll always have a place here, when you get back. Please come back to us."

Thad greeted him on the porch. First they clasped hands, and then embraced. Thad was aware of busybody Abigail watching from inside. It was a late fall day, fairly warm, and they sat on the porch.

"Thad, forgive me for not seeing you sooner. I know you've had a long siege to get better, but I've still been remiss." He pounded his fist on his knee. "I should have come to you as a friend, if not an employer. But I didn't want to give you false hope."

"It's all right, Sam. I really wasn't eager for the pity of old friends."

"I wanted to offer some encouragement of coming back, before I saw you. And I couldn't really." He sighed, and shook his head. "And I still can't, much. But maybe a little, Thad, if you'll be patient." He paused.

"Go on, Sam. Tell me the worst."

"I want you back, in your old position of Professor of Rhetoric, and be my right hand man. But we have so few students now. The boys are all off fighting, or have already made their sacrifices to the cause. For the girls still attending, I sometimes wonder how relevant our theoretical disciplines are to the far greater urgencies of the day." He tugged his beard and looked out at the scrubby pines, and shook his head. Then he turned back. "Thaddeus, do you think our school can survive this?"

"If we can just last a few more years, maybe we can," Thad ventured.

"We have little with which to pay you, or anyone else for that matter. You may not be interested in such an uncertain situation."

"I am, Sam, I am. We'll get by. If we can just find enough for basic necessities."

Turner sighed. "Yes. Basic necessities. Strange how unimportant everything else is at a time like this. Down to the elemental . . . and even that will be a challenge."

Thad was not surprised. After all, the South was practically defeated and its resources for the most part drained. An artificial leg to replace the crude peg would have to wait well into the future. If ever. But this was reality.

So they agreed that he would begin teaching the first of the year. A full load if possible. If not, well, some classes would have to be canceled.

Now with his future somewhat assured, provided the small college survived, and with six weeks on his hands before classes began, Thad could put his mind on more constructive things. Abigail helped him outside most days, except the coldest and rainy ones. He tried to extend his endurance walks in preparation for the classroom physical activity. He reviewed his old books and notes on subjects that had been out of mind for years. At first it was difficult to make the transition from harsh realities to flights of theoretical fancy.

The days passed quickly until classes would begin, and now Thad felt an almost forgotten excitement. There had been no excitement before battles, not even the first one at Manassas when almost everyone else was bound up in the thrill of it all, and had supreme confidence. No, the fighting brought him no excitement, only a stolid resignation, and a fear of somehow being found wanting—in courage, or judgment, or whatever.

Still, he was concerned about how the women students would react to him. Some would surely think he was a freak with that ugly peg leg; others would probably be oversolicitous and want to treat him like an invalid.

On the first day of classes, he was surprised, and rather delighted, to find his students found him attractive, despite his peg leg. Or maybe because of it. But these women were starved for men, he knew. Still, a Confederate hero—ha— seemed to intrigue them.

One, the daughter of a Quaker landowner, apparently regarded him as a good catch, and was quite obvious about it. Her name was Lucy.

"Dr. Barrett, don't you think you should have a little fun?" she asked one day.

"Fun?"

"Sure," she said gaily. "We need to forget this War for a little while. There's a dance, we girls have planned a dance for next Saturday. Trouble is, there aren't many men. So, you must come."

Whoa, he thought to himself, gaiety in a time of utter devastation and deprivation. "Lucy, I can't dance."

"Oh, no problem, Dr. Barrett. The dance is just an excuse to socialize a bit." She smiled teasingly. "You know, you're a very attractive man. We're all wild about you."

He looked at her, bemused. "I can't imagine what you mean."

"Oh, you know. You excite us. Such a wounded hero, and so good lookin' too."

With reluctance he made an appearance at the dance. After all, as one of the few faculty, he was almost compelled to come. His students treated him so nice, and he even clumped around for some slow dances, and it felt wonderful to hold a soft body in his arms. Lucy shared him with the other girls, until he had to plead that he was worn down. Sam Turner tried to fill in while he gathered his strength. That night, he had difficulty sleeping.

#

In this spring and summer of 1864, the War had not yet touched western North Carolina, but ominously it was not that far away. Chattanooga and eastern Tennessee, barely 200 miles to the west, had been captured by Grant and Sherman. Only mountains were between Chalfant and the Union invaders, and the stories they heard of Sherman scared them all. But the Union general turned out to have other objectives than the small rural towns in the hills of Carolina.

Word now surfaced that Sherman was moving on to Atlanta with a vast army. So Chalfant escaped destruction. Still, the economy was in shambles. Shortages of all kinds—food, clothing, medicines, essentials—plagued them, as they did all the South. The dreaded reports of wounded and dead loved ones brought the War to every hamlet and practically every household. Thad found himself feeling guilty that he was still alive and back in civilization while so many were not.

Fear of Union forces intensified as the Confederacy began collapsing late that year of 1864. How much longer could Lee hold out? And the valiant troops of Johnston? Atlanta, a mere 200 miles to the south, was under siege, and then they learned that it had surrendered September 2. Their fear was palpable that Union cavalry would sweep down and burn their town, and drive off what few livestock remained.

Christmas of 1864 was wretched indeed, with the deprivations and the fear. Then word came that the devil Sherman had entered Savannah in a 60-mile-wide path of destruction from Atlanta to the sea. Everything was said to be destroyed in the swath, with the puny forces the South could pit against him no better than fleas on a horse.

So, 1864 came to an end. Hardly anyone was optimistic about the future of the Confederacy, although a few still expressed a forlorn hope that Lee would win a great victory against Grant, and then turn his army on the devil. But the handwriting was there.

#

One day in March, word came that Union cavalry under Bradley had torn up the railroad only twenty miles from Chalfant.

It was then that a delegation of town officials sought him out. "Major Barrett, we need your help," the elderly mayor, Josiah Ripley, began.

"How can I help?" Thad asked.

"Well, as a senior Confederate officer, we need you to save us from being pillaged. We have a cache of arms and ammunition to defend ourselves. Will you lead us?"

Thad stared at him, shocked at what these naive civilians were proposing. "If the Yanks are intent on pillaging," he said, "there's nothing we can do except hide in basements, and if we have any livestock, to drive them into the hills. Any valuables should be hidden where they cannot be confiscated or burned. Any chickens, let them have them."

The mayor was wringing his hands. A woman whom Thad later learned was deputy mayor, spoke up forcefully. "Surely, Major Barrett, you don't advocate we hide like animals while the bluebellies burn our town?"

"What is your name, ma'am?" he asked.

"I'm Kate Burnham. My husband, a colonel, was killed at Gettysburg?"

"I'm sorry, ma'am. But if you and the other townspeople do not want to be killed, like your husband, you had better make yourselves scarce. Offer no resistance. Otherwise, you'll be shot without mercy."

As she started to protest, he went on, "What chance do you think a small town of mostly older people, womenfolk, and a few cripples like me have against a well trained and armed body of cavalry? Even if we have some guns? None whatsoever. Any resistance, and we'd simply be giving them an excuse to kill, pillage, burn. And even rape," he said, and saw her flinch.

They were silent, looking at him in despair. "Mayor Riply, Mrs. Burnham, the rest of you, let us hope they don't come here," he told them. "But if they do, we must offer no resistance. Not only no firearms but no outcries. Such may save us, even if we have to be humiliated. I think the War is almost over. What a shame it would be to lose lives just a few days from the end. Better buildings be burned, humiliation be endured, than lives lost."

The delegation prepared to leave, somber but impressed with his remarks, he could see. Mrs. Burnham lingered a moment longer. "Major Barrett—may I call you Thaddeus? Please call me Kate—I respect your remarks, and you, sir. I think you've given us sound advice." As she started to leave she turned back from the door. "Thaddeus, I would like to talk with you again. I suspect we have a lot in common. If nothing else, this terrible War has branded both of us."

He nodded. As she left he realized she was an uncommonly attractive woman. Maybe slightly older than himself, but he knew he looked older than he actually was. Her dark hair was tied rather severely back, lessening her womanly attractiveness. But her loose-fitting dress could not disguise the voluptuousness of her figure. He wondered if she and the colonel had had any children.

Now memories of Sarah came unbidden. He had not thought of her much these last months. It seemed such an impossible dream, one best repressed. Now, suddenly, he found himself comparing Sarah with Kate Burnham.

Sarah was more slender, more girlish, not as sensual as the widow Burnham. Her dark hair was shorter, whereas the widow's was long. Her face was smaller, more angular, not as full as this woman's. He still remembered the beautiful bone structure of Sarah's face. And her wonderful hands, so slender and gentle, yet firm and capable, that thrilled him with their touch and that he longed to hold. But physical features were only part. He knew so much about Sarah's character, her supreme dedication, her courage, her endurance, and most of all, her wonderful compassion. He was quite sure she had a wonderful capacity for love. The widow Burnham was unknown to him. But he thought she would have to meet high standards indeed to compete with Sarah Lindsey. He sighed. Sarah, oh Sarah, what has become of you? Will we ever meet again?

#

The Union cavalry never invaded their town. A short time later word reached Chalfant that Lee had surrendered on Palm Sunday, April 9th. The War was over.

Now it was final: the South had lost. It had all been for nothing, the piles of dead, the missing limbs, the mangled bodies, innards ravaged by disease.

Thad viewed this news with mixed feelings. To have the horrible struggle over with . . . but at such cost. For himself, a lost leg, a chest that still pained on exertion, an arm weakened by the muscle damage from the same wound. What an utter waste.

At least now it should be easier to put lives back in order, with the all-consuming effort finished. The worst days for the college also ought to be over, with some men likely returning.

Shortly after the news reached them of the end of the War, Kate Burnham sent him an invitation to meet with the mayor and the town council about the future of Chalfant in the reconstruction days ahead. Sam Turner was also there, by virtue of his position at the college. The meeting took place at her spacious home. Her husband had undoubtedly been wealthy, but little good it did him.

While the loss of the War hardly made an atmosphere for celebrating, still Thad sensed a general feeling of profound relief. At least the town and the surrounding country had been spared the destruction of most parts of the South. No more families would be losing loved ones, and others would be finding their menfolk slowly returning. He wondered if some of his old command were still alive to return to their nearby homes.

Kate brought out bottles of spirits. "I'd been saving these, to celebrate our victory. Now that can never be, so let's drink to our future. And to our perseverance in spite of the Yankee conquerors."

"Here, here," the guests applauded. Thad noticed that the town dignitaries went at the whiskey as though they had long been deprived. Perhaps they had been.

She introduced him. "We have an honest to God hero who's been living among us for the last two years. Quietly. Unassuming. Teaching at the college. But a person of great experience, wisdom, and vision," she went on.

Thad listened wonderingly at such effusive praise. It sounded almost as if she were building him up as a political candidate. For what?

Later, Mayor Riply told those gathered of Thad's judicious advice during the Union cavalry threat. "While the threat did not materialize, it certainly could have. He counseled us to lie low, to accept burned buildings instead of lives. Even to accept humiliation."

They urged him to run for mayor. Joseph Riply wanted to step down. "I think you, sir, could better handle these difficult days ahead. You will certainly have my support."

"I'm not sure that's possible, Joseph. The word I hear is that Confederate officers are not permitted to hold any political offices. By order of Secretary of War Stanton."

Kate disagreed with that. "The word I get from Raleigh is that the harsh decree of Stanton, from back in '63, is not being followed. Washington wants to bring stability as soon as possible. Confederate leaders, be they military or governmental, are the only hope for such quick stability. So, Thad, I don't think your concerns have any merit in the realities of the day. And we're not putting you up for more than local office, yet."

Others expressed the same thoughts. The rumors seemed to be widespread. "But I've heard that they've just imprisoned Jefferson Davis, even put him in chains. That doesn't sound to me like leniency and amnesty," Thad observed.

"Their main charge against Davis is that he was involved in the planning of the Lincoln assassination. There're also inneundos that he somehow approved the Andersonville mistreatment of prisoners. But I'm sure he'll be exonerated," Sam Turner said.

Thad was ambivalent. He was being swept along by wishes of other people, not his own. He had no interest in politics, despite those who maintained such was the ultimate achievement of life, the only way to make an impact. Well, he knew that the desire of most men, and most women he surmised, was to make some contribution to humanity, to make the world hopefully a tad better. It was easier for women with their children. For someone like himself, unmarried, such direct contribution was denied. So far. But, couldn't he make a reasonable contribution in the molding of young lives, as a teacher? Did it have to be limited to politics? The biggest contribution, the one he wanted most to make, was to influence society by his writings.

"I'm sorry," he said. "I'm not prepared at this time to run for any office."

They were shocked, and stared at him. "How could any one turn down such an opportunity?"

"Thad," Kate spoke up. "Don't let this be your final decision. Think about it."

Reluctantly he agreed to think about it.

Afterwards, as everyone was leaving, somewhat the worst for the unaccustomed imbibing, Kate asked him to stay a few minutes longer. He could see she was upset with him, even angry, though she tried to conceal it.

"You disappoint me, Thaddeus. I'd have thought you'd want to take advantage of your considerable talents. As well as assume a measure of responsibility for this community that you defended with your life."

He bowed his head. "I'm no politician, Kate. Nor do I want to be." Now he told her bitterly, "I certainly hope I can make a contribution to this community that I sacrificed my leg and body for, in other ways. But not in politics."

She shook her head. "Politics has to be the best way to make things better. Teaching, it may or may not have some long term impact. Who can say? I think you should reconsider."

"I'm no politician," he repeated. "I don't even like politicians." He shook his head disgustedly. "My experience with politicians is that they're all self seeking, trying to promote themselves. Little concerned with the greater issues, and with the people affected."

"See," she breathed. "You could make a difference. You could be a new kind of politician, one broader minded, unselfish, protector of the masses."

"Ha," he said. "And be shot down in debate like the naive fellow I am." He gave a twisted smile. "Not even you, I wager, would support my position of giving suffrage to the Negroes." She stared at him. "Yes," he continued, "I support giving them a vote. But I don't think we'll have a choice. It will be forced on us by the reconstruction people."

She changed the subject abruptly. "Thad, does your peg leg influence your decision?"

He reflected on this. "No, I don't think it does. Although it certainly reminds me, all the time, of the futility of conflict."

She murmured, "I understand Rafe Kessler makes artificial legs. But they're expensive. Would you accept a loan from me to get such a leg?"

He looked at her. "Why would you make such an offer, Kate? To someone who might take ten years to pay it off? Is my going into politics so important to you?"

She shook her head, rather indignantly. "It's more than politics. Don't you know? I'm interested in you. I want what's best for you. And I think an artificial leg would help you make a better decision about your life than a peg leg." She looked steadily at him. "I would like to know you better, Thad, politics or not. Is this so wrong of me? I can afford it, you know."

He put his hand on her shoulder. She made a strange sound, and suddenly reached for him and pulled him to her. He could feel her soft breasts.

#

Somehow he found himself in her bedroom. He was not even sure how this had happened. She had unfastened her hair so that it flowed around her shoulders.

"Undress me, Thad," she commanded in a husky voice.

His fingers were clumsy as he helped her undo her buttons and fasteners. Her garments slipped off her shoulders. "My handsome major," she murmured as she pressed his face to her. The last of her garments were scattered on the floor, and her white lush body beckoned. He tore at his clothes, as she stretched out on the bed and pulled him down to her.

The stick for a leg intruded. It did not bend, and was an awkward obstacle. Their passion momentarily cooled. "Thad," she murmured, "could we take the leg off? Could I help you with it?"

He winced. He had not attempted to make love since the amputation. He had expected this would turn off any woman, so was not surprised. "We can take it off," he said hoarsely. "But I'm not sure my stump of a leg will be any more pleasing." He moved to get off her.

She grabbed him, and would not let him get up. "Please, Thad, you turn me on, leg or no leg. Please, honey, don't leave my bed." She was almost sobbing. "I'm sorry I said anything. Forget it."

He stared at her, then at the configuration of their bodies. Damn it, the leg was an intrusive thing. He could see it was rubbing hard against her soft flesh. "All right, maybe it would be better off." They worked together to unfasten the straps and ease the device off his stump. It dropped with a thud on the floor.

Her passion was quickly rekindled. She was making small moans and stroking him. "Take me, please," she urged. But his ardour had cooled. Maybe her aggressiveness turned him off, or maybe his deformities affected his performance, both physically and emotionally. Or maybe it was something else. Afterwards as he looked back, he knew that Kate could never take the place of Sarah, and he wasn't sure he even liked her.

He didn't remember too much more about that night. Shortly after, he fell asleep in the haze of an alcoholic stupor. He woke sometime near dawn, at first uncertain where he was. But then he saw her awake besides him, looking at him. "My dear lover," she said, "let me help you try this again."

He pushed her away, trying to be gentle but firm. "Kate, I'm just not ready for this. It's been too long, and too much has happened. Would you just help me get my peg of a leg on, and I'll be on my way." At her protests, he said, "I'm really sorry about this, and embarrassed too."

"It's okay," she finally murmured. "I can see we must train you." She sighed. "There'll be other times, my dear major."

She fixed breakfast before he left. He felt badly hung over. He was not used to such indulgences. She tossled his hair. "I still want you to get one of those new artificial limbs. On me. Shall we go later today to arrange it?"

He hesitated. There was no denying he needed to replace this awkward peg. But something urged him not to become too beholden to this woman. Perhaps she was too skillful, not naive enough for him. Maybe too dominant a personality. Maybe too ambitious for her men. "Please, Kate, let me think about it. I'm reluctant not to do this on my own."

She appeared rather miffed. "Damn it, why the hesitation? Do you want to go through life with that stick of a leg? When you could have something less conspicuous and more comfortable? And be a better lover?"

He toyed with his grits. "Please bear with me, for a little bit. My mind's muddled from last night, and this morning. I'm not sure I'm thinking very straight."

She smiled now. "You really are quite unsophisticated, aren't you." She paused. "Maybe that's what makes you attractive. A diamond in the rough."

He tried to grin, and the effort hurt his head. "I'm not sure there's a diamond under all this."

CHAPTER 9

He knew he was introspective, a thinker. Perhaps a dreamer. But more likely only a brooder. Maybe this was not a bad personality for a philosopher, and even a writer. And perhaps an artist. But not for other pursuits.

In his youth, he had on occasion climbed Steven's Knob, an outlier of loftier mountains. There he could look to the west where the mass of the Blue Ridge etched the skyline, often with clouds piling up behind the summits, while eagles floated on updrafts and crows intruded with their cries.

In this splendid isolation he would wonder about his life to come, what he would be, and how he should get there. He had heard that Cherokee youth had also pondered their destinies from this same hill, before the Cherokees were forcibly evicted from these lovely mountains of their heritage.

Now it was a warm weekend in early May, and he had several days between classes. Of a sudden, he felt the need to go to the mountaintop again, perhaps to find direction and peace. He knew it was foolish to attempt this with his infirmities, but somehow he wanted to try.

Abigail was out socializing this morning, so he left a note telling of his plans, and that he would not be home that night. He made himself a quick breakfast, and put together a small pack of food, water, and a blanket so he could stay overnight. In his youth, it was no great challenge to make the ascent and descent on the same day, although he often even then liked to spend the night, and sometimes even several nights on the mountaintop before coming down. It was really no more than a simple, unchallenging hill. But with a peg leg, it assumed far more awesome qualities. He wasn't sure he would be able to do it, but vowed to crawl if he had to.

He hiked to town and then found Isaac, the blacksmith, willing to drive him the three miles to the foot of the hill. He told him he was trying to toughen up his stump with a hike in the countryside.

The ascent proved a terrible challenge.

His peg of a leg found purchase difficult amid the loose rocks. This strained his good leg, and by halfway up, this leg was aching and cramping. He slipped and fell half a dozen times, once wrenching his shoulder so badly he despaired of continuing. But he did. The last hundred feet the trail steepened, and he crawled on his hands and knee over the stones, with the stick trailing behind.

He was utterly exhausted when he reached the summit, drenched in sweat, with a bruised knee and hands, an aching shoulder, and his stump so sore he didn't see how he'd be able to use the peg for several days. But he would have to on the way down, unless he were to crawl all the way, and he hardly thought his hands and his one knee could cope with that. He chided himself about this foolishness, especially since he had classes in two more days. Somehow, despite the pain and exhaustion, he sensed a profound triumph. He had done it! He might be a cripple, but he was not a helpless cripple.

The day was almost gone and the sun was setting behind the ridges to the west, touching the scattered clouds with a feast of colors.

His breathing quieted and he sat with his back against a boulder, and gazed westward, and tried to capture the peace and the promise he had felt in his youth. So many years gone by. So many dreams destroyed.

Before full darkness came, he helped himself to some of the rolls and dried meat. It was not much, but he certainly had not come all this way for a feast. The water in his canteen was half gone, but he should have enough if he wasn't profligate. Even on this mountain top, the night was gently warm. Such a night would not have been to the liking of the Indian boys who sought to extend their physical endurance to the breaking point, and fasted for days in hopes of finding a vision. Well, his body had seen hardship enough.

After a while, he felt the spell of this childhood sanctuary enveloping him, maybe even purifying him. At least he felt he was on the verge of sorting things out. It was dark now although the night was clear and a three-quarter moon cast an eerie light. He finished the last of his food and wrapped himself in the blanket. Eventually he stretched out on the ground and gazed at the heavens and the panoply of stars that seemed so close from this elevation, and his troubles felt puny before such a universe.

Except for the blanket he had brought no sleeping equipment, but he made the ground reasonably soft with pine needles, and the elevation was high enough to not be bothered by insects. Exhausted by the climb, he fell asleep quickly.

During the night he dreamed of Sarah, a vivid dream, one that stayed with him after he awakened. In his dream they were on opposite sides of a narrow gorge, and her hair was blowing in the wind and her arms were outstretched, seeking him. She was yelling to him, but with the wind he couldn't hear her words, although he could see tears streaming down her face as he desperately tried to find a way to get to her. But the chasm was far too wide to jump and the vertical dropoff made climbing down and up impossible. He woke then to the caws of crows and other early birds, with a feeling of great love and profound loss.

He found he was so stiff he could hardly get up. Now he wished he had brought coffee and the implements for a fire, and more food. He still wasn't sure he could get down the mountain, and shuddered to think of Abigail having to organize a rescue team. That would surely be an ultimate humiliation. Maybe sliding on his butt over the steeper terrain would make it possible to get down unaided.

He realized suddenly that he had come to resolution.

He was not going to let Kate buy him the artificial leg. He would get by as is until he could afford to buy one himself, however long this might take. Furthermore, he was not going to jump into Kate's bed again. Not unless they were married, and he doubted that would happen. She was not the woman for him, and he was sure she was finding out he was not the man for her.

His life needed a new direction. He would try to find Sarah, if such was possible, and hope she had not gotten married. And the book he wanted to write, he had decided on the topic. He would write about Civil War medicine, and the doctors and nurses, both Union and Confederate. If nothing else, researching this book might help him cross her trail.

Ah, but what about money? Money for travel and research? Furthermore, he still needed the mobility that an artificial leg would provide. He realized that his goals would have to be suspended until he could save sufficient funds. In this time of economic shambles for the South, the likelihood of his amassing such money seemed impossibly distant.

The next morning, he tried sliding down the steeper terrain. The rocky trail was terribly hard on his butt, and on his trousers, but it could be done. About thirty feet down, the path leveled for a few feet before it plunged again. He stopped there and wrapped the blanket around his lower body, so that it could both cushion the descent and save his trousers. Thus he made it down the mountain, mostly sliding until the terrain leveled. By now his butt was as sore as his stump and his hands and shoulders, and the blanket was so shredded he abandoned it. But his trousers were still wearable.

Now he wasn't sure he'd be able to navigate the three miles to town. He was a wreck of a man, but he had to do it! Maybe he could if he both walked and crawled. He hoisted himself up using his already savaged hands and knee, and managed to cover a few hundred feet with his crutches before his stump was so raw he had to stop. He tried crawling until he collapsed face down in the dust. He wasn't sure which was worse, trying to walk, or crawling. He lay there awhile, covered in sweat, trying to gather enough strength to go on. He was trying to get himself upright using a tree for support, when a wagonload of Negroes came down the road. As the wagon came abreast him, it stopped and several men got off and approached him.

"Massa, can we help ya? Can we give ya a lift?"

He knew he couldn't make it all the way to town, and he gratefully accepted. They helped him to the wagon and made room for him on the seat. They even found a blanket he could sit on, to ease his sore butt. Aware of their curiousity of what he was doing out here, he told them about climbing Steven's Knob.

"Massa, Massa, why you do that?" they asked, really impressed.

"I used to climb that when I was a boy, with two good legs. To think, and to dream." He gave a short laugh. "I really needed to think and dream now. And see if I could do it with one leg. Well, I got up and got down, but I'm not sure I could have made it back to town. Without you coming along to save me."

They went out of their way to take him to Abigail's. He clasped each of their hands to express his thanks, and they touched their hands to their foreheads in a kind of admiring salute. Abigail observed all this and came down the porch steps to help him, and waved to the wagon.

As she scrutinized him, his raw and scraped hands and knee, his torn clothes, and dirty face, she shook her head unbelievingly. He expected her to comment on his foolishness. Instead, she asked, "Did you make it to the top?"

"I did."

"And down, by yurself?"

"Yes. I was on the way to town when the Negroes came along." He smiled wryly. "But I don't think I could have dragged myself all the way back to town today."

"I was wonderin' when we should come 'n get you." She helped him up the porch steps and into the house. "I jus' hope we can get you fixed up so's you can be ready for school in a few days." She snorted. "Still, if you can climb a mountain, a little classroom shouldn't cause you much trouble, should it?"

"No, Aunt Abigail."

That night over supper, she brought up something else.

"Did you do some good thinkin' on that mountain top?"

"I think I did. Maybe I needed to drive myself to exhaustion to do so."

"To do the good thinkin'?"

"Yes."

"Does some of it concern the Widow Buchanan?" She smiled mischievously. "I hear you two 'ave been doing some hanky panky."

"Hanky panky?"

"You know, rollin' in the hay."

"Aunt Abigail!"

She spat a blob of tobacco juice at a hapless beetle. "Thaddeus, your old aunt knows a thing or two about goings-on here in western Carolina, you know. Bet she wants you to run for public office."

He stared at her. "How did you know?"

"Wal, she's ambitious. I'll say that. She led her husband, dear Lord bless his ornery soul, into headin' for the state legislature. By whatever means possible, includin' buyin' votes." The old woman paused. "Would you like some more tea, dear nephew?"

"Yes, thanks."

"My advice to you is not to get into her inviting pants."

"They wanted me to run for mayor, but I've decided to turn them down."

"Good for you."

"Why, Abigail?"

She spat again, missing a bug this time. He thought her splats of tobacco were worse than any stray bugs. But who was he to criticize?

"I don' think you can git elected. Not if they give the Negroes the vote, for they'll vote against the South. An' there's a lot of Union sentiment in these western counties. Dear nephew, you know, there's people here who hate you."

He started. "What?"

"Yes. Both those pro and anti-Union have reasons to hate you. An' there's certainly a bushel of hate around. The pro-Unionists, of course, hate you for being a Confederate officer. But those against the Union hate you for being rescued by a Union nurse. The diehards think you should have refused her help."

"She saved my life. I was on the verge of death."

"I know. But the zealots think death would have been better than fraternizing with the enemy."

"My God." He pounded his fist on his peg.

She was silent, looking appraisingly at him. He nodded at her. "I'm going to tell Kate tomorrow of my decision not to run. I'm not sure how she's going to take it."

"Well, Thad, the worse she can do is ban you from her bed. An' she might not even do that. I suspect such would hurt her worse than you." She looked shrewdly at him. "Beware the overly ambitious woman. Or man either. That's my advice to you."

#

He sought out Sam Turner before he confronted Kate with his decision. "Sam, I've decided to turn down the invitation to run for mayor. I don't have any political ambitions. Not now at least." He looked concerned at his boss and friend. "My Aunt Abigail thinks there'd be no chance to win anyway. She thinks I'm the object of considerable hate."

"Ah yes, Abigail."

"What do you think about this hate thing? Could she be right?"

"She's a shrewd old lady." Sam paused. "Do you want my honest opinion?"

"Of course."

"I suspect she's read the situation right. I don't think you're a viable candidate for political office. I'm sorry to say this, Thad, but I agree with her that you're despised by the extremists of both sides, the pro-Unionists, and the secessionists."

Turner stroked his beard, and gazed out the window. "This is a time of much hate. And you're the most convenient object." He turned back to Thad. "I was an unwilling part of the group wanting you to run. While I've no doubt you would be not only capable but even an excellent mayor, and think you could be an attractive candidate sometime, I don't think this is the time. Perhaps in a few more years. When the hatreds have lessened. Furthermore, Washington is going to look with favor only on Union sympathizers, what they like to call the 'loyal southerners,' and on those denied the vote before the War. Not on Southern officers."

"But still, conditions will be better once there is a general amnesty. I hear that's likely to come in just a few years.

"Incidentally," he smiled, "I have some good news for you, too. I also hear the state legislature is on the verge of approving artificial limbs for our Confederate amputees."

Thad took a deep breath at this news. "God, how wonderful that would be . . . if it really happens. They cost so much, you know, more than I'm likely to afford for years." He had to be careful not to hope too much. "How soon do you think?" he asked.

"I'm told sometime next year, but knowing legislators and bureaucrats it may be a year later." Turner took off his glasses and absently tapped them on his chin. "Talking about hatreds, Thad, what the legislature is proposing . . . well, it's going to feed the hatreds."

"What do you mean?"

"They're only going to give the limbs to Confederate veterans. Not to those who joined the Union from North Carolina. Did you know that in these mountain counties enough men volunteered to fill more than four Federal regiments?"

"I knew some joined the Union. But I had no idea that many."

"Most of these veterans are isolated, uninformed, illiterate. They're incapable of applying for disability pensions from the federal government. Now their state refuses to give them equal treatment, still considers them traitors to the cause."

"I didn't know," Thad said.

"Well, things like this certainly don't promote reconciliation. Further, I hear that a secret organization is out to terrorize the Negroes, keep them from voting and from moving ahead."

"I can't think these hatreds will be lasting. There was no hatred in the hospitals among the wounded of both sides. Also, I hear at Appomattox there was no hatred."

"Yes, but there are always extremists, on both sides, whose great goal is to fan the hatreds." He paused. "Shall we change the subject, Thad?"

"Sure."

"May I ask what your long-term goals are, if not in politics?"

"Probably in academia, as a professor, or maybe an administrator. I do hanker to do some writing."

"Academic?"

"Probably some nonacademic as well, nonfiction and fiction."

"About the War?"

"Nothing will ever be as traumatic in our lives."

Turner steepled his fingers, thinking about this. "There'll be a lot of competition. So many people will want to write about it."

"I know. I must somehow write better. Or find a somewhat different slant." Thad paused, then asked the question that was uppermost in his mind. "Do I still have a job here for next year?"

"As long as you want, Thad. With the conflict over, we're getting more applications. I think we can even begin paying you more money this fall."

Thad nodded, though he was sure the amount would still be little more than subsistence.

#

"I've decided not to run for mayor or any other public office," he told Kate later.

She was shocked. "I hope you don't mean that."

"I've thought it over, Kate."

"You're repudiating this opportunity? Your rightful role and responsibility? I can't believe it!" Her voice was rising.

"I've been talking with some people about this. They think there'd be too much hatred against me to get elected at this time."

"Chrissake, who would tell you such a thing?"

"Sam Turner, for one."

She stared at him. "I bet."

"And my Aunt Abigail."

"What does that old woman know?"

"She has a good nose for public sentiments."

"Major Barrett, isn't the real reason for your despicable decision the fact that you're just a coward? Afraid to face up to criticism and public attacks?"

"I was not a coward on the battlefield."

"Then losing a leg must have removed your manhood, too," she spat at him.

"You don't really think that?" He was getting angry, too. "I don't have to put up with such insults."

"No, Major, you don't. I'd like you to go now."

"Surely our friendship means more than my lack of political ambition."

She laughed scornfully. "You're simply a weakling. When I thought you were a heavyweight. Well, Major Barrett, we know now."

"Kate . . ."

Her face was flushed in her anger. "And furthermore, Major Barrett, we both know that you're not even an acceptable lover. An utter disappointment you are!"

CHAPTER 10

A few weeks later, a man waited for Thad as he left his office at the college. "Do ya remember me, Major?"

Thad studied the man. He was short and wiry, with an unkempt beard and buck teeth. Of course. "Corporal Haskins, I'm glad you made it. And without injury?"

"A little flesh wound in the arm, Major, that's all." He gave a toothy smile.

"How many others made it, Isaac?"

"Not many, Major. Antietam took care of most of us. An' Gettysburg most a' the rest." He paused. "Those of us who made it through Antietam, we wondered 'bout you. Word was, you was almost dead." He nodded knowingly, "I see they got your leg."

"They got almost all of me."

"Major, the few of us left, we wondered, if ya might like t' lead us agin."

"What are you saying, Isaac? Lead you where?"

"There's a meetin' scheduled for t'morrow night. At Schindley's barn. We'll tell ya all about it there. We'd all like ya to come."

"What's this meeting about, Isaac?"

"Cain't tell ya now, Major. But, it's for our common interests."

Afterwards, Thad reflected on this strange invitation. He had never thought much of Isaac Haskins. While the man had performed his duties reasonably well, somehow he didn't trust him. He was the sort who would cut off fingers of the dead for their rings. Wartime often presented unusual opportunities for those out for personal gain who had no conscience. He wondered what Isaac was involved with now, but suspected nothing good. He decided to go to the meeting and find out.

Find out he did, the next night. The meeting was that of a secret society. At the door, Thad had to mention Haskin's invitation before he was admitted. About twenty men were milling around, talking and cursing. He looked around but the only person he recognized was Isaac, who waved and made his way to him.

Isaac shouted, "Boys, this is my major, who was almost killed at Antietam fighting the bluebellies."

They crowded around to shake his hand. The thought jarred his mind that most of these looked like the jetsam of society, men who would blame their own poor straits and prospects on others.

Now a burly man shouted for quiet. He stood on a box and began damning the Negroes and the pro-Union whites. "Fellow knights, we have to protect ourselves and our loved ones. Who else is goin' to, if we don't? The government? We know better. It only wants to protect the niggers. An' give 'em the vote. We know, if they all vote, whites don' have a chance." Now he shouted even louder, "It's up to us, knights! Up to us to defend our society. And our womenfolk. We 'ave to make 'em afraid to vote! Right?"

Loud cries of assent answered him. Now the group poured out of the barn and into the field where a wooden cross had been erected. Someone torched it, and the dry wood flamed in a demoniac symbol of hate under the guise of Christianity. Bottles of whiskey were freely passed around, and the men became ever more frenzied.

Now another voice asserted its demand for attention. Thad recognized Isaac. "We 'ave to put the fear of God in these niggers. We 'ave to remind them of their place. Let's torch Tooner's hamlet tonight." With a strident yell, he cried, "Are you with me, men?"

A chorus of cheers answered him. Now white hoods and robes were being donned. This was the Ku Klux Klan that Sam Turner had warned against. Thad was certain of this now, just as he knew he wanted no part of it. Of a sudden he sensed physical jeopardy: the beast of violence had been unleashed and no rational arguments would cage it.

He tried to make his way beyond the flickering light of the still-burning cross to the woods beyond. He would come back later for his horse.

But he did not make the woods.

"Major, aren't you with us?" Isaac shouted as the man ran up with several hooded figures at his side.

He thrust another robe and hood at Thad. As Thad backed away, Isaac snarled, "You wouldn't be a coward an' trying to run away now, Suh?"

"Isaac, I can't condone violence, for whatever cause."

"Dammit, Major, this is what we fought for, at Antietam n' elsewhere. To save our homes from the niggers and the traitorous whites. You, Suh, 'ave to be with us, else you're agin us. Now which is it?" he demanded, his face close to Thad's, showering him with spittle.

"I'm not with what you're proposing to do."

"Damn ya, Major." Isaac grabbed and shook him violently, while Thad tried to extricate himself.

Someone kicked his wooden leg and he fell heavily to the ground. Several more men in their white garments joined the fray.

Isaac shouted, "See men, them rumors was right! He's a turncoat. He's joined the nigger lovers. Saved by a Union nurse. I should've known!"

Thad tried to defend himself against a flurry of blows and kicks, but it was no use.

He sensed ribs breaking as he desperately tried to protect his face and head. His hands were being savaged in his futile efforts.

The animal cries of the men drowned out his feeble pleas. One particularly violent kick at his head smashed through his protecting hands and blackness rolled over him.

He briefly came to as he was being dragged along the stony ground, slipping in and out of consciousness, aware of pain and prepared to die. Was he to be killed by the very men he had been fighting with in the great struggle?

He felt himself being pushed into a ditch, the mud at first a welcoming cushion. Faintly, Isaac's curses filtered down: "Be damned, Major! Nigger lover! Traitor!" Now the men were laughing.

Isaac again shouted down, "We oughta git some nigger bodies to pile on top of ya 'n see if that Union nurse can save ya agin."

With that, he heard horses galloping away.

Now blackness threatened again as he vaguely realized that his life depended on getting face and head out of the mud before unconsciousness took over again. Otherwise he would choke to death in this ditch.

Summoning what little strength remained, he tried to push to the drier edge. The broken hands were numb now and his whole body was unresponsive, like a sack of potatoes.

Later, somehow his head was beyond the mud and he wearily let it rest on the drier edge. In the last moments of consciousness he knew the impossibility of escaping the ditch. The first rain would drown him. From somewhere came the memory of that night at Antietam and he suddenly felt a sense of peace and hope.

The next day Negroes found him unconscious and carried him to their quarters. He became aware of a soothing cloth wiping his face and gentle hands bandaging his wounds. His eyes opened to see a concerned black face trying to give him a drink of water. He struggled to get up, but the pain of the ribs almost brought darkness again.

"Jus' rest quietly," a soft voice said.

"How bad?" he managed.

"Ya're hurt, but it'll be all right."

Through cracked lips he whispered, "Abigail Simpson . . . Dr. Sam Turner . . . tell them . . . I'm here."

Abigail and Sam Turner arrived together later that day. "We was so worried about you, Thad," Abigail said. "Thought you mighta been killed. The Klan was active the night you disappeared."

"How long have I been here?"

"They said you was unconscious for 'bout 24 hours. I told you there was hatred around," she said.

"It was one of my own men," he murmured.

"He told me they wished they had . . . some dead niggers to pile on top of me. So the Union nurse could try to rescue me." He thrashed in his agitation.

"Easy, Thad," Sam Turner urged. "Was it the Klan?"

"Yes. They wore white garments, and burned a cross."

"They killed a Negro, that night. Whipped him till he was dead. And burned several buildings. Now many Negroes are afraid to exercise their right to vote."

"That was the intent . . . to take away their right by fear." Thad tried a deep breath, a mistake as the pain sent a veil of blackness. After a few moments he was able to continue. "Can I, can we, do anything? I'd be willing to testify . . . what I saw and heard."

Turner shook his head. "It would do no good. There's no proof since you didn't see them do anything. Even if you had, it would be their word against yours. And the courts would not likely favor the Negroes given unproven charges."

"God help us. Is there no stopping the hatred?"

As Abigail and Sam prepared to take him home, Thad reached out with his broken hands to express his gratitude to those who had saved him and nursed him. "You saved my life . . . How can I thank you?"

"Thank ya, Massa, for bein' on our side," they told him, as they gently touched his hands. They carried him to the carriage, and the neighborhood watched solemnly as he left.

Fortunately, Thad's injuries were not as serious as first thought, although it took him several months to fully mend. He wanted Abigail to keep the Negro community informed of his recovery, and she was glad to do it. This situation would have been far different if passing Negroes had not found him and rescued him from the ditch. At first it was thought his skull was fractured, but it turned out to be a concussion. The broken ribs healed fairly quickly. The broken bones in his hands took longer, and his hands were still in splints when he started classes for the fall semester.

#

The tactics of the Ku Klux Klan apparently worked that fall of 1865. In the state's first postwar general election, the old Confederates decisively triumphed over the Unionists. The provisional governor, appointed by President Johnson, went down in defeat to a bitterly anti-Northern opponent. The plight of the Negroes, newly freed under both the North Carolina constitution and the U. S. Constitution, was hardly improved either economically or in safety. The hatreds remained strong.

#

The year 1865 was finally over, and spring cloaked the land in 1866. The economy and the infrastructure were slowly improving. The railroads, so wrecked in the last days of the War, had been mostly repaired. Now opportunists from the North, carpetbaggers, were bringing themselves and needed money into western North Carolina. The aggressive actions of many of these, and their political aspirations, were exacerbating hatreds and jealousies.

After the acrimonious exchange with Kate Burnham, Thad had not seen her. "She's having an affair with a carpetbagger," Aunt Abigail was pleased to report. "The word is he's leased some land from the Quaker, Josiah Vanderhall. An' he's interested in politics. So, he's a natural for the Widow Burnham."

"Has he two legs?" Thad couldn't resist asking.

Abigail grimaced. "That he does, dear nephew. But don't let that bother you. The Widow is not your type, I know."

"What kind of girl is my type, Abigail?"

"Wal, maybe that Union nurse." She cackled.

"How can you say that? You know nothing about that woman."

"Don' need to know, nephew, don' need to know." She spit tobacco at some insect, real or imagined, but missed. "Dammit."

"Abigail . . ." was all he could say.

#

Things at the college were going better. With the end of the War, applications were rising. "It looks like we're going to make it," Sam Turner told him one day early in 1966. "Your loyalty helped us over these difficult times, and the students speak so highly of you. I think this is where you belong."

Turner looked out his window and mused, "I'm glad you decided not to go into politics. That episode with the Klan, perhaps it was a learning experience, for all of us, of the hatreds still around. I fear the South has not heard the last of this Ku Klux Klan."

"I've sent a manuscript to several publishers up in New York about this state of mind," Thad said.

Turner turned around. "Such may fan the flames of our divisiveness. But I fully approve. The extremists must be shown for what they are." The older man paused. "Thad, there's something I'd like you to consider." Now he frowned slightly. "I'll be retiring in a few years. And I want you to be my successor." As Thad was silent, contemplating this surprising development, the older man seemed compelled to give more encouragement. "We know this little college is nothing outstanding. But I hope it serves a useful service for these people. And I think you can make it better. Please, will you consider this?"

"I'm honored, Sam," Thad said solemnly. "Your support has always meant so much to me. It brought me hope, during difficult days. Yes, I think I'd like to be your successor, very much."

#

In early January the next year, 1867, Thad received word from the state capitol that he was eligible for a new leg. Now Rafe Kessler greeted him warmly.

"Major, I'm told to give priority for these limbs to former Confed officers, in the order of their rank. You're the top one in these parts. Shall we measure you up today?"

"The sooner the better." He looked around. The facilities had been greatly expanded since he and Abigail had come seeking help from Kessler several years before, only to find a new leg denied because of his lack of funds. Now more than a dozen people seemed to be engaged in production.

"It looks like your business is booming," he told Kessler.

"Yes suh, Major. I had thought of retiring. But . . . we've got to help our poor boys. Don't we now."

"And make a healthy profit, I wager," Thad said coldly.

"We all have to make do, best we can."

By the next month, Thad had his new leg. He had to admit it was a considerable improvement over the old peg, both in looks and operation. In particular, the knee joint was great. Still, the leg took some getting used to, and he needed a cane to balance himself. Occasionally he fell.

He had one extremely embarrassing such episode. Toward the end of the spring semester, he was lecturing in front of about twenty students. Intent on his subject matter he had not noticed that his artificial leg was slightly wedged against the desk leg. As he started to move to the blackboard he tripped and fell heavily to the floor. He was slightly stunned and had trouble getting up. Lucy Vanderhall and several other students rushed to help him.

"Dr. Barrett, are you hurt?" Lucy's face was contorted with anxiety, he realized as his mind cleared and he looked at her close up.

"I'm not hurt. Only my pride," he muttered. He wanted to laugh this off, but in truth he needed their help in standing up and moving to a chair. He finally joked, "These drat things have minds of their own." Lucy did not join in the forced laughter of the students. She simply looked at him unsmilingly. He wondered what she was thinking: pity, maybe? Now he noticed that she was uncommonly attractive. In the several years since he'd first met her, she had matured and was no longer a frivolous schoolgirl.

The class finally ended, and the students filed out, some of them inquiring if he was all right from his fall. Lucy was the last to leave.

"Professor Barrett, you hurt your hand, didn't you."

He looked down. His hand and wrist were swelling. "I guess I sprained it a bit." He looked at her. "Lucy, you're very observant. I wasn't even aware of this until now."

She blushed faintly. "Can I help you back to your office, carry your briefcase, maybe?" she asked softly.

He started to say no, that he didn't need any help. But then somehow he didn't. He let her carry his briefcase and books.

"Thank you, Lucy, that was kind of you," he told her at the door. She stood there a moment watching him seat himself. On an impulse, he asked, "Would you like to come in and visit a little while?"

She nodded and sat down across from his desk, not saying anything. "You must be close to graduating, Lucy," he ventured.

"In June." Now she smiled mischievously, "That is, if you don't flunk me."

"My 'A' student?" He smiled, too. "I couldn't do that." He leaned forward, "Tell me, what are you going to do when you finish here? Is there someone waiting to marry you?"

"No, no one's waitin' to marry me."

He was surprised. "An attractive . . ."

She interrupted him with a brief chuckle, ". . . girl like me. I know. I've heard it before. Well, I just don't think I'm eager to settle down, have kids, and take up running a house. Of course, with the right man . . . well. I may look into teaching, or the ministry. We're Quakers, you know."

"I guess I knew that." He looked at her, speculatively now. "Your family must have been against slavery, and secession."

"Yes, we were pro-Union. Actually, there are a fair number of Quakers in this part of the state. Pa has done quite well, owns a 750-acre tract west of here, as well as some other real estate. I suppose, indicative of our sentiments, Pa just leased some of his land to a man from the North, Harlan Pettengill. He wants to start a nursery, and also raise some cattle. I guess you'd call him one of those carpetbaggers."

"Ah," Thad teased her, "Maybe your father has a prospective beau in mind for you."

"Shame on you, Professor Barrett." She gave a quiet smile, almost a sad smile, he thought. "You know . . . no, you don't know . . . I've really found the man I want. Though he doesn't know it. And would be shocked if he knew it."

"Some lucky fella . . ."

She looked steadily at him, her lips slightly parted.

"Holy Lord, you don't mean me?"

She didn't say anything. No protest, no denial.

"I'm old enough . . ."

"To be my father?"

"I guess I'm not that old," he sheepishly admitted. "But I must be more than ten years older than you."

"Is that so bad?"

"Maybe not. But a man with one leg. With a terrible scar on his chest. A weakened arm. A cripple."

"But such a magnificent cripple," she whispered, her eyes suddenly tearing.

Suddenly he couldn't look at her. Seeing the emotion in her face. Wondering about the incredulity in his own face. He swiveled his chair toward the window. The blossoms of spring were near their peak. He could feel the pulse pounding at his throat. This lovely creature. "Have you told anyone about this?" he asked.

"No one, Dr. Barrett. And I didn't tell you. You just guessed."

He turned back to her, moving his face to a half smile. "It seems, after this revelation, that you ought to call me Thad, don't you think?"

"I'd like that . . . Thad," she whispered.

"And we probably should get better acquainted. After all, you only know me from the classroom. Maybe that's not the real me, Lucy."

#

A few weeks later, Lucy took him home to meet her father, Josiah. Her mother had died in childbirth some years earlier. The house was large and well furnished, reflecting the wealth of a prominent landowner. A long curving driveway wound up to the portico. As with all the houses in this rather isolated part of the South, it had escaped destruction by the Union forces.

Thad feared his involvement in the Southern cause would result in strong animosity. He had said as much to Lucy a few days earlier when she brought the invitation. But she pooh poohed such concern. "We're Quakers, Thad. Our religion teaches tolerance for all sincere views."

Josiah Vanderhall indeed showed no animosity whatever. "Pa, this is Thaddeus," Lucy introduced him.

Her father smiled as they shook hands firmly. "I've heard a lot about thee, Major Thaddeus. Many good things. It's high time Lucy brought thee around," he said in a soft voice that belied his girth. His face seemed to Thad that of a benevolent man, with smile lines around his eyes and white teeth that showed often. He suspected that Josiah doted upon his daughter.

He had been invited to dinner. It was a sumptuous affair, with Negroes in attentive service. There were a few other guests, most notably the carpetbagger, Harlan Pettengill.

Josiah introduced them. "Thaddeus, this is Harlan Pettengill, formerly a captain in the Ohio militia. He is down here to invest in our Carolina economy. Harlan, this is Major Thaddeus Barrett, lately of the 20th North Carolina volunteers."

They shook hands. The man was handsome, if turning to fat. He had a smooth polished way that bordered on the unctuous, or so Thad sensed. Harlan was quick to note Thad's war injury. "I can't compare myself to you, sir. I have not lost a leg or an arm for my country. I admire those who have."

"I'm not sure how much honor, and glory, there is in losing a leg or an arm."

"That makes you a hero, sir."

Thad frowned. He'd been prepared to make friends with this man. But this was politician's slavering. The words came too easily.

He was disappointed at the eager acceptance by Lucy's father of this smooth stranger bearing gifts. Now he remembered. This was the man Abigail had said was bedding Kate Burnham. Well, he was not surprised. This was her type.

Lucy sat near her father, observing the exchange. Thad wondered whether she was perceptive enough to have caught the essence of it. Her father obviously had not.

At the table they talked of the pressing political issues of the day. It was obvious this was a center of pro-Union sentiments. Thad knew that his own sentiments were moving that way. Still, he didn't like the selfishness that seemed to effuse these sentiments. It was not the blacks nor the neglected soldiers who were the prime considerations for aid, but rather political gain and ascendancy. This was why he had shunned the political career. It was too damned self-seeking.

Afterwards, he and Lucy sat on the porch, overlooking the hazy ridges behind which the sun was setting. "I'm not sure I impressed your father favorably. He probably thinks I'm an unrepentent rebel."

"Unrepentent? Did you do some fiendish misdeeds, my dear major?"

He tried to stifle a groan. "Not misdeeds, Lucy. But a mistaken cause. That is what so many of us fought and died for. A mistaken cause. I know it now."

"Did you like Pettengill?" she quietly asked.

He didn't answer right away. "Not particularly," he finally admitted. "You?"

"Dad's taken with him. But I don't trust him. He's too quick to praise, it seems to me. I don't think he's sincere."

"My thoughts exactly." Thad looked at her speculatively. Lucy was turning out to be a perceptive and mature young woman.

"Shall we take a walk?" she asked.

They strolled the spacious grounds hand in hand. The moonlight and the gentle breezes touched them. They stopped and she moved closer to him. Her soft body and perfume powerfully aroused him. He had to resist the urge to crush her to him. Instead, they gently embraced. They had not attempted sex, and Thad vowed not to now. But it tantalized.

"Oh, Major Thad, I love thee. Truly I do. Please take me in the bushes."

"Shush, Lucy, You know I will not defile your father's hospitality."

She was angry now, and she beat him on the arms and shoulders with tiny fists. "Why do you insist on treating me as a juvenile? Can't you think of me as a woman?"

"Oh. God, yes," he admitted.

"i think we should get married. Why don't you propose to me?"

"I think you're too young, that's why."

"I'm almost twenty, Thad. My mother was married at sixteen. I bet your mother was married by then. Many pioneer women were married by fourteen."

He took a deep breath. It was all he could do to restrain himself. But he knew it would not be right. Not at this stage of their lives. "I have something I have to do first, before I consider marriage."

"Will you tell me what?" she demanded.

He touched her cheek tenderly, trying to think how to explain without destroying their relationship.

"It's that Union nurse, isn't it," she said bitterly, before he could answer. "The one everybody says saved your life. You're in love with her, aren't you? Damn you, you're in love with a dream."

He tried to quiet her, to sooth her agitation. Finally he told her, "I want to research and write a book about certain aspects of the War. I'll need to do a lot of traveling. So I've taken a leave of absence from the college for next academic year. I can't consider marriage until I finish this project."

She was quiet now, trembling. He wrapped his coat around her in the chill of the late spring evening, and held her, trying to comfort her. She pulled away. "What are you writing about?"

"Civil War medicine. After all, who should know the deficiencies of this better than I. And what needs to be done to improve wartime medicine."

"You're going to research and write about the nurses?"

"Nurses, doctors, sanitation, medicines, operating procedures, the whole panoply of battlefield medicine."

"And one particular Union nurse?" The moonlight was backlighting her hair. He thought she had never looked more beautiful. Did he really want to put this relationship at risk, maybe sacrifice it? Yet, deep in his gut he knew he had to.

"I need to find her, if I can. To satisfy myself. Otherwise, a cloud would hang over our relationship, you and me. I need to resolve this, one way or the other." There he'd said it. He paused, and pulled her close to him. He could feel her heart beating, like a wounded bird. She tried weakly to push him away, but then surrendered. "I know this is asking so much of you, to wait, to give me a year," he said huskily. "It's terribly unfair of me." He paused and kissed her. "I'll just hope that you'll still feel the same way about me when I get back. If not, then the loss is mine, and I'll deserve all the disappointment."

"What are you going to do for money, for all your travels?" she asked.

"I just had two articles published by major magazines," he said. "Both of these are about the Ku Klux Klan. Seems that northern journals have great interest in this cancer in our society. And a publisher has given me an advance on the book."

"You're determined then?"

"Yes. But if you find someone else, I'll understand."

In the moonlight, he held her beautiful face, wiped the tears, kissed her softly. And berated himself for being a fool.

"You may find some nice young Quaker boy."

"No," she breathed.

"I have to do this . . . odyssey. Don't you see?"

"The pursuit of a dream," she said bitterly.

"Probably an impossible one," he admitted.

Then he heard her say, "But I guess I'll have to wait, Thaddeus. And hope your dream does not become reality."

"Thank you," he said softly. He tossled her hair and touched her nose, and they embraced urgently. He could feel her tears dampening his shirt. He had to restrain himself from not leading her to a roll in the grass.

Afterwards he reflected that such would have solved everything, taken the decision from his hands. For it would have meant marriage, and no more thoughts of a useless search for this wild odyssey.

CHAPTER 11

The Civil War had ended, the devastation and bloodletting finished. Why wasn't she feeling more exhilarated? Good God, did she only thrive on blood and gore, as those vampires in the old books?

As Sarah analyzed her feelings she realized she feared the unknown, the major changes of life now facing her. She had mastered the wartime scenario. Could she master the peacetime?

Sarah and Mother Bickerdyke made their farewells in Washington City, shortly after the Grand Military Review. "Are you going to try medical school now?" Bickerdyke asked.

"I'm not real sure I'm up to it, Mary Ann. To try to fight the prejudice and the barriers, the manmade obstacles. I feel so tired and weary."

The older woman looked keenly at her. "It's just the letdown, dear child. You'll get over it in a few weeks. I know you're a fighter, and you won't let a little male prejudice make you give up, will you?"

"Only a little?"

"Well, then a lot. But you can do it. If you don' give up. Perseverance, that's what it takes. If we're to find our ultimate destiny."

"I'm not sure perseverance is enough. If the obstacles are insurmountable, isn't this akin to endlessly batting our heads against stone walls? Until they're hopelessly mangled? Our heads, that is."

Mary Ann touched her on the shoulder. "Dear Sarah, the greater danger for all of us is giving up too soon, to fleeing the field of battle when it's on the verge of being won." She paused, as Sarah looked searchingly at her. "My dear, pursue every avenue you can. But if all else fails, let me know. I'll even go to General Grant in your behalf."

"Thank you, Mary Ann," Sarah murmured. "I just might need your help."

"Course, on the other hand, you might prefer to marry some nice fella and raise kids," she said feigning seriousness.

Sarah shook her head. "I feel that I'd like to make a difference, somehow. Anyone can raise kids."

Mary Ann frowned. "Don't ever downgrade the contribution of women having babies. For most of us that's the greatest contribution we can ever make."

Sarah was embarrassed. "I didn't mean that wasn't important. Only that women shouldn't be limited to it, while men can have unlimited possibilities. It's not fair to us women."

"Shush, Sarah. I agree with you." She took her hand. "Be of stout heart. I'm sure things will work out. What you need now, most of all, seems to me, is to have a little vacation. Why don't you go home and visit your father? And rest for a few months before starting the struggle for medical school?"

"I'm not sure he has ever forgiven me for rescuing the Reb. And I'm sure the town hasn't."

"My dear, time does a lot of good things. It heals sorrow, and it heals hate. Go home, dear, see if the hate hasn't diminished now that the War's over."

#

So it came to pass that before looking up Dr. Rizzo and actively pursuing her career, Sarah decided to see Pa. She had written him a number of times over the last several years, but he never responded. He must still be holding that grudge. But he was her father, and she was homesick to see the old homestead in Pleasant Valley. Maybe there she could subdue her restless spirit and quiet the demons still assailing her from the horrors of war and the seeming futility of her ambition.

From Washington City she took the train to Hagerstown and thence the stage to Pikeston. It had been over two frightful years since she'd been home, not too many months after South Mountain and Antietam, the turning point of her life. And how she remembered the unbridled hostility and prejudice of most of the townspeople, and her confrontation in the church with Preacher Williams who so smugly professed to know God's judgment of what she had done on the battlefield.

Now in the full blooming of early summer, the beauty of this land touched her more than ever before, and her eyes feasted on it as the stage carried her closer to home. Now, her memories of Antietam battlefield, barely twenty miles away, both horrified and exaulted her. How could she, a simple small-town girl, have done what she did? Suddenly she felt ashamed that her memories of the time with Sol that spring of 1861 had faded almost as if they had never been. Yet, he had been the inspiration for her being at Antietam in the first place. Now she remembered Pa's hand gushing blood as he had crushed a glass in his anger at her thinking of going to the battlefield to try to help. Ah, such old memories of a lifetime ago. She was so far different from the naive young woman of those days.

The stage clattered to a stop at the town square. It was but a short walk home, if it could still be called home. Maybe Papa would bar the gates to her.

Charlotte opened the door at her knock. "You!" her sister exclaimed. They stared at each other, both surprised. Charlotte looked older than Sarah remembered, though they were only five years apart, but her face somehow had lost the marks of youth.

"What are you doing here? Is Pa all right?"

"Pa's dying. With cancer."

Sarah groaned. "Why wasn't I notified?"

Charlotte looked at her sternly. "How could we know you'd want to come? After all, this isn't a battlefield. And Pa wanted no part of his Rebel daughter. Then we didn't know where you were."

"The Army knew where, and any letters eventually would get to me. Can I come in?"

The sister stepped aside, with visible reluctance. "This is such a surprise," she said.

Sarah dropped her two bags by the door. "Where is the cancer, and how long do they give him?"

"It started in his lungs. Now it's spread. Doc Wooten gives him two months." She paused. "He's bedridden. Very weak. Emily and I have been working in shifts to take care of him, and give him comfort. But he's very depressed." She looked at Sarah. "Now, what are you doing here? This is hardly one of your glorious destinations."

"Glorious . . . ?" Sarah choked on the word.

"Isn't that what you've been up to, dear sister, a glory seeker?"

"Good God, No! Is that what you think of me?"

They stared at each other.

"So, the prodigal has returned." A harsh voice broke in.

"Hello, Emily," she said turning around. Sarah looked at her two sisters. "Could I see Pa?"

"He's sleeping now. I can't let you disturb him." Emily, her oldest sister, looked hard at her, no welcome in her face. Sarah suddenly realized she reminded her of a younger Dorothea Dix. Her dark hair was pulled tightly back in a bun, and her face maybe had not smiled in years. Twelve years older than Sarah, she had run the household autocratically after Mother died.

Now Emily brusquely commanded, "Well, what are you standing there for? Take your bags up to your room. You'll have to dust it. It hasn't been used since you left so abruptly."

Her room smelled stale and musty. She opened several windows, and tried to wipe away the worst of the dust with a damp cloth. She looked curiously around this refuge of her childhood and adolescence. There were the dolls and stuffed toys she had once been so fond of. On the wall was the head of the deer she had shot while hunting with Pa when she was fifteen.

She took off her shoes and stretched out on the bed. She was surprised how exhausted she felt. She needed to digest the news about Pa, and adjust to the presence of her sisters who had always resented the favoritism Pa had shown his youngest.

Her thoughts went back to her sisters. Charlotte and Emily were enough older and enough bigger that they bullied her as she was growing up. Neither sister was very attractive. They were large boned like Pa, while she took after Mama in being small boned with more fragile facial features and slender hands. Charlotte had married a store clerk and they lived in Waynesboro, just across the Pennsylvania line. Emily had stayed here until a few years before the War when she moved to Hagerstown as a bookkeeper in a tannery. At age 38 she was still a spinster.

Sarah wondered if she'd look like Emily in another dozen years if she remained a spinster, which most likely she would. She hadn't looked at herself in a mirror since Atlanta when she was getting ready for that dismal date with the young doctor. She had had no time to think about her looks, and wondered if she were already getting to look like an old maid. Perhaps her mirror was still in the room some place, and she got up to look for it. She found it in a drawer and with some apprehension gazed at herself.

She wasn't particularly pleased with what she saw. Her hair was long and unkempt, her skin was rather weathered and her face had frown lines it never had before; even her eyes seemed more deepset and the cheekbones more prominent. Yet, her face must have had enough promise that three men professed love for her, and one had married her. She briefly fooled with her hair, then gave it up. Being a beauty queen was hardly one of her ambitions.

She must have dozed off, for she awakened to knocking. Charlotte opened the door. "Pa's awake now. He wants to see you."

"I'll go right in." As she fumbled with her shoes, she asked, "Charlotte, how is your family? Was Dan able to stay out of the army?"

The woman seemed startled. Then she said more softly, "The children are fine. And yes, Dan's asthma kept him out of the War." She laughed without humor. "Now that it's over, Dan complains that everyone conspired to keep him out. Otherwise, he would have been a war hero, so he says." She looked at Sarah. "But you should know something about war heroes."

"I never saw any heroes. Only poor frightened and dying men. Wondering what they were giving up their limbs and their lives for." Charlotte was still staring at her. "I still wake up drenched in sweat with nightmares. It was horrible, Charlotte, really horrible." She would have liked to have embraced her sister, but Charlotte made no attempt to draw closer. For a moment she had thought . . .

#

She was shocked at her father. So pale and gaunt. He had always been a fairly large man, not fat, but well muscled. Now he seemed unable to even raise his head from the pillow. She couldn't help staring at him. His eyes were bitter as he stared back at her. "So you finally came back to see your old Pa," he whispered hoarsely.

"I didn't know you were sick. Nobody notified me."

"You were probably too busy with your Reb."

"Papa," she cried. "I haven't seen any Reb. I don't know where he lives, if he's even alive. I didn't cavort with the enemy, despite what you, and my sisters, and Preacher Williams are so quick to believe."

"That's not what I hear."

"What have you heard?"

"That my daughter was practically a Confed spy."

"Good God, who told you that?"

"The word's around."

"That's not true. Any of it. Don't you believe me? Is that why you never answered my letters?"

"I don't remember seeing any letters." He was getting tired now, she could see. She wasn't sure this conversation was even registering. But the terrible falsehoods certainly had. A chill went through her, even though the room was hot and stuffy.

"Well, it won't be my concern much longer," he said weakly, and closed his eyes.

"Pa!" With his eyes closed she studied him more closely, more professionally. He had undoubtedly lost a lot of weight, obvious despite the scraggly beard that badly needed trimming. But his breathing was labored as well. The room smelled of stale urine, vomit, sickness. She realized now that her sisters were not really doing a good job taking care of him. All thoughts of seeking out John Rizzo and enlisting his support in her quest for medical school would have to wait. She must pen a letter to him asking for his patience. But he had not answered her last letters, and she wondered about that. Now she rolled up her sleeves and prepared to take care of her father.

"Would you like a drink of water?"

His eyes opened, regarding her. "Yes."

The chipped pitcher on the bedstand was empty, and she went downstairs to fill it. Her sisters were sitting at the kitchen table in serious conversation. "You don't seem to be taking good care of Pa," she told them, more sharply than she intended.

"Sounds like you're hankering to take over," Emily said coldly. "What are you planning to do, amputate his arms and legs?"

"Course not. But Pa does need to be better cleaned. He'd feel better also if he had his hair cut and his beard either shaved or trimmed. And I bet what you're feeding him . . ."

Charlotte interrupted. "He has no appetite. Doesn't want to eat. We have to force him to."

"What are you trying to feed him, for God's sake, meat and potatoes?" They stared at her. "What he most needs is hot soup, something that doesn't require much effort to eat." Sarah paused and looked sternly at her sisters. "He may be dying, but we can certainly make his last days more comfortable. Have any of you tried reading to him? To make the time pass better, without his staring at the ceiling?"

They looked at each other. Emily gave a barely perceptible nod to Charlotte, before saying. "Sarah, don't overstep your position in this family. Gone all this time and now coming back for a few days and wanting to run things. We know what you have in mind. You just want to impress Pa. So he'll leave you most of the estate. Well, Sister, it won't work. We won't stand for such!"

"What . . . ?" The idea of Pa's inheritance had never crossed her mind. Now she realized why she was unwelcome here. Suddenly the explanation came for Pa's persistence in believing she was a turncoat: her sisters had been planting misinformation about her. Probably they had even told him she was living with the Confederate major. She suspected that Father had never received the letters she had written periodically, and to which he never responded.

"Now I get it," she said through tight lips. "The lies you've told him about me. And probably the town as well?" She pounded her fists on the kitchen table. "You lying hypocrites!"

Of course they denied all such charges. But Sarah knew otherwise. She didn't particularly care what the community thought about her. But she would like Papa to realize the truth before he died.

She was badly delayed in getting upstairs with a fresh pitcher of water. "I'm sorry, Pa, for taking so long. I had a conversation with my sisters." She raised his head and gently helped him with the water.

"Are you up to my giving you a bath? And maybe shaving your beard, and cutting your hair? I used to do this in the hospital, you know. When I was supposed to be cavorting with the Rebs." Her father weakly agreed to her ministrations.

As she finished, she asked, "Now doesn't that feel better?"

"It does, Sarah, thank you." He looked at her. "Do you mean it, that you were not associating with the Confeds, spying for them, living with the Major?"

"Those are all lies put out by some who want to hurt both of us."

"Lies? All lies?" He couldn't seem to comprehend this. He closed his eyes, and she thought he had dozed off. Then he roused briefly. "But I heard these stories from so many people, from the Preacher on down."

"It takes just one or two persons to spread lies so that soon everybody is repeating them. That's what happened here, Pa."

He changed the subject. She could tell he was tired, but he wanted to talk. "How long will you stay, Sarah? A few days? A few weeks? Until I pass along?"

"I don't know. Until I feel I'm no longer really needed, I guess." She paused. "Right now, I don't think you're getting very good care. Maybe from ignorance. Or carelessness. Or damned laziness." She gave a short, bitter laugh. "If nothing else, I am sort of an expert, I suppose, on making wounded and dying men's lives a little easier."

"Could it be . . . could I have misjudged you, daughter?"

"It's not your fault. We both tried to do the best we could, under these terrible circumstances." She put her hand on his forehead. "Don't tax yourself, Pa. There'll be plenty of time to talk later. For now, how about some warm soup. I'll cook up something like we used near the battlefield."

But he would not stop, despite near exhaustion. "What are your plans, Sarah? Now that the War is done?"

"I want to try to get in medical school, to become a doctor." She quietly suggested, "Hadn't I told you that, when I was home a couple years ago, not long after Antietam?"

"I dunno. Maybe so. All I could think of was your 'sociating with that Reb major. And how disappointed I was." He closed his eyes momentarily. Then opened them again. "Maybe I was wrong, Sarah. Bullheaded. An' we both suffered because of it. When I should, rather, have been proud of you." His eyes were tearing. She gently wiped them dry.

"Try to rest, Pa."

"No. There's something else I want to say." He coughed violently now, mucus dribbling out of his mouth.

"Hush, we can talk later."

"No, No." He struggled against her restraining hand.

"It may be some months . . . 'fore the grim reaper gets me, you know. I don't want you chained to this passing. It's not fair to you. I wouldn't want it on my conscience . . . when I meet the Creator." He looked at her. "Do you understand?"

"No, I don't."

"Spend a few days here . . . to get things organized. To see if you can get those damned sisters of yours to give me decent care . . . without complaining all the time." A paroxysm of coughing shook his body. "I would hope . . . you could come back . . . a few days before the Almighty gets me . . . to tell me how you're doing. And to hold my hand. But, if our timing . . . is not right, Sarah . . . I'd go easier if I knew you were accomplishing something . . . something good, and maybe great."

She bent down and kissed him. "Oh, Pa, how I'm going to miss you."

Sarah resolved that she would not leave until Pa's good care was more assured. Now she thought of Mother Bickerdyke, and how she had bulldozed 1,000-bed hospitals into new levels of health care and cleanliness. If Bickerdyke could demand and get such high performance from a lackadaisical staff, surely she could do so in her own home and for her own father. It would mean, of course, that her two sisters must be both instructed, and somehow compelled, to perform the necessary level of care. But she knew that a honey approach would not do it with her sisters. Maybe if she tried to approach them rationally. After all, even though she was the youngest sister, she was the expert in these matters.

A few days later, a partial solution to the problem occurred. She was reading Shakespeare to Pa when Doc Wooten knocked at the door. Doc Wooten. He had delivered her, and doctored her childhood illnesses and injuries. He had ministered to Mama in her final bad days. Now he was taking care of Pa in his final days. He must be in his seventies by now, and she wondered if his vigor still matched the youthful thickness of his white hair.

"Well, I see daughter Sarah is home."

She rose and offered him her hand. "Hello, Doctor Wooten. I'm just trying to give Pa a little culture."

"Well, he certainly needs it." He looked at her closely, appraisingly. "I've heard all kinds of things about you. It 'pears you're either a heroine, or some kind of she monster."

"She's a heroine, Doc," Pa weakly said.

"Well, I don't believe all I hear. Example, I don't think she rescued a whole battalion of Rebs. And I don't think she chopped off hundreds of arms and legs." He winked at her, mischievously. "Did you really do all that stuff?"

She laughed. "It made a great story for some reporter's wild imagination."

Now Doc Wooten sniffed the air. "What I'm sure is true, is that Sarah is a dedicated nurse, probably a very skilled one. The conditions in this room tell me that. Everything smells fresh and clean. Ol' man, you look the best you have in some months. And the only new factor here is Sarah." He turned to her, his eyes crinkling.

Later, he asked, "How long are you going to stay, Sarah?"

"Only a week or two," Pa answered for her. "She has important business elsewhere."

"I hope the quality of care won't deteriorate too much then."

Now Sarah spoke up. "Will you help us, Doctor, in keeping better conditions?"

"Better conditions? Child, what can I do?"

"A gentle word or two from you would make all the difference in the world. My sisters would surely listen to your advice and recommendations."

"Well, of course, I can do that. Trouble is, Sarah, I'm not able to come every day to monitor things. Maybe only once a week. For now."

"I understand, Doctor. Perhaps I can get Julia Bledsoe to stop in every day. She'll be able to reach me if things get bad. And, of course, I'll come back. May she talk with you about Pa's care, if necessary?"

"Of course. But it sounds to me like you don't trust your sisters, young lady."

Sarah took a deep breath. "It's not so much that. But I haven't been able to convince them of the need for cleanliness. Of course, many people, even in the medical profession, still are not convinced. So, they're not likely to listen to me. But they would to you, Doctor."

"All right," he nodded. "We'll convince them."

Later, as he was leaving, he asked, "Sarah, what is so urgent that you have to leave, at this time?"

Again, Pa answered for her. "She's trying to get into medical school. She wants to be a doctor like you."

"You don't say." He looked at her, his jovial expression fading. She could see disapproval taking over his face. She realized sadly that old Doc Wooten also was prejudiced against women as doctors. How pervasive such prejudice was. Even here in the hinterland. It's all right for us to be cleaning women and helpers at the beck and call of men physicians, but beyond that . . . no way. She tightened her lips. She could see Pa watching her, his eyes dark and unfathomable.

#

The next day Sarah talked to Julia about trying to see Pa every day or two. "Of course, Sarah, I'll be glad to do it. I've stopped in several times already. But what if I don't think things are very good?"

"I asked Doc Wooten if you could keep in touch with him on Pa's condition. He agreed. And you must notify me if things get worse."

"Suppose your sisters won't listen to Doc Wooten or to me? Or if they decide there's too much interference, and won't let me in the house?"

"As long as Pa is rational, that shouldn't happen. When he gets worse, you'd better let me know. From Baltimore or Philadelphia I should be able to get here in a day or so after hearing from you." Sarah paused reflecting. "I really think my sisters just needed some coaching of good nursing procedures. After all, they're not trying to shorten his life. Or to get revenge at me." She sighed. "But how difficult it is for them to take any advice from me. It seems . . . I'm still a kid sister to be bullied."

#

Her final confrontation with her sisters occurred a week later. She and Pa had agreed that she shouldn't stay any longer at this time, but that she would keep in close touch through her friend, Julia. Sarah still didn't trust her sisters with handling communications. Rightly or wrongly, she was sure they had kept her letters from him.

"I'll be leaving for Baltimore tomorrow," she told them at the dinner table. "I'll keep in close touch through Julia. She'll know where to reach me if Pa should suddenly get worse, or need me." She looked at them steadily. Over the past ten days, the leadership position in the household had shifted to Sarah. She had the nursing expertise and now had Pa's support. She had warned her sisters in no uncertain terms about what she expected for his care. Old Doc Wooten and Julia would be checking on them and would notify her if there were lapses. Already Charlotte was talking about going back to her family, since "she was no longer appreciated 'round here."

"Well, little sister, you've finally done it, haven't you," Emily spat out the words.

"What do you mean?"

"You've wormed your way into Pa's good graces. Telling all kinds of lies about us. Trying to show us up that you know more than Doc Wooten does. Now I suppose you've got Pa to change his will in your favor. So now you can leave."

"You're still harping on your inheritance? Shame on you! I don't know anything about a will, or who gets what. And I don't care. I only care that Pa's final days are as good as we can make them. If you can't accept that, that Pa gets the best care, then leave. We can always hire somebody to take care of him."

"You'd like that, wouldn't you. For us to abandon him, and with it all hopes of being well remembered in his will."

"For God's sake, is that all you two think about? You make me ashamed to have you as sisters."

They looked sullenly at her. Now a persuasive argument occurred to her. "You'll have a chance, with me gone, to get yourself in Pa's good graces. Over the next several months you can make him think you really care. About him. Not yourselves." She smiled mirthlessly. "You can even sell yourselves as worthy of the lion's share of his estate. But please, dear sisters, don't lie about me again."

She realized now that this schism would probably never be healed. Siblings divided, not this time by the War, but by the jealousies of inheritance. But she swore to herself that she would not let Pa's care suffer, if she had to come back every week or so.

#

"I wondered when, and if, you'd come," John Rizzo said.

"Whether I'd see you before I left for a new life, if not a better life."

Sarah had stayed with her father for two weeks. When she took the train to Baltimore, she knew not what to expect. She had posted a letter to John early the second week at home, but probably could not expect a reply before she left. She didn't know if he were still at this huge hospital or not. But he was.

"John, I feared you'd already left. You never answered my last letters. I thought you might have left months ago." Somehow, she sensed that their relationship had distanced, that it was no longer the same.

"Things have been in turmoil here. The country needed many new medical facilities, and now suddenly the need is gone. For months we've been expecting this place to close, and it will, within a few weeks." He paced around his modest office, and looked out the window at the slums surrounding the building. "With the War over, the country doesn't need so many doctors and nurses. Now there're too many of us."

"John, are you about to tell me to forget about medical school?"

"Not forget it, Sarah. But recognize that it may be more difficult to get in with the War over."

"Will you still help me, John?"

"Of course I will. I said I would."

"But you don't have much confidence in my success?"

"Not now. Maybe in another five or ten years."

"Will you still give me a strong letter of recommendation? Your letter was so wonderful with Mary Ann Bickerdyke."

He sighed, rather relieved, she sensed. "Of course I'll do that. I'm your supporter, you know."

They were both silent then. She tried to lessen the gulf between them. "Do you still blame me for leaving you for the Western Campaign?"

"Sarah, certainly not. We each have to do what we must do. I'm sure you did far more good out there with Bickerdyke than you possibly could have here." He took a deep breath, and the silence lengthened. Finally he said, "I guess you need to know. Rachel has gotten better. She's no longer institutionalized. We're living together, again."

"How wonderful, John," Sarah breathed.

"But no one can take your place in my heart," he hastened to add. Now he rested his hand on her knee. She wanted to push it off, but refrained. This scenario was not quite played out, she suspected. "I still remember our time together, before you left for the West," he murmured. "That was special."

She bowed her head, saying nothing. "Sarah, could we get together again, tonight, for the old times? Have dinner with me. Please."

She could feel the old passion rising. Half of her wanted to refuse. But the other half was drawn to having a man catering to her, being nice to her, helping her forget the strains and disappointments of the past. And the possibility that it might result in a better chance at medical school. It would not pay to antagonize this man. Maybe he held the key to her future.

"All right, John, if you want."

That evening, if it had not been for the revelation about his wife, she could have imagined a repeat of their nights together some two years before. The good dinner in a fine restaurant, a pleasant and romantic evening, the just stopping short of going too far. It had been so long.

She noticed that he was drinking more heavily than he used to. He wanted to dance, and they swayed to soft music, but he seemed more forceful and less tentative than in the past.

"You're more beautiful than I remembered," he whispered.

She murmured a thank you and suggested that maybe his memory had faded a bit. "After all, it's been a long time."

As soon as she could without offending, she said, "It's late, and I need to go back to my hotel."

As he reluctantly escorted her back, she asked, "What about Rachel tonight? Isn't she expecting you home?"

"I sometimes have to work late at night," he explained. "On those nights, rather than taking the long ride home, I sleep on a cot in my office. Rachel understands."

"How nice."

At the door to her room, she gave him a quick kiss on the cheek. "Goodnight, John. Thank you for another nice evening." She turned to go in.

She was surprised when he pushed into the room with her, and shut the door.

"Please don't leave it like this. Our love is stronger than a peck on the cheek. Won't you let me spend the night with you, my dear Sarah?" He put his hands around her waist, and bent his head to her breasts. She pushed him away.

"John, you're married. And I haven't been with a man since my poor husband. Don't destroy our long and wonderful friendship."

He stepped back. "You're still faithful to the memories of your husband?" he asked incredulously. "After all that you've seen and done?"

"Yes. We mustn't do this. Please go, John."

"All right," he muttered gruffly, and opened the door.

"John, don't be angry. Will you have breakfast with me, like you did before?"

He paused, and turned back to her. "I'd like that." Now he touched her face gently. "Sarah, I'd give anything if you could be my wife."

"I know, John, and I'm honored."

In the morning John evidently thought he owed her something for his actions the night before. He discussed her strategy for medical school. "I've made out several copies of this letter of recommendation. It should help at least to get them to talk to you. I still doubt that you'll find much interest in the bigger schools. But in some of the smaller ones, possibly. I've been trying to find the whereabouts of Elizabeth Blackwell for some time, but she may still be in England. If all else fails, she could be of help when she gets back." He smiled sadly, and covered her hands with his. "Sarah, I can never forget you and will only want the very best for you."

"Thank you, John, for all your help."

"You must keep in touch with me. I may wind up in Philadelphia, at the big hospital there. But I'm also looking at some opportunities in small town private practice." He scribbled a name and an address on a piece of paper. "Here, Sarah, this is the address of my sister. She will always know where I can be reached."

He kissed her then, long and tenderly. She could feel herself responding again. But finally he loosened his hold. "I have to go, dearest. May you realize your dream."

Later in her room, she sensed she was at as big a crossroads as she had faced that long ago Sunday afternoon in September as a river of a massive army flowed through Pleasant Valley to the passes of South Mountain. The next few days changed her life completely. She wondered if what was yawning before her was another such threshhold of new horizons and opportunities, or more a crevice that would swallow her and her hopes.

CHAPTER 12

"Young woman," the sharp featured young doctor frowned at her. "Even if we were to accept you for medical school, and you were bright enough to finish, do you think anyone would have enough confidence in you as a woman to be your patient? You would have no credibility. Outside perhaps of being a midwife, under the most ideal conditions."

Sarah looked at this man, this smug young man, and she detested him. Her hopes had risen when she was first ushered in to see him, after her experience at the other school with the older doctor. She had briefly hoped that the new generation of physicians would not be so biased against women entering their profession. What a joke that was! She should have expected this. She remembered now the insufferable young doctor with whom she went to the ball in Atlanta, after Sherman had captured the city.

The letter from John Rizzo, and the older one from Dr. Randall after the battle above Chattanooga, lay barely read on this man's desk. "My wartime experience under great stress and endurance means nothing then?" she asked, the pulse pounding in her ear.

"This is peacetime The War is behind us. You and women like you rose to heroic heights, for a few years. But it required no special training to change bandages, to wipe fevered brows, to ladle soup, to arrange bed pans, to maybe write letters."

"Were you in the War, Doctor?"

He appeared startled at that question. "Yes, of course. I was in a base hospital for fourteen months before coming here."

"Not in a field hospital, though?"

"No, not on a battlefield. Where the butchers held sway." Now he looked at her grimly. "Are you questioning my credentials, Miss?"

She looked down, slightly flustered. "No, of course not. But nursing in the field of battle was vastly different than apparently it was in a base hospital."

"Still, this experience hardly qualifies you for medical school, nor for ever being able to develop a practice should you somehow finish."

As he droned on, explaining in detail the common reasoning of the male dominated medical profession why women were not suitable for becoming doctors, her mind went back to her experience of the week before. Dr. Rawlings, his name was, a man probably only a few years younger than old Doc Wooten back home. He was not as smug nor as obviously condescending as this young man across the desk. No, he was more fatherly in his listing of reasons why no woman should ever consider becoming a doctor, and why no reputable medical school would accept a woman as a student. A faint smile touched her lips as she remembered how he had treated her almost as a favorite child who was somehow on the verge of straying into danger or into social disgrace.

"There are so many womanly pursuits, my dear," he had said, "that would be more suitable for you, than trying to break tradition to try to enter a field that historically women never have. Perhaps for reasons of emotional unsuitability. Or insufficient physical strength and endurance." She stared at him trying to come up with arguments against these staid old perceptions. She knew the utter falseness of such beliefs, from her own experience and from those of other women she had encountered during the War. Emotional unsuitability? Not sufficient physical strength and endurance? How damn unfair and untrue such beliefs were! But she realized that nothing she could say would convince this man, this father-like figure, that women were more than fragile objects to be sheltered and protected.

Now this young doctor, this cock of the walk, was summarizing his denial of her admission. "So, you see, Miss, your aspirations have no practical possibilities." He smiled then. "Sometimes we have to tone down our ambitions, to those things reality based. Dreams have no place in the field of medicine." Now he extended his hand to Sarah. "So, I wish you well in whatever womanly pursuits you direct your efforts."

She stared at him, ignoring the hand.

She stood up, resisting the impulse to spit in his face. The bastard. "It had seemed to me that helping the sick and injured was a womanly pursuit, Doctor. Now you have clarified that mistake in judgment. Good day, Sir."

With that she turned and left his office, seething. Exiting the building, she sought a bench in a nearby park to try to calm herself. She was overwrought from the disparagement, not so much to her but to all woman. That we are not worthy of this profession. Perhaps he is right, the thought briefly crossed her mind: we are too emotional to handle the stress of medicine. But the better angels of her nature quickly dispelled that random thought. Righteous indignation was not the same as debilitating emotional distress.

Now the idea occurred to her. It was even more heady than the idea nurtured at Antietam of medical school.

Perhaps she should devote her life to elevating the status of women beyond the traditional pursuits of childbearing, homemaking, and mundane occupations. Why could not women have the scope of men in their choices of work and life pursuits? Mary Ann Bickerdyke had shown her what a resolute woman could accomplish. And while she had never met up with Clara Barton, she knew she had accomplished great things. As her anger diminished, Sarah felt a new commitment. She would not give up. Damn it, she would not!

#

A letter from Julia Bledsoe awaited her at general delivery at the post office. Father was failing. Perhaps she should come home in the next few days. He wanted to see her very badly, before it was too late. And, yes, her sisters seemed to be giving him very good care. She must have really inspired, or coerced them, somehow.

Sarah quickly made preparations for the trip back to western Maryland. Everything was at an impasse here in Philadelphia, and maybe it would have been better if she'd never left Pa's side. Still, she felt some satisfaction that she'd succeeded in goading her sisters to give him better care.

When she saw Pa, she was saddened at how much worse he had become in the two months since she had last seen him. Emily told her, "Doc Wooten only gives him a week. We didn't want you to get here too late."

Sarah touched her arm. "Thank you, Emily. I would have felt terrible not to have gotten here in time." On impulse, she opened her arms to Emily and the two hugged. "I didn't mean to be so bossy," Sarah said.

"You knew what should be done." Emily took a deep breath. "I think Pa's last days have been as good as they could be."

"I'm sure they have been."

Sarah sat and held his hand for a while that night. But he was only dimly aware of her presence. Doc Wooten had given him pills to lessen the pain, and they made him groggy and somewhat delirious. "He's not always this way. He has moments when he's lucid," Charlotte told her.

Later, as she and her sisters had coffee in the kitchen, Sarah learned at least a partial explanation for her sisters' change of attitude toward her. "Pa said we'll all be sharing equally in his estate," Charlotte told her.

"That's good," Sarah said drily.

"Of course, Emily and I did most of the taking care of him during these difficult months," she pointed out petulantly.

Sarah didn't say anything.

"But we don't have any hard feelings," Emily said.

"I'm glad."

"We really don't know how big the estate is. He's not sure, and doesn't know how much his debts are."

Good God, Sarah thought, have they been interrogating the poor man on his death bed about his estate and finances? But she didn't say anything. No use antagonizing these sisters.

Doc Wooten was coming in twice a day now. Nothing more was said about Sarah's ambition to go to medical school, but she could sense his disapproval of her. Despite this, she asked on the third day, "Doctor Wooten, couldn't you lighten the pill intake, so Pa can talk to us rationally before he dies? As it is now, he's out of it. And we need to communicate before it's too late."

The doctor frowned. "Your father's in terrible pain. I won't condone reducing the pills. Young lady, you're asking too much."

Without Doc Wooten's approval, Sarah nevertheless took on the responsibility of reducing Pa's medicine. As he became more coherent and conscious, she told him the situation. "Pa, the medicine Doc Wooten wants you to take is putting you out of it. If I reduce it some, your pain is going to increase, but you'll be more mentally alert. What do you want me to do?"

"Reduce, reduce," he whispered. "The pain . . . I can stand. But I want . . . to talk . . . 'fore it's too late."

She sat with him as the daylight faded, and a single candle was the only illumination. She held his hand as his breathing labored. Occasionally he would briefly squeeze her hand. "Is the pain bad, Pa?"

"I can stand it," he muttered. He seemed to be gathering his strength for more conversation. "Tell me . . . 'bout medical school."

She sighed. "Nothing yet. All I'm encountering is male prejudice. And closed minds. Even Doc Wooten has the same mind."

"Don't give up . . . Sarah. Do it . . . for me." She looked down at his ravaged face, contorted now with the difficulty in breathing. "Promise me," he managed to get out. She shook her head sadly. "Promise me," he was more insistent. Slowly she nodded.

Somewhat satisfied, he relaxed on the pillows. Then he roused again, seemingly with great effort. "Sarah . . . God willing . . . I hope to see you . . . as a doc . . . from above."

Now utterly exhausted, he closed his eyes. The raspy sounds of his breathing filled the room. She put a wet compress on his forehead. Now she offered him several more of the pills. He did not resist.

#

A steady downpour cast an even more depressing aura on the funeral day. The church was full, and most people with their umbrellas accompanied the casket to the cemetery. Pa was a prominent citizen, so this was not surprising. Sarah was surprised though at the people who greeted her and offered their condolences. Evidently the earlier hatreds had subsided. Or else Julia and others had managed to discredit the bad rumors about her. Still, Preacher Williams would not greet her, nor even extend the basic courtesy of condolences.

Julia remarked about that. "Isn't it strange how men of God can forget so easily the golden rule?"

"They're not unlike much of the medical profession. Self righteous, closed minds. Unwilling to bend, or admit that they might be wrong." Sarah grimaced. If she were a man she would have spit to show her disdain.

"Sarah, I've become very interested in nursing, because of you. I wonder, when you become a doctor, would you consider hiring me as a nurse?"

"What a nice thought, Julia. I'd be delighted. But, I don't know if I'll make it to become a doctor. Still, Pa, in almost his last conscious words told me not to give up, that he would be watching me." She paused, then asked her friend, "Do you believe the dead can still keep track of what we're doing on earth?"

"Oh, I do, I do. Don't you?"

"I don't know. But I'd like to believe if a dead spirit wants to bad enough, that he or she is entitled to at least observe. How truly sad it would be not to know how your loved ones are faring."

The two young women held hands as the casket was lowered into the ground and the last prayers were said by Preacher Williams.

Later in the lawyer's office, Sarah and her sisters learned the extent of their inheritance. It was not as much as her sisters had expected, and they were bitterly disappointed. While Father had had considerable property, his debts had grown considerably with the War. While property would have to be sold to realize the full extent of their inheritance, it appeared that Sarah would have a few thousand dollars. Still, this should be enough to live modestly and perhaps pay for some of the costs of medical school. If only she could find one willing to admit her.

#

With the prospects of getting into a medical school in Baltimore and Philadelphia now seemingly denied, Sarah turned her attention to New York City. She had heard that Dr. Elizabeth Blackwell was back from England and practicing there, and she hoped the woman might give her some advice, and even sponsor or recommend her.

"I'm trying to meet with Dr. Blackwell," she told the receptionist at the New York Infirmary for Women and Children. The hospital was a large house on Second Avenue that had obviously been adapted to medical use. This day, perhaps a typical day, it was crowded and noisy with women and children patients.

The woman at the desk seemed harried. Rather curtly she asked, "Are you one of her patients?"

"No, I wanted to see her, on a personal matter."

The woman frowned and checked some papers. "We don't expect Dr. Blackwell in for several days. She mostly works out of her office on 17th Street now, and only comes in when she has patients here that she needs to see. I'll give you her address if you'd like."

"Yes, please." Sarah looked around. "Is it always this busy?"

"We could use twice the space and twice the doctors."

"Are most of the doctors men?"

"Gracious, no. We have several women, in addition to Dr. Blackwell."

The receptionist jotted down the address of Dr. Blackwell's office. "Without an appointment," she said, "you'll probably have a long wait. She's very busy."

"Thank you. I've been waiting a long time to see Dr. Blackwell. A few more hours won't hurt."

Her office was about ten blocks away, so the receptionist said. Sarah walked the crowded, noisy, dirty streets with wonder. She had never been in a city as big as this, with such a crush of humanity. She leaned against a building, as a sudden longing to be back in the green hills of western Maryland was almost more than she could bear. The neighborhoods became worse as she neared the office: more squalid, more depressing. Many of these wretched people, she realized, must be immigrants, for she heard snatches of many different languages as she moved through the mass of people. The day was hot, made worse by the heat rising from the sidewalks and the congestion. This combined with the foul stench of garbage and the leavings from horse-drawn vehicles, made her faint and nauseous, and she leaned against a building trying to fight this off. Now she had a vision of that savaged horse that had made her sick on the way up South Mountain, when she would have abandoned the beginning of all this except there was no way to turn back. That would have been the end of this odyssey. A horse could have ended it. Now she steeled herself. Dear Lord, she whispered, give me strength. After bearing up so well under the stench and sounds of the battlefield, don't let a big city defeat me!

At last she reached the small storefront with the sign, Dr. Elizabeth Blackwell, MD. The inside was almost as hot and noisy as the sidewalks had been. Now much of the noise was crying children rather than the babble of a dozen dialects, and the smells were of sweat and vomit.

She pushed her way to the desk. "Do you have an appointment?" the woman asked.

"No, I wanted to see Dr. Blackwell on a personal matter, not for a medical problem."

The woman waved her hand vaguely toward the room. "Well, you can see it'll be a long wait. I doubt she'll get to you until the end of the day."

"This is very important to me. I'll certainly wait."

The woman appraised her. "Could I ask what you wanted to see the Doctor about? I could relay this to her."

Sarah hesitated. Why not? "I wanted to see her about getting into medical school. Get her advice. See if she might be able to help."

"You're not the first, you know, about such."

Sarah started. "Have there been others?"

"Dozens. She broke the ice for women. Now they all want her to help them."

Sarah took a deep breath. "Was she able to help any of them? Get into medical school, that is?"

"A few, shortly after she finished in the 40s. Now, there're just too many women trying to get into so few openings."

"Then I'm wasting my time, trying to see her. And her time, of course." Sarah rubbed her eyes, vaguely conscious of a baby crying just behind her. "I should go, then. But I don't know where else to turn, or what else to do."

More kindly, the woman said, "Why don't you wait, Miss? Since you're here. Dr. Blackwell, I'm sure, will want to talk with you."

It was almost seven before Dr. Blackwell's appointments were finished. For hours Sarah had stood in the crowded room. Finally it had thinned out and she could sit. It made no difference. Her mind was numb with the news of the surfeit of women now seeking to be doctors. She'd thought she would be one of the few.

A short dark-haired woman came out from the back. She bade the receptionist goodnight. "I'll close up, Gertrude."

She wore a dark gray suit, and her face reflected tiredness bordering on exhaustion, Sarah thought. She sat beside her on the bench. "You're the young woman wanting to talk about being a doctor? Gertrude didn't get your name. I'm Elizabeth Blackwell." She extended her hand for a firm handshake.

"I'm Sarah Lindsey. I'm so sorry to take any of your time. After you've had a long hard day. Please excuse me."

A smile flashed across the woman's face, and was quickly gone. "I try to talk with the aspirants. But there's getting to be so many. And so few positions available." She looked at her. "Can you give me a quick rundown of your experience, and why you want to be a doctor?"

Sarah fumbled in her purse. "I have a letter here, from a doctor I worked with on the battlefield. I helped in field hospitals. It was then that I realized medicine was my calling, and that I had experience and skills—yes, and the dedication needed—to become a doctor." She gave John Rizzo's letter to Dr. Blackwell. She quickly scanned it. Then read it a second time more slowly. Then she looked up, her face inscrutable. "Very interesting. Dr. Rizzo says you even did some surgery."

Sarah nodded. "Do I have any chance . . ."

"I don't know. But I can see why you aspire to be a doctor. Do you have any academic credentials? Any formal college coursework?"

"No. But I think I'm reasonably smart. That I could handle medical school."

Blackwell nodded, as she closed her eyes in thought. "There are several medical schools that will accept a few token women. One of them is Geneva College in western New York. Where I went. Another is the Cleveland Medical College in Ohio, from which my sister Emily graduated a decade ago. You should contact these, and there are a few others whose names and addresses Gertrude can give you if you come back tomorrow. The big schools, such as Harvard, they just will not accept women. Some European schools have recently begun admitting a few women." She sighed. "But so many want this." She looked at her watch. "It's getting late, and I must go. Sometimes I wonder why anyone would want to go into medicine, the hours, the exhaustive work."

She put her hand on Sarah's shoulder, "But we know, don't we, why someone would aspire to this."

Sarah nodded. They stood up. "Thank you so much for giving me this time. May I ask a quick final question?"

"Of course, dear."

"These medical schools that do accept some women, would it be best to go in person to see them, or to send them my application first?"

"It's always more difficult to turn down someone face to face than by mail. If you can afford to, I'd see the two I mentioned and the several others that Gertrude can give you. But I don't think there's any hurry right now. The fall classes will soon be starting, and they won't be considering applications for next year's classes until spring. You might consider giving us some help at the Infirmary. It will give you a taste of big city civilian nursing."

#

Sarah decided to accept Elizabeth Blackwell's suggestion to join the Infirmary's staff for at least a few months. Her efforts at entering medical school could have no payoff until next spring, if then. She rented a small housekeeping room on the fourth floor of an old building within walking distance of the Infirmary. It seemed best that she have a mailing address where she could be reached. For she had correspondence she needed to send and receive.

First, she wrote a letter to John Rizzo, addressed to his sister, telling him of her getting nowhere in Baltimore and Philadelphia, then her seeing Dr. Blackwell, but still little hope. She wrote to Julia Bledsoe, her dearest friend. Finally, she wrote to Mary Ann Bickerdyke, hoping it would reach her, wherever she was. She wrote about the darkness of her spirit, the forlorn hope, and the bitter realization that her ambition to be a doctor might be forever barred.

The New York City environment was not one to give her comfort. In later years she was to remember these months as some of the worst of her life. Far worse than the battlefield, which had its moments of supreme fulfillment. Now there was precious little feeling of fulfillment, as she helped with the multitude of patients suffering from all kinds of ailments day after day, most of them due to neglect, carelessness, and lack of adequate hygiene. The hours were long, not just for a few days as battlefield conditions necessitated, but the weariness of day after day, seemingly without end. She began to wonder whether she was cut out for regular medical practice.

She never heard from John Rizzo. Whether his sister did not forward her letter, or whether he simply wanted to break all contacts, she did not know. Julia's letter coming at a time when she was near the depths of depression from her lonely and frustrating life, amid the grayness and drudgery of a New York City winter, was as welcome as the first blossoms of spring. Julia had no particular news to impart. Sarah's sisters were still complaining about the leanness of their father's estate. So what's new. But Julia's faith in her, and Julia's desire to be her nurse some day, comforted her. Had the distances been closer, Sarah would have journeyed back to Pikeston to see this dear friend. Almost the only friend she had in this austere and unrewarding life.

But the last letter really buoyed her spirits. From Mary Ann Bickerdyke. She should have known that she had another true friend besides Julia. And this one was far more influential and her strength of purpose poured from the pages:

> My dear Sarah,
>
> It was so good to hear from you. I've thought about my dear companion in the great struggle so many times. And wondered at your fulfillment of your dream.
>
> Dear Sarah, your letter reeks of your frustration with the many obstacles. Please, do not give up. Do not let your noble ambition wither. For I never met a more dedicated and talented person. You have so much, my dear, to offer. So much of a contribution to make. It must not be denied!
>
> If those damned doctors won't admit you, you may have to try a flanking approach. (And we should know about such things, from our battlefields, ha ha.) I have a name for you, a prominent woman doctor up in Boston. Marie Zakrzewska. She's in a position of some influence up there. And I believe she knows me. I wrote her today in your behalf. I told her all about you and that you'll be up to see her. I think she's a kindred spirit. And I think she might be able to help you, my dear Sarah.
>
> I'm having difficulty adjusting to life after the War. But my children are offering challenges I never expected. As you can see from the address, we are in Kansas now. Always seeking a better life, pursuing a dream, too.
>
> Dearest Sarah, please keep in touch. Let me know how things go up in Boston. Incidentally, do you ever hear from that doctor in Baltimore, John something? And Sarah, have you ever seen that Reb major again?
>
> Your devoted friend
> Mary Ann

#

It was several weeks before Sarah could arrange to go to Boston to try to see Dr. Zakrzewska. The Infirmary was unwilling to spare her for the three days necessary for the visit. The alternative was to resign, and burn her bridges in New York City. Sarah was prepared to do that when one night after dragging herself to her room after a long day, she was astonished to find a letter waiting for her from Dr.

Zakrzewska. She hastily tore it open. Her hands were shaking so much she could hardly read it in the dim candlelight. Then she had to sit down and try to calm her raging pulse. Now she read it again, marveling:

> Dear Sarah,
>   Mother Bickerdyke has written me about you. I was tremendously impressed. While I cannot promise you medical school yet, still I think it's highly probable in the not distant future. As you may or may not know, we have established the New England Hospital for Women and Children, here in Boston. It's well accepted, and has been a springboard for several young women to get into medical school. With your wartime experience, I would like you to join our staff as a surgical nurse. You might even call this an internship before you get into medical school. Sarah, please come to Boston as soon as you can. It will be hard work, but rewarding. I know you are not unfamiliar with hard work.
>
>   Sincerely,
>   Marie Elizabeth Zakrzewska, MD

#

The Infirmary would not permit Sarah to leave without two weeks notice. She prepared to take the train to Boston the next day after that. She penned a letter of acceptance, and appreciation, to Dr. Zakrzewska. Then wrote to Julia and finally to Mother Bickerdyke: "My appreciation, Mary Ann, is boundless. You have salvaged my career, and my life. How can I ever thank you?"

#

Sarah arrived in Boston the evening before her appointment with Dr. Zakrzewska. Curiously, and fearlessly, she walked the twelve blocks to the New England Hospital that evening.

The building on 14 Warren Street was old but seemingly well kept up. It was somewhat larger than the Infirmary in New York City. The neighborhood was on the edge between slums and middle class. She ventured in the front door, but did not approach the reception desk. She only wanted to get a feel for this place that might soon be so important to her life. What most impressed her as she entered the building was the cleanliness. It was the cleanest hospital, or even major building, she had ever seen. It even smelled fresh and antiseptic.

The next morning at her hotel, she asked the housekeeper if she knew anything about the New England Hospital.

"Indeed I do, dearie. I've been there, as has my daughter. A wonderful place. It's so nice to be treated by women doctors rather than always by men. And that

Dr. Zakrzewska, she's something." She looked at Sarah with interest. "Why are you asking, dearie. Are you going to be a patient?" Before Sarah could respond, she looked at her shrewdly, and asked, "Or maybe a doctor?"

"Not a patient. Hopefully, a doctor some day. For now, a nurse."

The Irish woman touched her shoulder. "Good for you, dearie. You'll probably be working some with Dr. Z—that's what we call her. Would you like me to tell you a bit about the good doctor?"

"I sure would. Yes."

"She was an immigrant, you know, just like me. 'Cept she wasn't Irish. I think she's Polish, or maybe Prussian. Anyways, she came to this country when she was 'bout your age, I would say. Didn't speak any English, either.

"She went to medical school somewheres out west. Then set up shop in New York City for a few years. After that she came up here and opened this hospital. Now there's no better care a woman can get anywheres in the world than Dr. Z's hospital. Believe me."

The Irish cleaning woman could not stop talking about Dr. Z. Sarah listened fascinated. "When she had night calls to make, first she walked in any type of weather. She wanted to prove that women are tough as men. Maybe tougher. In bad neighborhoods she'd walk with the messenger who called her. If he couldn't go with her on her return home, she'd walk with the local policeman to the end of his beat. Then go from one beat to another till she gets home." The woman sighed. "Ah, dearie, there's one to look up to."

#

Dr. Zahrzewska was much younger than Sarah had expected. She was hardly forty, she would judge, and her face looked youthful. Not at all like Mother Bickerdyke in looks. But from what she had heard since coming to Boston, she must be very much like Bickerdyke in temperament.

"Sarah, please call me Marie," she said, smiling.

"I'd like that. Thank you." Sarah looked at her appreciatively. This was a woman you could quickly feel comfortable with. She hoped she had found another good friend. "Your hospital is impressive. Big. And so clean, Marie."

"You should have seen it four years ago. We had only a few iron bedsteads, a few chairs, some straw. But donations kept coming, sometimes only scissors and bandages, but sometimes furniture, and money. We never refused any gift, however small. Then two years ago we gained enough grants that we could move here. Now we're not ruling out the possibility of moving to still larger quarters. There seems no end to the number of patients seeking us out." She smiled again. "We are the cleanest hospital in Boston. Those male doctors have never quite understood the value of cleanliness. But I'm sure you know about that. From the battlefield."

"I truly do. The wonder was that so many men did survive with their wounds amid the filth, not only in the field hospitals but even in base hospitals."

"We don't have any men as patients here. We have a few men doctors, although we're mostly staffed by women, and a good part of our popularity is providing women with medical care from doctors of their own sex. We're unique at this time among the Boston hospitals in specializing in both obstetrical and gynecological treatment of patients, as well as pediatrics. We also offer a full range of medical treatment, including surgery."

Now Marie paused and looked down at the papers on her desk: Mother Bickerdyke's letter, the "To whom it may concern" letter of John Rizzo, and the letter of recommendation from the administrator of the New York Infirmary that Sarah had given her. "Have you thought about what field of medicine you would like to practice?"

"I think right now any field. Just to be a doctor. Still, if I had a choice, I think it would be surgery. Yet, I wonder whether there are any women surgeons?"

"I don't know of any, yet. But someone has to be first. After reading Mother Bickerdyke's letter, and now this one from Dr. Rizzo, I think surgery might be a good choice. Maybe the best." She paused and looked at Sarah, then her eyes shifted to her hands. "Do you mind if I look at your hands, Sarah?"

Sarah offered them and she examined them closely. "Now grip my hands as strongly as possible. Good." Marie leaned back in her chair. "A surgeon needs good dexterity, with strong yet gentle hands. It is a big asset if these characteristics can be found in small hands with long fingers. Which you have. Of course, a surgeon needs the mental toughness to go with the hands." She smiled again. "I would suspect that you have all these attributes. That's why we want you as a surgical nurse, for now."

Now Dr. Zakrzewska frowned. "I'm afraid this means you'll have to go to Europe for your medical education. No American colleges are willing yet to enroll women in surgical training. However, Zurich and Paris universities have recently opened their doors to women. But we'll talk more about this later."

She stood up. "Now, Sarah, let me show you around. By the way, if you haven't already found a place to stay, let me give you several nearby possibilities. Nothing elegant, of course. But convenient, and clean. And safe."

CHAPTER 13

Sarah quickly fitted in as surgical nurse. Dr. Dreyfus was the main staff surgeon affiliated with the hospital. His backup was Dr. Manning, a younger man who helped out mostly with emergencies and when Dr. Dreyfus was otherwise tied up or had more than he could handle.

It took Sarah but a short while to become acquainted with the various surgical tools and the procedures for sterilization and anaesthesia. Within a week she and Dr. Dreyfus were working as an effective team. Within two weeks she was often even anticipating his order for instruments.

Her steady and dexterous fingers quickly came to his attention. As John Rizzo had on the Antietam battlefield, Dr. Dreyfus soon was having Sarah close his incisions. She found the time spent in the operating room flowing by so fast she often hardly realized the day was over. Except by the time she got back to her room she was almost too tired to fix something to eat.

"Sarah, I imagine our insistence on cleanliness here is a far cry from what you saw a few years ago," Dr. Dreyfus remarked one day shortly after she had started.

"In the field hospitals there was no sanitation whatever," she said. "The blood on instruments was simply wiped off with a hand or a bloody cloth, or else the instruments were dipped in a bloody pail. There was little time for even primitive cleanliness. Still, I suspect the doctors were not aware of the dangers of lack of sanitation."

"Well, Marie has always insisted on maximum cleanliness, with sterile instruments and our well scrubbed hands. You know, Sarah, we have the lowest operating deaths of any hospital in Boston." He laughed. "And I don't think it's just because we have the best surgeons."

Aside from injuries, most operations dealt with complications of childbirth; some involved removal of tumors. These were medical problems Sarah had not experienced as a war nurse. She eagerly sought to increase her knowledge here, and Dr. Dreyfus carefully explained, even if the surgery had to be slowed to do so.

About six weeks after Sarah came to New England Hospital, a messenger, a young hospital worker named Tony, came to her door on her day off. "Dr. Dreyfus requests you to assist him on an emergency operation. On a woman's face. She's been slashed."

"Good God! Of course, I'll come."

"I have a carriage waiting outside."

"I'm not used to such first class treatment," Sarah told him as they drove off.

"This is Dr. Dreyfus's carriage. It should be faster than walking."

"How bad is this woman, Tony? Have you seen her?"

"Pretty bad, I think. She was all bloody when they brought her in."

"How old is she?"

"Quite young, I would think. Maybe 'bout your age."

Sarah felt chilled at this. She wondered how such a terrible injury could have happened. She could imagine herself in this tragic scene.

"So glad you could come, Sarah," Dr. Dreyfus greeted her at the hospital. "I hated to call you in on your day off, but I need your deft fingers. Or rather, this poor woman needs them."

The woman had already been anesthesized. Now they could see the full extend of the wound as it extended from her cheekbone to her jaw. Blood was still oozing from the wound, although it had slowed. She had been a pretty girl, Sarah realized with a sinking feeling, but no more.

Dr. Dreyfus carefully worked on the wound as Sarah assisted him. Then he said, "Sarah, I want you to stitch her up. If you do it carefully, the scar may not be too noticeable. You will need to have very close stitches with the wound drawn up tight, but not too tight."

The wound required many stitches, and Sarah concentrated on this while Dr. Dreyfus hovered nearby. Soon she was drenched with sweat, and the doctor and one of the other nurses wiped her forehead every few minutes. The stitching was taking a long time, and the patient was now beginning to moan. The Doctor touched her on the shoulder. "Stop and rest for a few minutes. We need to give the patient more chloroform."

They sprinkled the liquid onto a sponge and held it tightly over the woman's nose and mouth for a few minutes. Now she was quiet again, and Sarah continued with the stitching.

Finally it was finished, and Sarah sagged against the operating table in relief.

"That was very well done, Sarah. Better than I could have done. This woman owes you for saving what was possible of her beauty." Together they carefully bandaged her face.

The next day, Sarah stopped in to see the woman, whose name was Amy Panelli. Her face was heavily bandaged, and while she was sedated, she was conscious. Sarah explained, "I'm the one who sewed you up. I just wanted to see how you were doing."

The large brown eyes searched hers. "Is my face ruined, Doctor? Will I be a freak the rest of m' days?"

Sarah closed her eyes, momentarily, trying to find the words to give this woman, about her age, hope. "I tried to stitch the wound . . . so very carefully. At best there may be a slight scar. But not bad."

"And at worst?" the woman asked bitterly.

Sarah sighed. "Then there will be a more prominent scar." As the woman groaned, Sarah struggled to reassure her. "Miss Panelli, even if there's a noticeable scar, I don't think it will destroy your beauty. You will not be a freak, or ugly. In fact," and she paused, trying to find the right words, "I think it might add to your attractiveness to some men. A woman who has faced trouble, and not let it destroy her, who has great strength of character."

"You think men are looking for that?" Amy asked sarcastically.

Sarah pondered this. "I really think the better ones, the real gems, are."

The woman nodded, not convinced, but still wanting to be, Sarah suspected. "How did it happen, Amy? Was it a boyfriend, or a husband?"

"I was mugged," she said bitterly. "Two men attempted to rob me almost in front of my building. I resisted, and this is what they did to me."

"Dear Lord, where do you live?"

She named an address only a block from where Sarah was rooming.

"You could have been me, Amy."

"Then God help us all. These hoodlums who care nothing 'bout killing and maiming women." She took a deep breath. "I sometimes wonder whether all men are the same. They only want t' get and not give. Do it, or we'll hurt you."

Sarah took Amy's hand in hers. "Thank God, most men are not like that, Amy. Believe me."

#

One evening a few weeks later, Marie Zakrzewska approached Sarah as she was preparing to leave for the day. "I see you're working late, Sarah. I understand you often work late."

"There's so much to do, Marie, so many people needing help. It's hard to break away when you're needed."

Marie smiled. "I know it is. To feel so needed, it's what makes this a wonderful profession. But an exhausting one, too." She paused as Sarah was putting on her coat. "I've heard very good things about you. From Dr. Dreyfus, as well as other people. He tells me you did a superb job in sewing up that poor girl's face. He thinks you have a great talent. And I do, too."

At this, Sarah's eyes teared. She tried to wipe them away unobtrusively. But Marie noticed. "I also understand," she said softly, "that you did a great job of comforting that poor woman, Amy Panelli."

"I tried to give her hope."

Marie Zakrzewska stared at her. Then she asked, "Sarah, would you like to go with me on house calls from time to time? They're often in the evening, so I realize this would take away from your spare time. But these can be great medical experiences."

"I'd love to." She smiled into Marie's sober eyes. "I'm honored that you asked me."

Now the older doctor smiled. "I thought you'd be willing."

Only a few days later, as Sarah was ending her shift, Marie asked, "Can you join me on an emergency call right now?"

Sarah looked up, her breath coming faster. "I certainly can. Thank you."

"A young boy has accidentally been shot. The bullet may still be in his shoulder. We may have to do something before bringing him to the hospital. We don't have much time to spare."

Marie expertly maneuvered the carriage through the crowded streets. Sarah said, "I've heard you used to go on foot to these calls, sometimes late at night."

"The sick and injured couldn't wait. But I usually found a policeman." Marie laughed. "I've come up in the world, now with my own horse and carriage. Just like those big time men doctors."

They reached the flat. A teenage boy waited anxiously for them. "It's my little brother. We was playing with a gun. Didn't know it was loaded." He looked beseechingly at the doctor. "Please save my little brother."

"We'll do our best," Marie said as she quickly shouldered past him into the room where several people were hysterically waiting.

She looked briefly at the weakly whimpering victim, then gave rapid orders to the spectators, "Quick, we need more light in here. Bring as many candles as you can find. Also get some towels and some boiling water. Quickly now! His life depends on you!"

"Sarah," she commanded, "Look at this wound. There's no exit. The bullet must still be in there. Take that vial of chloroform from my bag. We're going to have to do an emergency operation here. The jarring of the carriage might move the bullet into a vital organ."

Quickly they put the boy under, and painted the shoulder with antiseptic. Marie tried to probe for the bullet. "Get back," Sarah yelled to the crowding spectators. "We have to have room. Back to the wall, please!"

Now Marie said urgently, "I can't get it, Sarah! Can you try?"

Sarah dipped her fingers into the near boiling water. Then took the probe and forceps from Marie. She put her hand into the now extensive wound seeking the bullet as the blood obscured any chance of seeing it. She was vaguely aware of a woman crying in the background. At last, a finger found a hard object, deep in the wound. She hesitated. A scalpel would do more fearsome damage. As would forceps. Could she draw this out, with her fingers?

She inserted her forefinger and middle finger into the wound, and tried to move the bullet closer to the surface. If it was not too trapped in sinews. Her fingers repeatedly slipped on the bloody tissues. It seemed hopeless, without a massive incision with the scalpel. But at last she felt it moving a bit. Her two fingers moved it enough that her thumb was just about able to reach it. She strained toward the bullet. What damage this must be doing to the wound. At last she was able to grasp it with her thumb and forefinger, and triumphantly drew it out.

"Well done, Sarah," Marie breathed. They quickly bandaged and arranged for the boy to be made comfortable in the carriage.

No MD surgeon could have done it better, Marie told her on the ride back to the hospital. Later, as she was about to leave for a few hours sleep before the new day, Marie asked, "Would you like to borrow some of my medical books, and my notes? I don't know that you'll have much time to study these. Somehow, I think you'll find the time, though."

Sarah was profoundly grateful. And she did find time to pore over the books and notes and marvel at this wealth of human knowledge. Sarah sensed that she was receiving special treatment, but she was sobered by the memory of her sisters' jealousy because of her imagined special treatment and favoritism by Pa.

One woman on the staff in particular worried her: Elaine Cassidy. She had been at New England Hospital a year longer than Sarah and also was hoping to get into medical school. Tall and spare, not very attractive, she was one of Dorothea Dix's nurses during the War. As such, she had had extensive experience in the base hospitals at Baltimore and Washington City. Her resentment of Sarah became evident early. In fact, a few days after Sarah had sewed up Lucy Panelli's face.

"How do you manage to get these choice assignments?" she had asked benignly. Then spat out, "Are you bedding some of the male doctors? Is that it? How you get such choice assignments?"

Sarah had stared at her, appalled. "Of course not." Then as the full implication of Cassidy's accusation struck her, she moved closer, livid. "How dare you! What gives you the right to accuse me of such?"

"Bitch!" Cassidy snarled, and shoved her into the wall. Sarah had to struggle to keep from falling. Then she moved closer, prepared to fight the bigger woman. Cassidy might be surprised how much fisticuffs she had learned as a bullied child. But before they came to blows, others stepped between them.

Cassidy glared at her, before she turned away. "You haven't heard the last from me, bitch," she said over her shoulder.

Sarah heard herself shouting at the woman's departing back, "Then you'd better bring your boxing gloves." But Cassidy was gone, with her dignity intact. On the other hand, Sarah thought she had come out second best in this encounter. But she knew now she had at least one enemy. She wondered how many others were jealous of her standing with the administration.

#

Several times a week Sarah was now accompanying Zakrzewska on evening house calls. "Have you had much chance to look at the medical books and my notes?" Marie asked toward the end of January as they were going to a more distant patient.

"Every spare moment I study them. I can't tell you how much I appreciate . . ."

Marie interrupted. "I think we should try to get you into medical school for this coming fall. We will need to send in the paperwork within the next month. Most schools make their decisions for fall classes by May. And they need time to process the applications."

A thrill went through Sarah. She looked at the Doctor but didn't say anything. Dr. Z was looking straight ahead.

Now Dr. Z continued. "As I told you when you first came, no U. S. medical school will offer a woman training in surgery. Some day, yes. But not now. Which means you'll have to go to Europe. Either to Zurich or more probably Paris." She paused. "I don't suppose you speak any French?"

"I had some in high school. Of course, I would have to do some strong reviewing."

"Good. That's one problem that can be handled. Most of the lectures will be in French. But, still, many people will speak some English." She looked now at a wide-eyed Sarah. "But the bigger problem is money. Having to go to Europe costs many times more than if Harvard would accept you." Then she asked, "Do you have any sources of income?"

"I got a small inheritance when my father died last year. But it's mostly gone, outside of a few hundred dollars."

"That's not enough, of course, for three years of study abroad." Now Sarah's spirits fell. They had reached their destination, but Dr. Z was in no hurry to leave the carriage. "This isn't an emergency," she said. "So we can talk a few minutes before going in."

"Could I work my way through?" Sarah asked. She was conscious now of thickening snow flakes covering the dirt of the city and muffling the harsh sounds.

Finally Dr. Z said, "No, work would not do it. Medical school is a full-time commitment. While you'll be expected to work in a hospital, medical students are lucky to get room and board." Suddenly she was smiling, and Sarah wondered why. She put her gloved hand on Sarah's. "Don't give up, my dear. There are several wealthy women in town who earnestly want to further women in medicine. I don't think we'll have any difficulty finding some to fund the formal medical education of my prodigy."

"Your prodigy?" Sarah said stupidly.

"Didn't you guess?"

"I couldn't even think of such a possibility. For fear of being far too presumptuous."

"Well, I'll take you to meet some of your probable patrons. We must make your application as strong as possible. Surgery is where you should specialize. Don't you agree?"

"Yes," she said numbly.

"Now I think these patrons, as I do, will want you to come back here after you finish abroad, for perhaps three to five years. To give us the benefits of your training. Would that be agreeable?"

"That'd be wonderful."

"Good, then let's go in and see what medical problems we can solve tonight."

\#

Only a few days later, Marie told Sarah to bring her best dress to work the next day. They would be having lunch with two wealthy women interested in sponsoring her for an European medical school.

"I'm not sure I have anything suitable to wear," Sarah told her nervously. "The few clothes I have weren't meant for something like this."

"Don't worry," Marie assured her. "Anything clean and modest will be fine. These women won't be judging you on your fashion elegance."

Another confrontation occurred the next morning with Elaine Cassidy. Sarah was hurrying down the hall after changing to her best dress, when Cassidy blocked her way. "Well, look at Lindsey. All fancied up. Probably going with the good Doctor to meet the high society. While your colleagues sweat in the wards."

"Let me by, Cassidy."

"Maybe we should just throw some blood on your dress. So those society bitches could be impressed: 'I just had a quick operation to do before lunch. Sorry about that, ladies,'" she mocked.

"You've had your fun. Now let me by."

"Try and make me."

They were on the verge of a pushing and shoving match when Dr. Z's voice sounded down the hallway. "Sarah, I'm waiting. Get a move on!"

Reluctantly, Cassidy moved aside, glaring at her. "Another time, Lindsey."

"What was that all about?" Marie asked as they left the building.

"Elaine doesn't approve of me. She thinks I don't deserve special consideration. That I haven't been here long enough."

"Oh."

Sarah said slowly, "I think the crux is that she resents me being your prodigy."

The Doctor touched her arm. "Sarah, do you think Elaine should be my prodigy, and not you?"

"She's been here longer. I'm sure she's worked hard. She has war experience same as I have."

"Are you suggesting I make her my prodigy, and not you?"

Sarah sighed. "Now you're testing me, Marie. My unselfishness. My lack of ambition. Maybe even my confidence in myself. What can I say?"

"I think you've said it, Sarah," Marie said softly.

#

"Mrs. Putnam, Mrs. Cabot, this is Sarah Lindsey, the young woman I've told you about."

Sarah smiled shyly and took their offered hands. She really felt intimidated and ill at ease in these luxurious surroundings. The house was a mansion. They had driven in a gated entrance, up a curving driveway to a covered portico, where a man came out to take care of their carriage, and a uniformed doorman escorted them inside where the women waited in a spacious foyer. She was a simple country girl, the daughter of a small town lawyer, a rustic. What was she doing here?

But the women did their best to put her at ease. Marie Zakrzewska smiled reassuringly, and even winked several times. "Sarah, please call me Donna," Mrs Putnam, the woman of the house, told her. "And this is Rosalind," she said, nodding to Mrs. Cabot.

Despite her initial trepidation, Sarah soon felt more and more comfortable with these women. They were doing their best to put her at ease. She sensed they were admiring. But so much was at stake with making the right impression. She still felt fearful.

As they approached the table for lunch, Marie whispered to her, "They're already sold on you. This is no test. Just enjoy."

After that she felt better. At the table, Donna Putnam asked with wonderment, "Is it true, Sarah, that you saved a high ranking Confederate officer at Antietam?"

Sarah momentarily closed her eyes. Would she ever live this down? "I did. But it was pure happenstance. He was under some dead bodies, badly wounded. I just happened to find him."

Donna Putnam seemed as giddy as Julia had back home. "That even reached the Boston papers. Did he know you saved his life? Was he handsome? Have you seen him since then?"

Sarah looked at Dr. Z. She nodded at her. "Yes, he knew I saved his life. He was nice looking, although badly wounded. I saw him once several months later in the Baltimore base hospital. Not since then. The papers made far too much of this. They sensationalized a simple battlefield foray to find any wounded who might have been missed."

The women looked at her. Sarah felt embarrassed. They acted like she was some kind of heroine. As she toyed with her dessert, Rosalind Cabot asked her, "Marie has shown us the letters of recommendation, from a Dr. Rizzo, and from Mother Bickerdyke, that you are gifted with your hands. that you would be a wonderful surgeon. Sarah, do you truly aspire to this?"

She said slowly, "I hope this is the talent the Lord has given me. And that I may use it well. Yes, I aspire to this, however difficult it may be."

She must have said the right words. For the women both seemed to have something in their eyes. Marie put her hand on her knee and squeezed reassuringly.

Before they left after the lunch, both women solemnly affirmed their support of Sarah and their financial commitment. "After all," said Rosalind Cabot, "what better use can we make of our husbands' money than to further the training of worthy women in medicine. The noblest profession of them all. One that women should be so suited for. If only the male doctors could be dethroned from their self-imposed dynasties, and their arrogance.

"And if Harvard won't admit women, we'll seek out the most prestigious European universities."

"Hear, hear," said Donna Putnam and Marie.

As Marie drove the carriage back to the hospital, Sarah asked, "Do you really think there's a chance I can be admitted in Zurich or Paris?"

"I hope for the best, Sarah. Your credentials and experiences are so good. You'll have the very highest recommendations. But one can never be sure, for pioneering women threaten the status quo. We think the male establishment in Europe is not as rigid and biased as here. But one prejudiced doctor could close the opportunity. What I am sure about, Sarah, is that you must never give up. If this doesn't work out, we'll pursue other avenues. Even abandon surgery for a while. The important thing is to get the M.D. Still, we mustn't give up planning for Europe."

"It looks like it takes more than money."

"Money alone might not be enough to do it." She smiled sympathetically at Sarah. "But I think you better redouble your efforts to refresh your French. If you get admitted to either Paris or Zurich, this is the language of choice. You mustn't let an opportunity be lost."

#

Two weeks later Marie asked Sarah to go with her on another emergency. "This is a young woman who has been knifed, not on the face but in the abdomen. She's pregnant. It sounds like we'll have some work to do before she can be transported back to the hospital."

They rushed to Marie's carriage. The messenger rode with them and directed the way. Somehow, Sarah became suspicious of him. He was too evasive. Supposedly the brother of the victim, he didn't know how advanced the pregnancy was. He was vague as to the circumstances of the injury. He contradicted himself as to whether the young woman was conscious or unconscious when he left. Now he seemed increasingly nervous as they neared their destination.

The weather on this mid-February night was a mixture of sleet and snow. A high wind whined eerily down the mostly deserted canyons of the city. The route took them deeper and deeper into the slums. Finally he directed them to turn into a dark street. "It's in the middle of the block," he said.

"Don't you have any street lamps here?" Marie asked him.

"The wind must've blown them out," he said.

"I don't like this," Sarah whispered.

"I don't either," Marie answered.

"Here it is," he suddenly said, and leaped from the carriage, and quickly fastened the horse to a post.

In the darkness, Sarah was aware of running footsteps and men's muted voices. Before she and Marie could step down from the carriage they were roughly grabbed and thrown to the pavement.

Now someone lit a lantern and they could see four men surrounding them, including the messenger.

"What's this all about?" Marie demanded. "We're here to give medical treatment to an injured woman."

The men laughed uproariously. One smirked, "You'll have to give treatment to yourselves, then, that is if we let you live."

Sarah tried to sit up and get to her feet. But a vicious blow drove her face down into the cobblestones and she was briefly dazed. She knew then that she and Marie were going to be raped, and probably killed. Strangely, she felt very calm about this and she wondered how that could be. But calmness did no good without weapons.

She thought about screaming for help, but knew this would do no good in this dark and deserted street. She tried to shield her vital organs with her arms against their vicious kicks, but above all she tried to protect her hands.

Now a wild-eyed man with a dark scraggly beard grabbed her hair and pulled her head up from the cobblestones. She thought he was going to break her neck, but then he grabbed one of her arms and flipped her on her back. He came down hard on her, pressing his knees against her shoulders immobilizing her. In his hand he had a knife, which flashed in the light of the lantern.

He bent over her, his spittle spattering her face.

As she cringed helplessly, he laid the blade against her cheek. "I should slash you 'n let you work on sewing yourself up. You're so good with a needle 'n thread I hear. C'mon, plead with me, you bitch."

"Please, Please don't," she whispered, as he raised the knife. She closed her eyes at what she knew was to come.

The knife did not descent. Now she dimly heard a voice saying, "Don't kill them! We weren't hired to do that. Grab their belongings, and the horse, and let's get out of here. But first, we have to smash the young broad's hands and fingers. Todd, hold her hands flat on the pavement, while I smash them with my boot."

"Oh God, no . . . !" Sarah cried as she tried to fight a vice hold on her wrist. Now she was whimpering, "Oh God, no. I wanted to be a surgeon. Please, don't do this. God help me!"

But it was no use. Her strength was useless against that of the several men. She cringed at the thought of what was to come. Not so much for the pain, but for the ruined dreams. "Please, slash my face, but leave my hands alone," she pleaded.

The bearded man, Todd, giggled. "The broad's more concerned 'bout her hands than she is 'bout her face. Maybe we should do both?"

The other man gruffly ordered, "Let's get the hands first. Good and smashed."

Dimly through the blood seeping into her eyes from a scraped forehead, she could see him raise his boot.

Suddenly there was an animal cry of rage. And a scream from one of the assailants. "Holy Jesus, she cut me!" Another man stumbled away clutching a bleeding arm and shoulder.

Sarah's hands were suddenly released.

"C'mon, let's get outta here before the old bitch cuts us all!" somebody shouted. Sarah could hear the rapidly receding footsteps. Miraculously, her hands were still intact.

"Sarah, Sarah! Are you all right? Did they smash your hands?" Marie was at her side, reaching for her hands, then cradling her head.

"I'm okay, now." Sarah suddenly felt nauseous, and bent over and retched on the pavement. Marie moved over to help her, and held her trembling body.

"I was so scared," Sarah sobbed. "I thought sure they were going to ruin my hands."

"So was I, Sarah dear. So was I."

As Sarah became calmer, the wonder of their escape set in. "What on earth did you do? Where did you find a weapon?"

"I was suspicious. As I know you were, too. I hid a scalpel under my blouse. I wasn't going to use it if this were a simple robbery and assault. Too much danger of them killing us, if I did, I thought. But then when they were going to smash your hands . . ."

"Was that you that made that wild animal sound?"

"I was so damned enraged. I bet they thought I was a crazy woman."

They held each other again, now laughing and crying, almost hysterically. "I guess you showed those hoodlums," Sarah said.

"Let's get out of here, before they decide to come back and get revenge."

The horse was nervous at first, but settled down to Marie's soft voice. Once they were out of the dark street into more light, they could see the full extent of their ordeal.

"Do I look as bad as you do?" Sarah asked. Marie's face was bruised and bleeding, and she knew her's was, too.

"I wouldn't be surprised if we both have broken ribs. They kicked us pretty good. But your hands were the big concern." Marie squeezed her hand. "The thought came to me that your hands were what this was all about. They wanted to destroy your hands, so you couldn't be a surgeon. I don't think these were ordinary hoods. The setup was too suspicious. They knew too much about us, about our procedures. Evidently even about you sewing up that woman's face."

"I know."

"Do you have an enemy, that you know of?"

"Nobody I can prove. But I have my suspicions."

Marie looked at her, the glow of a street lamp casting shadows on her bruised face. "Cassidy?"

"I wouldn't have thought she'd go this far. Now I don't know. But I can't think of anyone else."

"I doubt we'd be able to prove anything. Not without one of the attackers getting caught and confessing. And that's most unlikely."

"Still," Sarah mused, "I wonder whether Elaine will be able to look us in the eye and act normal. If she really conjured up this whole thing."

"I don't know. If she's hardened enough she might be able to cover up any involvement."

"I have an idea," Sarah said. "Why don't we let on that the police have found a clue about one of the assailants, and that he's about to be picked up? Wouldn't that make a guilty person likely to flee?"

Marie thought about this. Then she quietly laughed. "I think, Sarah, that maybe you missed your calling. You should have been a detective, a female Sherlock Holmes."

"Well, it was just a thought."

"And a good one. I think we should talk this over with the police. If Elaine, or whoever is involved, suddenly leaves the hospital, this makes for a strong suspicion. The police might be able to follow up on this, and maybe apprehend all the participants."

CHAPTER 14

Thad left Carolina shortly after the bittersweet farewell with Lucy. He felt guilty about his relationship with her even though she'd promised to wait for him. Still, it was unfair to expect her to wait, while he sought another woman. They both recognized this involved that Union nurse Sarah who was so much in his thoughts that he couldn't give his heart to any other woman until it was resolved. The quest was like an obsession.

He took the train to Baltimore. There he hoped to talk with John Rizzo to see if he might know of Sarah's whereabouts. The idea of seeing Rizzo worried him, for he had reckoned him to be his great rival, with Rizzo having all the cards. He would not have been surprised if Rizzo and Sarah were already married. It seemed such a natural. All he, Thad, had was the most presumptuous hope. Just because she had once saved his life, why would this beauteous creature feel attracted to him? He wondered if she would even remember him, after so many years.

His inquiries in Baltimore were not very fruitful. Dr. Rizzo had left for parts unknown. But one of his former nurses tried to be helpful. "Do you know where he is now?" he had asked her.

"Perhaps in western New York state," she replied. "He was planning to start a private practice in a small town. After all those years for a great cause."

"Yes, a great cause it was," Thad assured her. "He helped save my life in that cause."

She looked at him, her eyes large. He sensed that she had a crush on Rizzo, maybe almost as Lucy had on him.

"He was a wonderful surgeon and physician," she said softly.

"That he was, wonderful," Thad admitted. "I would so like to find him, and thank him."

"I wish I had more information of his whereabouts. I do know that his wife who had long been institutionalized had gotten better. I believe they're living together again." She sighed. "I wish them both well."

Thad's heart leaped. Sarah and Rizzo must not have married! Could there really be hope for him? Could Rizzo provide a clue to her whereabouts? "Could you guess where in western New York he might have gotten established?" he asked the woman.

"As best I know it would not be a big city such as Buffalo or Syracuse. On the other hand, a very small town probably would not support a good surgeon, do you think?"

"You're right," Thad said. "You've been very helpful, more than you know."

#

He resolved to go to western New York and investigate the larger towns for a Dr. John Rizzo. The task did not seem particularly daunting, provided the doctor had indeed settled in upstate New York.

Ten days later he found a Dr. Rizzo listed in the town directory for Ithaca, a nice university town on the shore of Cayuga Lake. The address of his clinic was not far from downtown.

He checked in at the Inn and walked to Rizzo's clinic that afternoon. About a dozen people were in the waiting room. "I'm an old patient of Dr. Rizzo. From the War," he told the receptionist. "I just wanted to stop by and say hello to him." He could see she was impressed.

"What is your name, sir?"

"Thad Barrett, ma'am."

"I'll tell him you're here. I'm sure he'll be delighted to see you again."

Rizzo strode into the reception room only minutes later, and quickly recognized him. "Major Barrett, how wonderful to see you." They embraced, in front of the wondering patients. "Please come in my office. We must make arrangements to get together after I'm through here."

He ushered Thad into a nice-sized room, light and cheerful looking, with diplomas and certificates gracing one wall, and books another. The doctor waved him to a comfortable chair and sat down next to him rather than behind his desk. He looked appraisingly at Thad. "Thaddeus, you look good. Well, maybe a little thin. But healthy. And I noticed you're walking well. Hardly a limp. We must bring each other up to date. I'd invite you to the house for dinner, but Rachel isn't much up to entertaining, yet. Although she's getting a hell of a lot better."

"Whatever you say is fine. I certainly don't want to impose. I couldn't tell you I was coming since I didn't know where you were exactly. A nurse in Baltimore thought some small town in western New York. I found your name in the directory when I got in this afternoon."

"Then you must have really wanted to find me, to go to all this trouble."

"No amount of trouble would be too much, to see the man who saved my life." Rizzo waved his hand in modest deprecation. "But I do have some things I'd like to ask you, John."

Rizzo scribbled an address on a piece of paper. "Thaddeus, let's meet at my house for a drink and then we can go to the Inn for dinner. You can meet Rachel, but this way we won't put her to any trouble."

Thad easily found the house that evening. It was a rather imposing large frame structure on a street with similar large homes. The lot was well treed, and Cayuga Lake could be seen through the trees a block away. The good doctor must be doing well for himself, Thad reflected, as he ascended the front steps and touched the door knocker. Rizzo opened the door and ushered him in.

A dark-haired very slender woman waited inside. "Rachel, this is Major Thaddeus Barrett, who I've told you about."

She extended a thin hand and he found himself gingerly gripping it. "Welcome, Major Barrett." Her voice was low and husky. "I understand you met during the War, under the worst circumstances."

"Yes, your husband saved my life. But please call me Thad."

"Then you are certainly welcome here. I'm sorry I didn't know in time to invite you to dinner, Thad."

"We didn't want to impose, my dear, especially on such short notice," John Rizzo interposed. "So, I've already made reservations for Thad and me at the Inn. I'm sure you won't mind, Rachel."

"We have so few visitors, John," she said wistfully.

"We should do our socializing rather slowly, my dear. You know that."

"Yes, of course."

"I'll be back about ten o'clock, then, dear." He kissed her on the cheek.

"Goodbye, Major Thad," she said as they left.

#

"Rachel has had some problems," Rizzo explained, as he drove the carriage to the Inn. "She had to be institutionalized for some years and while she's a lot better, I must be careful she doesn't try to take on too much. She especially has problems with new situations. I hope you understand."

"Of course. She's a very beautiful woman."

"Yes, that she is. But very fragile."

Later over dinner, Rizzo again complimented him on how well he was handling his wooden leg. "Except for a slight limp, no one would take you for having lost your leg. Does your chest bother you at all?"

"Not much. Only if I have to lift something very heavy. I never expected my wounds to have turned out as well. Thanks to you and Sarah I'm almost a whole man."

Rizzo stared at him. "Why really did you go to all the trouble to look me up, Thad? Not merely to thank me for saving your life? After all, you were one of many."

"No."

"It's about Sarah, isn't it?"

Thad toyed with his coffee cup. "I had thought you and Sarah would be married."

Now the doctor examined his hands. "One never knows what God has in store for us. What route he has laid out for each individual. I think . . . God has in mind for Sarah more than simply marriage to a country doctor." He looked at Thad, his voice maybe wistful. "Her destiny may be greater than married to either one of us."

Thad felt a chill go through him. He was vaguely aware of his stump suddenly throbbing. He stared at Rizzo, unable to speak. Now the doctor averted his eyes and quietly continued. "After being institutionalized as a hopeless mental case for years, Rachel suddenly got better, able to leave the institution. Some of her doctors said it was a miracle." He was quiet, thinking. Thad could hear some laughter in the background, but he was engrossed with John Rizzo's revelations.

Finally the doctor continued. "I had wanted to divorce Rachel and try to persuade Sarah to marry me when she came back to Baltimore again. I don't know if she would have consented. But I felt obligated to go back to Rachel, to help her recover her life. I was able to buy a practice in this small town, and it has been a satisfying life. But I sometimes wonder how Sarah's doing."

"Do you know where she is?"

"No. I do know she tried to get into medical schools in Philadelphia and New York City, but failed to break the male dominance. I tried to help her as best I could. I put her in touch with a pioneering woman doctor in New York, but evidently nothing came of it. She has a letter of recommendation from me. I wrote it in the strongest language I could, for I think she is truly gifted. Dedicated. Would make a wonderful surgeon." He took a deep breath. "I would truly like to know if she succeeds."

"So would I."

"Tell me about yourself, Thad, how life has treated you. We have all been scarred by that War."

"I'm a professor at a small town in the hills of North Carolina. I was there before the War. Like Sarah I guess, I also have a dream, to be a writer, to maybe be an influence for the better, to maybe touch the heart." He paused as the waitress brought more coffee. Rizzo was silent watching him. "That's partly why I wanted to see you. I want to find Sarah, of course. But I'm also researching a book on Civil War medicine." Thad laughed. "I certainly should know firsthand about that, shouldn't I?"

"Yes, from the patient's perspective, but you need it from the doctor's and the nurse's perspectives, too, don't you?"

"Right. And from the perspectives of both the North and the South, although I doubt there was too much difference in medical care. To begin with, I was hoping to interview you."

"I'd be most happy to tell you all I know. I'm afraid most of my remarks will be critical. As you know, medical care was abominable during most of the War. Yet, I suppose the very process of gearing up to handle thousands upon thousands of injuries was a tremendous accomplishment."

"Even if they threw amputated limbs out the doorways like firewood."

"Yes, that was surely part of it. As Sarah can attest." Rizzo stopped and looked around. They were the only ones left in the dining room. "Thad, why don't you come home with me tonight. Let us put you up. We can talk more about this there. If you need to stay another day or two, that would be fine."

"Won't Rachel object?"

"I think it would be good for her to have a pleasant house guest."

"I've already checked in at the Inn."

"We should be able to cancel that."

The front desk of the Inn presented no objections and it was a simple matter to transfer Thad's two suitcases to Rizzo's carriage. They drove back to his house along the quiet tree-lined street. The evening was balmy and people were strolling. An almost full moon cast shadows and the lake glistened through the trees. "This is a pleasant town in the summer," Rizzo remarked.

"Where was Rachel hospitalized? Nearby?"

"At Binghamton, about fifty miles away."

"Is that why you moved up here?"

"I had an opportunity to buy a practice in Ithaca, and it seemed better for Rachel not to be thrust into too big a city."

"You must love her very much."

"I found out I do. But I also loved Sarah. The two women could not be more opposite—one so vulnerable, the other so strong. Yet both beautiful women."

"Yes, that they both are."

"Ah, here we are." An attendant came from the shadows and took over the horse. Rizzo led the way into the house.

"I'll tell Rachel we have a guest."

She did not reappear that evening. Soon Rizzo came back with some brandy. "Rachel is fixing up a spare bedroom." At Thad's expression of concern, he assured him, "It's no trouble. She told me to tell you welcome. She'll see you in the morning. Meantime, this is a good opportunity for us to talk about war medicine. Brandy always loosens my tongue."

Thad took notes and asked questions, but mainly Rizzo talked volubly. Thad could see the skeleton of his book project emerging.

Sometime around midnight, there was a lull. Then Rizzo said quietly, "We haven't tackled your hopes to find Sarah, have we."

"No. Any ideas?"

"I've given this some thought, Thad, since this afternoon. I may have a lead for you. You probably don't know this, but Sarah couldn't get a decent nursing job at an Army hospital."

"She saw me in the hospital the day before they shipped me home." He saw Rizzo's eyes widen. "Yes, and she told me the hospital didn't want her. Even with her battlefield experience. I believe she was going down to Washington to try to see a woman named Dix, who I guess was in charge of military hospitals. I never saw her again."

"I didn't know you saw her then."

"I told her I was in love with her. And that you were too."

Rizzo stared. "What did she say?"

"She said she was overwhelmed, that she didn't want this."

"Yes, I can see her saying that."

"Evidently the trip to Washington to see Dix did no good?"

"No. Dorothea Dix who ran the entire Army nursing organization wouldn't have her, wanted no young attractive women. Said she could scrub floors if she really was dedicated to helping."

"Dammit, what a waste that would be."

"Yes. Well, I was able to put her in touch with a rather remarkable woman in the West with Grant and Sherman, Mary Ann Bickerdyke. Sarah worked with her for the rest of the War and I understand became her understudy and associate. I wonder whether Bickerdyke might know something about Sarah's whereabouts. You should talk to her anyway for research for your book."

"John, that sounds like a great lead."

"The only trouble is I don't know where Bickerdyke might be found. During the War she operated out of Chicago with the Sanitation Commission, but with the War over I doubt that it's still in existence. But you might get some information in Chicago. After all, she was a rather prominent woman. I believe she came from a small town in western Illinois and could be back there, or else corresponding with some friends there. You'll need to find out which town."

"I should be able to do that."

"Another brandy, Thad?"

"One more would be fine. You've stimulated my mind more than it's used to being."

Rizzo poured the drinks, and they sipped them appreciatively. After all, much had been accomplished, even if Sarah's whereabouts was still unknown. But Thad felt that his odyssey to find Sarah was getting closer to the end. Now he sensed that Rizzo still had something more to say about this.

"Is there something else, John?"

"Another possibility occurs to me. If all these leads come to naught in finding Bickerdyke, one man in Washington might know where she is. General Sherman."

"Sherman?"

"He and Bickerdyke were very close friends. She and Sarah did great things for his men. Bickerdyke even rode with his generals at the Grand Review. Incidentally, I hear that Sherman will likely be named General of the Armies, so he should be in Washington now."

"I doubt he'd want to talk to me."

"Just mention the name Bickerdyke to his aides and I'm sure he would."

They sipped their brandies reflectively.

"You've been a wonderful help. How can I ever repay you?"

"If you could write me sometime and tell me how Sarah's doing, that would be repayment enough." He stared at Thad. "You know, it is said that if you save someone's life you are forever bound to that person. I sometimes wonder if the same is not true for someone's great career: if you help make it possible, you are forever bound to that person. I just hope I may have helped Sarah's dream come true. If so, I'd truly like to know."

"I'll keep in touch, John."

#

The next morning when Thad came downstairs, Rachel had breakfast waiting for him. John had already left, having an early surgery. Again he was struck by her uncommon beauty, dark hair encompassing an elfin face dominated by her brilliant eyes, her body slender to the point almost of emaciation.

"Good morning," she greeted him. "I hope you slept well."

"I didn't want to be an imposition," he said gently.

Now she smiled. "It's no trouble. I'm glad to have some company. John is so protective. He thinks I'm not strong enough to do any socializing." She sighed. "I guess I can't escape the lodestone."

"He loves you very much, you know," Thad said.

"Does he?"

"Of course."

"No he doesn't," she whispered. "He's in love with someone else, a nurse from the War."

Thad stared at her curiously, his pulse quickening. "Why do you say that?"

"If he didn't feel sorry for me . . ." She snuffled, and tears gushed from her eyes. Thad started to rise from his chair, to try to comfort her. She motioned him back. "No, I'm all right. I'm so sorry. I'm trying to control my emotions. But it's so hard sometimes. If it wasn't for me . . . he'd marry that nurse. I know." She was again sobbing.

Thad rose this time and took her in his arms. Her body was so thin, so vulnerable. He tried to kiss her tears away. And she was responding. He pushed her gently away and raised her chin to look directly into her eyes. "Let me tell you something, Rachel. Your husband loves you very much. At one time when you were away he thought he was infatuated with this nurse. With Sarah. As I was, and still am." Her eyes were searching his face. "But when you needed him, he willingly came back to you and gave up all thoughts of Sarah. I on the other hand am still pursuing a phantom love."

She touched his face. "You are indeed a nice man, Major Thad. Thank you for telling me this. Was she very beautiful?"

"Beautiful, yes. But no more beautiful than you."

Rachel sighed and moved away. She sat down at the kitchen table and rested her chin on her hands, still staring at him. "Then Major Thad, I wish you success in finding your phantom love."

"And you, Rachel, rest comfortably in the embrace of your husband's love."

Thad departed soon after to catch the train for Chicago. He was eager to follow up on this Bickerdyke connection. Bickerdyke should not be impossible to find. After all, she was a prominent woman. He had the feeling now that she would be the conduit to lead him to Sarah. Somehow, the eyes of Rachel, the pain in them at first and then their changing with the hope he had given her of the love of her husband, stayed with him on the tiring journey. Perhaps he had brought something positive to her life. Might God be smiling on him.

#

"Mary Ann should be home. She was in heah just a few days ago to do some shoppin'. She doesn't do much travelin' these days. Says she's had enough for three lifetimes durin' the War." The shopkeeper squinted at Thad. "She's a purty great lady, you know."

"I know she is. That's why I want to see her. To interview her about her efforts during the War."

"You're a newspaper man, then?"

"No. I'm writing a book about Civil War nurses and medicine."

Thad could tell the older man was impressed. "Wal, she's the one who knows."

"Is her place easy to find?"

"Jus' take the pike road west 'bout four, maybe five miles. There's a little road that comes into it from the north. By a single cottonwood tree that some homesteader planted years 'go. If'n you look closely by the tree you'll still see the foundation of their shack. Wal, take that road three, four miles and you come to her place. It's painted white—Mary Ann always says that white signifies cleanliness and purity. Most people 'round here never painted their houses till Mary Ann showed them."

"Does she have a ranch?" Thad asked curiously.

"Wal, 'round these parts folks don't call them ranches. Jus' large farms. She does raise some cattle though."

"Thank you. Much obliged." Thad turned to go.

"If'n you hurry, you oughta make it by supper. Knowin' Mary Ann, she'll be glad to feed you and put you up."

Thad rented a carriage for the drive out to Mary Ann's. He was beginning to think of her now as Mary Ann, rather than Bickerdyke, as everybody he had contacted had called her Mary Ann. He was rather reluctant about starting out now for her stead. If the owner of the store was right as to distance, he would be arriving at suppertime. Poor timing, this, he thought. But he hated to waste another day before trying to see her.

The drive was long enough to allow him plenty of thinking time. He wondered what kind of a welcome he would get, an enemy officer. Would she hold that against him? He wondered if Sarah had ever mentioned him to her. But his greatest concern was whether this was a wild goose chase: did Mary Ann have even the vaguest idea where Sarah was? His optimism at Ithaca two months before had faded.

It had not been easy getting to this point. Only with great difficulty had he tracked Mary Ann to Galesburg, Illinois, a small town about thirty miles east of the Mississippi. He had about given up finding her roots. But inspiration finally came to him to check with an editor of one of the Chicago newspapers: after all, she was a famous woman, or at least deserved to be.

He was surprised at the cooperation of the people at the paper. They were eager to talk about Mary Ann Bickerdyke. Her exploits had been widely publicized and had evidently impressed many in this interior of the Union. He wondered whether Mary Ann realized how venerated she was.

Unfortunately, her esteem in Chicago did not immediately translate to finding her present whereabouts. But the clue of Galesburg did. It took little time there to find any number of people who at least knew about where she was: somewhere in Kansas. The specifics took longer. The minister of a church in Galesburg finally supplied the specifics needed. Thad was profoundly grateful that he did not have to approach General Sherman to find her. He could imagine how that might have gone.

On the train across Iowa and into Kansas he had found this land so different from the mountains and green fertility he knew. The land was empty, practically without trees, and the sky was huge. It awed him. He wasn't sure if he could ever love this land, or whether with more familiarity he would detest its emptiness. Yet, somehow he felt that the closeness to God that he had always felt in the green and fog-shrouded mountains of Carolina was also present in these vast expanses. The mark of God was on the land. But why had He permitted the terrible War?

The directions of the storekeeper were accurate. He had easily made the correct turn off the main pike. At least he thought he had. Now to watch for this white house near the road, the one that Mary Ann had painted as an example to her neighbors.

There it was! No mansion for sure. But about what he expected from the stories of Mary Ann. Well kept up, clean, rising white above the starkness of the plains in this late October. With some apprehension he pulled his horse in front of the house and stopped there. It was dusk now, and the sun was about to set in a ragged sky. A woman had come out on the porch and was quietly watching him.

"Mary Ann Bickerdyke?" he called.

"Yes," she responded, and came down the steps peering at him.

"You don't know me," he said, "But I've been looking for you for some time."

"What in goodness sakes for?" she had come up to him, a short, stocky woman, who had to look up to his tallness.

"I'm seeking information, and I think you may be my last hope." Now he stopped, rather embarrassed. "Oh, please excuse me, my name is Thad Barrett, although you don't know me."

She stared at him as the setting sun turned the side of the house reddish. "Major Barrett. How could I not know you? You're the man that Sarah saved."

He started. "She told you my name?"

"Many times she mentioned you, and wondered what had become of you. How you were doing, and whether you ever thought of her. She wanted to find you in North Carolina immediately after the War ended. But we discouraged her. We thought it too dangerous with the roaming bands of still armed men." Now she took his arm. "Please come in the house, Major Barrett—I'll get somebody to take care of your horse—and let us feed you after your long ride and prevail on you to stay the night, and maybe longer. I sense we have a lot to talk 'bout."

"The burning question I have, the main reason I sought you out, Mary Ann— may I call you Mary Ann? Please call me Thad." As she nodded, he continued, "Do you know where Sarah is, where I might find her?"

His heart leaped as she said, "I think I do, Thad. But we'll talk 'bout this after supper."

Mary Ann's two tall sons joined them for supper. Talk was mostly light banter, but Thad learned something about the economics of farming in this country where rainfall could not be depended on, and where cyclones were a fearsome threat in the spring and summer. During dessert, Trapper, the youngest son, curiously observed, "You and Mom were on opposite sides during the War." He looked at Mary Ann. "I don't understand how you can now be friends when you were once enemies."

"There was no hatred among wounded men, Trapper," she said. "Just as there should be no hatred among brothers. For we were all brothers, fighting for different causes. Isn't that right, Thad?"

He answered slowly. "I think today there is more hatred in the South, among different factions, than there was for those who fought on different sides during the War. Then we were all fighting for some cause bigger than we were, even though we only vaguely understood what that was. We were fighting other brave men, to save ourselves but also because of the pride in our army and with it, ourselves.

"Now a scourge is sweeping the land, the Ku Klux Klan, the hooded ones, whose hatred toward Negroes and those whites they think sympathize with Negroes knows no bounds." Thad stopped. They were all staring at him. "I'm sorry. I'm talking too much. But I've had some bad experiences with hatred and the Ku Klux Klan."

"Trapper, you shouldn't ask such profound questions. Not at the supper table anyways," she admonished her son.

Later, Thad and Mary Ann talked quietly in her parlor. He told her about his research for his book on Civil War nursing and medicine and she promised that if he stayed another day or two she would give him enough material to fill several notebooks.

Then they talked about Sarah. "She wrote me about her great troubles in Philadelphia and New York City in trying to get into medical school or even into a satisfactory nursing position. I put her in touch with a wonderful woman doctor in Boston. Her name's Marie Zakrzewska. I've had several letters from both Sarah and Marie. Marie's really impressed with Sarah, thinks she has a chance to get into medical school and study to become a surgeon. I haven't heard in the last few months, but there's some thought that if she can't get into school in this country she might go to Europe to study. Until then, she's working with Marie at the New England Hospital for Women and Children in Boston."

Thad listened intently. He wondered whether Mary Ann noticed his excitement, for he felt like getting up and pacing around the room. He took a deep breath. "I must go there as soon as I leave here. Maybe I've waited too long to try and find her." He looked down and without realizing it tapped the wood of his leg.

She stared at him, concern etched on her face. "I don't think Sarah has a man," she said softly. "But I don't know with medical school that she has time to think of romance. Her quest to be a doctor is so all consuming."

He gnawed on his knuckle now, all pretense of self-control seeming to have fled. He finally said, "I guess now that I'm so close to finding Sarah any hope I had of winning her . . . well, you just dashed it."

She put her hand on his arm. "I'm sorry, Thad. But all may not be lost. If you're patient with her and supportive. And not try to discourage her wonderful talent, her gift, for that's what it is."

He stared at her, as she continued. "Go to her, Thad. I've always thought a woman can be more than a loving wife and mother. A wonderful career doesn't have to be sacrificed." Now she looked at him shrewdly. "Or do you think it ought to be?"

"No, no! Certainly not." He sighed, and gnawed his knuckle again. "Nothing should destroy her wonderful talent, and the contribution she can make. I think a career and a family would be wonderful."

"Well, then, you may have to tell her that."

Thad spent the next day and evening with Mary Ann, tapping her great knowledge and criticisms of medicine during the War. She suggested he contact Dr. Randall, the doctor Sarah helped with surgery at the Lookout Mountain battle near Chattanooga, "although I don't rightly know where he is now." She also suggested he contact Dorothea Dix, head of Army nurses during the War, for her "biased" thoughts. "You certainly will want to talk with some nurses and doctors from the South, won't you?" He agreed. This was necessary for a thorough study of the wartime medicine.

He left the following morning to drive into town and flag down the once-a-day train that led to parts east.

"Give Sarah my love," she told him. "Tell her I approve," she said mischievously.

"Approve what?" he couldn't help responding.

"She'll know," was all she'd say.

#

He arrived in Boston five days later to an early season blizzard. It was only the second week of November but the city was paralyzed for two days. He had trouble getting from the depot to a nearby hotel. There was no chance of pursuing Sarah at New England Women's and Children's that day.

Now that he was here and on the verge of seeing Sarah, he was scared. This would be the first time they had seen each other since 1863 in the hospital at Baltimore, some six years ago, and he doubted she would recognize him. She might not even remember him, even though years ago she had spoken of him to Mary Ann. So much had happened, to both of them, so many years gone a slithering. Even if there was a flicker of something, surely his wooden leg would turn her off. For, while he was able to get around tolerably with it, there was no disguising that he was crippled, not a whole man. Added to all this baggage was the worry that Mary Ann had planted in his mind. That Sarah was so dedicated to her odyssey to become a doctor, and a truly wonderful quest it was, that she would have no time to consider romance. Maybe some time far in the future. But not now. Still, this was not a new worry. It had nagged him years ago in Baltimore.

He had great difficulty sleeping that night. The hotel room was stuffy and noisy. Part of the trouble had to be that he was not used to big city hotels and on a frugal budget you had to put up with some discomfort. But his concerns about Sarah would probably have kept him awake even under luxury accommodations.

Toward morning he finally fell asleep, and again had that strange dream of years before. He was standing on the brink of a canyon or crevasse. On the other side he could see Sarah crying out to him. But he could not reach her. There was no way they could be united, no matter how much they wanted to. He awoke, shaken and drenched in sweat. God help me, he prayed. Don't let this dream be a prophesy, that we can never be together.

The next day found little transportation moving yet. Thad wondered if he could reach the hospital on foot. He found the place on a map. It was about thirty blocks from his hotel. He thought of trying to walk there but bitterly discarded that idea. Were he an able-bodied man he might be able to, even though the depth of the snow would make walking difficult. With his artificial leg, it was out of the question. He would have to spend another day and night in this miserable hotel, alone with his worries. He tried to look over his notes from John Rizzo and Mary Ann, and organize them. But his mind was not on this. He couldn't concentrate.

He finally went down to the bar off the lobby. The place was rather quiet, not surprising for this snow-bound city. But a few women seemed to be appraising the customers. He suspected they were prostitutes.

One moved to the bar chair next to him. "You look lonely."

He looked at her. She was nice looking, but rather heavily made up even in the dim lights of the bar. Her face somehow reminded him of his memories of Sarah. And after all these years, her perfume was the same as he remembered Sarah's, a wonderful relief from the smells of that terrible hospital in Baltimore "Do you think every man sitting alone at a bar is lonely?" he asked her.

She laughed, a little like he remembered Sarah laughing. "Probably most are. But some more." She started to get up.

"Can I buy you a drink?" he asked, surprising himself.

She sat back down, and nodded to the bartender. She looked at him appraisingly. "Are you a talker or a doer?"

"Only a talker."

"Okay, just for a little while." She had a nice smile, but her perfume was strong. "You look sad. As though you lost someone close to you. Is that it?"

"You're very perceptive."

"It's my job to be. Do you want to tell me about it?"

Thad found himself telling her: saved by this Union nurse, then the many years apart, now on the threshold of finding her, but the unlikelihood of love winning out over her career.

"Do you love her?"

"I'm afraid I do. But it may only be of a dream woman."

"Never give up, never." She touched his wrist. "Now I must go." As she stood up, she asked, "What is her name?"

"Sarah . . . You remind me of her. That's why I wanted to talk with you. What is your name?"

"Clara. My name is Clara." She placed her hand on his shoulder. "When you see Sarah, tell her that Clara thinks she's a lucky girl." With that the woman left, leaving her perfume behind.

#

Things were getting back to normal by the next morning and Thad was able to get a taxi to the hospital. "My wife thinks the docs and nurses there are the best there are," the driver told him.

"Why is that?" Thad asked curiously.

"They're more caring. And the place is so clean. And they specialize in women and children. Ah, do you have someone there, sir?"

"A nurse, who saved my life in the War."

"Ah, man, have you seen her since then?"

"No."

"Jeez, wait'll I tell my wife about this."

They pulled up to the building. It appeared to be a large three-story house. It looked sturdy and had a nice yard surrounding it. Thad learned later that this main structure was connected by a covered passage with three smaller houses behind it.

His heart was pounding as he navigated the steps and entered the front door. The lobby was full of women and crying children. As he looked around, somehow he had the impression not of confusion but of a well organized operation. While the room was not large, there were enough chairs and people were waiting patiently. Some were conversing with each other as they waited. At first he thought he was the only man here but then he spied several waiting with their wives.

He approached the desk. A blond woman looked up and slightly frowned at him. "Did you wish to see someone, sir?"

"I'd like to see Sarah Lindsey, when she has time."

She looked at him curiously. "Sarah's not here. Can someone else help you?"

His disappointment must have shown in his face, for the woman looked sympathetically at him, he thought, or was it pity? "I'm an old friend of hers, from the War. I haven't seen her since then. Didn't know where she was." He took a deep breath to quiet his racing pulse. "Is she only gone for the day?" he asked hopefully.

The woman looked at him keenly. "I think maybe you should talk to Dr. Z. Just a minute, sir." She motioned to a white-clad woman who had just come into the lobby, evidently to call someone into an examining room. "Rose, would you see if Dr. Z could talk with this gentleman? What is you name, sir?"

"Thaddeus Barrett."

"He wanted to see Sarah."

"I'll see if she can spare some time."

As the woman left, the woman at the desk smiled at him. "Mr. Barrett, why don't you sit over there. I'm sure Dr. Z will want to see you as soon as possible."

"Has something happened to Sarah?" he asked anxiously.

She smiled. "Nothing bad, Mr. Barrett. Only good, very good."

In his concern, and maybe the realization of this long odyssey nearing an end, he couldn't sit. He wandered over to the window and gazed out, his mind a turmoil of conflicting emotions. Out of nowhere came the memory of the woman named Clara who had the same perfume as Sarah so long ago. What had she said? Ah yes, Never give up, never, she had told him.

A voice spoke up behind him, "Major Barrett."

He leaned against the window frame, almost overcome with emotion, for he had not used that title today. Sarah must not have forgotten him after all these years.

He turned around. A dark haired petite woman smiled gently at him. "Major Barrett," she said, "I'm Marie Zakrzewska." She extended a small hand and gripped his firmly. His confusion must still have shown in his eyes.

"Sarah's told me a lot about you, how you met and all. But please, let's go to my office to talk." A smile illuminated her face. As she led the way he realized that this woman was younger than he'd expected. But from what Mary Ann had told him, she had accomplished so much against an entrenched establishment.

The room was small, with a desk, rather uncluttered, and two plain chairs. There were no pictures on the walls, only one framed diploma, an MD, he could see, awarded from Cleveland Medical College of Western Reserve. He couldn't see the date. "Sit down, please, Major Barrett," she said kindly.

"Ma'am, please call me Thad."

"All right, Thad, and call me Marie." She looked appraisingly at him. "Sarah often wondered what had become of you. Whether your wounds healed sufficiently. Whether you were able to work again—I believe she told me you had been a professor before the War. She had hoped to try to find you afterwards, but then the opportunity was gone.

So perhaps you can bring me up to date about your life, and what brings you here." As he started to speak, she held up her hand. "But first I know you wish to hear about Sarah."

Thad nodded. "The woman at the reception desk said it was good news."

"It is good news. Then perhaps not so good. Tell me, how do you feel about Sarah? As a friend . . . ?"

"I think I've been in love with her, ever since she found me on the battlefield." He wondered if she was testing him before she would reveal Sarah's whereabouts? "In these years since then my love has not diminished. If anything, it's grown stronger." Now he looked down at his hand resting on the wooden knee. "But my confidence in her feeling likewise has never been very strong. I've long thought I was only tilting at windmills."

"How did you find this place?"

He explained his long search, and the clue supplied by Dr. Rizzo, and the final resolution to the search given by Mary Ann Bickerdyke.

"Ah, yes, Mary Ann. She's the one who brought Sarah and me together. She wrote me of this wonderful battlefield nurse, and surgeon. And how she was unable to find a medical school that would even consider her."

She looked solemnly at Thad now. "This brings us to where Sarah is. Wonderful for her career dream. Maybe not so wonderful for any romantic inclinations."

Thad stared at her, and his suspicions now of what she was to say faltered his heart. "She's in medical school?"

She nodded, "Yes. A wonderful opportunity. She started two months ago."

"Where is it? Maybe I can at least see her. At this point I'd be willing to go anyplace."

"She's not in this country. She was accepted by a prestigious school, the Sorbonne in Paris, France. She'll be there for three and a half years."

Thad gnawed on his knuckle. "Well, I guess that's it," he finally said. "The end of a dream for me." He looked up, trying to present a brave front. "But the beginning of a wonderful dream for dear Sarah. How can I be anything but pleased for her." But he suspected that his face belied his words.

Marie was staring at him, saying nothing. Finally she suggested softly, "Thad, it doesn't have to mean the end. You two have been apart for six years now. Three more years is far from a lifetime, and may be worth waiting, for both of you." Now she asked sternly, "But are you willing to wait?"

He was silent a long time, trying to sort out his turbulent thoughts. He looked up and said resolutely, "I'd be willing to wait longer, if I could be sure she wanted me to wait."

"Then why don't you ask her? You can write her, you two should have so much to write about. I can give you her address. If you really love her, you can court her by mail."

CHAPTER 15

With trembling fingers, Sarah opened the letter postmarked from Paris, France. This had to be the acceptance or rejection, that momentous missive that would so profoundly affect her life! At first, she was afraid to look at it. So much depended on these few sheets of paper. She gritted her teeth, expecting the worst, and steeled her nerves. Now, with wonder, she read the verdict.

> Miss Lindsey, it is our pleasure to admit you to the Fall of 1869 class at Sorbonne. Your achievements and the powerful letters of recommendation have been duly noted. Should you decide to specialize in surgery, as you indicated, this should be possible. Congratulations.

The letter went on with further details, but she was too excited to read this carefully. After all, the important thing was the acceptance. She had to tell Marie as soon as possible.

Now she was glad Marie had so strongly encouraged her to study her French. For these many weeks she had thought it a futile exercise, one with no payoff. Better her time be spent in studying Marie's medical books and notes.

Now the payoff was at hand. Still, she had serious doubts about her facility in French. After all, she'd only studied it from books and vocabulary lists. She had never heard anyone speak it. And she wondered whether she would be able to understand lectures.

She took a few minutes to look out the window of her flat, to calm her racing pulse. The view was of a busy city street, dirty and noisy. She had often contrasted this with the tranquility and beauty of Pikeston, the small town in Pleasant Valley where she had grown up. At first she had never thought she could get used to the big city. And God knows, she thought, since the War she'd seen plenty of big cities: Baltimore, Washington, Philadelphia, New York City, and now Boston. Somehow, since she'd been in Boston she'd grown to love the city. She knew this was partly because she had been so accepted here. She had to ruefully concede that the prejudices and even hatreds that festered in her small town under the veneer of hills and green fields were magnified far more than they were in the diversity of the city. Now in early June the scene below her window seemed redolent with optimism and hope.

She sighed and turned away from the window. She had herself under control now. Soon it would be time to leave for the hospital and Marie.

#

They hugged and stood with tears streaming down their cheeks. "Such wonderful, wonderful news!" Marie finally managed. "I wasn't sure we dared even hope for this."

Together now they studied all the instructions that had come from Paris. She was to report the second week of September. She would need to get there at least a week ahead to arrange for accommodations and get oriented. The college could provide information on suitable accommodations.

"How long do you think it'll take to get to Paris?" Sarah asked.

"I understand a steamer takes about two weeks to get to a French port. Then probably a day or so by train to Paris. You probably should plan to leave here early in August, to give yourself a little time to get settled." She laughed happily. "We certainly wouldn't want you late to your first classes, would we?"

"I'll miss it here, and you."

"We'll miss you, but it's such a breakthrough." Marie took her arm, "C'mon, let's tell the staff the news. Then we must get word to the good ladies, Donna and Rosalind. I'm sure they're waiting eagerly for this."

The congratulations appeared sincere, Sarah thought. Everybody seemed genuinely pleased and excited about one of their own having this glorious opportunity. She hoped none were harboring secret resentments and jealousies. Like Elaine Cassidy. Her thoughts briefly went back to that fearsome experience in a dark alley when she and Marie were almost killed by hoodlums. It must have been Elaine who planned the assault, for she abruptly left the hospital for parts unknown right after. Sarah tried her best after that to be humble and unassuming, to do nothing that might arouse any animosity from her co-workers. Marie had been careful not to be too obvious in her preferential treatment and esteem for Sarah. At least in public. But Sarah wondered, how could you ever be sure that someone did not harbor bitterness and jealousy, but hid it well until the opportunity came to do harm?

Her friend, Dr. Dreyfus, told her, "Sarah, I must say I didn't really think you had a ghost of a chance for such a prestigious school. You know, it puts Harvard to shame. Well, a pox on Harvard." He kissed her then, full on the lips. "Girl, you go over there and show them what a good woman can do. Come back here after, and be the brilliant surgeon I know you can be."

"Thank you, Dr. Dreyfus, for all your help and support," she murmured.

#

"We're invited to a celebration party at the Cabots," Marie told her over coffee a few weeks later. "You'll be the guest of honor. They want to give you a sendoff for the journey to Paris." Marie had, of course, told the two women the news, and they had invited her and Sarah to another luncheon shortly after. Such a luncheon apparently was not enough in their eyes. Now they wanted to throw a party.

"I don't need this," Sarah told Marie. "I've no desire nor aptitude for high society."

"It can be developed, Sarah. With a little practice you'll find it a nice experience. A beautiful young woman like you can benefit from the right contacts. Especially when you become a physician."

"I don't want to become a doctor for the rich and famous."

Marie put her hand on her arm. "Listen up, my dear. These contacts have made this possible for you, and for all women who might aspire to become physicians." She lowered her voice. "Now let me confide something else. It looks like through my contacts with the Cabots and the Putnams and their friends we're going to get the money to build a new and much bigger hospital. Not to help the rich and influential. But the needy."

Sarah stared at her wide eyed, overwhelmed with the persuasive ability of Marie. "I think you should have been a politician. How great, Marie."

Marie laughed. "Now do you think you and I don't need this socializing?"

"I'll do my best," Sarah promised.

"That'll be plenty good enough."

#

They drove to the Cabot mansion in Marie's carriage.

The building was imposing, just like the Putnam's, with big stone portals and a curving driveway. Tonight there were lights in every window. Attendants were efficiently taking care of the horses and carriages, and well-dressed people milled around the front entrance.

Marie had prevailed on Sarah to buy a new dress, a bright green affair that highlighted her dark hair and eyes and showed off her shoulders. "Think of it as an investment, my dear," Marie had told her as she almost choked at the price.

She knew she'd be self conscious wearing such a gown, but now as they climbed the stairs and entered the massive parlor she felt more at ease. The room was already crowded with men and women in elegant attire. Rosalind Cabot and Donna Putnam must have been watching, for they quickly came forward to greet them.

"Sarah, how lovely you look," Rosalind said smiling. "You too, Marie," she added as an afterthought.

Marie winked at Sarah. Rosalind caught the wink, and grabbed both their arms. "Let's introduce you to the guests." She and Donna led them to one end of the room where an ensemble of musicians were tuning their instruments. She had them stand on a platform while she clapped for attention.

"Dear friends," she said. "Welcome to Cabot Manor. As you know, this occasion is to honor our first woman admitted to the prestigious Sorbonne College of Medicine, one of the great medical universities in the world. This pioneering woman's credentials were so impressive they simply had to admit her. Of course, Harvard wouldn't," she couldn't help adding, with a pointed look at someone in the audience. "So, we're most pleased to introduce Sarah Lindsey."

The applause was polite, but Sarah noticed a few men were not applauding. She gave a brief bow. Apparently she was not expected to make a speech, and she was thankful for that.

Now Donna Putnam stepped forward. "Another honored guest is Dr. Marie Zakrzewska, who many of you already know, founder and leader of the New England Hospital for Women and Children. Dr. Marie was instrumental in bringing forth Sarah Lindsey as our candidate of merit."

The applause was stronger now. Evidently Marie had really won the hearts and pocketbooks of many of these people. She was not surprised at this. But she was rather discomfited that several men still did not join in the applause.

Afterwards, Sarah mingled with the other guests. Most of the time either Marie, Donna, or Rosalind were with her to make introductions and smooth the way. So many names and faces, she knew she could never remember them all. But she tried to be friendly and modest at their congratulations. In truth, she would rather be administering aid in the vilest slum than be here. She chided herself for not enjoying this.

Sometime later, as Sarah had a chance to sip a cup of punch between the socializing, a man approached her. He was of stern visage, with deep-set eyes framed by heavy eyebrows, his craggy face topped by unruly graying hair.

"Miss Lindsey, my wife hasn't seen fit to introduce us. But I'm her husband, Jonathan Cabot." His voice was very deep, and his eyes were difficult to meet for any length of time.

Sarah's voice faltered as she tried to make conversation. "My deepest thanks to you and Mrs. Cabot," she managed to say.

He peered at her, unsmiling. "You may as well know," he said, "I was not in favor of . . . this violation of the Biblical injunction for the role of men and women. I do not think any woman is suited for the life and death decisions of medicine. At least not in the role of doctor. And especially not in the role of surgeon. I was against this from the start."

"Why, then, did you permit it to happen?" she asked curiously, forgetting to be intimidated.

He stepped back slightly, surprised at her modest aggression. "My wife is stubborn in her way, a woman of strong convictions. She has the misguided idea that women can do the same things as men, that their roles are interchangeable, rather than complimentary." He sighed then, and Sarah wondered if this man's formidable presence was only a facade. "Miss Lindsey, I love my wife. I have no desire to sacrifice my happy home for the cause of women in medicine." Now he peered at her, his face that of an eagle surveying his prey. "But mark my words, young woman, I think this . . . adventure into a man's world is doomed, and I'll be quick to pounce on any evidence of your unsuitability."

Sarah stared at him, her hackles rising. "Let me guess, sir. You're on the board of Harvard University?"

He fell back again, a step, a brief hesitation. "How did you . . . ? Yes, I am."

"Then that explains why I have to go to Europe to get my medical education rather than here."

He glared at her for a few moments. Then, "Excuse me, Miss Lindsey, I have other guests to attend to."

The evening finally ended. On the ride back with Marie, Sarah told her about her confrontation with Jonathan Cabot, and her fears that she may have muffed her opportunity to receive support.

Marie was quiet a long time. Sarah was aware of the clapping of the horse's hoofs on the cobblestones and wondered if this presaged the trampling of her opportunity.

At last Marie spoke to reassure her. "Jonathan Cabot is a well-known chauvinist. That's probably why Rosalind didn't want to introduce you. But for all his bark, she rules the household."

"Well, he certainly intimidated me. Doesn't he intimidate his wife also?"

Marie laughed. "She has more money than he does. And she's an independent thinker. He doesn't control the decisions where Rosalind's involved." She was still chuckling. "I sometimes wonder how she puts up with him, his prejudices and inflexible mindset. But you have nothing to worry about that source of funding."

"He admitted he's on the board of trustees of Harvard."

"Now did he. You must have been quite aggressive in your probing. Good for you. Yes, he's one of the ones who so adamantly oppose any women being admitted to medical school at Harvard. He may be the biggest obstructionist."

"He threatened me. He said he'd be quick to pounce on any evidence of my unsuitability."

"Well, you'll just have to give him nothing to pounce on. Being in the top ten percent of your class should do that."

CHAPTER 16

In the immediate months ahead not many things stood out in her memory. Much of the time was spent in unremitting studying. No recreation, no socializing. She was determined to show these arrogant men, both back home and here, that she could do the work as well or better than any man. But it was more than that. In the depths of her soul she hankered so much to learn all she could about the human body. She yearned to perfect her surgical skills, to make the most of the talent she believed God had given her. The advances of some of the young men, her fellow students, as well as a few of the instructors, she rebuffed, trying to be tactful and not to make enemies, but not always succeeding in that.

She had tried to keep at bay her trepidation since the notification of acceptance. But it broke through, before the ship even reached the French port of Havre. The French language was the first major concern. She had spent the several weeks on shipboard frantically reviewing her French. Despite studying the language every chance she could back in Boston, she still had little confidence. She was able to practice on several French passengers during the voyage, but was appalled at her difficulty in understanding them, especially when they talked at normal tempo. She realized now that being able to read French was a far cry from understanding it when spoken. She knew this was going to cause great trouble unless she could quickly master it. But she didn't know if she could.

"My child," an older French woman tried to assure her, "You must board with a French family that will be willing to coach you. In a few weeks you'll get by reasonably well, I'm sure." But Sarah had no such confidence.

Upon reaching Paris, she went to the University for her class schedule and the list of recommended places to board. She was very thankful that Marie had insisted she get to Paris ten days before classes. She spent several days looking for lodging and settled on staying with an older couple who promised to help her with the language, especially at meal times.

But with the first day of classes so close, she was scared. Not only of language problems, but of how well she could handle the class material. But even more than that, she worried about how well she would be accepted in this dominion of males. She was sure some would try to make life miserable for her, maybe even in fiendishly clever ways. Would she have any supporters? In her pessimism she doubted there would be any. Oh, maybe a few tacit ones, reluctant or afraid to go against the mainstream.

This new situation—a foreign environment, nobody she knew and could confide in or ask for advice, the uncertainty of it all and of her ability to cope successfully—brought her awakening at night drenched in sweat and pulse pounding, as in a nightmare.

Her conversation with Dr. Ranvier, the top administrator of the College, helped not at all. At first she had thought he was the kindly, fatherly type. Perhaps he was, but his prejudices still seemed just below the surface. She wondered how she had ever gotten accepted here.

"You will be the only woman," he had told her, speaking slowly so she could comprehend. "We're not sure how our students will react."

She stared at him silently. He must have interpreted her silence as fear, for he hastened to reassure her. "Do not be afraid. If the men are too unruly, or if they are too much distracted by your presence, we may have to make arrangements for you to sit away from them."

"I would hope they'd soon get used to me."

"Yes, that is the hope, but we'll have to see, won't we, young woman?" He gazed at her speculatively. "There is another possibility that the faculty has discussed. You could disguise yourself as a man."

Despite her trying to maintain a calm demeanor, her face must have betrayed her thoughts of this option. Dr. Ranvier again tried to reassure her. "That wouldn't be so bad, would it? At least it would enable you to conduct your studies without provocation. You should think about it."

"I will not attend school under false pretenses!"

"Very well, young woman," he said pompously. "The faculty and I wish you the best."

Afterwards in her room, she sorted out her apprehensions. Not being accepted by her classmates didn't bother her so much. She could live with that. After all, she was not attending this university for the social benefits. Or to find a man, she wryly thought. Still, too much disturbance might cause the school to cancel her admission.

Not the least of her concerns was that the academic studies might be beyond her. After all, her formal education was limited. Would she ever master this language, so essential for the important lectures? Above all she feared what her failure would mean to all those who had supported and financed her and, hopefully, for those who would come after her. She was doing this not only for herself but for women in general—to break the bastions of male dominance of this highest profession. That was why she could never consider hiding her sex under male garments. She ruefully recognized that she was carrying a heavy burden. "Dear God," she prayed, "let me be up to it. Please guide me so's not to let down all those wonderful people in Boston." Now of a sudden, her plea to God reminded her of that time so long ago, the eve of the battle of Antietam, when she feared letting down the brave men about to face the terrible battle, and fervently prayed.

#

One of the events that was to stay in her memory was that first class. The subject was anatomy and it was conducted in a large lecture hall with perhaps 150 beginning medical students. All men, of course, but for her.

Professor Bernutz saw fit to introduce her to the class. "Gentlemen, this is Sarah Lindsey, from America, our first woman medical student. Please make her welcome."

The class erupted into bedlam. Some were cheering, but most were booing and pounding their chairs and even shouting obscenities at her. Sarah was not sure but what she was going to be physically assaulted. Several men moved to protect her, however. One asked her during the height of the disturbance, "How can you be so calm about all this, mam'selle?"

She stood quietly watching the commotion. As it began to die down slightly, she told him, "After being a battlefield nurse, this should hardly faze me." The young man raised his eyebrows, then stared at her without saying anything. Sarah wished she hadn't said that. It smacked of bragging out of weakness. No one would probably believe this anyway.

After about ten minutes, Professor Bernutz tried to restart his lecture. "Are you here to learn, or to agitate?" he shouted at the still unruly class. Gradually they settled down and became quiet, although many were still glaring and shaking their fists at her.

"Miss Lindsey," he said before getting into his lecture. "Perhaps you would feel safer up here on the platform with me." He had brought out a chair that he placed to one side of the lectern.

Sarah stood up and said, "Professor, I prefer to sit here with the rest of the students, if you don't mind." This raised another howl of protests and obscenities. Finally, Sarah was forced to take her seat away from the other students if there was to be any lecture and learning this day.

Afterwards, Professor Bernutz talked to her. "Young lady, you see the difficulties your presence is making for us. Do you still want to continue this maybe futile effort?"

"I didn't expect things to be easy, sir. I'm prepared to stick it out, even if I'm an outcast." Now she grimaced. "I just hope, sir, that you won't deny me this chance. I've been pursuing it, oh for so long."

He studied her. "I admired your calmness today. You didn't seem afraid at all."

"I was afraid. Not of physical harm. But very much afraid that you wouldn't let me continue in the class."

"Still, maybe you Americans underestimate the explosiveness of the Frenchman. Some critics would even say the complete lack of control."

"I don't think your country has the patent on rowdyism."

He laughed then. "No, I suppose not. Well, if you're willing to continue despite what may come, I'll certainly not deny you the opportunity. Incidentally, it looked to me like you had several young men prepared to defend you."

"Yes, a couple of brave souls."

He laughed again. "Some Frenchmen are chivalrous, you know. We're not all rowdies."

She laughed, too. "I know it. And I was counting on that."

"You are plucky," he said more seriously. "Still, I think it best that you sit up here in front for a while—you'll be on public display, of course. Does that bother you?"

"I'd prefer not to be. But if you think it's best, then for now, I suppose."

"I also think you should enter and leave by the side door, the same door that the professors use."

So in subsequent lectures Sarah sat in front, off to one side as far as she could place the desk and chair, but still visible to most of the student body. She diligently strove to maintain a calm demeanor and to take copious notes. She didn't know it then, but her studious concentration was to influence these and future students. She was setting a higher standard, strictly by example.

A little over a month later, Jacques, the student who had been one of her protectors and to whom she had mentioned her wartime nursing under the stress of the student protests, caught her in a hallway. "Miss Lindsey, do you remember me? I'm Jacques Lavelle."

"Yes I do, Jacques, although I didn't know your name. I never got to thank you for protecting me. But please call me Sarah."

"Okay, then Sarah. Quite of few of us have been talking about our treatment of you that first day. It was terrible. Many of the men are ashamed. I've been spreading the word about your wartime nursing. And your not getting rattled with all the insults. Well, many of us would like to have you join us, rather than sitting up there in front. Would you ask Professor Bernutz to have the class vote on your becoming a regular student?"

Sarah felt her eyes tearing. Damn, why couldn't she control her emotions better. She tried to wipe the tears away unobtrusively, but knew she had failed, as Jacques was watching her closely. She touched his arm. "Thank you, Jacques. I'll tell Professor Bernutz what you said."

So it came to pass that Sarah rejoined the students to a rousing round of applause. A few dissenters still raised their voices but they were drowned out by her supporters. She found out later that information about her Civil War exploits had become common knowledge among the student body. She wondered about that, for she had not mentioned it on her application and only briefly with Jacques. Was this to plague her the rest of her life? She couldn't seem to escape it. But was that so bad?

#

Despite her eventual acceptance by most of her classmates, that winter of early 1870 tested her mettle to the core. Long, cold, gray and wet, the weather was made worse by the lack of adequate heating. She shivered in her room despite wearing as many clothes as she could muster. Added to the misery was the grinding tedium of work if she were to achieve her goals. She had no time for recreation, and hardly enough for eating and sleeping. She would get up in the cold predawn and try to study by candlelight for several hours before going to the children's hospital for four hours until noon. Then to the library for research and further studying until late afternoon. In the evening were various classes, lectures and laboratories. A chemistry class in particular was causing a lot of work. She had never had chemistry, unlike most of her classmates. Despite her commitment, all this was getting her down.

The only bright spot was her French. Her understanding of the spoken language had greatly improved, thanks to the conscientious help of her landlady. She remembered the first time she attended church in Paris. The sermon was beyond her. Now she could understand almost all the words.

Around Christmas, Jacques had asked her for a date.

He was a rather handsome fellow, with his dark hair and beard, and his intense eyes. But she had no time for a romantic interest. It was all she could do to try to cope with her studies. She reluctantly turned him down, trying to be as nice about this as possible.

"I'm sorry, Jacques, I just have too much work to do, too much studying."

"You can't study all the time," he had said, rather peevishly.

She tried to mollify him. "I have to, Jacques. Otherwise I'm not going to do well. So many people back home have staked me, and are counting on me to do well."

But it seemed no use. "You just think you're too good for the rest of us. A hell of a way this is to treat a friend! Well, I know better now." He had stormed away. Now she wished she hadn't turned him down. She wondered whether she could have been more tactful. She hoped she hadn't made an enemy, but feared she had. Only a few letters from supporters back in Boston sustained her in the difficult times.

#

Then in February a letter came, postmarked Chalfant, North Carolina. It was from that Confederate major. In the last few years she had almost forgotten him, even though he had once filled her thoughts. They were only ships passing in the night she had come to think. He wrote:

Dearest Sarah,

After all these years maybe I have tracked you down. If you receive this, then this part of the odyssey has been successful.

My great congratulations for gaining admittance to medical school, and a most prestigious one from what I hear. I had hoped to visit you, but Europe is beyond my means.

Please permit me to say that you have been in my thoughts ever since Antietam. I have not been able to banish these thoughts. Nor would I want to. For, dearest Sarah, I love you. For all these years since Antietam.

Ah, but I am so presumptuous. Riding the slender hope that you might somehow feel the same way toward me—someone you haven't seen except in the mud of a battlefield and the barrenness of a hospital for these many years.

I hope your wonderful quest to be a doctor may still leave room for love. I could be proud of a famous doctor wife.

A brief note about me. My wounds have all healed, although I have a wooden leg with which I get around quite well. I have gone back to being a professor at the small college here. And I have become a writer with modest success. The green and blue hills of western North Carolina still comfort me, but the hatreds around here are appalling.

If you ever have time, please write me, dear Sarah.

Your great admirer, and more,
Thad Barrett

The letter brought solace to her these bleak winter months.

She tried to analyze her feelings about him.

It had been so long, she could hardly remember what he looked like except that his face was kind and gentle. Now the thought of him brought a stirring. The spark must still be there, she thought. Or was it simply that she was so deprived of male companionship? What was it he intimated? That he could live with her career aspirations? Many men could not, she was sure. Even these young doctors-to-be who were her classmates. She would be willing to wager that most could not tolerate a successful doctor wife.

She must pen a letter to him, soon as she could, she resolved.

But it was several months before she did. She was studying very hard for the first major exam of the five she would need for the medical degree. The candidate made the decision when he felt ready to take these exams. They would be both written and oral, and might also include some laboratory exercises, perhaps anatomical. The oral would be conducted before a board of three professor doctors, and spectators would be welcome.

She had already taken and passed several preliminary written exams, required before one could sit for the medical ones. One of these that she had worried about was chemistry. But her work ethic had placed her near the top of her class. In retrospect she thought her lack of good facility in French was less drawback in chemistry where so much emphasis was on symbols rather than the meaning of words.

The first crucial medical exam though, that was something else, she knew. Especially the oral part where she would be interrogated and any weaknesses probed to the probable delight of the audience.

She dared not think of Thad before this was out of the way. Then she would write him, and express, what . . . ? She didn't know. How was it possible to express your love when you had only seen a person two or three times and that was many years before? But she marveled. Thad had done so. He must be a dreamer, indeed.

#

It was late May before she had enough confidence to think about sitting for this first exam. Two other students would also be doing so at this time. One was Jacques. As they gathered to go into the testing room, she whispered to him, "Good luck." He looked at her with seemingly no recognition and did not deign to reply.

The first part of the exam involved several hours of written questions. After this the papers were gathered and the candidates immediately escorted to the amphitheater, open to the public. This day it was crowded with onlookers. Sarah wondered how many had come to see her flub it. She observed a flat table in the center of the stage, with a cadaver stretched out. Each candidate was asked to describe various arteries, nerves, and muscles for different parts of the body and cut into the tissue to demonstrate. The third student, a young man named Jules, at this point bolted from the room, evidently sure he was not sufficiently prepared. She and Jacques remained.

Next, each was questioned before the board. The chairman turned up an hour glass and the interrogation lasted until the last grain had fallen. Jacques was first, and as she watched she became more and more apprehensive as she saw him falter before the barrage of questions. But most of these she knew, if she could only express herself adequately in this language. Finally, Jacques' time was up and he left the center chair. Now he looked at her and shrugged, his face wretched.

Somehow, now that the time had come, she found herself with the same icy detachment she had experienced in other traumatic situations: the battlefields, the sewing up of Lucy's face, the hoodlums in the alley, yes, and even the first anatomy class here and the near riot of the students opposing her admission. As the questions came, she realized all her months of preparation were paying off. She felt reasonably confident and entirely knowledgeable. Several times her French let her down as she misunderstood a sentence or did not make her reply quite specific enough. About half way through the interrogation, she realized suddenly that the professors' attitudes had swung strongly positive.

Several were smiling at her, nodding at her answers, looking at each other in agreement. When her time was up, they each shook her hand, congratulating her. "Miss Lindsey, if your written work confirms what we've seen here, you will have passed this first exam with highest honors," the chairman told her. She shook her head in wonderment, her eyes tearing again. God, how she hated this expression of her feminine vulnerability.

Jacques accosted her in the hallway, his face dark and menacing. "Well, Lindsey, you succeeded in showing me up. How dare you?"

"Jacques, I was only trying to pass the exam. I'm still not sure I did." She tried to place her hand on his arm but he abruptly pulled away.

"I won't forget this," he muttered as he stalked off.

She shuddered at this latent display of animosity. Why do people resent it so when she was only trying to do her best? Her sisters had, and Elaine, and now Jacques. Why?

That night she tried to compose a letter to Thad. She wanted to apologize for not answering sooner, she wanted to express her appreciation for his interest, she wanted to share with him her present triumph, but she feared to do this. And she wanted to try to tell him that she was interested in him but didn't know if it was love. After all, they hardly knew each other, and it would be additional years before anything could possibly come of this.

She didn't know if she would be able to convey the right blend of promise, yet hesitation. The thought struck her that she probably would turn Thad off just as she had Jacques. She shivered at the probability that in the interest of seeking and hopefully attaining her career quest she might be relegating herself to old maidhood: no husband, no children, no real home.

As she posted the letter to Chalfant, North Carolina that May evening, she had no way of knowing that communication with America would soon be closed down for months.

#

On July 19, 1870, France declared war on Prussia. France had hoped for support from Italy and Austria but did not receive any. Still, the French army possessed modern equipment in some respects superior to the Prussians. But Prussia was better led, with Otto von Bismarck, and quickly pushed through Alsace and encircled a French army at Metz in August. Another French army, attempting to relieve Metz, was severely defeated at Sedan in September. There Napoleon III surrendered and was taken prisoner. Prussian troops quickly pushed on to surround Paris, but the city held out under a long siege, not capitulating until the end of January at which time Prussian troops marched down the boulevards into a silent and prostate city.

An armistice was declared, but the tribulations of Paris were not over. As the Prussians watched from the heights controlling the city, but did nothing to stop it, a civil war raged until the following summer between the mobs of Paris and government troops from Versailles.

The impact of the war was immense in Paris. Except for Sarah and other foreigners, medical students were all called to arms. Even hospitals were stripped of interns. The fortunate ones were assigned to the medical service; otherwise, their lot was as common soldiers.

While there were no formal classes during these months, Sarah was able to pursue her studies and preparation for the second medical exam. However, distractions were on all sides. The city was full of soldiers preparing to defend it, some 400,000 she had heard, but most of these were untrained and not even well armed. They were called the National Guard, but they really were more a rabble, and were joined by the radicals and misfits of society.

It was impossible to send or receive letters with the outside world, although she heard that some mail had gotten out by balloons. Most foods, especially meat, potatoes, green vegetables, butter and bread soon became in short supply. Sarah found to her surprise that wine, chocolate, and coffee remained plentiful the whole time. But desperate to find meat, Parisians slaughtered their pets and horses—just as Sarah remembered the people of Vicksburg doing under Grant's siege. Even the zoo was emptied of its animals as the starving city continued to resist.

The winter was as severe as any on record. In this coldest of winters, fuel became even more scarce than meat. The trees of the boulevards were cut down for firewood. The gas was cut off in November and the nights were spent shivering in darkness while sporadic and indiscriminate shellings brought civilian casualties and forced many, including Sarah, to huddle in basements when the guns were pounding their part of the city. It was, of course, impossible to leave, whether you were native or foreigner. The last chance to leave had been back in September.

Sarah found herself spending more and more time at the hospital, what with no formal classes and the difficulty of studying. With the absence of interns and some doctors, and the steady inflow of casualties, both military and civilian, as well as those suffering from pneumonia and other afflictions of deprivation, her services were well needed.

With the capitulation and occupation of Paris the end of January, Sarah had thought the worst of the ordeal would be over. But that was not to be, as the city became engulfed in its own revolution, reminiscent of the reign of terror in the original French revolution of the late 1700s. Except that now, thank God, there was no guillotine.

Sarah continued to devote most of her time to the hospital, although now with long winter fading into spring and more daylight she was able to do more studying. But Paris was still under siege, this time from the troops loyal to the French government at Versailles. The university had not reopened as yet and she feared for the lost productive time. What she was doing was primarily repetitive nursing duty at the hospital, and hardly adding to her knowledge or skill.

The situation came to a head in the latter half of May.

A sudden influx of wounded men flooded the hospital. One was Jules, the young man who had taken the first exam with her and Jacques and who had fared so miserably. He was not wounded too badly, although one hand was wrapped with a bloody rag.

"Sarah, I hoped you'd be here. The Versailles troops are breaching our barricades. The city's lost!"

"Never mind that, Jules. Let me look at your hand." She gently unwrapped the bloody cloth. His hand was smashed by a rifle bullet. She looked at him soberly, and suddenly remembered that dark alley in Boston and her hand about to be crushed.

"It's not good, is it?" he asked quietly.

"I don't think you're be able to be a surgeon," she said. "I'm so sorry, Jules."

He smiled grimly. "Don't be, Sarah. I quickly found out that wasn't for me."

"But you can still be a doctor."

"Sure, sure I can."

Soon the resources of the hospital and the doctors and nurses were taxed to the utmost with the wounded pouring in. All were despairing that the city could be saved from the Versailles troops. "They're showing us no mercy," some said. "They're far worse than the Prussians."

Sarah and the other medical people worked to the limit of their endurance. When they could go no further, they dragged themselves to a corner and curled up for a few hours of exhausted sleep. Sarah had not worked this hard since her Civil War days. But at least now there was adequate drugs and water, and sanitary conditions were far better than a decade before. No cannon balls and small arms fire was threatening them.

But something else soon did.

"Fire! Fire! The city's on fire!" the cry went through the hospital.

Sure enough, flames and smoke were spreading throughout the city. Even the hospital buildings seemed in danger.

Now the cries became more frantic, and Sarah could smell the acrid smoke. "We have to evacuate the hospital! Everyone has to be moved outside! Hurry!" The word spread quickly throughout the hospital.

Racing against the spreading smoke, Sarah and the rest of the staff evacuated everyone.

No nearby buildings were any safer from the spreading fires, so they used the yard outside to place the wheelchairs and litters. Sarah and some of the doctors braved the increasingly dense smoke to save badly needed medical supplies. Fortunately the weather was warm and fair, and unless a sudden storm blew up the patients should be relatively safe for the night.

Toward dusk as Sarah was helping some of the patients outside, a strangely familiar voice harshly sounded in her ear, "Lindsey, so I find you helping the rabble."

She whirled around. There stood Jacques in the uniform of an officer of the Versailles, the conquerors of Paris. He was staring at her, his face a mask.

"Jacques, I wondered what had happened to you. It's good to see you," she bravely tried to say.

Her remarks seemed wasted as he continued to stare at her, with that same intensity she well remembered and had come to fear. "I'm not surprised to find you on the side of the insurgents." He spit out the words. "And we're prepared to punish those who are!"

"Punish?" she asked in bewilderment, her pulse racing at the implication. "What are you saying, Jacques? I'm simply being a nurse and helping the sick and wounded, whoever they may be. I haven't taken part in any insurrection or whatever you call it."

He grabbed her arm, his face close to hers. She shut her eyes momentarily to hide from the hate she saw in his face. Why, she asked herself, why such hate, when all she had done was turn him down for a date?

"Woman, we're rounding up thousands, nay, tens of thousands. They'll all be executed or imprisoned," His spittle was striking her face. "Just like you!"

She was really scared now. "But I'm an American," she weakly tried to say.

"Bitch, you're coming with me!" He grabbed her by the upper arm, and began forcing her across the lawn, oblivious to any wounded in the way. She struggled to break away. "Bitch!" he growled. He smashed her face with a fist, and she was on the ground, blood pouring from her nose and mouth. Now he gripped her by one ankle and an upper arm, and bodily began dragging her. His grips were like vices and she was powerless, his strength that of a madman.

She desperately looked around for help, but saw no medical people or attendants at all, only people on stretchers. "Please, Jacques, please don't do this," she begged. "I thought I was your friend."

"You sorry bitch!"

"Why, Jacques, why?" He continued to drag her across the grounds and then into the darkness beyond. She wanted to resist, hoping to catch him by surprise, but it was no use. Her strength was not up to it.

Finally, in a deserted alley he stopped, and flung her down on the cobblestones. She was dimly aware of the smell of garbage and putrification. Another alley, her mind screamed. "You bastard," she choked out.

Now from somewhere she summoned enough energy to fight back, to claw at his face, to kick his legs. Momentarily she was able to fight him off, and drew blood from his face. But she still couldn't break away from the merciless grip on her upper arm, and now his knees pinned her to the pavement.

"You bitch, you bitch," he kept muttering and suddenly hit her hard across the face with his free fist.

Her last conscious thought was regret for not having a scalpel as Marie had in that other alley.

She came to.

He was on top of her, his weight threatening to drive the breath from her body. Her clothes had been ripped off and he was pounding into her, grunting with the exertion, a madman.

She could not even feebly struggle now.

At last he spent himself. But he was not finished yet. His hands gripped her breasts and squeezed and pulled as if to rip them off. "God damn bitch. I should kill you," he muttered. "But I'll slash your face instead."

She felt a sharp intense, almost-burning pain across her cheek, and momentarily her mind flickered to Amy Panelli, the girl whose slashed cheek she had sewed up so many months ago.

She sank into a fog of pain fading to numbness.

Sometime later he must have finally tired of her, for she was aware that his weight was gone.

Then she felt a sharp pain as his boot attacked her prone body, and she retched, the pain driving her back into unconsciousness, dimly aware of blood everywhere.

She did not hear the sound of his boots fading away.

How long she lay there, Sarah did not know. She felt something wet on her face. A gentle feeling, not unpleasant. She heard sounds. Someone was moaning, and someone else was panting.

With a supreme effort she opened her eyes. A dog had been licking her face! He must have been the one panting. But who was the one moaning? It took her quite a while to decide that she must have been the one doing the moaning.

The dog, a short-haired mongrel, mostly terrier perhaps, had backed away, not sure whether to flee or to stay.

She tried to call out to him, and could not. But he came back and began nuzzling her.

Now she was aware that it was getting lighter in this filthy alley. Dawn must be coming. She must have been here all night!

Still not trusting herself to try to sit up, she finally gathered enough strength to attempt to assess her injuries.

She felt rather detached about her body, almost as if it belonged to someone else. Her breasts were bleeding and she knew she must be bleeding down below. The last kick must have damaged some ribs, for breathing was painful.

The back of her head felt wet and ached. Evidently she had struck her head on the cobblestones when he knocked her down.

But her face. What had he done to that? It burned and throbbed, but then her whole body was a mass of pain. She tried to raise a hand to touch her face, but felt too weak to do that. Something in her mind urged her not to try, that she was better off not knowing.

But the little dog was still with her, his tongue and wet nose, and his presence, a comfort.

Finally she struggled halfway to a sitting position against the side of a building, trying to fight off nausea and the blackness that wanted to engulf her.

She knew she didn't have the strength to drag herself from this wretched alley. She doubted she could even sit up like this for very long.

Now she wondered if the dog had a master who might come looking for him, and find her. But she discarded this hope. In this wretched city, all the pets had long ago been killed for meat. The few who were left, who had escaped such a fate, were the wild ones, too clever and too fast to be caught.

Unless by some miracle someone would come into this dark alley and find her, she was sure she would be another of the thousands of victims of this insane siege and rebellion.

Suddenly a joyous and wondering thought came to her. He had not destroyed her hands!

And he could have so easily. In his insane rage to do her harm, he somehow had forgotten about her hands. "Thank you, dear Lord. Thank you," she prayed. Her soul was uplifted with hope. Could it be that He had something special in store for her? Then like the stealth of an assassin, the merciful blackness crept in.

CHAPTER 17

Thad did his best to fight off the discouragement at learning Sarah was in Paris pursuing her career. He knew he should be pleased for her, knowing she was on the verge of attaining her dream. But he couldn't help the selfish presentiment that this meant the end of his dream. Maybe God had some greater purpose for her than simply being married to him, a humble professor and writer of little consequence. Well, he didn't know about that, but Rizzo had speculated as much, and Bickerdyke and Dr. Z also had thought her destiny was to achieve great things in medicine.

But couldn't there be a place for love in her life, even though her life might be on the verge of greatness? He would have liked to grasp this sliver of hope, but he well knew the perils of optimism: dashed dreams.

He knew he must have looked stricken when Dr. Z told him about Paris. It was obvious the good doctor thought Sarah's career as a surgeon transcended any other considerations, including marriage. He remembered almost word for word what she had told him: "Sarah's mind, her tremendous dedication, and not the least, the wonderful dexterity of her hands, will make her a brilliant surgeon. All she needs is this God-given chance."

As a morsel tossed to a dog, Dr. Z did tell him, "You can always write her," and had given him her address in Paris. But he saw this long quest as now virtually hopeless, and he did not rush to write Sarah.

He had further research to do in New York City, and then he would give the editor his partially completed manuscript. He left Boston shortly after talking with Dr. Z. Early in 1870, his work was finished in New York and he decided to return to Chalfant, the first he'd been back since late the previous spring.

#

As the train chugged across Virginia and into Carolina, he couldn't help comparing his impressions now with those of seven months before. Then the countryside was green and the trees fully leafed. His hopes, too, were fertile and beckoning. Now the country was denuded, with barren fields, bare trees, patches of snow and ice. And his hopes? They were as dashed and destroyed as summer's green by winter's hand. Oh, he still would pen a letter to her, but with little expectation of anything good coming from it.

He suddenly realized how much he had been out of touch with home. He had written Aunt Abigail twice, but since he was traveling with no set destination he could hardly expect mail. And Lucy. He'd thought little of her during these last months, had only written her once, from New York City. In the short letter he told her that he expected to be home in a month or so.

He knew his written words were not those a love-starved girl would cherish. He who wanted to be a writer, how uninspired he was. He reflected now that if she had gone and married someone else in his absence, it was his own fault, and he realized now his actions, or lack of actions, were inexcusable, even if he didn't love her. But, in truth, he wasn't sure about love, and doubted he would ever find it again.

A grizzled veteran was sitting next to him. He also had a wooden leg, but in addition a missing arm. At first they had traded memories of the War. But Thad was tired of the prattle and pretended sleep. When he was depressed he was less sociable than usual.

At last, the conductor opened the door to the car, banged it closed, and shouted, "Chalfant! Chalfant!"

As the train lurched, Thad and his companion grabbed the back of the seat ahead to steady themselves for the deceleration. With a screech, the train jerked and rattled to a stop. Thad bade farewell to his compatriot, and made his way down the aisle, his wooden leg giving him a queasy feeling of insecurity after the long hours of riding.

#

"Golly, Thad, you weren't doin' a very good job of tending to business back home here, with all your gallivantin'."

"What do you mean, Abigail?" Thad had come back to her place as soon as he reached Chalfant. While he didn't want to say it, he did wonder whether Abigail would still be her usual perky self. But he needn't have worried. She'll probably outlive me, he thought amusedly.

Abigail was saying, "Wal, rumors are that Lucy is goin' with that carpetbagger fella. Maybe they're engaged by now. Didn't she write you 'bout that?"

Thad groaned. "No, she couldn't. I didn't leave any address to reach me. Just as I didn't with you. I was on the road almost all the time, you know."

"Did you write her at all, while you were gone?" She looked sternly at him. "Bet you didn't. Your face doesn't lie."

"I wrote her a few weeks ago from New York. Told her I'd be coming home soon."

"Wal, as slow as mail is out to these boondocks you prob'bly beat the letter. You haven't seen her then, since you got to town?"

"I wanted to see you first."

"I know. To see if I was still kickin'." She smiled affectionately at him. "And now I betcha' don't have anybody on the string."

He shook his head. "I don't think so. Sarah's over in Paris and will be for several more years. I doubt anything will come from that." Now he laughed, trying to seem nonchalant. "It looks like your nephew is bound for spinsterhood."

"Wal, I think you should at least see Lucy, 'n get the news from the horse's mouth. Maybe seein' you agin will change her mind about that carpetbagger. That's if you don't foul it up again."

"I'll see her, Abigail. And I'll try to be charming. Trouble is, I've had little practice being charming."

"Wal, I thought with most men it came natural." She sniffed. "And your old flame, Kate Burnham, she's still around. Available I guess. Looking for anybody she can chew on and spit out. Rumors are she's goin' to run for the state legislature, the first woman to do so."

"I'm impressed," Thad admitted. "She ought to do well in politics."

"Are you goin' to look her up?"

"I don't think so. I don't want to be chewed on and spit out." He tried to chuckle.

Abigail looked at him closely. "You're hurtin', Thad, ain't you? Is it Lucy?"

Thad sighed. "Not Lucy, Abigail. But yes, I'm hurtin'. But I'll get over it."

"You can't get over that Yankee nurse, then?"

"I will. I will."

"Is she married yet?"

"No."

"Wal, nephew, what's so bad 'bout that. You'll just maybe have to delay your gratification for a few years."

"There's more to it than that." He hesitated, trying to choose his words. "There's some question whether she has time for romance and marriage in her quest for a great career. You see, they think she's very talented."

Abigail looked at him soberly. Then she put her hand on his arm. "Thad, I didn't mean to try to be funny. Not for somethin' serious. An' maybe it is for both of you, don' you see? She'd be a splendid woman for you, 'n you for her. An' she's not taken. Probably never will be, 'less you give up. If'n it were me, I'd sure go after that filly."

"You mean that, Aunt Abigail?"

"Never been more serious. A woman, out of the ordinary, maybe a great woman, still needs a good man. A supportive one, and a lovin' one. And you, think how excitin' life would be with such a woman."

"I have her address. I could write to her."

"Go for it then, dear Thad. Remember, you're a good catch yourself." She studied him. "Still," she said softly, "If I was you, I'd want to see Lucy. See if that affair is really dead. Don' you think?"

#

"Lucy, did you get my letter?" Thad had ridden out to the Vanderhall farm the next day to talk to Lucy and try, as Abigail suggested, to see just how serious this thing with Harlan Pettengill was. He immediately sensed a coolness. For a brief moment he wasn't sure whether he was glad or sad. If she had leaped into his arms, what would he have done?

"I got it, day before yesterday, I guess."

"I would have written sooner, and more often. But I was traveling the whole time," Thad tried to explain.

Now she smiled. "It's all right. Things have a way of workin' out for the best."

He shook his head. "No, they often don't, I've learned."

"Well, for me they have. Harlan and I expect to get married this spring."

"I thought you were going to wait for me, Lucy. That's what we promised."

"What a one-sided promise that was." Her voice rose. "You exact a promise from me. You, well, you were free to pursue your dream nurse and go to her, if she'd have you. What kind of deal is that? Harlan calls it a promise based on victimizing."

"I'm sorry, I didn't mean it that way. I guess it was unfair. And I'm sorry." He studied her face. At his apology it had softened. She was indeed a beautiful young woman. And rich besides. A man would be a fool to leave such a woman dangling with no firm commitment while he was on a lengthy absence. Unless he loved someone else.

She was saying, "Why don't you have a drink before you go. Harlan will be coming shortly, and I'm sure would like to meet you again. He's running for city council, and is really becoming an important man in the community."

"No thanks, Lucy. I must be going. Of course, I wish you and Harlan the very best."

He started to put his coat on, but it was too late. The carpetbagger just drove up.

As Harlan came in, Lucy went up and kissed him. Thad tried not to wince. "We have company, dear," she nodded toward Thad.

If Harlan was surprised, he didn't show it. He strode over to Thad and firmly grasped his hand. "Hello, Barrett," he boomed. "How good to see you back in town. Are you here for long?"

"Probably permanently. The traveling is about over, except for a few short trips."

"How's the leg, my good man?"

"It's fine. Hardly know it's not my own." Thad had always thought Pettengill was too glib, too smooth, too much of a big voice. Now he realized he was a handsome devil, prosperous looking, and with that supreme self-confidence he detested. He wondered if Lucy would find ultimate happiness with this man, or whether she would only be a waystation to his ambitions.

Harlan was going on about how Chalfant had turned itself around in the last six to eight months. "But it's not only Chalfant," he said, "but the whole South is resurrecting, is a phoenix. Or hadn't you noticed?"

Thad mumbled something. He had to get out of here. He expressed his congratulations to both of them, and fled the scene.

#

The next day Thad sent the letter that Sarah received that bleak February day. He waited and waited for a reply. Each week that went by seemed to dim the chances of any reciprocity of interest. Finally, in early July he received her letter:

> Dear Thad,
>
> It was so good to hear from you. It came at a time when I was feeling low, and it cheered me up. To think someone from my past was still thinking of me. Yes, I remember you. I'm honored that you saw fit to track me down. I'm so glad you're doing well, healthwise and careerwise.
>
> I'm sure Marie, Dr. Z, told you all about this wonderful chance that somehow came to me. Unbelievable. But work has been so hard. To make it much worse, my French was hardly good enough to handle the lectures, and I've had to really work on that. There's so much to learn, chemistry for example. I never had chemistry before, and everybody else had.
>
> I'm sorry I waited so long to answer your letter, Thad. I've just been studying all the time. The first major exam was a week ago, and I prepared months for it. Somehow, it went well.
>
> I can't expect you to wait for me. I'm sure we've both changed mightily in these years apart. Still, I'd be most grateful if you would continue writing to me. I wish you the very best, Thad.
>
> Your sincere friend,
> Sarah

The letter did not assuage his depression. It offered faint hope of anything beyond distant friendship. He showed it to Abigail.

"Wal, at least it didn't close the door. An' you certainly don't have another man to compete with."

"Maybe a dream is harder to compete with than a person."

"Only if such a dream is contrary to what you want. An' Thad, I don' think it is."

Whatever. In any case, a slight flicker of hope remained. He penned another letter to her, trying to give it the right blend of interest and detachment. After all, she had not mentioned any love for him. He should not bare his soul so readily.

As the weeks went by with no answer, he felt again the despair of rejection. She was not even enough interested in this relationship to respond to his letter within a decent time.

Then he learned of the possible explanation for her lack of response. Sam Turner told him one day, "Did you hear about the latest war over in Europe?"

He shook his head, but his pulse began racing.

"The French and Prussians are fighting each other again. It looks like the French are losing."

"How do you know this?"

"The newspaper got it on the wire service from New York. They're calling it the Franco-Prussian War." He looked at Thad, suddenly aware of his concern. "Isn't your friend, that nurse, now over in Paris?"

Thad nodded. "How serious do they say it is?" he asked tensely.

"Not good for the French. Two of their armies have been destroyed, they say. And Paris is under siege."

"That sounds bad."

"Nobody, no supplies, and no mail can get in or out."

"How about the people of Paris? Are they in danger?"

"No one knows. Still, they must be hard pressed because of the siege. I'd suspect food and other necessities are short,"

"It sounds like the siege of Richmond," Thad recollected. "The populace suffered mightily then."

"Paris is many times bigger," Sam Turner reminded him. "They surely have more resources to draw from in a siege."

"But no mail service, is that what you heard, Sam?"

"Yes. Nothing can get in or out with the Prussians surrounding the city."

In one way, this revelation comforted Thad. It meant her lack of response to his letter might not be her fault. But was she in danger? He tried to put that thought aside. After all, she was hardly practicing medicine on a battlefield. Or was she?

#

One weekend in early October, Thad decided to climb the mountain of the Cherokees that he had climbed six years before when he was barely recovered from his wounds, and had the peg leg. He remembered his difficulty then in making the climb. It would be easier now, but still a challenge without two good legs. He hoped the ordeal would help him sort out his emotions, as it had before, and maybe find solace in the situation with Sarah.

He packed a little food and water, a blanket, and a sleeping bag and planned to again spend the night on the mountaintop. The leaves of the hardwoods were in all their falltime splendor, but he barely noticed.

That night under the stars, weary from the climb, his mind was a profusion of thoughts. He remembered vividly the heights of South Mountain on the chill of a September night, a night much like this, as his men prepared to fight for their lives against an enemy poised to throw vastly superior numbers at them the next morning. He remembered the defeatism and bleakness of spirit, almost hopelessness, of his return to Chalfant after his injuries. His present feelings of despondency had to be almost as nothing compared to those days.

After all, his career was well settled now. Sam Turner had offered him the presidency of the college, wanted him to be his successor, and he had agreed. He would be not only a professor but an administrator. As for his writing, while he would hardly have a best seller, still the early reviews of his manuscript were favorable. So, why this bleakness of spirit? But of course he knew. Now memories of the last time he saw Sarah, in the noisome base hospital in Baltimore, when she brought freshness and hope with her, and gently stroked his cheek and kissed him, brought tears to his eyes. So many years ago. God, why can't I shake this enduring infatuation for a woman who is bound to be only an impossible dream?

The night air was becoming chilly, and he roused himself enough to prepare a small campfire and finished the scant provisions he'd brought along. Then he wrapped a blanket around and sat with his back against a tree, staring into the night while the flames flickered at the periphery of his visions and a pale moon poised low on the horizon. He was vaguely aware of a few night birds crying in the distance, as he tried to leave his mind receptive to whatever comfort might come. But nothing came. He finally crawled into the sleeping bag, his emptiness of spirit still with him.

The next morning he trudged back down the mountain. His stump ached from the unusual exertion, but his mind was even more stricken. He had found no solace. Unless it was that we have to go on, no matter the adversity, and couldn't there still be hope?

He began to realize that maybe that was the message from the mountain, not coming to him there, but only on the way down: there could still be hope; he must never give up.

But did he need to climb a mountain for this revelation?

He remembered now that woman in the bar in Boston when he had tracked Sarah down to Dr. Z's hospital, just thirty blocks away, but was unable to get there because of the snow storm. He was depressed then wondering whether Sarah would have any interest in him after all the years. The woman, whose name was Clara, who looked kind of like Sarah, whose name sounded similar, and who even had the same perfume, had told him never to give up. Could this be some sort of portent? Abigail had told him the same thing, not to give up. So had Bickerdyke. Dr. Z. gave him the least encouragement, but she only closed the door to hope for the next few years while Sarah was in Paris.

#

Thad took over for the retiring Sam Turner the first of the year 1871. The work as administrator was challenging, but entirely satisfying. In the aftermath of the postwar reconstruction, students were flocking to the school. The difficult days were behind. Now, Thad's biggest challenge was to hire enough capable and qualified people to handle the increased enrollment.

The book would be published in June, and now the editor and the reviewers were predicting it would be a modest success. While the payoff in money might not be all that great, the prestige could be significant.

Sam Turner told him shortly before he stepped down, "Your book may bring more publicity to the school than anything I could ever have done."

Thad had put his hand on the older man's shoulder. "We certainly had our tough days, didn't we?"

Sam sighed, "I must say, there were days when I never thought we'd make it. You made the difference, you know."

"No."

"Without you, I couldn't have staffed the school. I couldn't teach all the classes myself. I was about ready to close the college, until you came back. Then I just wanted to hang on until you could get better, and hope you would join me, despite practically no pay."

"I bet you wondered if I'd ever get well enough to be able to work again. I certainly wondered that myself."

"Abigail kept me informed of your progress. She assured me you'd be able to teach again, except she kept moving back the date."

"Yes, I can see Abigail doing that." Thad shook his head. "Aside from the physical problems, I wasn't sure psychologically I would ever be fit enough to come back and face a classroom of students, girls no less."

"Every one of the girls came to tell me how wonderful you were—they simply adored you—and were awed by you being a hero and all."

"Yes, I guess that turned out all right," Thad said sheepishly.

"So, Thad, I fully believe your being wounded at Antietam is what saved the college."

"Without your faith in me, I don't know what I would have done those days."

Now, Thad immersed himself in work, trying to escape his ambivalence about Lucy and her marriage—he had not attended the ceremony, under the excuse of out-of-town research—and, of course, the lack of communication from Sarah. He wondered how she was getting along under the siege, and whether she was in danger.

In February news came that an armistice was signed the end of January when Paris capitulated. Now the siege of Paris should be over and the populace able to communicate with the outside world, and also get needed supplies. But only a few weeks later, further word from Europe told of civil war between the government in Versailles and the Parisian "mob." The city was again isolated, and worse, violent and fanatical factions were fighting in the streets.

Even more chilling news came in May. Now the government forces had broken through the barricades of Paris and tens of thousands of people were being killed in the fighting or subsequent summary court-martial-ordered executions.

His nightmares about Sarah reoccurred. He would be standing on the edge of an abyss, and the great love of his life, Sarah, was on the other side, pleading for him to save her, as lightning and thunder crashed around them. Rescue lay with a narrow rope of a bridge swaying in the storm, but he hesitated, fearing to brave the bridge, only to see her fading into the mist, her plaintive cries dying away. He would wake sweating in twisted sheets feeling an almost unbearable sense of loss, with these emotions lingering.

One morning in early June, after a particularly bad night, Abigail finally remarked about it over breakfast.

"Thaddeus, you look like you was dragged in by a polecat."

"I'm having that dream again. Seems almost every night now."

"The one 'bout Sarah bein' across the chasm?"

"Yeah. She keeps calling to me, but I can't get to her."

"What'd you think it means? That she's in danger?"

"I have to think so, Abigail. We know from the news reports that thousands of Parisians are being killed in this civil war. Other thousands are being executed for having chosen the wrong side. I don't see how there could be any classes, and who knows what Sarah may have gotten herself into."

"I'm afraid there's nothin' you can do about it."

"I'm really tempted to try to get passage over to a French port, and see if I can make my way into Paris."

She stared at him. "That sounds like somethin' an adolescent boy would dream up."

"I have been a soldier, or had you forgotten?"

"But, dear nephew, you haven't been a spy, you don' know anythin' about France or Paris. You don't even speak the language. An' you certainly ain't as nimble as you once was. An' last, just 'cause you're havin' nightmares sure don't mean Sarah's really in trouble. Even if you could find her, would she welcome you, d'you think? After all, she ain't your wife, or your betrothed."

"I don't know, of course. Still, I feel I should be doing something." He massaged his forehead, but finally nodded. "You're right. Absolutely right."

The highpoint of the summer was the publication of the book. It looked impressive in its shiny binding and its thickness. Thad knew this should have given him great satisfaction and pride. But his worry over Sarah's fate dominated his mind.

By the end of summer, order apparently was restored in Paris. Thad wrote several letters to Sarah now, and anxiously waited to hear from her. But no correspondence came from Paris. In October he wrote to Dr. Z in Boston to inquire whether she knew anything about Sarah, if she had survived the siege and civil war and was back in school.

In early December he received a letter from Dr. Z:

> Dear Professor Barrett,
>
> I'm sorry to be so long in answering your concerned letter about Sarah. The siege and the civil war was very hard as you suspected. She worked in a hospital during most of this time since medical school was shut down. She was rather seriously injured during the last days of the war, but she is recovering and we hope will be able to resume her studies before long.
>
> Thank you for your interest.
Marie E. Zakrzewska

The letter only added to his concerns. Except that he knew she had survived. The "seriously injured" phrase was scary in itself. But the further phrase, "is recovering," sent a chill up his spine. She had not recovered yet, and the civil war had been virtually over for almost six months. And she was still not able to go back to school. They only "hoped" she would be able to before long. The thought occurred to him: What if she is crippled?

He immediately wrote another letter to Sarah. He was going to address it to her old address in Paris but then thought better of this. With the Prussian bombardment and the subsequent civil war that raged through the city, there was no assurance her old residence was still there or was habitable. Accordingly, he addressed the letter in care of the Medical College at the Sorbonne. Perhaps they would know of her whereabouts. Hopefully, she would soon be starting back to school and at worst would get the letter then. In this letter, he expressed his love and plaintively asked her to write him to relieve his grave concerns about her welfare.

But months and years were to go by with no word from her.

#

He did receive other mail. Mary Ann Bickerdyke wrote congratulating him on the book and praising his efforts.

Then she asked about Sarah:

> I have not heard from Sarah for a long time. She did write to tell me she'd been accepted for medical school in Paris. I presume she still is there. I had rather hoped to hear of wedding plans for you two by now. Please keep me informed.

John Rizzo also had seen the book and wrote to congratulate him. He also asked about Sarah and their relationship. He invited Thad, and Sarah if possible, to visit Rachel and him.

In May of the following year, 1872, in desperation Thad wrote to Marie Zakrzewska again asking for further information about Sarah. In particular, how she had been injured and how serious it was, and when she might be coming back. He even enclosed a copy of his book, which he hoped might spur a reply. But he received no communication from either Sarah or Dr. Z.

CHAPTER 18

"You gotta give up this obsession with Sarah," Abigail was saying. "Find someone else." She laughed, or maybe it was a cackle. "It's not that I mind havin' you 'round, you know. But you really oughta be warmin' some lassie's bed."

"I don't have any obsession, Abigail. I've long ago recognized when I'm licked. I am looking. But they're all either too young or too old."

"Then you're jus' not lookin' hard enough. A handsome man like you. A famous author. President of a college. Gawd, what a catch. For starters, I hear there's a single woman professor you got there. What's her name? Mildred Twitty, I think. What 'bout her."

"You really are trying to get rid of me, aren't you. You just want the house to yourself, I can tell."

"Nah, I jus' think . . . what's that word you sometimes throw 'round when you're tryin to act smart—empa . . . ?"

"Empathetic?"

"Sure, that's it. I gotta lot of empathetics for all single women. They need to be comforted by some man."

"Abigail, Professor Twitty is almost as old as you are."

Abigail cackled again. "Wal, what's wrong with that?" As Thad shook his head, she went on, "There's plenty of nubile students, I bet, that could really be hankering for you."

"Abigail, don't you remember Lucy? She was a young nubile student who had a crush on me. And by the way, where did you pick up that word 'nubile'?"

"Nephew, you jus' never knew how learned I really am." She took a chaw of tobacco. "Wal, I still think you could 'ave done a better job of pursuing that one."

More than three years had gone by since Thad had written Dr. Z imploring any information about Sarah, with no response. He had reconciled himself to the futility of this long quest. Abigail was right, he should try to find somebody else. Or else resign himself to never having a wife and family.

Abigail was getting older, she wasn't as spry as she used to be, even though her mind and tongue were as sharp as ever. He had felt very comfortable staying with her these years since coming back to Chalfant, but this would not go on forever. Still, it wasn't easy finding someone. It was as he told Abigail, they all were either too old or too young, or else married, or perhaps widowed. He still shuddered when he remembered his adventures with the widow Kate Burnham.

#

One day, two colored men came to see him. He recognized one as Reverend Brown of one of the Negro churches in town. He rose and shook hands. "Reverend Brown, it's good to see you."

"This is Reverend Davis, one of my competitors," the tall heavy-set man said, his eyes crinkling, as he introduced the shorter, white haired man.

"Please sit down, gentlemen. I still remember and am grateful for your help, Reverend Brown, those many years ago when the Klan got their ire up at me. And almost killed me."

"Yes, who could forget the hatred. Which is still with us, by the way. The Klan is still lurking out there behind their white hoods. Only maybe not quite as obvious as in the late 60s, but it wouldn't take much to arouse them, I fear."

Thad nodded. He had always had good rapport with the black community. He hoped they felt he was on their side, trying to bring their standing to as near equality as it could possibly be in this day and age. He estimated his position regarding racial equality was close to that of the Quakers, and a world removed from the Klan. Except that the Klan used the power of violence and undeviating hostility in promoting their side of the issue.

"How can I be of service?" Thad asked.

The two ministers looked at each other. Finally, Reverend Brown spoke. "There is a young black girl in our community who shows outstanding learning potential. She must truly be of genius intellect. She has just finished colored school, as far as we can go with her, and she's only fifteen. She desperately needs to have her potential furthered by college. We wondered if . . ."

Thad stared at them. Admit a black student? What a breakthrough that would be. But would it be possible, or would all the white students desert the college?

"Tell me more about her," he said.

This must have been somewhat encouraging to the two ministers, for he could see them relaxing a bit. Reverend Davis now spoke up. "Joan Washington learned to read when she was three—don't ask me where her mother got the books; she must have smuggled them in, somehow. She went through the grades and the colored high school always at the top of the class, far exceeding her classmates. Her interest is science. I, no, we believe she has a very great talent. But it must be nurtured, and this would have to come from colleges like yours that can feed into the great graduate schools." The man had a melodious and expressive voice. Though it was low pitched, it was charismatic and Thad was impressed. What a far cry from the booming rhetoric that characterized most politicians such as Harlan

Pettingill. Rev. Davis seemed sincere and absolutely committed to the cause of this girl.

Reverend Brown spoke up now. "There is one other thing you should know, sir. This girl, Joan, is crippled. She gets around in a wheelchair."

"Good Lord," Thad exhaled. "A brilliant mind, in a wheel chair, and black. What tremendous handicaps." He paused, studying the ministers. They looked at him, their eyes expressionless, revealing nothing.

He sighed. "What does Joan think about all this?"

"She would do anything in her power to further her education. She would like to be a great scientist, to help humankind."

Thad kneaded his forehead. "I would truly like to help this gifted girl. Still, I have to think of the impact enrolling a colored would have on the college. It might destroy it, if no whites would send their children because of this." He mused, "On the other hand, it might be the breakthrough needed to advance the cause of equality and opportunity for all." He paused, thinking about this and all it portended. "I can't give you a decision on this now, gentlemen. I have to talk it over with the board of trustees and many of the parents. I just cannot sacrifice the college for the just cause of your Joan Washington. Give me some time."

The two men nodded. "Dr. Barrett, that is all we can expect. And don't forget the Klan, who we're sure would love to get wind of this and don their hoods. But please, keep in mind this great talent and how it may well be utterly wasted."

"I know. I realize that." With mounting excitement he knew this was the greatest issue he might ever encounter in his years as president. "I wonder if I could meet Joan? Could you bring her to see me in the next few days?"

"Of course, Dr. Barrett."

#

The next day he met Joan. Reverend Davis wheeled her in. The first thing that struck him was her eyes. They dominated her face, and seemed to reach out to him with eagerness and intelligence. As she was introduced, she stretched out her hand and he grasped it, a bony little hand that firmly gripped his.

"Dr. Barrett," she said in a low, husky voice, "Thank you so much for seeing me." Each word was distinct, the slurred words common among both blacks and whites in the South were not evident here. As they talked, her face was animated, and she smiled frequently but not excessively as many nervous people have a tendency to do. Her hands were restless, however, fluttering, gesturing, as though to make up for an otherwise frail and unmoving body. He was becoming tremendously impressed with this young woman as she answered his questions and intently listened to him.

"Joan," he asked, after explaining the difficulties he might have in getting her enrolled in the college, "In case I can't get enough support for admitting you, what are your plans, what would you do?"

"Dr. Barrett, I have to face the reality that this dream of mine, to get an education, may not come to pass." She looked at Reverend Davis. "Still, I think God has something better in store for me than being a vegetable. With this hope in my heart, I'll continue reading everything I can. Maybe someday things will change, and I can make a difference in some small way."

Thad felt his pulse quicken with emotion. This little black girl and her seemingly impossible dream was not unlike the dream quest of Sarah. And even his own dream quest. Her expression of hope in God's will reminded him now of the hope that flooded through him on the way down from the mountain those months ago. "Joan, I have a very dear friend who faced a seemingly insurmountable barrier. She wanted to be a doctor, a surgeon, and go to medical school. An unheard of thing for a woman. Yet she finally succeeded, even though she had to go to a university in Paris."

She was staring intently at him, her eyes luminous. "How wonderful," she murmured.

"Joan, if the worst comes to pass, that we just can't get you in, I'll see that you have all the books you can possibly read."

Tears were suddenly rolling down her cheeks. "I'd be profoundly grateful for that, sir."

Now he took her fluttering hand. "But let's not give up on your formal education yet. I'll talk with the board and some of the parents. See what the sentiment is, and whether it can be changed."

They left a short time later. He leaned back in his chair and tried to plan his strategy for getting Joan admitted. He'd learned from the preachers that money would not be a problem. Their congregations were prepared to handle the tuition. Still, Thad thought it might be a nice gesture if she could be given a scholarship.

#

Sam Turner, even though retired, was still a member of the board. Thad sought him out the next day.

"Sam, something has come up. I need your advice, and I'm sure I'll need your support, if you agree."

The older man looked at him questioningly. "It must really be serious, Thad. I'm sure you could handle most things, better than me."

"There is this young colored girl . . ." Thad described the meeting with the preachers and with the girl herself. He described her dream quest, and his impressions of her. "We believe she's a genius, Sam. She could make a contribution with her life."

"But she's black and she's crippled."

ROBERT HARTLEY

"Yes." He looked steadily at him. "Will you support me before the board?"

"You really feel strongly about this, don't you?"

Thad had thought about this before, and was ready to state his convictions. "Sam, I think this could be the greatest thing I'll ever accomplish in academics, and maybe in my whole life, if I could somehow give Joan this dream opportunity."

"Then of course I'm with you." He frowned. "But there are four other board members, besides ourselves. We would need to win over two of these, since a split vote would not do it. You'll have to convene the board, soon as possible, and give them your pitch. I'll be a strong supporter."

"I know it won't be easy."

"This is an issue where passions will run high. The issue may tear the board apart." Softly he added, "And it may tear the school apart. All we've tried to build up."

"I know."

"You should talk to some of the parents, feel them out about this."

"Yes, I intended to do that."

"I think you should also talk to some of the students. And don't forget your faculty, Thad. Those who would have to teach this girl, if we should get her admitted."

"Good suggestions, Sam."

#

Thad conferred with his faculty first. Rather than call a meeting, he decided to do this individually. He was glad he did since attitudes were extreme. Some faculty were violently opposed; most, thankfully, were lukewarm at best to the idea but not bitterly opposed. Only a few were in favor. One of these was his only woman professor, Mildred Twitty, the one Abigail had with tongue in cheek suggested as a possible love interest, except she was only twenty years older than him. But while she had some gray hair, he found her a compatible personality with his own, and increasingly trusted her judgment.

She told him, "I think this is a marvelous gesture on your part, Thaddeus, whether it's successful or not. But I don't think it will be. I've heard faculty talking in the halls and in the cafeteria. Some are so upset about this they are threatening to quit."

"Nobody told me anything about quitting," Thad said, gritting his teeth.

"Well, it's easy to make such threats but not always so easy to carry out. 'Specially when it means giving up a good job and trying to find another job somewhere else. Still, we may be fifty years before Southern society will accept blacks and whites going to the same schools."

"This is only one little black girl, a one-of-a-kind little girl."

"Admitting one little black girl makes a tremendous difference in many people's minds, Thaddeus. It would be a great breakthrough in principle, would set a precedent many people would shudder to think of. It's like, with a dam holding back the flood, one leak unless quickly plugged could destroy the dam, and the community."

"You don't think it can be done, then?"

"I'm sorry. But, I would be very pleased to tutor Joan. You said her greatest interest is science. So let's plan on this if the other doesn't work out."

"Thanks, Mildred. Now I have to see what kind of a reading I can get from some of our students and their parents."

"I can already give you a reading on the students. I've heard them talking among themselves and some have talked with me about it."

"How quickly the word spreads," he observed with wonder and sadness.

"This is a hot topic, Thaddeus. Now most of the students are not as sharply negative as the faculty is—though I'd bet their parents are—but some are very much so. Still, most are lukewarm. None volunteered to be a friend or to help this little girl, however."

"I see."

"So that means, unless these attitudes change—and they may when they get to know Joan—that her life here, should she gain admission, will hardly be comfortable."

"I don't think that would dissuade her."

"No, I don't think so either."

#

Thad's sampling of students' and parents' opinions confirmed the conclusions of Mildred. What he was most concerned about, however, was whether enough parents would be so incensed they would withdraw their children and the tuition money needed. He judged that a few would; most of the rest would mask their resentment and quietly work to oust him and any other members of the board who approved this "sacrilegious" idea. He was truly putting his career on the line for this cause.

Now he began getting hostile letters, all anonymous, of course. Some threatened bodily harm to him, even death. Others threatened to burn down his house, or rather, Abigail's. This deeply concerned him. Still others threatened the college.

One letter in particular worried him greatly:

Dear Major,
    Guess who this is. Your old friends aint happy with you. We werent happy with you one time before. Member that. An you know what happened then. This time will be worser. If you dont stop this shit. An you know what we mean.

An ol army buddy

This could only be from Isaac Haskins and the Klan. He well knew their threats were not idle threats. They were certainly capable of killing anyone they saw as their enemy, white or black.

He showed this letter and some of the other messages to Sheriff Jenkins.

"I'm sorry, Dr. Barrett, but there's nothing we can do. We can't lock up a fella for makin' idle threats, now can we? Besides, we don't know who wrote any of these."

"I know this one is from the Klan and one of my old enlisted men."

"Wal, I'm not surprised the Klan is interested in this. But we can't arrest anyone just on suspicion. There's no proof. An' no crime done."

"Yet."

"Wal, yes." The man spat on the ground. "You know, what I'd do, if I was you?"

"Leave town?"

"Wal, yes, maybe that to. No, I'd pack a gun. Give myself a little protection."

"I see," Thad said.

"You being an officer would certainly know how t' handle a pistol. But I'm sorry. That's all we can do for now."

"Could you at least have a man watch the college buildings and my Aunt Abigail's house?"

"Tell you what, Dr. Barrett. I'll have someone patrol past the college several times each night. Can't do more'n that. You may want to hire a private guard. But I can't spare anyone to watch your house. I'm sorry."

"Thanks, Sheriff. I appreciate the help." Thad wondered how Jenkins felt about this controversy. He suspected he was strongly on the side of those against Joan and the threat they thought she posed to their way of life. Who knows, under those masks and robes, the sheriff could even be one of the Klan.

#

"What're you doing, Thad?" Abigail had come up unexpectedly to find him packing his valise.

"It's best if I move out, until all this blows over, Abigail. I don't want to put you and your house in danger because of me."

"Nonsense. Don't let the bastards have us runnin' scared. 'Sides, my house and I'd be a lot safer with a man here than in some hotel room. I might be of some help, too." She winked at him. "I've got Ol' Annie next to my bed, you know."

"Ol' Annie?"

"Sure. My trusty shotgun. I used t' get a fair number of birds back when I was a young lass and this here was mostly wilderness."

"I bet you did."

"You never knew what a rambunctious old gal I used to be, did ya?"

He chuckled. Praise be, Aunt Abigail. "I never did. But I can imagine."

So he stayed, but they made plans in case of terror in the night. Still, what could an old lady and one man and a pistol do against a yardfull of white hooded devils?

He did hire several students to be night watchmen for the campus. He did this with some trepidation, fearing that they could well be in jeopardy along with the buildings.

#

He was rather shocked to find a few days later that the stage had widened substantially. Newspaper reporters were flocking to the little town of Chalfant. Word had gotten out there was a major controversy brewing here that could affect the rest of the country, but especially the South. Furthermore, this controversy hinted at violence to come, always a big attraction for the press.

The board meeting was several weeks away, but already reporters knew about this and were speculating on the outcome: would Joan Washington be admitted to the college or would she be denied this opportunity? Thad Barrett was both vilified and praised. This public spotlight he detested to the uttermost.

One aggressive reporter, Leo Konstanzo, accosted him one afternoon as he was leaving his office. "Dr. Barrett, sir," he demanded attention. "I'm from the Baltimore Sun newspaper. The nation needs to know more about your motivation for this adventure into educational equality. Are you a nigger lover, sir?"

His path was barred by the reporter. He would have had to physically challenge him to pass. Thad sighed. It had been a hectic day, what with the board meeting coming up soon. Still, maybe some publicity for their side of the issue would not hurt. "Sir, I'm not a Negro lover, and I'm not a white supremacist. I believe in equality. What's more," he said peering solemnly at the man who was rapidly scribbling, "I believe in opportunity. I believe in the greater social good that can come from letting someone with great talent develop this to the fullest. Whether black or white. Or red or yellow," he added.

The reporter nodded. "Dr. Barrett, do you think this . . . integration . . . is possible, this day and age?"

Thad looked at him keenly. "That is very perceptive, sir. I don't know if it is. Perhaps we're half a century too soon for this. But God help us, I hope not."

The reporter looked at him and prepared to let him pass. Then another thought came to him. "Dr. Barrett, can a handicapped person really make any contribution to society?"

Thad halted, his hackles rising. "Mr. Konstanzo, if you had a handicapped daughter, wouldn't you want the best for her, for her to reach for all she can achieve? Wouldn't you, man?"

Now the reporter was on the defensive. He tried to evade the question. But Thad persisted. "Wouldn't you, Mr. Konstanzo?"

"Yes, I would," he finally murmured. Then more strongly, "Yes, I would!"

This exchange received national attention. The writeups of the press were in general very favorable. But then most of the reporters were from northern newspapers. Southern papers, that would be something else. But even their reports were only moderately critical.

#

The Klan arose to intimidate two nights before the board meeting. Sam Turner was accosted and threatened, but then the Klan backed off. Thad learned later that even Joan's household was threatened by the Klan, but their attempt at intimidation was quickly countered by neighbors who rushed to her defense.

That was not the case with the confrontation at Abigail's. It was after midnight when they were awakened by shouts and gunfire outside the house.

Thad's pulse was racing as he groped in the dark for his clothes and his pistol.

Now Abigail was at his door with a lantern in one hand and Ol' Annie in the other. "Thad, they're heah. The devils are heah!"

"Douse that light, Abigail. We'll stay in the darkness, and inside."

"What if they break the door down?"

"Then we'll use our weapons. But we mustn't let them lure us outside where they can surround us and torment us."

He looked out and could see a dozen or more white hooded figures, some on horses, some milling around on foot, all shouting obscenities and threats and waving torches.

A sudden premonition came to him and he groaned. It was too late, but he should have anticipated this. "They're going to try to burn us out, Abigail. Quick, can you get some blankets we can use to beat out the flames?"

"Here, take Ol' Annie, and I'll get some." She thrust the shotgun at him and scurried away. She was soon back. "These'd be better if they were wetted. But I couldn't get to the pump for water."

"These'll have to do. Remember Abigail, we mustn't go outside unless we absolutely have to. Even with our guns, we'd be sittin' ducks against all those men."

"Devils in white robes," she muttered.

They positioned themselves by the windows on the first floor. Thad was prepared to race up the stairs if they attacked the second floor with their torches.

Now he could see several spurring their horses up to the porch. They threw rocks and shattered the front windows. As quickly, torches were tossed inside.

Thad fired his pistol several times over their heads and they retreated, shouting more obscenities.

He and Abigail worked desperately to beat out the flames. But the house was filling with smoke. Torches must also have been tossed through other windows and maybe on the roof.

"They're burning it down 'round us!" Abigail had a fit of coughing.

"On the floor, Abby! By the front door. Keep your gun handy if we have to leave the house."

The smoke thickened. "We 'ave to get out, Thad!" She was coughing badly. He held her against him until the spasm passed. But they had no option. They had to get out or die in this burning house.

"Abby, don't stand up! We'll crawl out," he ordered. "And give me your gun for a moment."

He used the tip of the shotgun to push the door open. Then he gave the gun back to her. "You'll likely only have one shot with that before they overwhelm us. Wait until someone is almost on you before firing."

Now they could see a cross burning on the front yard. Then he heard cheers and gun shots as they were spotted.

As they crawled to the edge of the porch, a group rushed toward them.

He heard Ol' Annie discharge beside him and one of the white clad figures slumped to the ground cursing. Thad was able to get off only two shots before he was overpowered and the gun wrenched from his hand.

His leg was again a handicap in hand-to-hand fighting. Someone shoved him and he was thrown to the ground.

Now he saw Abigail on the ground unmoving. This gave him new energy. He struggled up shouting, "You killed her! Killed an old lady! Murderers!"

In the distance he heard a whistle and a man shouting, "Let's go, boys!" The figures began to filter away.

Thad grabbed one man and tried to detain him. He ducked a wildly swinging fist and drove his head into the man's midsection.

Now they both were on the ground rolling and clawing at each other and he realized the wooden leg was no longer a disadvantage.

He managed to rip the hood off. It was Isaac Haskins. His face was bloody from Thad's fists, and his teeth were bared in a vicious snarl. "Damn you, Major! You broke my nose!"

"I might have known," Thad grunted.

"I'n gonna kill you yet!" He struggled to escape Thad's grip.

"Like you killed an old woman!" Now Thad was aware of loud voices coming in the yard. But his attention was concentrated on trying to hold the slippery and desperate

Haskins. He saw Haskins eyes suddenly focus on something behind him.

Too late, he reacted. A sudden blow to the back of his head cast him into darkness.

He must have come to a few minutes later. As his eyes opened, Sheriff Jenkins was stooping over him and someone else was holding a wet cloth to his head. "He's comin' round," he heard a voice.

He struggled to sit up, but the pain in his head forced him back. "Abigail?" he whispered.

"I'm sorry, Dr. Prentice," the sheriff said.

Thad groaned. "They killed her then."

"We'll not sure 'bout that. We haven't found any injuries, any bullet wounds or knife wounds. Abigail was an old woman. She may have had a heart attack."

"If so, it was certainly brought on by the Klan." He tried to look around. "Did you get Isaac Haskins? He was one of them."

"They'd all left, before we got here. How'd you know one was Haskins?"

"I tore off his hood and tried to hold him until help came."

"Somebody must've come back and clobbered you then an' gotten him away."

Thad struggled to sit up, and made it this time. He could see the bucket brigade trying to save the house.

The burning cross was mostly a blackened skeleton. While he looked, someone pushed over what was left. "Can they save the house?" he asked dully.

"Most of it, it 'pears," the sheriff answered. "Mostly smoke damage, except for the kitchen which is pretty well blackened. You'll be able to fix it up . . . excuse me, Doctor."

One of his men had come up and wanted to confer with the sheriff. He went out in the yard with him, and Thad could see them examining the ground in several places. The sheriff came back. "Looks like you and Abigail bloodied a couple of 'em."

"It won't bring Abigail back."

"No . . . but if someone seeks medical attention for a gunshot wound, wal, it'll be mighty suspicious."

#

Abigail's funeral was the morning of the board meeting. The church was full, and many stopped to offer condolences. Sentiment was running strong against the KKK. The preacher gave a glowing eulogy, praising Abigail as a pioneer woman, one of the first settlers of this area. "And despite her age," he thundered, "she would have had many years still ahead of her, except for the dastardly misdeeds of men too cowardly to show their faces. Our hearts go out to her nephew, Thaddeus Barrett, who was by her side as they tried to defend themselves."

From the sentiments expressed at Abigail's service, and the general denunciation of the aggressive prejudice of the Klan, Thad wondered whether any of the board members might be swayed. If so, then Abigail's death might have some purpose.

The board meeting that afternoon was crucial. The decision of the board would determine whether Joan could be admitted or not. It looked like his side had three votes: Himself, of course. And Sam. And a Quaker friend of Josiah Vanderhall, Jacob Hull.

The other three, well they were something else. Unless one of these could be won, Joan would not receive permission to enroll. The man most likely to switch was Charles Penwick. He had a prosperous retail business in town, with many black as well as white customers. Thad thought it would be in Charles's best interest to go along with this singular integration, and told him so.

But Charles saw things differently. "Thad, if I went along with this proposal, I'd lose all the business of some of these wealthy white folks. What I might gain from the coloreds would not come close to making up for this."

"But where would these wealthy whites go? There's no place else as convenient for them to shop as Chalfant."

"There's other places. Little farther, but not that bad. For example, Hickory and Morganton. These offer at least as much we do here, maybe more. No, in the interest of safeguarding my business, and my family's best interest, I have to vote no to this. I'm sorry Thad, but the family must come first."

There was no dissuading him, Thad quickly realized.

His appeals fell on deaf ears for the other two members of the board who were wealthy land owners. The board finally voted three to three on the proposal. Joan was denied admittance. Abigail's death was of no purpose.

#

He went out to Joan's house to tell her the news. He asked Mildred Twitty to go with him, and she eagerly agreed. The house was an unpainted shack on a dirt street next to others like it. Its yard was grassless, and a dead tree graced the front, like a stripped sentinel guarding a forlorn outpost. A thin black woman with high cheekbones answered the door. She seemed to know him, though he had never met her. "I'm Joan's mother. Please come in, Dr. Barrett." She looked at Mildred and Thad quickly introduced them.

They entered a dark and barren room. A wheelchaired figure sat hunched next to a candle-lit table in a corner.

She propelled her chair toward them. "Hello and welcome, Dr. Barrett," she said, and again offered that small but so firmly-gripping hand. She looked at Mildred Twitty, and said without being introduced, "Hello, Professor Twitty. Welcome to our house."

Mrs. Washington brought several chairs. "May I offer you some tea?" she said in a deep melodious voice.

"That would be nice."

"They denied me," Joan said without preamble, after the tea was served.

"Are you surprised?" Thad asked.

"How could I be? The hope was such a slender tendril."

Thad looked at Mildred. She was staring, fascinated at Joan. Suddenly Joan smiled at her, and at him. "It's all right, really. I truly appreciate what you've tried to do for me. Maybe this is for the best. The college survives without distress, and your job has not been sacrificed. I really felt badly that it might be, you taking up my cause and all." Now her eyes began tearing. "Dr. Barrett, I'm really stricken that your aunt lost her life in this futile endeavor. I pray the good Lord will bless her, and that He will forgive me, for being the cause of it."

Thad shook his head. "Don't blame yourself, Joan. In no way are you responsible for the actions of evil men," he said gently, wiping her eyes with his handkerchief.

Mildred spoke up, "Don't give up hope, Joan."

"Oh, I won't," she said.

"Mildred here has volunteered to tutor you in the sciences and whatever else seems best." Thad explained. Then he wondered why he had used her first name before this child instead of calling her by the more formal Professor Twitty. Was Joan casting a spell on them? If so, it was certainly a benign spell.

"Thank you, Professor Twitty," she acknowledged, repudiating his unintended informality.

They sipped their tea in silence, somehow uncomfortable. Mrs. Washington strove to put them more at ease. "We don't often get white folk visitin' us here. I'm sure the whole neighborhood is watchin', 'n wonderin'."

"Do they know you have an exceptional daughter?" Thad asked, curious.

The mother stared at them, then looked at her daughter.

"They'll be thinkin' Joan is a caster of spells, bringin' you white folk down here."

Joan laughed at this. "Those who are different, perhaps deformed, have been viewed by primitive peoples as special, even God's chosen." Now she sighed audibly. "How different it becomes with civilization. Now we become the outcasts, the dregs of society."

Thad tried to protest. But she continued. "Well, I certainly don't think we're necessarily God's chosen, though we hope He has merciful feelings toward us, but we certainly aren't the dregs of society either."

Mildred couldn't take her eyes off Joan. The child dropped her eyes modestly. Thad could see a pulse beating in Joan's neck. Mildred said then, "Joan, we absolutely have to further your education." She sniffed and massaged her eyes. "I think we can ready you for a northern graduate school, without any formal classes here. I'll be glad to tutor you, two, three times a week. It may well be that you'll learn more and quicker than in a classroom full of average students. Child, I have a feeling that you'll be able to go as far as your dreams can lead you. And I'm sure that's a long ways."

"How wonderful, and I'm so grateful," Joan murmured, barely able to keep from breaking down. Her mother moved to her side and took her hand. Thad and Mildred looked at each other, profoundly moved by all this. They both tried to hold back their own tears.

On the way back to the college, Mildred was so quiet Thad wondered if she were upset about all this. He was about to ask her when she touched his arm. "What a special person this is, Thad. I feel privileged to be able to work with her. I've . . . I've never felt this way about any student before."

Thad said slowly, "I've been thinking quite a bit about this. Especially since I doubted we could get her admitted. Do you really think you can give her a good enough academic foundation that we might get her into grad school up North in years to come."

"She'll be an eager learner. I truly think such may indeed be possible in some northern schools where there's less prejudice."

"There still is prejudice," Thad reminded her. "Especially concerning higher education for women."

"Yes, but I sense the walls are crumbling, at least in most academic fields." She paused. "We have another need in Joan's scientific education. She'll have to have lab experience, especially in chemistry, biology, and physics. Do you think we could use some of the campus facilities, after hours, of course? I would hope we wouldn't have to go through the board for that."

"We'll do it, Mildred. Just tell me when. Weekends should be all right. Even nights, sometimes. I don't think we need to clear this with anyone but us."

As he dropped her off, he said, "One last thing, Mildred. Tell that little girl never to give up hope. Tell her that from me. She resurrected it for me, you know."

CHAPTER 19

The brief letter from Dr. Z came a little over eight months later. It was late April, and dogwoods bloomed in the valleys and were creeping ever higher. Strangely, all the controversy with its abundant publicity about his failed efforts to admit the little colored girl, Joan Washington, had not hurt enrollment at the college. It was the highest ever.

More than five years had gone by since his last letter to Dr. Z with its fervent plea for information about Sarah, and she had never bothered to answer. Now this. Why now?

He couldn't help the adrenaline rush, and his fingers trembled and were clumsy as he opened the envelope from Boston. The message was terse and cold. It promised nothing but puzzlement. And yet . . . ?

Dear Professor Barrett,
    If you still think you might have some love for Sarah, she is here working in the hospital, having finished her schooling in Paris.
    If you should decide to come, please see me first as Sarah does not know I have written you.

Marie Zakrzewska

#

After reading this strange and cryptic letter, Thad sat for a long while gazing out the window at the blossoming campus with its streams of students seemingly oblivious to the beauty of the blue and greening hills beyond. He had told his secretary not to disturb him except for an emergency. He needed to sort out his roiling thoughts.

Did he really want to go to Boston, to follow up on this spare message? Possibly to reopen old wounds that after five years had crusted over? He missed Aunt Abigail at times like these. Her earthy advice and wry humor never failed to put his perspectives in their proper places. He was still bitter that the authorities had never found the men responsible for her death.

On impulse, he went to the door to tell his secretary, "Cathy, would you check Professor Twitty's schedule? If she's finished with classes, would you ask her to see me?"

214

"I believe her last class is over in twenty minutes. I'll give her the message. Do you still want me to hold all other appointments?"

"Yes, unless it's very important. I've got a major decision to sort out."

Of late, he had been grooming Mildred Twitty as his administrative understudy, and she certainly could take over if he decided to go up to Boston. Despite her being considerably older, he felt a deep affection for her. It was not hard to understand. She had latent managerial talent, was compassionate and easy to talk to, and her dedication to the education of Joan matched his own. Mildred Twitty arrived thirty minutes later.

"Come in, Mildred. Please sit down. I've something I'd like to get your thoughts on . . . something rather personal."

She seated herself, looking expectantly at him. "Is it about Joan? She's doing very well, by the way."

"No, it's not Joan, although I'm glad to hear she's doing well. I doubt either of us is surprised at that. No, it's something else."

She sat quietly as he tried to sort out his thoughts and how much he wanted to reveal.

Finally he asked, "Mildred, do you know anything about how I got wounded during the War?"

"You've never discussed it with me, Thaddeus. But it's rather common knowledge that you were severely wounded at Antietam. That a Union nurse saved your life."

"Is that all?"

"Well, I'd heard a rumor some years back that you were in love with this nurse but could never find her again. I didn't know if this was true. But if true, how sad for you."

"The rumor was partly true, Mildred. Except that I did finally locate her. In medical school in Paris, studying to be a doctor and surgeon."

"Joan mentioned a woman you had told her about whose great dream was to become a physician, but medical schools all refused her because of being a woman. Finally, a prestigious school in Paris . . ." She peered at him. "That was the nurse you loved . . . ?"

"Yes." Thad swiveled his chair to gaze at the distant hills, to hide the emotions that his face surely must show. Maybe this answered his question: he still held deep feelings in his heart, despite the years gone by. He turned back to Mildred, his face now composed. She was staring at him, wide eyed.

"I'd not been able to get any information about her, about Sarah, for more than five years. Today I got this letter." He fumbled with the papers on this desk and handed her the letter from Dr. Z.

"What are you going to do?" she asked after reading it.

"I wasn't sure until we started talking. I'd thought I was long over Sarah, but it appears I'm not. I must go to Boston, to somehow resolve this thing, one way or the other. I . . . have the feeling that the consequences may not be easy to take."

"But you still feel you have to go," she added softly.

"Yes. Soon as possible. Maybe even tomorrow. Could you take over here for a few weeks? There are no crises looming that I know of."

"Except your own personal demons."

"Yes, there certainly are those."

"Of course I'll take over for you. I'm honored you want me to."

"I'll give Cathy the hospital address in case you need to reach me. Though I'm not sure how long I'll be there. Maybe one afternoon of rejection. Or maybe the rejection will take several days."

She touched his hand. "Thaddeus, remember the hope you told Joan to have. Don't abandon it for yourself."

#

He arrived at Boston weary and sore from the long train ride. The jerking and bouncing and the confinement as usual aggravated his stump and brought unpleasant feelings of helplessness. Despite what Mildred had said to comfort him—about not abandoning hope—still the thought prevailed of the hopelessness of it all. Too many years gone by, too much water over the dam, for both of them.

It was too late to go to the hospital so he checked into a hotel and had a quiet meal. He remembered the last time he had been here, back in '69, almost eight years ago. He had such hopes then of finding Sarah at the hospital, since Mary Ann Bickerdyke was sure she was there. And she had been, until a few months before. He remembered the blizzard that delayed his getting to the hospital for several days, days in which his hopes had changed to worry about what kind of reception he would get from her. Would she be eager and welcoming? Or, more likely, would she be appreciative of his efforts to find her but cool to anything beyond friendship? He had the same misgivings now. After all, she didn't know he was coming. Dr. Z hadn't told her. What ominous thing could account for her not telling Sarah? That thought nagged him through the night until it became a mountain of doom and foreboding, and he began to question his decision to come.

The next day was cloudy and cool. He took a taxi to the hospital, and learned from the driver that it had moved and expanded from what he had known. The congestion of a big city again assailed him, but somehow Boston was less frenetic than New York, a little more polite perhaps, and a prettier place. Even some trees. But he saw that only traceries of greenery could be seen on trees. Spring was weeks behind Carolina.

The New England Hospital for Women and Children was now a substantial establishment. Thad was impressed at the brick and mortar evidence of the driving force that was Dr. Z. He couldn't help but compare this tangible achievement with his own at the college. No new buildings there, no additional facilities under his administration. Perhaps he was only a caretaker, not a builder. A flaw in his character?

He was surprised that the receptionist must have been alerted to his possible appearance, for he was ushered immediately into Dr. Z's chambers. How did they know he would come? Her secretary offered him coffee, which he accepted gratefully. "Dr. Z will be with you shortly. She has a meeting, but should be able to wrap it up soon. She wished to express her apologies."

"It's all right. She couldn't know when I was coming. If I was coming." The secretary looked at him strangely. What did that mean?

Dr. Z rushed in, about fifteen minutes later. "Professor, Major Barrett, I'm sorry to keep you waiting. My secretary explained, I hope." She offered her hand in a firm grip, and pulled another chair in front of her desk and sat down facing him.

"Yes, she did. Please call me Thad. The "major" is certainly a long time in the past, a past best done with."

"But not forgotten, Thad," she said. "Friends call me Marie."

He couldn't resist asking, "Are you suggesting that I might be a friend?"

She stared at him. "I surely hope so. Even though you must have thought I was not. But there were reasons for not responding to your sincere concerns."

"Why the change, Marie?" he asked. "It's been over five years, you know."

"I know. How well I know." The woman looked off into space, before turning her attention back to him. "How much do you love Sarah?"

"Hasn't my long quest to find her attested to my love?"

"Yes. I would say so. But how about now. After so many years. Do you think you still feel the same way?"

"Dr. Z, Marie," he said slowly. "I've had to inure myself to my one-sided love. I'd thought . . . that I'd succeeded, that I was calloused to this loss. Then your strange letter came, offering little encouragement, but still something . . ."

Now his emotions almost overcame him. He suddenly got up and walked over to a window, staring out unseeingly, hitting his hand against his leather-covered stump. He turned back to his tormentor, yet also the source of hope. "I think I'm sorry to say it, fearing more rejection, opening old wounds." He shook his head. "But I'd be a fool to try to deceive myself. It's still there, the love, after all these years. What a wonderment."

"She's not the same as you remember," she said softly. She sighed. "Her self esteem, her zest for life . . . I truly believe she needs your love, badly. But she would never admit it, nor ask for it now. That's why I didn't tell her I'd written you. But I hoped you were still unmarried, and that you'd come. Your coming would prove your love, it seemed to me . . . at least for the woman you used to know. And you came."

He sat down heavily. "Tell me, Marie."

"During the civil war for Paris, she was attacked, by a jealous classmate." She took a deep breath. Thad had the feeling this proud and dignified woman was on the verge of breaking down, and his pulse pounded in his ears in anticipation of what she was about to say. "She was raped, brutally, and her face slashed. She was left for dead in a Paris alley, not far from the hospital where she was working." Now her words poured forth, as in a release. "A stray dog saved her life, licked her wounds and brought her to consciousness. Then when morning came, this strange mongrel attracted passersby to her in the depths of this dark and filthy alley.

"They saved her life, bound up her wounds. But her face still bears the livid scar." She mused, almost to herself, "If the wound had been more carefully sewed up . . ." Now she looked directly at him, almost challenging. "Does all this turn you off? You can see why I didn't want to raise Sarah's hopes about you coming."

"Dear Lord, no wonder she didn't answer my letters. Now I understand. No, Marie, it doesn't turn me off." He paused, another thought striking him. "Tell me," he said urgently, "Were her hands destroyed, her surgeon's hands."

He could see that Marie's emotional reserve was breaking down. She absently wiped tears away.

"Thanks to God, no. The devil, in his hatred and passion, forgot to destroy her hands." She took a ragged breath. Thad reached for her hand and she gripped his tightly. "She had such a splendid future in medicine. After the first year, she was the very top of her class. It took her a year to recover from the assault. She was thinking seriously of giving up becoming a doctor. I went over to Paris to persuade her to keep persevering, and she did start again. But she was never the same, and she had other problems, too. She finished ten months ago, but well in the middle of her class. She's been back with us for about eight months. She's still a good surgeon. But her spirit is broken."

"I'm surprised," he said quietly. "I always thought she was so very strong. So did those who worked with her during the War. She should have been able to recover from some facial scars, some blemish on her beauty. With her hands intact . . ."

"There's something else, Thad. She has a child from this assault. The only child she can ever have." As Thad stared, she went on. "A little girl, crippled and in a wheel chair."

Thad groaned. "I had such a girl who wanted to enroll in my college. A black girl. But there was too much prejudice. We couldn't do it. What a coincidence . . ." He rubbed his eyes.

"I know about that. It was in the Boston and New York papers. About your efforts to enroll this girl, and your confrontation with the Ku Klux Klan, and your aunt being killed. That is what finally gave me the courage to write you, Thad. Your championing another girl who was crippled. I hoped . . ."

He stared at her. "You mean my trying to help a little black girl may have brought me to my beloved, after all these years?"

She nodded, not trusting herself to talk.

He kneaded his forehead, overcome with emotion and with hope. He looked up. "Tell me, have they been able to assess her intelligence, yet?"

"They think she's very intelligent."

"So is this black girl, actually at the genius level." Almost to himself he murmured, "Do you sometimes wonder, Marie, whether Divine Providence is acting in this world?"

Marie nodded. "Sometimes we call it embraced by an angel, or a miracle, or God's will. But yes, most physicians have seen wonderful coincidences."

Now she said so softly he could barely hear her. "I think Sarah's hands, not being destroyed, is also such a thing. You know, this happened once before, too." He looked at her fascinated. "Yes, before she went to Paris. Sarah and I were accosted by hoodlums bent on smashing her hands. We suspect they were hired by a jealous coworker."

"But they were not touched, her hands?"

"Almost. But no, they were spared."

"Thank God. I can still remember those hands, binding my wounds, caressing my fevered brow . . ."

"Do you still want to see her, after all this?"

"Dear Lord, yes."

"Then come with me." She looked at her watch and took his arm and led him from the office and down a corridor. "In here," she whispered. "We can watch her finishing up from this balcony."

Four white clad figures were standing over a form swathed in white sheets. With the masks, Thad at first couldn't tell which was Sarah. But then he could. She had to be that small figure who was working swiftly and with such deftness. The others were handing her instruments and doing other things that he could not readily determine.

In about fifteen minutes the operation must have been successfully completed for the patient was wheeled out and the doctors and nurses began removing their masks as they left the room. Thad caught a brief glimpse of a long white scar.

"Why don't we go back to my office? I'll leave word for Sarah to come there when she gets cleaned up. That will give you two a quiet place to get reacquainted."

"Thank you."

#

In her office, Marie said, "If you don't mind, I think I'll leave. My secretary can send Sarah in when she gets here. I'll see that you're not disturbed." She suddenly stood on her tiptoes and kissed his cheek. "You know, Sarah's very dear to me. I only want the best for her."

"Thank you, Marie, for all you've done."

"May God approve," she said as she left.

In the few minutes before Sarah showed up, Thad paced restlessly around the room. As always when he was extremely agitated his stump began acting up; it seemed to swell and chaff and made him very much aware of it. There was a gentle tap at the door. He quickly moved to one side and grabbed the top of a bookcase, not trusting himself to stand alone. The door opened and she entered.

"Marie," she called. He couldn't miss the livid scar that covered the length of her cheek. He thought it made her even more beautiful. She looked around, and saw him. She started violently, and quickly put her hand to cover her cheek. "You! Thad, is that you?" she whispered.

Now he came to her, his leg forgotten. He held out his hands and she put her wondrous hands in his. In a moment they were in each other's arms. He was aware that someone had closed the door to the outer office. And he was aware of the pulse pounding in his ears and her pulse throbbing at her throat. After a while they kissed. But then she pushed him away.

"We better . . . sit down, Thad. My knees have suddenly gotten weak. And your leg . . . ?

As they sat down he realized that Marie must have moved the two visitor chairs so they would be very close to each other. Sarah noticed, too. "It looks like Marie has been up to something," she remarked with a faint smile.

He easily reached over and took those hands again, and his eyes dwelt on her face as she looked at him. For a while neither of them spoke. Then he swallowed. "You look beautiful."

She shook her head, perhaps in disbelief, and closed her eyes briefly. Now she tried to remove her hand, perhaps to touch her cheek, but he held on tightly. Her voice came out strained. "I suppose Marie told you all about me, all that happened."

He nodded. "She did, but not until a few hours ago. Is that why you never answered my letters, you thought my love was so shallow?"

She made a small bitter sound. "Things were changed. I thought God had other plans for me. Plans that didn't include romance and a man."

"Do you still think that now?" he ventured.

"I don't know. I'm confused." Now she pulled her hands away, briefly touched her scar without probably even knowing she did so. "Did Marie tell you about the child?"

"Yes. She said she is crippled and in a wheel chair, but that she's very bright."

"She's the last child I can ever have, you know."

"Yes, Marie told me. May I see her?"

The door opened now and Marie looked in. "I just wanted to see if everything's all right. It's past lunch time. I'm having some coffee and sandwiches sent up."

"Marie, please come in," Sarah pleaded.

"I thought you two needed your privacy, didn't need anyone to chaperone you." But she came in and sat down behind her desk. "You think you've had enough privacy?"

"I think you owe me an explanation for inducing Thad to come up here, without even telling me."

"That was kinda sneaky of me, wasn't it?" Marie chuckled.

"I don't think that's funny," Sarah said. "And yes, it was sneaky. I'm surprised at you."

Marie frowned slightly. "Are you glad I did?" Her voice was husky.

"I . . . I'm not sure." Sarah momentarily touched her scar. "He wants to see Ginny."

"I'm not surprised." Marie looked at Thad, her face innocent.

"He tells me you didn't tell him my troubles until after he got here."

"That's right. I didn't."

"She didn't have much faith in my love," Thad interjected now.

"That's right," Marie admitted. "I was afraid he'd never come, if he knew. But I was mistaken." She smiled now at both of them. "Don't you think it's time you let him see Ginny? See what a wonderful little girl she is?"

Sarah looked exhausted, Thad could see. The emotional strain of this encounter had left her like a rag doll. She collapsed against the chair, all resistance gone. "Yes, yes," she murmured.

#

Sarah and Thad spoke little on the way to her place. They rode in Marie's carriage, and held hands on the way.

"Do you know anything about the crippled?" she asked.

"Quite a bit," he answered, surprising her. "In fact I was deeply involved with such a girl who wanted to enroll at my college. She has a brilliant mind, but she's colored. Marie knows all about this. She said it was in the papers up here."

"Oh?" Sarah breathed. "She didn't say anything to me about it. What happened?"

"The prejudices were too strong. We weren't able to let her in the college."

"How sad."

"But we are tutoring her in private. Some day I think she'll be accepted in a grad school up North."

"How old is she?"

"Just about sixteen now."

"Is she really smart?"

"A genius I would say. Someday I hope you and Ginny can meet her. She's a very special person."

"Is she in a wheelchair?"

"Yes, she's never been able to walk."

They were silent after that until the carriage stopped. Her hand tightly gripped his.

The building was on a quiet residential street. A few trees paced the sidewalk. Sarah's apartment was on the first floor. A woman in a white uniform greeted them as they came inside.

"Is Ginny sleeping?"

"No, I believe she's looking at her favorite book in the bedroom."

"Martha, this is Major Thaddeus Barrett, a very dear friend of mine, from South Carolina." The woman was black. She momentarily reminded Thad of Joan's mother. She was unsmiling as she nodded her head at Thad.

Sarah opened the door to the bedroom and motioned Thad in. It was a light, airy room, with cheerful colors, and guarded by stuffed toys and dolls. A child sat in a wheelchair near the window. "Hello sweetie, I've brought someone who wants to meet you."

The little girl smiled and said cheerfully, "How nice. I don't have many visitors. My name is Ginny. What's your name?"

"I'm Thad. How nice to meet you, Ginny." He took one of her little hands and gently squeezed it. He looked at her and saw she was intently appraising him. She was a pretty child, but her disability was apparent. A big collar encircled her neck. She was strapped in the wheelchair, and below her skirt he could see legs hardly bigger than his middle finger. Her arms seemed to be active, just as Joan's. "Are you another doctor?' she asked.

"He's not a medical doctor, Ginny," her mother explained. "He's a professor doctor. He teaches at a college."

Thad knelt besides the chair. "What are you reading, Ginny?" he asked softly.

"It's a book of fairy tales," she said, and handed it to him. "See."

Thad examined it very seriously. "Such a big book. Can you read some of it?"

"Oh, Doctor Thad, I can read all of it," she said proudly. "I'm reading it for the third time."

"Wow," he said. "I'm really impressed." He asked, looking at Sarah, "Do you go to school?"

"No. Mommy teaches me."

"I know a little girl, Ginny, who's a lot like you. She's a little older, and she's very smart."

"Is she in a wheelchair, too?" Ginny's eyes were wide.

"Yes, she is. The only difference, other than age, is that she's black."

Ginny thought about this. "Like Martha?" she asked.

"Yes. Martha reminds me of her mother."

Thad handed the book back. "I like you, Dr. Thad," she said suddenly. "Could you be . . . would you . . . mommy's boy friend?"

Thad looked at Sarah. She was embarrassed and started to protest. He quickly said, "Ginny, I hope to be more than your mommy's boy friend. And also . . . something special to you."

Thad could see that the little girl was almost overcome with emotion, for her arms were fluttering uncontrollably.

"We'll going now, sweetie," Sarah told her. "I'll see you a little later."

"Goodbye, Dr. Thad," she said.

He took her hands and gently held them quiet a moment. "Goodbye, Ginny. I think you're a beautiful young woman."

"Gee, Mommy, did you hear what he said?"

#

"She's a lovely child," he told Sarah later. She nodded, without saying anything. They were having dinner at a quiet restaurant several blocks down the street from her apartment. In truth, this night he wasn't aware of what they were eating. Somehow this whole day had an ethereal quality, unreal. The culmination of his dream all these years might be at hand, and he could barely believe it. Still, his quest was only partially fulfilled. He had found her and was talking with her. He knew absolutely that nothing had changed in his feelings for her, that they were as strong—nay, even stronger—than ever. But what about her? Did she feel the same way? Even if she did, would she consent to marry him carrying the great handicap, as she saw it, of her crippled daughter and her own scarred face? No, the quest was still not completed, he realized.

He was suddenly conscious of music. Someone was playing a violin. He noticed now a small dance floor, and two couples began to dance. She had said very little since they left her apartment. But her eyes were attentive to him. "Shall we dance, Sarah?"

She nodded. They got up and stepped over to the smooth surface. To his chagrin, he suddenly realized something. "I've never danced with this leg. I forgot about it. I don't know if I can dance."

She moved close to him, and rested her head against his cheek. "It's all right. We can just sway to the music," she murmured. A fourth couple soon joined them on the dance floor, and now there was little room except to stand still and sway.

He was aware of her softness, yet her thinness—he could feel her ribs through her dress—and some subtle perfume. The lilting sounds of the violin helped create a mystical mood. As the piece ended, she looked up at him with her lips slightly parted. And he kissed her, and she didn't draw away. Not like she had in Marie's office.

He led her back to their table. "I think we should talk about our future," he said as they sat down.

"Don't you think it's too soon. We hardly know each other."

"Sarah, I've known you for almost fifteen years."

"But that wasn't the same me. Probably not the same you either."

"Are you saying there's nothing between us?"

She took a deep breath. "I think there is. Yes, there is. But one of us has so much baggage to bring to any relationship. Damaged goods. It wouldn't be fair to the other person. To you."

"Are you the best judge of that?"

"No, but I . . ."

He touched her lips to stop her, and moved his hand up to cover her scarred cheek. "I think I should be the judge of baggage. After all, I'm damaged goods, too." Her hand moved up to touch his hand on her cheek. "I can see Ginny as my daughter. A truly loved daughter. As I truly love her mother."

"I can't have a child by you," she said so softly he could hardly hear.

"Ginny is enough for me."

She sighed audibly. "You have to give me time, Thad. I'm hardly thinking straight today. This is all so sudden. And so overwhelming." Another thought occurred to her. "And I'm just not sure if Ginny and I would be happy in a small town in Carolina. I'm not sure if I'd be able to use my medical training. I don't think I want to give it up, even for the man I love."

"I've thought about this a lot, dear Sarah. I've always thought you'd be reluctant to give up a big city hospital and medical practice. To come to a small town where there may still be prejudice against women doctors." He laughed cynically. "They're certainly prejudiced about everything else, so I'm sure they'd be about women doctors.

"No, Sarah, I don't expect you to come down to Carolina, unless you truly want to. I'm prepared to come up here to Boston, or wherever else you want to locate."

She stared at him. For a long time she said nothing. "This is too much to ask of you."

"I've been grooming someone to take my place. Our only woman professor. She's handling things while I'm up here, but is perfectly capable of taking over completely. Perhaps I've been in Chalfant long enough. Maybe too long. I'd kind of welcome a change. Though I would miss the mountains."

"There're mountains not too far west of Boston. They're called the Berkshires."

He looked at her. Did she realize that she'd just made a subtle pitch for him to come to Boston?

Maybe she did. But now she raised another objection. "But what would you do up here, Thad? Could you find another satisfactory job?"

"I should think I could get a job teaching at some college."

"But you don't know."

"Tell you what, Sarah, let's talk to Marie about what she thinks of me moving up here. Whether I likely could find a good job. That would also give you a little time to think this over. But you should know, my dear, I came up here to marry you." Now he grabbed her hands, her wonderful hands. "And sweetie, I'm not going to take 'no.' Do you understand? It's about time I became forceful. Don't you think?"

"I don't think I should answer that. I might be putting myself in some jeopardy," she said with a crooked smile.

They danced again and held each other close and kissed when it was over.

At her door, Thad held her face between his hands, one hand so gently touching her scar. "The good Lord must have been truly helping us, guiding us, don't you think?"

"I've always thought He was. Until those terrible days in Paris during the civil war. Then when that evil man assaulted me, and raped and slashed me, I thought God had abandoned me." Her voice faltered. "Then a little dog saved me and, miraculously, my hands were not injured. And I was sure God or his angel must have been watching out for me. Not permitting the worst to happen. But then the bitter months afterwards . . . I turned away from God again. Now that you've come . . . maybe God has not abandoned me."

"Nor me either," he said.

She turned to the door. "I must go in. Martha will be needing to get home." She hesitated, then turned back. "Please come in for a few minutes, Thad . . . maybe some coffee?"

"I'd like that."

Martha was not particularly friendly to him as she let them in.

"Is Ginny still awake?" Sarah asked.

"She should be sleepin' now," the woman said brusquely. She frowned at Thad.

Sarah noticed the coldness. "Martha, Dr. Barrett is sort of a hero. He fought off the Ku Klux Klan some months ago. They were after him for trying to enroll a brilliant colored girl in his college. In the fight, his aunt was killed."

Martha was impressed with this. Her grim face suddenly softened. "I thought you were another slavery-lovin' Southerner."

"I told Dr. Lindsey that you remind me of that girl's mother," he said.

"Did'ya now?" The woman seemed pleased.

Later over coffee, after Martha had left, Thad said, "Marie told me something else about you. She was quite concerned about that. That's why she finally wrote me."

Her eyes widened. "What else did she tell you?"

"That your self esteem, and your zest for life, had been destroyed in that alley."

She opened her mouth, as if to speak, but her lip trembled and she closed it.

"Marie hoped I might help, that our love might help." His voice came out low and strained. "I do so much want to help, dear Sarah. That description of you describes me too, for these many years. My zest for life, my self esteem, even my sense of purpose, well, I think I had it once, when my search for you seemed near the end. I had just been to see Mary Ann Bickerdyke, and she was sure you were here in Boston."

"You saw Mary Ann?" she whispered.

"And Dr. Rizzo."

"Dr. Rizzo, too." she repeated. She shifted her position. "Then you lost your zest . . . ?"

"When I learned you were in Paris, probably gone from me forever, I lost some. I lost the rest when I never heard from you, through the months of chaos in Paris, and the years after."

She was crying now. "My troubles seemed so bad," she struggled to talk, "I didn't want to burden anyone else with them . . . I had such a difficult pregnancy, and then trying to care for a sickly crippled child . . . and cope with the severity of my injuries."

She took a deep breath and fought to gain control of her emotions. "I didn't even want Marie to know, but the doctors there wrote her about me, and she came to Paris to help me try to put my life together." She closed her eyes briefly, then gave a wan smile. "But maybe I've been . . . feeling sorry for myself . . . far too long. And ignoring my wonderful blessings."

"How could you, ignore your wonderful blessings?" He smiled at her and moved over to put his arm around her shoulder. "Do you really need time to think about marrying me? Why don't we tell Marie tomorrow about our decision and plans?"

As he held her, Ginny awoke and called from the next room. "Why don't we tell Ginny now that she's going to have a daddy," he suggested softly. "Then maybe I should fix some more coffee. Our coffee is cold."

She laughed now. "We sort of forgot about the coffee, didn't we."

#

Marie gave Sarah a few days off, "to begin planning for a new life." The next day dawned a beautiful spring morning. Could this be an omen, Sarah wondered as she and Thad had breakfast together? "Shall we go down to the river, and see if there are any sailboats?" she suggested.

"Sounds good. We don't have any sailboats, or much water except mountain streams, in western Carolina."

Near the water the fresh breeze had the tang of salt water as it blew against their faces and ruffled her hair. They left the carriage and found a bench and she leaned against him as he put his arm around her while seagulls wheeled overhead. He thought this was as near to heaven as a mortal could attain.

After a while, he brought up the subject of their honeymoon. He had thought she might mention it first, but she evidently wanted to defer to him. "For our honeymoon, wouldn't you like to go to the seashore?" he asked. "Maybe get a suntan and do a little swimming in the ocean."

She was quiet for a long time. He looked at her, wondering. "You wouldn't be able to go wading and swimming with me, would you?" she finally asked.

"Probably not, but I would enjoy watching you, and maybe covering you up with sand, except for your toes, which I could tickle."

She didn't see this as funny. "Have you been in a swimsuit in recent years?"

"Not since the War," he admitted.

She became very serious, then took his hands in hers. "Dear husband soon to be. How could I enjoy the ocean when you could not easily join me on the beach or in the water?"

"Well . . ."

"I think I'd like to go to the mountains. Why don't we explore the Berkshires in the western part of the state? Maybe you can introduce me to the magic of the mountains, how they must have inspired you, maybe brought you to tranquillity and acceptance of God's majesty . . . how they brought you to become the man you are." She touched his cheek with those wonderful hands. "Teach me to see the mountains as you see them and feel them in your heart."

Thad felt a tingle go up his spine. The gentle Sarah. How like her this decision on the honeymoon, to subordinate her leanings to accommodate him. He didn't realize he had mentioned his love of mountains, but she had sensed it. "I didn't tell you," he huskily said, "but at the battle of South Mountain just before Antietam, I thought I was going to die on the mountain, and somehow dying there didn't seem so bad." He chuckled without humor. "Instead, I just about died on a dusty road full of bodies. If not for you."

"Shush, Thad. These bad memories are all behind us. Just as mine of a filthy alley in Paris should be."

"But they are part of what honed us to become the persons we are today," he said.

"Yes, they are that."

They stood gazing at the waters and boats before them, then turned without regret to embrace the new life that awaited them.

CHAPTER 20

Later, Sarah began to have second thoughts as Thad's difficulties finding a job worthy of his experience and ability mounted. The first few days of job searching were not too discouraging. After all, she well knew the arrogance of the big universities such as Harvard and could imagine their disdain for a professor and even a president of a small college in the hinterland of South Carolina. "Thad, these people are like the doctors I faced trying to get into med school. They are so sure no outsider can possibly meet their standards. But there must be other colleges around here that would welcome you."

"Well, if nothing else I can appreciate what you went through on a much bigger scale." He looked at her and tried to smile. "Sure, I'll survey the college market for miles around. Something will turn up. I don't have to be a college president. A professorship would do just fine."

So Thad spent the next few weeks going from school to school, extending his search into Rhode Island and Connecticut. She could see he was discouraged after he came back to town from a week on the road. He shrugged. "Nothing really. Well, one school did say they might have a parttime beginning position, an adjunct assistant professorship, later in the school year, maybe. Most had no openings at all, and nothing in administration." He tried to smile. "I'm ready to consider anything, to be up here with you."

She couldn't allow that, to have Thad sacrifice his own wonderful career to be with her. It was so unfair, such a waste. Just like her own confrontation with Dorothea Dix, when the woman pompously told her she was only fit to be a scullery maid and scrub floors and other mindless tasks. "I can't expect you to sacrifice your career this way," she said. "I just can't. It's not fair to you."

"Hush, Sarah. I'll find something. It's only been a few weeks, and there must be plenty of jobs out there. It doesn't have to be in academia."

She could see he was distraught at the danger of jeopardizing their relationship. "But most are not deserving of your talents." She had to say it.

"That remains to be seen."

"Maybe we're rushing things too fast. You've said before that you need to go back to Chalfant to put things in order." He nodded, his face ashen. "We've waited this long. Another month or so shouldn't be too hard to take." He was staring at her, his eyes expressionless.

She gave a faint smile. "Maybe you could survey the situation in Chalfant and neighboring towns to see if any would consider a woman doctor. It wouldn't have to be in surgery."

He groaned. "What a waste of your God-given talent that would be."

They couldn't settle anything that night. Later, as she lay awake, dark thoughts and doubts assailed her. Was she the right woman for Thad, or for any man? Despite his rapport with Ginny, was marriage the best thing for them? Now she thought of her inability to have another child, a child with Thad. The long forgotten emotions she'd experienced after hearing of Solomon's death and realizing she never could have his child swept over her mind. She felt again the intensity of those emotions. Wouldn't Thad feel the same way at her inability to have his child? Then she touched her scarred cheek. She rolled and tossed in her despair: the tantalizing hope of a long-delayed future now seemed in danger.

#

The next morning Marie noticed the ravages of Sarah's sleepless night. "My dear, you look peaked."

"I didn't sleep well last night. Too much thinking."

"Is Thad still having trouble finding a suitable job?"

"I'm afraid so. I just don't think I can let him sacrifice his own career to be with me. How unfair that would be."

"Your happiness needs to be considered," Marie said softly.

"I could not be happy if Thad is unhappy, or at least frustrated in a job not fitting his talents."

Marie paced her office. "Sarah, I think you two are giving up too soon. Surely in a big city like Boston there must be good opportunities for his talents. If not in academia at the present time, maybe in some other field, such as business." She paused, thinking about this. "Yes, in business. Maybe Thad could sell a firm on the need for better employee training. Surely there's a need for that."

"His education is more in linguistics and philosophy."

"But he also has good administrative skills developed under trying conditions."

"Yes, he has that . . ."

"So, don't give up, you two. I'll try to put out some feelers, see if I hear of any job opportunities that might be fitting." The older woman gripped her hand. "We can't let this little hurdle defeat us after all the major ones you two have surmounted over these many years. Can we now?"

#

Sarah told Thad about Marie's comments that evening. They were dining at the same quiet restaurant of their first evening together. Tonight, Thad seemed curiously optimistic after his depression of the last few weeks.

"She's absolutely right, dear. I have to be flexible in this job search, and I haven't been so far." He smiled at her.

The flickering light of the candle cast passing shadows over his face. Such a good face it was, strong and kind, honed by years of adversity to hollow cheeks and deep-set eyes, the darkness of his hair and beard now scattered with gray. She truly loved this man. "We're getting older, dear," he was saying. "We must grasp this opportunity. I'll eventually get a suitable job, but our love is surely not dependent on that."

"No, it isn't. Still I want you to be happy, not frustrated."

"I'll be deliriously happy." He took her hands in his. "I think we need to dance, don't you?" She nodded, and they swayed to the soft music, and she felt her passions rise. They had not been intimate yet, both feeling that this should wait until they were married, but neither had expected this much delay.

Back at the table as they sipped wine after dinner, he placed a ring on her finger. "I should have done this the first night I saw you," he said. "Then the damned job search got in the way." She took a deep breath. "Let's set a date tonight. I'll go down to Chalfant for no more than a month. Let's plan our wedding for six weeks from today."

She slowly nodded, watching his eyes light up. He raised her hand to his lips and gently kissed it.

#

The stay at Chalfant would not be the easy transition he had expected. Mildred Twitty looked worried and haggard when he met with her at the college.

"For weeks I've been hoping every day you'd come," she said. "I penned a letter to you a week ago but I suppose it didn't get to Boston before you left. Thank God you're here now."

"Why Mildred? I thought everything was running smoothly."

"It's the Klan, again. Somehow they found out that we've been tutoring Joan. Now they've threatening her and me and the college as well. Their crosses have been burning on campus and all over town. Joan is terrified. Several of her neighbors have been injured. She's afraid of causing more trouble."

"Isn't the sheriff any help with this?"

"He claims he can do nothing without some specific evidence of a crime. And with their hoods, who knows who they are. Maybe the sheriff is one of them."

"I've always wondered about that," Thad said. He stood up and offered his hand to Mildred. "Let's walk outside, while we discuss this further. I think better when I'm moving around."

It was summertime and only a few students were on campus. Everything seemed quiet and peaceful, until Mildred pointed to a blackened scar on the lawn near the administration building. "There are half a dozen such burnings we've had at the school. This was blazing two nights ago."

"Did the sheriff come that night?" he asked.

"Oh, he did, a half hour after all the excitement, and nosed around, but offered no help except to tell us that maybe we should move Joan to some secret place."

"How's the staff taking this, and any students on campus?"

"Not too well. None are eager to leave, yet. But most of us feel that bodily harm is just a breath away. Some of the men are carrying pistols . . . I have one too."

Thad frowned and shook his head. "It worries me, our carrying guns. It could be just the tinder needed for blood to flow."

"They've already injured defenseless Negroes. Surely you're not against self defense?" Mildred countered.

"No I'm not. But I'm not sure guns are worth the risk—to you, the staff, our students. We don't want a pitched battle over this. Somehow I doubt the Klan does either, and maybe they can be made to see their folly." He was quiet, trying to think as they made their way back to the office.

Finally he said, "Mildred, I need to talk with various people about this. Maybe even try to find an old soldier who served under me, and who I know is deep into the Klan, maybe even the grand knight by now."

"Wouldn't that be dangerous for you?"

"Probably. I may have to take that chance to try to reason with the man."

#

He sought out Reverend Brown the next day. They had last talked when they were trying to get Joan Washington admitted to the college, an effort that failed as board members refused to stand up to community prejudice, and the Klan.

"How good to see you again, Dr. Barrett. It seems that hatred and prejudice in our small town just will not go away, as you must have heard from Mildred Twitty."

"Mildred was quite upset when I got in yesterday . . . the threats to her and the staff, the crosses burning on campus and around town. She said several of your people were injured and Joan had received death threats."

The minister sighed. "The threats to Joan bother us a lot—the poor girl, who only wants to make the best of what God gave her, having to face such hatred."

"Is the community trying to protect Joan and her mother?"

"Yes, neighbors are guarding their house. That's how two were injured a week ago, struggling with the white-hooded devils storming down the street to torch their house."

"I didn't know that."

"You can imagine how bad Joan felt that people were hurt because of her."

"Yes, I certainly can." Thad was silent.

"Why did you come to see me, Dr. Barrett? I understand you're moving up to Boston, having found that Union nurse who saved your life, the one who became a surgeon despite discrimination of the worst kind by the male establishment."

"We're planning to get married in six weeks and live in Boston. But I still have strong feelings for Chalfant, the college and, not the least, for Joan." The minister was staring at him. "I don't know . . . if I can make any difference in this atmosphere of hatred, but I want to try." He caught himself. He was pounding his wooden leg, a nervous action he still could not control in moments of stress. "I've several ideas I'd like to get your thoughts on."

"Please go on, sir."

"First, I was concerned with Joan's safety. But it looks like her neighbors should be able to protect her if she stays near home." The minister nodded. "Still, I'm not sure how safe Mildred or other faculty members would be going to her house." He looked at Reverend Brown who nodded again. "In this atmosphere, I doubt that Joan can get the best education, even though Mildred should be able to keep her supplied with books."

Thad paused again. "Please excuse me, Reverend. I'm trying to gather my thoughts . . . What would you think if I brought Joan and her mother up to Boston, to live with my wife, Sarah, and her little crippled daughter?"

"Crippled, like Joan? How old is she?"

"Let's see. I think four or five."

"What a Divine coincidence that is! Dr. Barrett, this is a generous proposition, one that I truly think would be in Joan's best interest, as well as the community's. Of course, we'll have to check with Joan and her mother, but I think they'd be joyful about this. Furthermore, I'm sure our community will want to contribute to her stay up there." Now he frowned. "But what about tutoring? I think she'd miss Mildred's and some of the other faculty's efforts."

"I think we should be able to get her in a regular college." Thad laughed sarcastically. "Probably not Harvard, though. They're as prejudiced against women and minorities as anyone down south."

"Does your wife know about this?"

"I didn't know about this situation when I left Boston, so no she doesn't know. But I'm sure she'll welcome Joan and her mother. Incidentally, she knows about them, and her little girl, Ginny, is eager to meet Joan."

So Thad had the support of the Negro community for this move. The Reverend said, "I just hope Joan doesn't forget us, that she'll write often to let us know how she's doing. But I'm sure she'll do that." As they shook hands, he said, "Would it be all right if Reverend Davis and I and maybe a few parishioners come up to your wedding? And see your beautiful bride?"

"We'd be truly honored, sir."

#

Sheriff Jenkins was the next person Thad visited. "I'm not surprised you've come, Prentice, after the unrest."

"And cross burnings, and death threats, and injured Negroes," Thad added.

"Yes, yes, there's that to cast a blight on the town."

"Did you ever find the persons who caused the death of my Aunt Abigail?"

The sheriff spread his hands. "There was just no evidence we could use to arrest anybody. Even though you thought Isaac Haskins was one of them, there was no proof we could use in a court of law with a southern jury, your word against his."

Thad stared at him. "Sheriff, may I ask you a personal question? Would you give me a straight answer? It won't leave this room."

Jenkins took time to light a cigar, before answering.

"I suppose I know what your question is. Will I answer truthfully? That depends on what you're going to try to do with this."

"Are you a Klansman?"

"Why do you want to know?"

"I want to confront Haskins—I understand he has a small farmstead up in the hills—and try to get his pledge to leave the college and staff alone, and also Joan Washington and her mother until I can get them up to Boston. Which I intend to do as soon as possible."

"You're a brave man, Prentice."

"I need your help, Sheriff. I have to be sure of it. My life will be at stake. If your ties with the Klan keep you from helping me, then I must know this now."

"I am a Klan sympathizer. Frankly, Prentice, I believe we have gone too far in giving freedom to the niggers, giving them the vote and all. But I can't accept Klan violence, and would have arrested Abigail's killers if I thought it would do any good. Does this answer your questions and your doubts about me?"

"Maybe. If I'm to confront Haskins, and live to tell about it, I'll need you to back me up and come to my rescue if I don't make it out of his shack in one or two hours. Can I trust you with that, if you sympathize with their cause, even if not their methods?"

The sheriff relit his cigar before speaking. "I say it again, Major, you're a brave man. I guess I should have known that from your battlefield experiences. Yes, you can count on me. Let's work out the details in a few days—I'll try to find out if Haskins will be home. And I'll back you up." They shook hands on this pact.

#

Thad drove a buggy out to Haskins' farmstead four days later. The sheriff had told him Haskins would probably be there with a few of his cronies. "So you'll be outnumbered, and maybe bad things will happen before I can get to you. But I'll be close as I dare, and also have a deputy with me. Will you be carrying?"

"I've thought about a gun, but decided not to. What do you think?"

"I don't know. Go with your instincts."

Thad was still doubtful whether he'd made the right decision. Especially with Haskins emboldened with several cronies. He knew he'd have to rely on his persuasive skills. He certainly didn't physically have a chance against at least three adversaries.

The road had deteriorated to a two-rut pathway winding through weeds and scrub pines. Ominous clouds were bullying the sun, and he felt the valley closing in around him, stifling him with its menace.

The weatherbeaten house and its few scattered sheds reflected Isaac Haskins' personality. Thad momentarily wondered what the man lived on, for no crops appeared to be planted, and two horses in a corral were as unkempt as the rest of the premises. He must be living on hate. As he drew nearer, he could see three horses tied near the porch. Isaac must have not two but three guests. Thad wondered whether the sheriff had alerted him to his coming, and whether the sheriff was indeed backing him up.

As he approached, the door opened and Isaac came out, briefly shading his eyes to identify the visitor. He started, and turned to shout something to those inside. Three men joined him and they moved to the carriage.

"Wal, Major, my old friend, what brings you heah to my mansion?"

"We need to talk, Isaac."

"Jed, help the major down. We don' want him to injure hisself with that wooden leg, gettin' out of his carriage, do we? Ha Ha."

They grabbed his upper arms and propelled him into the dim interior, and Isaac kicked his wooden leg so that he fell heavily in a corner. One of the men roughly searched him for a weapon. "Nothin' on 'im," he announced.

"Fellas, this is my high and mighty major, nigger lover, and traitor to the cause," Isaac shouted. "What do ya'all think we should do with him?"

"String 'im up!" several shouted.

"I came here to talk," Thad muttered through a bleeding lip.

"Okay, talk."

"As you can see, I came here in peace, no weapons. I want to reason with you, not to harm the college or its people, and not Joan Washington and her family."

The men howled, and Isaac slapped him hard, drawing more blood.

"Or else," Thad said softly.

The room quieted. Isaac stood over him with his fist raised. "Are you threatenin' us? How 'bout that men? This sorry specimen of manhood is threatenin' us."

"Yes, I am."

Isaac pulled up a chair. "You're a bold one, that's for sure. What're you goin' to do to us? Beat us with noodles? Ha Ha."

"More than that. I'll have reporters from major newspapers swarming around here, just like a few years ago. Only this will be a lot worse. They're all looking for sensational news of abuses, threats, burnings, attempted killings, intimidations, violations of federal laws. The feds will be coming, maybe even the army. You're be rooted out and sent to federal prisons or worse."

"You're assumin' you're gettin' out of heah alive, ain't ya?"

"If I'm not out of here in an hour's time, the sheriff and deputies will be coming to get me. They're close by, and if there's any hint of violence they'll bust in sooner."

This brought raucous laughter. The men had been passing around whiskey, and were laughing so hard Isaac could barely talk. Finally he said, "Sheriff Jenkins is one of us, has been wearin' the white robes for a long time, you fool."

"Are you absolutely sure he's one of you? Absolutely?"

Now Haskins turned quiet, looking appraisingly at Thad. Suddenly he turned to one of his men. "Jed, take a look outside, sniff out any other visitors. Let's see if our major is telling the truth, or jus' scarin' us to save his hide."

After Jed left, Thad said to Haskins, "If your biggest resentment is that we're trying to teach that little colored girl, then that should soon be removed. I'm planning to take her and her mother far from here, up to Boston. I want you to leave them alone until I can do that, probably in a few weeks." Haskins made a face, and spat on the floor, but didn't say anything. "You also must stop burning those crosses on our campus, scaring the faculty and the students. And no more killing or tormenting the blacks."

"You're making a helluva lot of demands for somebody whose life is goin' to end soon."

"Isaac Haskins, you don't dare kill me. Too many people know I've come out here to talk to you. If I disappear, it'll be hell to pay for you and your organization. Did you ever think of that?"

The man turned away and was conferring with his two cronies when several shots were heard in the distance. Isaac cursed and he and the others grabbed rifles and rushed outside.

Thad got up from the floor, wiped the blood from his nose and lip, and sat down to await their return. He was not injured seriously, and felt that he might have reached a resolution with the Klan today, even if the sheriff did not show up. But he wondered about the gunshots.

About a half hour later he heard voices outside and went to the door. The sheriff and two deputies were escorting Haskins and his three companions to the house. The rifles were in the hands of the deputies.

"Hello Major," the sheriff said as they came inside. "You seem to be none the worst for the encounter. Jed here got a little flesh wound when he was slow in droppin' his gun, but otherwise everything is peaceful. Did you have a good conversation?"

Thad looked at Haskins. "I think we came to an understanding. No more tormenting and burning crosses and death threats. I will get Joan and her mother up north as soon as I can, probably in a few weeks, so that sore spot for the Klan should be removed. Isn't that right, Haskins?"

He muttered something inaudible. Thad went over to stand face to face with him, and demanded, "Yes or No, Haskins?"

He finally said yes.

Thad looked at the sheriff. "Should we get this in writing and signed?"

"I don't think that's necessary. The source of the Klan's resentment will have been removed."

Haskins bitterly renounced the treachery of the sheriff. The sheriff told him firmly, "You brought it on yourselves with your violence. I have to protect the town."

Thad had one final warning. "Remember, if violence flares up again, I'll have the reporters down here, eager for such a story. We'll all suffer if that happens. The college will have fewer students, Chalfant's reputation will be blackened, and most of all you and the Klan will be broken as the feds get wind of this." With that he took his leave.

#

Thad felt drained as he left this confrontation. Yet things had gone better than he ever expected. He had reconciled himself to being severely beaten before the sheriff arrived, if he came at all.

It was twilight as he drove his buggy into town. Tired though he was, he felt compelled to tell Reverend Brown of the hoped-for outcome of all this. He stopped at the Reverend's modest house in the Negro community.

The preacher came out to meet him. "Thank the Lord you're back in one piece," he said. He reached up and helped Thad down from the buggy. "And it 'pears without any injury but a puffed lip. Please come in and tell us about it."

The preacher and his wife were very solicitous. In truth, he needed succor. They listened in rapt attention as he related the events of the afternoon and the preceding meeting with the sheriff. "I think, no, it's more of a hope, that this confrontation with the Klan will result in peace in this community," he told them. "But it depends on Joan and her mother agreeing to leave, to come up north to Boston. I didn't think that would be any problem. But now I wonder. What do you think?"

"Why don't we ask them? We could do that tomorrow."

As Thad nodded, Rev. Brown said to his wife, "Martha, why don't we let this brave man rest a bit while we prepare a good meal for him?"

"That would be nice." Now Thad realized how tired he was. He fell asleep before dinner, but then awakened to a sumptuous feast of chicken and dumplings and all the trimmings.

As they finished and Thad was preparing to leave, the Reverend said, "Dr. Barrett, why don't you stay with us tonight? It's getting late and you've certainly had a hard day. We have room upstairs. I'll take care of your horse and bring up some water and soap if you want to wash up."

"Thank you. I think I'd like that."

#

The next day, as the Reverend drove them over to the Washington house he said, "I've told my parish and also Reverend Davis of your intentions. The whole community is in favor of this move and deeply appreciative. There will easily be enough money for the family's transportation and living expenses in Boston."

"Have you said anything to Joan yet?"

The minister hesitated before answering. "I was going to, but then thought it better not to give her hope, just in case this didn't work out . . ."

"And the Klan incapacitated or killed me."

"Yes, that was a concern."

The house was as he remembered it, unpainted, with a grassless yard on a dirt street with other unpainted and grassless habitats. The same dead sentinal tree guarded it.

The tall thin black woman, Mrs. Washington, answered the door. She greeted Reverend Brown with some surprise, then started as she recognize Thad standing to one side.

"Dr. Barrett, I thought you had left Chalfant," she said in her melodious voice.

"I did. But I had important business to come back to Chalfant for a short time."

"Let me get Joan . . . Is it about her?"

Rev. Brown interjected, "Yes, but really about both of you."

Joan wheeled herself into the room. "I thought I heard your voice, Dr. Barrett. How wonderful of you to stop and see us." She was about as he remembered, a frail figure of a girl, with eyes that dominated her face, and a bony little hand that firmly gripped his. "How can I ever thank you for the dream you've given me? And your kindness and that of Professor Twitty and all the other faculty who have been helping? I just hope I'm worthy of such encouragement."

"I found my dream, at last," he told her. Her eyes were bright.

"The one who wanted to be a surgeon and go to medical school, and had to go to a university in Paris?"

"Yes, I finally found her, partly because of you." And he told her about Sarah, and how the publicity from the Klan's efforts to prevent Joan's admittance to college brought him the contact needed. And he told her about the little crippled daughter, Ginny.

"I know the bad men wanted to take your dream away, and almost succeeded. But not anymore." She was watching him intently, her hands fluttering like he remembered. He expected her to ask why, but suddenly realized the extent of her faith in him.

"I would like to move you and your mother up to Boston with Sarah, Ginny, and me, and very possibly to attend college up there, just as soon as we can arrange it. It may take several weeks to get everything ready, but you can start preparing now."

Now Reverend Brown told the Washingtons how their neighbors and churches would handle all the expenses of such a move, and how the Negro community would be uplifted if her dream and talent were realized.

Now Joan and her mother had tears in their eyes. Mrs. Washington hugged her daughter, then hugged Rev. Brown and Thad. "Thank you, oh thank you," she said.

Joan asked, "Dr. Barrett, would we be living with you?"

"Probably at first. Then you may want your own apartment. But we can see."

"Please, would you kiss me, Dr. Barrett?" He knelt beside the chair, and her thin arms raised up to embrace him.

"I think I'd better wipe your tears away," he told her gently.

The next day Thad penned a long letter to Sarah, trying to explain all that had happened in these several weeks in Chalfant, and of course the plan to have Joan and her mother come up to Boston, and perhaps stay with them for a few weeks or more while they found a suitable apartment. He hoped the letter would reach Sarah before he did. But he was sure Sarah would approve.

#

The next several weeks passed quickly. He had long chats with Sam Turner about the college and his handling of the Klan, and about moving Joan and her mother up to Boston. But he spent most his time describing how he had found his enduring love, Sarah, and the trials and tribulations of her great odyssey to become a surgeon. He also asked Sam to be his best man, and he eagerly accepted.

He had much to talk about with Mildred Twitty to allay her fears of the Klan, and of his plans for Joan and her mother. "Joan was concerned that you would no longer be able to tutor her, but I told her we could probably get her into a college up north," he said. They talked about the future of the college, and he listened to her ideas to start the college on a growth mode. He talked with various other faculty to listen to any problems and suggestions, and also to allay their fears of the Klan. He was so pleased that Mildred wanted to come up to Boston for the wedding, as might several other faculty members.

Before he left Chalfant, he visited Abigail's grave, a simple stone in a weedy cemetery. Its inscription said "Pioneer Woman." He put some flowers on her grave and knelt to pray: *I owe so much to you. You saved my life when I dragged back from the War, and gave me hope, and strength for the challenge ahead. And wisdom too. I owe you so much, Abigail. And now my odyssey is almost ended. The woman of my dreams is waiting for me, and I thank God for you and His blessings.*

As he got up, he looked to the west and could see Steven's Knob in the distance. The urge to climb the mountain again came hard over him. Twice, momentous decisions or inspirations had come to him on that mountain top, during times of crossroads and near despair. But the situation was different now. Sarah's and his long odysseys were about finished, and wonderfully so.

He leaned against a tree, still looking at Steven's Knob. No, I don't need to climb you now. I don't need to drive myself to exhaustion to find guidance to the right path. Still, there was something still lacking. He had not settled on a career path for himself. He did not yet have control of his destiny.

#

He left Chalfant a few days before Joan and her mother would be doing so. Reverend Brown promised to take care of arranging for them to get to Boston, and Thad and Sarah would meet them there. He needed to get back to Sarah now, as quickly as possible. It was getting close to the planned wedding date, and Sarah surely needed some help from him. His mission at Chalfant was finished, successfully, for the Klan was subdued and the college with Mildred Twitty at the helm now seemed in steady hands.

On the train back, an idea that had been formenting in his mind since the visit to the cemetery and his gazing at the mountain that had so influenced his life began to crystallize. He could hardly wait to see Sarah and get her reactions to it.

#

That first night back to Boston, he began talking about it slowly, gradually developing the idea. "I told you long ago, in the Baltimore hospital, that I had a dream, to become a writer. Do you remember? I bet you don't."

She nodded slowly. "Yes, I do remember."

"I had in mind, not being an ordinary writer, but one whose writings might have some impact on society, might in some way make it better. My articles about the cancer that is the Ku Klux Klan were a step in that direction. So too, this book on Civil War medicine, its terrible deficiencies and how it could be improved, may help future generations never have to go through what we did." She was watching him intently, her hand unconsciously touching her cheek. "The idea has come to me for a novel, a work of fiction, but fiction based on a reality that might have even more impact, and truly touch the heart."

"What?" She had a sudden premonition.

"About the fictional adventures of two people like you and me, who are changed by Antietam to odysseys of hope and striving."

"Yes," she breathed.

"One, a Union battlefield nurse who finds her great talent to be a surgeon, and her heroic odyssey to achieve this against almost impossible obstacles. And the other, a Confederate officer, saved by her, whose odyssey is to find her, and be worthy of her. I think I'll call this novel Odyssey From Antietam."

"What exactly is an odyssey? It's Greek, isn't it? From Homer?"

"Yes. Homer's *Odyssey* was the tale of a Greek king's perilous and lengthy journey home after the defeat of Troy. An odyssey is an adventurous wandering in search of a dream."

"Your novel does sound like us, Thad." She looked very thoughtful, but he could see the stirrings of excitement.

"Why not?" Don't you think our lives would make a great novel? We'll disguise the names, of course."

"Were we so noteworthy, Thad, in that time?"

"You were, far out of the ordinary. And your great strivings have opened the way for women, generations earlier than they could have otherwise. So, yes, you're an intrepid figure. I'm sure Dr. Z would agree, and Mary Ann Bickerdyke, and don't forget Dr. Rizzo."

"Your long efforts to find me would certainly be an epic odyssey. And your confrontations with prejudice and violence in the South so very brave indeed."

"I was only one of many in those bad days," he demurred.

#

The wedding would be at the Boston Hospital for Women and Children. Now that he had returned from Chalfant he was overwhelmed at the elaborate preparations. Marie, the Hospital, and the wealthy patrons were making this a lavish affair.

Sarah's eyes glistened. "Isn't this wonderful? And so many people from our past are coming. I never dreamed of anything like this."

"I never did either," he gruffly said. "I thought we could have just a little ceremony. Maybe we should have eloped. Is it too late for that?"

She looked at him with mock seriousness. "It certainly is too late, Thaddeus."

He knew that Mildred and Sam Turner were coming, with Sam his best man. But he didn't know that a number of professors, and even a few students, were making the trip. Mary Ann Bickerdyke would be there, and Dr. Rizzo and Rachel. Even two of Sarah's professors in Paris were making the journey. Julia Bledsoe came from Pikeston to be Sarah's maid of honor, and surprisingly, half a dozen others came from Pikeston, including Sarah's sisters who seemed awed by all this. And, of course, Reverends Brown and Davis came and brought Joan and her mother with them, and others of the Negro community as well.

Thad was particularly pleased with the way Ginny and Joan had taken to each other. Two little girls in wheelchairs, one 16 years old, the other 5 years old. They were soon holding hands. He had told Ginny, "I would never have found you and your mother if it hadn't been for Joan."

At this, Ginny looked at him wide eyed. "Yes, when we tried to get Joan into my college, and weren't able to, well, there was a lot of publicity about that."

"Is that how Dr. Z could find you?" Ginny asked.

"You knew about that?"

"Yes, Mommy told me."

Joan said now, "Dr. Barrett, Ginny, that makes me kind of an angel, doesn't it, to bring people together."

Ginny laughed delightedly. "Yes, a chocolate covered one."

EPILOGUE

Fall 2004

The manuscript of Odyssey explained many things about the lives and character of Betsy's ancestors. She and I made a careful search of the attic and other storage places for relevant letters and clippings, and then investigated public documents and old newspaper records in libraries and courthouses in nearby counties. In the process we learned a great deal more about Sarah and Thaddeus. We also visited Chalfant and the college there, now for many years a university. It was not far from Sanctuary, and we learned that Thad had indeed taught there in his later years, though apparently did not go back into administration. Why, we wondered, for he was not that old a man? We even went up to Boston to trace their lives there, and this provided further details of the years after they were married. We found some of the rejection letters for his Odyssey, letters that I am so familiar with, and I could feel the disappointment of this man who seemed to me almost as a living person.

But we still did not know the "why" of some of their actions, such as the major one of leaving Boston and building this mansion in the hills of Carolina.

They were both heroic figures, far more than either of us had imagined. I wondered why their story of their long odysseys had not been passed along better to the future generations, and asked Betsy about that.

"I've been wondering about that, too. I think it must have been that they were both modest and unassuming people— that comes across in the manuscript— and didn't talk much about those days, which I'm sure they didn't view as all that notable. If Thad had been able to get this published, things would have been much different. As it was, it was just a closet manuscript, as you are so fond of saying about yours, and almost lost for all time."

"You're probably right. Then I suppose after a generation or so, any stories would become hazy, as you found as a young girl, with no one sure what to believe, and maybe suspecting that most such tales were wild fantasies or exaggerations."

"I never heard either when I was a child that I had two such notable ancestors, not just Sarah."

We pondered for a while which was the more heroic, Sarah or Thad. "I think they were equally so," I told her. "Thad was certainly not a trailblazer like Sarah, but his long pursuit . . ."

"But he was a trailblazer, too," Betsy interrupted. "How about his attempts to enroll a young colored girl, at the risk of jeopardizing the college and even his life and that of his aunt? At a time when such was unheard of in the South."

"I guess that was plenty brave, too." In truth, I was awed by both of these great ancestors of Betsy. I wondered whether their blood presaged great things for our children. For Betsy was six-months pregnant with our first child. Could he or she possibly turn out to be a heroic figure? I mentioned this possibility to Betsy.

But she pooh poohed it. "I don't think my ancestors since then have been particularly notable. Mom and Dad had no claim to fame, did not accomplish much with their lives, and I think my grandparents squandered whatever modest fortune they inherited."

Now we speculated again on why Sarah and Thad decided to leave Boston and move down to Carolina. We found no information at the hospital in Boston that would be helpful. "Sarah must have had a very successful medical practice in Boston. Why would she give that up to move down here?"

Betsy was quiet for a few moments, wrinkling her nose again. "This may be the gist of a wonderful love story. Maybe in their later years, Sarah decided to sacrifice her practice and move down to the land her husband hungered for and that he had given up these many years to be with her. Maybe he never found a job up in Boston fitting his talents. Especially since his book efforts went for naught. Can't you see a loving wife doing that?"

"I'm surprised he would let her do it."

"Maybe she found she could love this land as he did."

We pondered these decisions of her ancestors so many years ago. Not easy ones, involving fulfillment but considerable sacrifice. The "why" of this major life change still eluded us. But maybe it was better this way. "Our speculations could be a sequel to the first book, if we can ever get the first one published." Another thought occurred to me. "What about the crippled little daughter? Was she able to live a good and productive life?" We looked at each other. "She must have gotten married, else how would you and your past generations come about?"

"In one of the old letters it tells of another child, a girl who was born some years later. I haven't investigated the birth records in Boston, but I presume that's where we all came from."

"Wow," I said. "I thought Sarah couldn't have any more children."

She smiled. "Sometimes God doesn't listen to learned medical people."

I nodded, then took her hand and examined it. "I guess I have also been mesmerized by your long and beautiful fingers. Now I know they came from Sarah."

"Dost thou think I should have been a surgeon?" she asked whimsically.

I squeezed her hand.

In our research, we were disappointed not to find any information about Joan Washington. We had thought she might have become a famous scientist. Sometime we'll have to pursue this trail again.

\#

While we had not heard anything promising from the agents we initially sent the manuscript to, we decided to keep Sanctuary. It belonged in this family. Maybe we will even decide to move down there permanently some day, just like Sarah and Thad did a century earlier. I couldn't get the beauty of this land out of my mind. It beckoned me, as it must have beckoned Betsy's forebears.

HISTORICAL AUTHENTICITY

While the major characters are fictional, some of the supporting ones are real indeed, and I have tried to portray them as realistically as possible. For example, Dorothea Dix, dictatorial Superintendent of Nursing for the Union Army; Mary Ann Bickerdyke, a famous Union nurse and confidant of Grant and Sherman, described in Nina Brown Baker's *Cyclone in Calico*; Elizabeth Blackwell, one of the very early women physicians, described in *Blackwell's Opening the Medical Profession to Woman*; and Marie E. Zakrzewska (Dr. Z), founder of the Infirmity for Women and Children in Boston, a place ahead of its time in cleanliness, efficiency, and compassionate service, described in Agnes C. Vector's (ed.) *A Woman's Quest—The Life of Marie E. Zakrzewska*. Also, Stephen Oates' *A Woman of Valor (Clara Barton)*.

The depiction of the events and battles are as accurate as we could make them, realizing that in a novel of this type we cannot be as detailed as in a history.

I have tried to be as accurate as possible in describing the medical practices and problems of the day, and used a number of sources to verify this. For examples: Harold Straubing's *In Hospital and Camp*; Walsh, *Doctors Wanted—No Women Need Apply*; Robt. E. Denny's *Civil War Medicine*; and Steward Brooks' *Civil War Medicine*.

Other important sources that helped frame the plotline of the novel, especially in the aftermath of the War include Richard Nelson Current's, *Those Terrible Carpetbaggers*; Paul Harman Buck's, *The Road to Reunion 1865-1900*; and Arthur Bining and Philip Klein, *A History of the United States, Vol II*.

local author